CHARMED VIGILANCE

SKYLAR DIETSCHE

Copyright

Charmed Vigilance

© Skylar Dietsche, 2024
All rights reserved.

No part of this book may be reproduced, stored in a retrieval system, or transmitted in any form or by any means—electronic, mechanical, photocopying, recording, or otherwise—without the prior written permission of the author, except in the case of brief quotations embodied in critical articles and reviews.

ISBN: 978-1-0672576-4-4

Cover Design: Skylar Dietsche in collaboration with Moonlight Magic Design
Illustrations: Skylar Dietsche

This is a work of fiction. Names, characters, places, and incidents either are the product of the author's imagination or are used fictitiously. Any resemblance to actual persons, living or dead, events, or locales is entirely coincidental.

Disclaimer:
While the story is set in a location that is not explicitly identified, it is intended to represent a fictional world outside of
US territory. The language used in this book adheres to
UK English conventions.

Published by:
Self-Published
Cape Town, South Africa

For permissions, requests, or inquiries, please contact:
info@skylardietsche.com

First Edition 2024

Note about Language

This book has been written and edited in UK English, which may differ in spelling, grammar, and usage from American English. Readers may notice variations such as "colour" instead of "color," "realise" instead of "realize," and "favour" instead of "favor," among others. These choices are intentional and reflect the author's preference for UK English conventions. Additionally, while the precise location of the story is not explicitly revealed, it is implied to take place outside of US territory. This setting further aligns with the linguistic and cultural nuances found within the narrative. We appreciate your understanding and hope it enhances your immersion in the world of the story.

Foreword

When I first embarked on the journey of writing *Charmed Vigilance*, I never anticipated the profound impact it would have on me. This book began as a simple idea sparked by a fleeting moment of inspiration after seeing a moonlit garden scene on the TV, but it grew into something much more significant. I smile and shake my head when I think back to that rainy December day in Wilderness, running to my mom to share the idea that had just revealed itself to me. I told her, "I don't want to be a writer, but I have to write this story." Famous last words.

Writing is a lonely road. Throughout the writing process, I faced numerous challenges—moments of doubt, endless revisions and rewrites that sucked the will to live right out of me, and unexpected revelations that continue to this day. These obstacles only deepened my connection to the story and its characters. It feels like a gift that keeps on giving. I am grateful to those who stood by me, offering encouragement and support. Their enthusiasm for this story kept me going at times, even when the path seemed uncertain. I am honoured to be the conduit of this story.

In terms of inspiration, my sources are numerous. As a teenager in the 2000s, bands like *Evanescence* and *30 Seconds to Mars, POD, Stone Sour, Staind, System of a Down, Linkin Park,* and *Korn,* were part of my formative years. Movies and series also played a part in my early creative development: *Lord of the Rings, First Knight, Queen of the Damned, Xena: Warrior Princess, Smallville, A Knight's Tale, Underworld, Blade, Pirates of the Caribbean, Pride & Prejudice, August Rush, Twilight,* and *Pan's Labyrinth.* These works shared a dark yet genuine and deep atmosphere that I aimed to recreate. Visually, *Pan's Labyrinth* was the biggest influence. While *Queen of the Damned* has been widely criticized, the movie and its soundtrack had a profound influence on my creativity. To this day, I find the soundtrack deeply moving. And of course, old-world architecture and culture played a huge role.

The world of *Charmed Vigilance* is one of mystery and wonder, where every twist and turn reveals deeper layers of intrigue. It reflects themes of self-discovery and the delicate balance between beauty and danger, reflecting how easily we brush things aside or rationalise what doesn't make sense. As you read, I hope you find yourself drawn into Josilyn's journey and the enigmatic town of Ostia.

Thank you for joining me on this adventure. May the story captivate and inspire you as much as it has me.

Dedication

G, the real MVP

Mamma—thank you for being there from day one of this story.

Johan—Jy was gereeld reg. Ek wens jy was nie reg oor die feit dat jy nooit hoofstuk 7 gaan kan lees nie.

One night, I woke up in a dream,
or so it did seem.
The light around me held a strange gloom
Resonating—bouncing—all over the room.
I rose slowly, stood up straight,
the curiosity in me could no
longer wait.
My mirror misted into a dark doorway,
By some strange compulsion,
I couldn't stay away.

Prologue

The river rippled under Kierivi's touch as she played her hands over the surface, submerged up to her thighs. Laughter and splashes echoed from the children playing on the bright, warm day.

Her name, whispered from across the waters, drifted towards her and goosebumps rolled over her arms. Heart thumping, she turned, looking at the mountain, gaze drifting over the treeline across the water. She saw nothing there and shielded her eyes against the sun. The whisper came from behind her now—closer this time. She recoiled, almost falling into the water, but she found herself no longer in the river, no longer in daylight.

Mist oozed through the darkened trees, a subtle luminescence glowing from within as it rolled in around her, slow and thick. Rattled, she stood frowning as it circled and enclosed her, obscuring everything from sight. The vapour clung and precipitated on her exposed skin, and she looked down. She looked at her bare arms, noting how dark they were, the blackest of black, and how her blue smock had somehow transformed into a brighter shade. Disturbed by the sudden change, she gulped and took a deep breath, but coughed as the dense fog choked the oxygen from the air. Breathing was toilsome, but her disorientation soon distilled into fear when an awareness dawned on her.

Eyes were watching. She could feel them pressing into her. Not knowing where she was, and unable to see anything around her, she gave a tentative step forward. And then a few more.

The silent presence followed.

Anxious, she hastened to get away, but no matter which direction she went, it stayed close. As if it lurked inside her mind, a perpetual presence right behind her, even though she saw nothing wherever she turned. A burning tear escaped, but she suppressed the hysteria welling up inside her and stayed mum.

From deep inside the fog, she heard someone call to her. She halted, and turned.

In a straw hut, with increased desperation, the little girl tried to awaken her mother. The whimpers and tossing beside her had roused her, and she knew her mother was having a nightmare again as she had been for weeks. She shook Kierivi's sleeping body, yelling, concerned by how damp her mother was. Her heart thundered inside her.

"Trejeki! Trejeki, soe tjici!"

Kierivi's eyes shot wide open, and she bolted upright with a desperate gasp, coughing. Frantic and bewildered, her wild eyes roved over the room, fumbling hands searching for a weapon.

"Trejeki!" Xorvelca was afraid, but Kierivi's eyes met hers after a second and recognition came. Kierivi held her breath, not trusting her sight, but a second later she pulled Xorvelca into a tight, desperate hug and relief flooded them both.

A rustling outside froze them into place. Kierivi's widened eyes stared at the entrance, waiting, listening. The rushing blood was loud in her ears, but no other sound came.

"Trejeki?" Xorvelca whimpered, not knowing what was going on. Kierivi pressed a finger to her lips. She trembled but gleaned what courage she had and grasped her daughter's narrow shoulders.

"Xorvelca," her voice caught, and she cleared it, "Xorvelca, teturi, haceh," urgent, she ordered her to hide, and pushed her away, but Xorvelca shook her head and clung to her mother, unwilling to be separated. Kierivi shared the reluctance, but she loosened her slim arms and pushed her again, as gently as she could. Slowly, terrified, Xorvelca backed away, unwilling to take her eyes from her Trejeki.

She stopped.

Hearts drumming, their gazes locked as the fear and love shone from their dark eyes, flowing between them in silence. Xorvelca couldn't bear it and wanted to close the distance, but Kierivi noticed and held her hand up to stop her. Suspense hung in the air as the silent seconds dragged on.

A twig snapped outside.

"Xor—" Kierivi didn't complete the sentence.
A violent gust ripped through the hut, a crackling surge of energy, which disappeared as fast as it came. Kierivi was gone.

Silence descended as if it were all imagined, and Xorvelca, bewildered, looked around the hut, searching for Kierivi, or whatever had entered. As she did, unbeknownst to her, her pitch-black eyes, her mother's eyes, turned icy blue. The surge had thrown her back and onto the floor. She jumped up, running from the hut.

"Trejeki!" she kept screaming, but the rest of the village remained silent, dark, and sleeping. Xorvelca stopped and watched in terror as the fog pulled back into the trees and disappeared.

Chapter 1

I remembered the day we received the unexpected call almost a year ago. Late summer brought temperatures that dipped lower and lower after midday. I had spent most of the day in my room, sorting through schoolwork and discarding clothes I'd kept for too long. Music permeated my room and created a tranquil cocoon, like some sensory isolation chamber or a warm womb. I felt elevated, detached from time and my physical self; a disposition of music-induced euphoria.

The phone rang down the hall, causing a breach in the tranquillity. Sitting on the wooden floor, I steadied myself, closing my eyes. But I still saw the room. I heard footsteps hurry from the kitchen to the hallway. A strange time for a phone call, late afternoon on a Sunday.

"Hello?" My mom's subdued greeting and the inclination in her voice inferred the same confusion I had. I tried to identify the caller, but my mom had lowered her voice and it all became too muffled to distinguish any real meaning. As the disruption dissipated, I fell back into my warm, elevated state. Bathed in an otherworldly glow which transformed the room, I returned to the business of filing. The call lasted a while.

At dinner that evening, I asked who had called. My mom and dad exchanged a significant look before she told me it had been Catherine, my mom's aunt. She was the eldest of three sisters, but somehow, she had outlived her younger siblings by almost a decade. I had only met her once, at my grandmother's funeral, when I was around ten. Even then, she had appeared old, yet refined and well-dressed. She was already a widow by that time and child-free. Though she was never a strong relational individual, she took a liking to my mother. They sometimes spoke on the phone, but never too long. Our family travels were rare, and she lived too far away to visit, an almost twelve-hour drive.

Catherine had fallen down the stairs at home and fractured her hip, which brought about the decision to move out since the house had multiple storeys. My mom was a real estate agent and had talked at length about the stunning home. Catherine, however, could not sell the house. Not because no one wanted it—quite the contrary. By law, the house had to stay within the bloodline until either the bloodline ended or the building no longer existed. As it stood, my mom was the closest blood relative to Catherine, so by order of inheritance, she was next in line, and then it would be me, and so forth. My mom didn't think about it much since Catherine seemed fashioned from immortal stuff. But the reckoning had come early. They debated whether renting out the house qualified as a business, since transforming it into one was unviable. The decision rested on my parents moving into the house to inherit it.

Otherwise, they had to decline, and the opportunity would pass to another distant relative. Naturally, this was not an appealing alternative.

My brother and I had lived in Weatonburg our whole lives. My parents moved there because of the favourable property market two years before I was born. An isolated mining town in a desert-like nowhere, far from anything significant. In my final year of school at the mature age of twenty, I hadn't considered where I would go after graduation. My desperation to leave Weatonburg behind and never return was immense, yet the idea of going terrified me. I knew I had lived a sheltered life, but the notion of freedom paralysed me. Like a captive animal staying rooted even after the leash is removed, since that was the only state it knew.

The news, however, had set things in motion. Choices had to be made.

A month later, my parents informed us they had accepted the offer and would move there in a couple of months. It had a respected public school for Andrew, my younger brother, and a decent property market. My dad was an accountant and writer, so it didn't matter so much where he lived.

I had decisions to make.

My singular certainty: I would not stay in Weatonburg. I discovered that Ostia, the town where the house was, had a decent university that offered a few main degrees, including a Music Degree. People and school were never my strong suit, but I always had a knack for music.

My whole life, a subdued energy lay dormant inside me, but the day I got the acceptance letter, it stirred.

~

After I walked out of our home for the last time, a peculiar pressure built inside my chest. My heart raced faster and faster the closer we got to Ostia. At first, I attributed it to sadness and nostalgia from leaving my old life behind and starting anew. After a while, I wasn't so sure.

Having never travelled far from Weatonburg, I found the varied landscape during our trip baffling. We drove through quaint, solemn towns and cold, concrete cities. I watched as the flat desert expanse I had known my whole life became greener and denser. I fought sleep, fearing I'd miss something. Knowing an entire world lay waiting out there versus seeing it yourself was quite different.

The last road sign we passed indicated we were five kilometres away—my palms were clammy, and my right foot was bouncing. I listened to music on my phone, attempting to distract myself from the pit in my stomach that yawned wider with every passing moment.

My foot stopped when the next song came on. One of my favourites, if not my most favourite. A Minor instrumental ballad by an alternative metal group of cellists, named the *Colour of Autumn*. Autumn carried a comforting melancholia which soothed the soul with the promise of warm fires and lazy afternoons. The colours showcased by nature emanated those feelings well. Though there were dead or dying leaves scattered around, they wore glorious shrouds of their own eulogies. No matter how many times I had listened to it, it never ceased to bring me to tears and give me goosebumps, transporting me to a cosmic, abyssal plane. I couldn't recall a time, before or after the first listen, that equalled how utterly berserk my senses went. *What an experience that was.*

Andrew sat absorbed in a book, his glasses slipping down his nose every so often. He pushed them back up out of habit. Despite not having a troubled relationship as siblings, clear divides existed beyond just the age gap. Ever since I could remember, he was always reading. Dad often joked that he came into the world holding a book. Most kids in Weatonburg played outside in the heat, but he never wanted to. I had often wondered whether he faced bullying, and I asked him quietly one day, but he shook his head and continued reading. Whether by choice or necessity, his reading habits made him a bit of an outcast. We shared the outcast label.

People, closed-minded people, reject or attack things they don't understand. I have a… peculiarity about me, and I couldn't resent people for their negative reaction to something I myself, or anyone else, didn't quite understand. I *could*, however, resent them within reason for diminishing me when it made them look like less, even just in their own eyes. But kids are cruel, and they don't understand. I longed for this facet of mine to be known. But we all long to be known, whether strange or ordinary. The fact that I was a twenty-year-old in high school did not help my cause either. Circumstances had kept me in school until a few months ago. I was a late bloomer in certain regards, but not all. Which made me a bit of a conglomerate mess that didn't quite fit in anywhere. Neither excelled nor struggled in school, not ugly or awkward enough to get targeted for it. I didn't do sports, but I wasn't exactly nerdy, neither a child nor an adult. Perhaps no one knew what to make of me. I fell under the radar, occupying the outer fringes of people's awareness, except for one aspect about me.

My one friend, Anna, lived across our gravel street, but I wasn't her only friend. She was three years younger and as divergent from me as one could imagine. She was brash, hyperactive, and courageous around family and strangers alike, and I envied her for that. Although she was uninhibited by social cues, somehow it caused keen fondness in the people afflicted by her. I often wondered if, perhaps, we were only friends because she lived so close to me. As we got older, she drifted away even more with each passing year. Though our friendship did not entirely end, a noticeable transition took place. Daily visits and playing in the fields dwindled into barely seeing each other except in passing, and many unanswered messages. We never discussed my *'condition'*, and she ignored my fits whenever they came over me.

I wasn't too unhappy on my own, though I wouldn't deny I got lonely sometimes, but I could tolerate it. With our permanent departure, I had to leave Anna behind in more ways than one. I didn't know if I'd ever see her again. I doubted it. An unspoken hope burned within me that everything would change once I was in Ostia. Where I'd meet like-minded people who enjoyed my ability and accepted the strangeness I carried because of it.

The trees and road blurred past while I stared at nothing. An unfamiliar awareness tugged at my subconscious and forced me to focus. My eyes were cloudy from daydreaming, and I blinked myself into the present. My breath caught.

Ostia.

A plethora of visual information rushed at me all at once. A massive volcano stood to the left, an imposing force of nature. We descended into a natural basin at its foot, the compact, reddish town across the lake to the right. Ostia was still quite a distance away, and the broad highway snaked towards the waters. Buildings lined and receded from one half of the enormous, perfectly oval-shaped lake. The lapis lazuli blue lake shone crystal clear and bright like a polished stone. The surface glittered in the sunlight, and I looked away when my eyes stung.How green and dense the forest around the town and lake was. The viridity was complete, an intense heaviness of nature's dominion as I had never experienced before. Bright wildflowers fought for visibility beside the road, a welcome deviation of colour to the otherwise green palette. Heavy, tentacle-like trees encroached on the highway like some monstrous green creature.

I was in Neverland.

I pinched myself to verify that I wasn't dreaming. The closest I'd ever been to a fairy tale. My eyes burned. A sinister presence, or awareness, pressed into me. It had been there the whole drive but grew stronger the closer we came. Though it seemed adamant to be noticed, I couldn't quite place it. It lent authenticity to the fairy-tale aura of the whole place. I still couldn't pinpoint the feeling in the pit of my stomach, but it disturbed me. My pulse drummed against my neck.

Mom nudged my knee, pulling me from my thoughts. Her enlarged eyes were questioning—she didn't want to startle me. I smiled in acknowledgement and removed my earphones.

"Sorry," my voice caught, and I cleared it. "What did you say?"

"You'll hurt your ears at that volume." My dad said, looking at me in the rear-view mirror with a mocking smile in his eyes.

His words sounded yellowish-red. Colours were frequencies, after all—and I picked up on all manners of frequencies.Sometimes voices, tones, and sentences had hues. My mother simplified it as a *talent*, but it was much more than that.

"Oh!" Mom gasped, sending a jolt through me. I leaned over and my attention was soon seized. We had turned off on a side road, headed towards the volcano, with broken white stones, engulfed on both sides by an impenetrable forest. The road slithered up the massive volcano's foot, left of the town and lake. It carried us deeper and deeper into the *terra incognita*. Dad drove at a glacial speed, uncertain we made the correct turn—trespassing in a different world, a different time. Gawping at the steep, imposing volcano, I felt unsure about getting any closer. I expressed doubts about its dormancy, but Mom confirmed it had been inactive for almost a thousand years. Its incline rose, sharp and steep, covered in a blanket of trees right to the top, where it flattened out like a table. I wondered if it could be hollow on the inside.

An awareness tugged at my inward parts again, refusing to be ignored. *Something lay ahead.* I didn't know what it could be and didn't want to linger on the thought, so I forced it back down. But it kept pushing up.

Despite the broad daylight, the forest was a ghostly dark passageway. Ahead, a large and ancient, white-stoned arch—cracked and covered in moss and vines—framed the exit of the forest. Moss covered the huge prehistoric tree trunks next to the road, as well as the road itself. It saw little traffic it seemed. The car crept forward at a sloth's pace. As we sat there, absorbing everything, all four of us remained silent.

My senses slipped for a second, and I closed my eyes. When the darkness behind my lids lightened, I opened them again just as the car crawled out of the forest into a generous field with the greenest grass I'd ever seen.

My breath caught.

The manor house I had heard so much about awaited us like a noble guard, forever built into the sharp mountainside. Embedded there as if nature had formed it, along with the volcano it resided upon. I had seen nothing like it before. The façade was Art Nouveau and Victorian influenced with some distinct Baroque markers, but still of a singular style unbound to one period or region.

Sounds of wonder escaped from us all as the car closed in. I put a hand over my mouth, flabbergasted.

"Oh, wow! Look at this!" Mom gasped, her voice tight with emotion. "The pictures didn't do it justice at all!" She made a couple of unintelligible sounds of wonder before joining the silence. We were at a loss for words.

I nigh pressed my nose to the window, devouring every curve and plane, every exquisite and foreign detail. It held a roundish quality, and the dark grey roof existed out of multiple styles at different heights and directions, belled, canopied, tented, bowed, bellied. With all its levels and faces, guessing the number of storeys it had proved difficult, but I reckoned around three, maybe even four.

"I have the *perfect* room for you, Josilyn. It's separated from the rest of the house, so we won't bother you when you need to study or practice, and you'll have more privacy." Although somewhat disappointed that I couldn't choose my room, I was sure I'd have the option to change if more rooms were available.

"Thanks, Mom. I'm sure I'll love it. I mean, just *look* at this house!" I'd be happy sleeping on the porch. My dad blew affirmative grunts and nodded as he hunched and investigated.

"Evelyn, I'll admit I didn't expect this. I thought you had doctored the photos you showed me in some way. This is something else." He shook his head.

The light sandstone stucco walls and windowsills contrasted against the surrounding greenery. The left side was a large silo shape, about two floors high, yet the lowest part of the house, with the gabled roof facing different wind directions. Ivy covered half of this structure on the side closest to the mountain, swallowing it like a forest monster from grass to overhanging eaves. The car inched closer and came to a stop a little way from the porch steps, but none of us were prepared to get out yet.

Unabashed, I gaped at the beautiful house. No one in their right mind would pass on living in a place like this, so I was relieved I had made the right choice in joining them. Living solo could wait a couple of years. I wondered if it had hidden rooms or hallways where lovers met, or dark secrets lived—surely a house this old would. The thought of such a mysterious place was exhilarating.

"Oh, wow, look at that," Dad breathed. We all followed his gaze to the right—the lake. The light fractured and shimmered on its surface and stung my eyes. It appeared much larger from this elevation. The vivid blue water looked unnatural, like an artist had cleaned their giant ink brush in the water. Separated from the house by a steep, densely wooded area, it was still quite close. I didn't mind the forest voyage in the least. Since I was little, the idea of a fay forest captivated me. Weatonburg lacked nearby forests, so I had no experience with them. The thought of entering the trees enthralled me.

Though we all itched to explore our strange new world, Andrew broke the ice first and got out. Everything so contrary to what we were all used to. Showing no interest in the house, he ran into the forest to the left without hesitation, drenched in the mountain's shadow. I confess, the image of him running into the trees twisted my insides a bit. My dad stared after him as though he wanted to yell something, but he stopped himself. I saw his neck muscles relax and his eyes losing the momentary strain.

"Don't worry, Joseph. The wild animals don't come close to the mountain. I asked Catherine. And confirmed with the rangers. I needed to know, since the forest is so close." Mom touched his shoulder. I wondered why that would be.

"I mentioned to him a relaxing spot Catherine used to talk about." She followed up. He nodded and stared around him.

The partial stone pathway leading to the house was almost indiscernible under the cover of moss that clung to it like skin and the tall grass around it. I removed my flip-flops and wiggled my toes on the soft grass beneath my feet. It tickled, and I smiled. My eyes closed, and I inhaled the scent of the moist soil and crushed plants. Rich earth permeated my lungs, fresh and dark. I had never smelled anything like it.

My senses drifted. Holding my breath, I waited a few seconds for them to fall back into order before opening my eyes again. I had phased out, it seemed, because when I opened my eyes, my parents were already on the porch at the front door when they'd been right next to me a second ago.

From where I stood, I took a full view of the house again. A tall tower perched at the top, higher than the others. Parts of the walls seemed to have grown into the mountain or even from it. I wanted to see that room first. The view would be incredible.

The wide porch stretched from the silo to the right, ending with a gazebo. The bowed roof hung onto pillars and balustrades, which were also light sandstone. Stairs dipped from the porch and curled outwards with well-manicured round bushes in dark mason pots at the curve.

I didn't want to miss anything and scampered to where my parents were. The moss on the stones was soft and tickled my feet, making me smile again as I ran towards the steps. I looked up and saw Dad frowning at me when he noticed my novel glee. A smile puckered at the corner of his mouth. I grinned back.

The stairs fanned out and had stone balustrades. Weathered, tapering stone cast columns with engraved ornate details repeated along the length of the porch. Stonecast balustrades connected them with bellied middles tapering to the top, broad enough to sit on uncomfortably. I climbed the wide cold steps, which had large smooth stones like the porch floor, also of light sandstone. Sturdy, that's for sure.

I looked at the floor for a break; there was too much to process. Somehow, Mom was still rummaging through her bag for the key. My father and I exchanged a glance, eyebrows raised, not for her struggle but for the house. My dad nodded and looked out over the lake again, and I looked at the arched, dark wooden double front door and noticed the detailed carvings. Palace doors. One side had a detailed lotus carved out, and the other had a tree. Below the tree, the roots under the ground were visible. They reached down to something that looked like an underground cavern. I stared at that side for a long time. *Peculiar.*

"Are there caves in the mountain?" I asked my dad. He gazed out over the lake seeming to pull himself back from deep thought. He looked at the door and then at me.

"I'm not sure, but I'd reckon there'd be. An underground spring feeds the lake. We should find out and go caving." He winked at me and looked at my mom, still struggling to find the key.

I looked at the door again. To its right was a window. The dark wooden vine frame covered the glass partially, as if it had been a plant once, fighting its way to the light.

Mom finally found the key. Why she took so long was anybody's guess, considering it was as big as my hand. The head of the key had a lotus carved into it. Strange. It had probably been planned that way. The grooves were twisted and odd. Beautiful and ancient.

"How old is that key?" My voice had an odd edge that threw me off.

"This is just a replica of the original, which is housed in the mayor's office. This house is about three hundred years old. It's a town monument, so they've taken good care of it. It was a summer home for a duke. This was the first house to be built here." She pushed the key into the keyhole. "So, it's old world. It has a master's bedroom with en-suite, and three other bedrooms, three bathrooms, a study, two parlours, a sunroom and of course, a ballroom." The inclination in Mom's voice denoted the thrill she had relaying this information, which was totally justified, yet it made my stomach churn. I felt maybe we shouldn't be living here; no one should. It should be a museum or something.

She turned the key, and the lock made a jarring, loud *cluck*! She pushed the doors, which opened to the inside and revealed a grand and spacious foyer. Light cascaded down from somewhere above. We stood at the threshold, staring in. My heart hammered faster. The floor was sandy marble, and the wallpaper was a very subtle green with golden filigree. A broad stone cast sweeping staircase nestled against the left corner with sandy marble steps. The deftly carved dark wood resembled thick, twisted vines.

"Wow," I breathed, and my voice echoed through the house. I gulped. The opening where the stairs landed on the floor above was oval. Light streamed down as if the sky was open, the gold and crystal chandelier glistening.

My mom hesitated another second but stepped inside, and we followed her. For a moment, we just stood there, taking it all in. My dad blew out a loud breath.

"Well," was all he said.

I turned in circles, absorbing everything. Below the stairs, on the opposite wall, was a door, and beside it a hallway that led to the right. The right wall featured a framed, closed double door that mirrored the front door. I wondered what room lay behind it and why the doors were closed. A doorway to my left opened into a room inside the silo with tall, wide arched windows flanking the wall. Occupied by couches and sofas, I reckoned it must be the first parlour.

Though some part of me wanted to linger below and explore the rooms, I had an urgent pull that drew me to the stairs. The marble was icy beneath my feet, and a cold draught gave me goosebumps. The light above shifted as if bird shadows or a branch had intercepted it, making the marble floor seem to move for a moment. I touched the twisted wooden balustrade, feeling its smooth heaviness as it roped and twisted over and under itself. I looked up and gave a small gasp. Far above was a glass-domed skylight; I could see trees and a part of the mountain through it. I found myself walking up the steps, almost drawn into this beautiful and unexpected feature. My heart was so full that the surplus overflowed through my eyes. Below, I heard Mom and Dad crack open the door to the room behind the double door. By the sound of their echoing voices, it had to be huge.

My hand glided over the vined wood as I continued up, my gaze never leaving the glorious skylight as I felt my way up. Outside, I saw the impression of a taller structure. The closer I came to the landing, the more intense the tingles became until I shivered. On top, I tore my gaze away, turning back to look down the stairs. The light cascaded down, shifting and changing like a waterfall made of sunbeams—the marbled stairs looked like moving sand. I found myself leaning forward, mesmerised, only held back by the budding-flower-shaped railing knob. I took a deep breath to pull myself from the trance as I felt my senses on the cusp of falling out of order.

The landing opened to a broad, long hallway with a barrel vault ceiling, light coming from the farthest end. Above, the dome skylight connected to a coved ceiling leading to expansive windows at the front. They overlooked the town and the lake, situated above the front door from where I stood. On the right was a door to another room that would be part of the silo. Another hallway stood between me and the window, opposite to it. I saw no other set of stairs and I stepped deeper into the hallway; curious about the light.

A hand touched my shoulder, my senses rushed, and I gasped. Dad! He knew he shouldn't sneak up on me.

"The tower?" He speculated, ignoring my rapid breath. I nodded, swallowing down my heart.

"Well…" He trailed off and inspected the hallway. "Secret rooms and towers were supposed to be difficult to discover, so they hid the stairs." He swept his hands over the right wall as he entered the hallway, his eyes seeking intently. Being a historical writer, I could only imagine how exciting this must've been for him. The walls on both sides had the same green and gold wallpaper, with dark wooden spars creating a grid. He paused about two metres down the hall – touched a horizontal wooden bar—and then pushed his fingers into an invisible button of sorts. What unfolded before me seemed difficult to even believe. The hinges revealed a smaller-than-normal door shape in the wall. He gently pulled it towards himself, and the narrow door opened into a dark nook. You don't see that every day.

Pitch black inside, I squinted to see any shape or form in the darkness. My eyes didn't adjust much, but an icy breeze flowed over me from somewhere inside. The hairs rose all over my body as I stepped closer. I saw some steps straight in front, and my brain filled in the blank. A winding staircase. The area was just a tad larger than a square metre.

Dad stepped in halfway, peered upwards for a moment, and then retreated.

"Well, up you go." He smiled widely, and I returned it.
I searched for a light switch but found none, so I placed my hand on the left wall as I stepped in. The steps were steep and narrow, the cavity dark as night. The walls were imposing, and the dark had texture. No light came from above either, and I raised my right hand, afraid to hit my head. The stairs made a full rotation before I felt a wooden texture above me. Assuming it was a trapdoor, I pushed it. With a loud thud, it hit the floor above. Violent light streamed in, and I shut my eyes. Giving them time to adjust, I opened them after a few counts, too eager to climb into the room.

I froze at the landing and felt the air on my tongue as my jaw dropped. I had stepped into another era.

"No way," I breathed with a raw voice, my heart hammering in my throat.

A bedroom, adorned with furniture not from this decade or century, although kept in pristine condition. The front wall facing me was crescent-shaped and flanked by windows with broad window seats around half of the room with grey, crushed velvet cushions. It would be an idyllic place to read. One window was open, and the voile curtain swayed delicately in the soft breeze. The fresh scent of plants flowed in.

In the middle of the room, against the crescent wall, was a foresty Blackwood canopy bed with slender vine pillars curved to meet each other in the middle, soft grey voile draping cascading down like a dream. I approached and touched the pillar of the bed as if it would disappear at any moment. The ceiling was groin-vaulted with a dark wooden chandelier hanging from the pinnacle. My heart thrashed inside me, too overwhelmed to absorb it all.

The crescent wall took up half of the room and revealed the postcard-pretty view outside. Looking towards the back of the room, I could see the skylight to my left, lower than the floor. The room's back half, squared and windowless, seemed to extend into the mountain, based on its proximity to the outside.

A deep sense of privilege to have access to such a dreamy place overcame me, the emotions rising in my belly. If someone had told me a few months earlier I'd be standing in a place like this—living, no less—I wouldn't have believed them. It felt surreal. I took a wobbly step forward to explore further.

At the foot of the bed was a low-profile burgundy chaise lounge. In the windowless corner, a Blackwood vanity desk and grand wardrobe faced each other.

I turned to the crescent window again. To the left was another, slightly lower, tower. The roof of the rest of the house was lower than the floor and of all shapes and sizes.

Down the slope, the lake's crystal clear water lay smooth as a mirror, surrounded by green forest. It looked deep, with varying degrees of blue stained across the surface. I felt like it would pull me in and drown me if I stared too long. I looked beyond the lake. On the other side of the water, the town's reddish buildings with dark red roofs looked like corals on a mossy ocean floor. Similar to other old towns, the town plan was circular, with a small harbour and canal encircling the historic parts. The divide between old and new was clear: the recent parts didn't embank the canals but stood apart, expanding beyond them into the land towards the forest and quarries. The foot of the mountain on either side of the lake waned until it blended with the rest of the landscape, keeping the rolling terrain. In the farthest part of the town, I could just make out the quarry.

My eyes drifted back to my immediate surroundings. Our BMW X3 below seemed dissonant against the backdrop. Too black. Too crude. For a precious moment, I was not in the twenty-first century anymore but transported to a land of fairy tales, high teas, and passionate romance.

"Do you like what you see, Honey?" Dad pulled me from my reverie. I hadn't heard him come up, which was his intention, I'm sure. I wondered how long he'd been there. It took a moment to pull myself back into the room.

"Yes… I don't think anyone wouldn't like what they see. The view is unbelievable," I paused, "This room is fantastic. The house is out of this world. I… don't even really have the words. How did they get all these large pieces in here?" I couldn't wrap my head around it. Not with that small staircase.

"All of this came with the house. I figure it's been here since the beginning; probably built in this very room, or at least assembled here. The nobles didn't bother thinking about how convenient something will be to execute. They just threw wealth and status at it… I guess not much has changed since then."

I smiled at his little political jab, took an involuntary deep breath, and absorbed the room some more. Perhaps a room for a paramour or something desired but preferred hidden. What other purpose would a secret bedroom like this serve? My eyes focused enough to notice the vines and moss outside had grown onto the windows closest to the mountain face, leaving green trails on either side. Those windows definitely wouldn't open again.

"Why would they go through the trouble of blasting into the mountain just to build so little inwards? It seems like a waste of time and money."

"Well," he pursed his lips and stared at the back wall, "The story goes… They wanted to build the house completely into the mountain, but when they began the excavation, this was the deepest they could go. No matter what they tried, it was impenetrable." He frowned at the back wall.

"Hmm, I guess they didn't have the equipment to break into a volcano back then."

He paused, as if he had a secret he couldn't afford to let slip. "Yes…" he trailed off, "But they had dynamite. Even that couldn't breach the rock." *Unexpected.*

"That's interesting. Maybe it's an ancient bomb shelter and not a volcano." I tried to make a joke, but my voice sounded distant. A smile hinted at his pursed lips as he gazed down at the floor. I couldn't place his expression.

"Anyhow, I'm glad you like it. This is your room." He turned around, attempting a dramatic exit as he headed for the trapdoor. A chill trailed down my neck.

"What?" He just grinned as he descended. "But what about you and Mom? Or Andrew?" My voice was shrill. He continued his descent until I only heard his voice echoing in the confined space of the stairs.

"You haven't seen *our* room, and Andrew needs to be closer to the bathroom… and I want to check up on him without climbing stairs."

I heard him close the secret door below and gazed into the shadowed hollow. A strange feeling, an almost-fear, came over me. Taking a few steps back, I sat on the windowsill. I pushed the intrusive feeling away and instead absorbed my new life. *Definitely dreaming.* A dream I never knew existed had now come true. My heart was so full.

I couldn't believe they had given the room to me. Unreal. I waited for my dad to return and say, *"Ha, just kidding."* But he didn't. Houses and rooms like these had only existed in storybooks and movies for me, and now I lived in one. What an indescribable sensation.

Within a few moments, with no external reason I could perceive, the hairs on the back of my neck rose in the sudden, imposing silence I found myself in. I had been staring out the window at the trees swaying on the mountain side when my eyes snapped back into the room as if expecting to see something. They landed on the towering mirror for the first time. I just stared at it. Stretching from the floor to just below the ceiling's ornate cornice, it could not have been more obvious. *How had I missed that?* The room suddenly appeared expansive, doubled by this large axis. I got up and approached it, stopping right in front of it. I stretched my arms to the sides as if preparing for a hug, trying to touch the frame on either side with the tips of my fingers, but I couldn't. It was *gargantuan.*

The ornate silver frame looked like a twisting vine, just like the balustrades. I tapped it—unsure why—and got the impression the creation was solid silver and not just plated wood.

For a scant moment, so scant I barely noticed, my senses shuffled. A frown puckered. *Why did that happen?* When they fell back into place, I dug my fingers behind the frame and tugged at it. Built into the wall. I wondered for what nefarious, tricksy reason the builders would've done something like this. It went beyond pure ostentation and tipped closer to the edge of the eerie. The thought crossed my mind: perhaps this was a two-way mirror, with another room on the other side from which one could stare into this one. It gave me the creeps, and I pushed the idea away immediately.

I needed to unpack.

Before I headed downstairs, I gazed at the room—*my room*—again, but it was the mirror that kept drawing my attention.

Chapter 2

Five days passed in a dreamy blur, and we were happy. Happier than we had ever been as a collective. My heart felt so loaded it might burst, euphoria flooding me from simply existing in a place like this. The rest of the haul arrived on Monday with the grey Lexus UX—an exhausting few days of unpacking. Thursday afternoon, around 2 p.m., Mom and I were outside gardening. She plunged her fingers into the rich soil and massaged it like she was kneading dough.

"Hon, get some water for these, please."

The last seed rolled from my hand into the ground. More plants in a place so green seemed outrageous to me. Mom, however, had always wanted to try gardening. She thought there was too much green and wanted flowers for variation.

"I'll get it, Josilyn. Don't get up." I was not aware my dad was behind us. *How long had he been there?*

"Oh, thanks, Dad." My smile turned into a wide grin when I saw him sucking on a lollipop. It looked comical; a grown and serious-looking, bearded man sucking on a child's sweet.

I inhaled a breath of contentment and gazed up at the clear blue sky. The weather was lovely; the sun was bright with soft clouds overhead. A whimsical breeze passed through the forest every so often, swirling my hair around like strands of living things.

Mom inhaled a sharp breath. "Josilyn, don't move; you'll startle it," she whispered desperately. I solidified. At least I knew that if it was something gross, she would have attacked it—me— with some foreign object by now.

"What is it?"

"Shh!" she hushed, "There's a rare butterfly on your shoulder. I want to get a camera. Stay still." She ordered and backed away towards the house. Great; if I scared it off now, she would be sad about it the rest of the day. I could feel the light movement on my shoulder and took shallow breaths to not frighten it. Carefully, I turned my head towards the minuscule sensation on my skin. I didn't have to turn much before I saw the tiny blue speck. Its small body faced me. It was *tiny*.

My eyes barely grazed the beautiful critter when my senses became disorientated. It caught me by surprise, and my eyes fluttered in response, trying to sober them. But my delirium lingered, and it wouldn't shift back. Panic rose in my stomach as the *Pulse* continued crashing over my skin.

I accepted the probability that I had frightened the butterfly away with the jolts rolling through my body. Befuddled, I glanced at the spot where it had been. To my surprise, it was still there, but now it shone with a brightness that was absent just a few seconds earlier. Everything around me had turned into my familiar *other* world. The contrast seemed cranked up, making everything glow brighter. I couldn't tell if it was day or night, as it appeared to be both simultaneously. I often perceived the world and things around me differently than most would deem normal—a type of energy, a *Pulse,* that shuffled my senses, inverted them, one might say. Like I could see in ultraviolet, with blue and purple always being the most dominant hue. Though the *Pulse* never lasted long, it took complete control of me when near anything euphonious—*any* form. Sometimes, like now, it happened without sound being the reason.

The butterfly's wings flapped and with each downward motion, a slow, viscous, glowing mist rose in swirls around it. My eyes pounded and my ears sang—I kept blinking, but nothing changed. It would not shift back. None of my usual soothing tics worked. People found it unnerving when I gawked at everything around me as if I were looking at things they couldn't see. Which I was. When I resurfaced, they always looked troubled—*disturbed*, even. That, of course, made me feel *right* at home. They assumed that something was off with me mentally, or that I had epileptic or schizophrenic episodes. As I got older, I'd managed with self-control to keep my composure to a certain extent during these spells. People did not notice so much anymore, but the damage had already been done.

BOOM! A noise blasted in slow motion without warning, as if I was underwater. It sent a shock through my body, and the butterfly flew away. As it did so, my senses flipped back to normal, and the world around me back to its usual muted self. I gaped after it, swirling into the forest. *That was a first.* It had never lasted that long. I came to my senses, wondering what the sound was and if I had cause to worry. I turned to find my chuffed mom smiling at the camera in her hand.

"Did the camera make that explosive sound?"

She frowned at me and shrugged.

"I didn't hear any explosive noises, but I took a photo. I'm so glad I got it! That was a Dwarf Blue Butterfly, one of the smallest and rarest in the world. I'm surprised it stayed there for so long. When I got back, you were staring at it like it was poisonous; I would've flown away faster."

I stood up. A nerve in my neck twitched when I thought of what the photo might look like. "Can I see it?"

She handed it over, eyeing me with suspicion, and my heart sped up as I pressed the display button. *My camera.* A part of me wondered how she got it.

But of course, the photo revealed nothing odd, just the tiny blue stain on my bare shoulder gazing at me and me gawking back. *No fluorescent-mist cloud. No bright colours.* Everything was dull; normal. I didn't know whether I was relieved or disappointed. I didn't know what I expected to see; of course, no one else would see what I did. Like taking a picture inside your dreams, expecting it to be there in the morning.

Dad descended the steps with a water canister, glancing at Mom and me. My frown must have tipped him off. "What's happening?" He asked in a mild, nonplussed tone. Anyone unfamiliar with him might have thought him unexcitable, but that could not be further from the truth.

"You missed it! A Dwarf Blue Butterfly was on Josilyn's shoulder. It sat there for five minutes!"

"Wow, Mom, it wasn't five minutes. More like forty seconds." She looked at me, frowning, and her expression relayed to me she was not exaggerating.

"No, it was definitely closer to five minutes. I went upstairs but couldn't find my camera, so I had to go to your room and get yours. Obviously, I had no *clue* where you would have shoved it in. But I found it in your desk drawer, rushed downstairs and called your dad. Not forty seconds. I'm not Superman." She Chuckled.

Unnerving—It honestly felt like such a short time. However, an abrupt loss of time was nothing unusual for me.

"Dwarf Blue, huh?" Dad gazed towards the forest. "You know, according to local legend, if a butterfly lands on you, it signifies that the forest accepts you, recognises your presence, and welcomes you." He seemed caught up in thought after speaking. I wondered what went on in that head of his. Every so often, he spilt drops of knowledge that were beautiful in their brooding triviality.

Ruminating, the three of us gazed into the shadowed forest and listened to the murmuring leaves. "I guess the forest likes you, Josilyn." Mom teased. Right at that moment, Andrew emerged from the trees where we were staring.

He looked up and stopped dead in his tracks when he saw us looking at him. Uncertain, he turned back halfway, but then turned back to us.

"What?" he mumbled, a pout just about to form. I had not seen that expression in a while. The three of us stared at him briefly before spontaneous laughter erupted, and we walked towards the house. Andrew, still trying to make sense of what had just happened, followed us.

After our arrival, I kept noticing more details of the house—too much for my brain to process all at once. As we stood on the porch, I realised the ceiling was quite high. It curved from the house wall down to the overhang like a half-bell shape. The windows were almost as high as the ceiling and had stone outer frames, but the inner frames were dark wood. Catherine had left most of her furniture, including a dark cane set with blue cushions, a flat coffee table, and a couple of potted plants. The porch was about four metres wide. I had utilised the large, comfortable hammock by the gazebo often.

"Honey, when did you say the decorators will arrive again?" Dad asked, stepping aside for us to go through the door. The cool air inside contrasted with the heat outside.

"Um," she stopped, eyeing her watch, "they said by four, so in about two hours. I should probably make some lunch." She handed me the camera. "There's some stuff laying around in your room, maybe put it away? I don't know if they might want access to it, since it's the tower."

"M-hmm." I was not fond of the idea of strangers in my room, but I didn't have much of a choice. Some preconditions came with living in a historical house: traditional social events must be unaffected by our presence. Luckily, only one such event existed per annum: *The Forest Masquerade*, a fundraising ball in honour of the indigenous Forest Emperor Butterfly. The town used the funds to restore historic buildings, conservation efforts for the butterflies, and all other wildlife in the area. This meant masked strangers would infest our home the following evening. Fortunately, we were not the hosts, so we—I—could fade into the obscured crowd without feeling guilty, and I planned to. I didn't even have a dress yet. My mom loved surprising me and saw this as an excellent opportunity to do so in an elaborate fashion. She'd taken my measurements a while ago, but that was the extent of my knowledge. It was the day before the ball, and I was getting nervous about not having anything resembling a ballgown yet. But I didn't say anything.

A shiver ran up my spine when my bare feet touched the cold stone steps of my hidden staircase. Though I had used them often in the past week and a half, they still held a mysterious air. Every time I entered the hollow, it felt like the first time using it. I loved that feeling. A smile spread over my lips, and I pushed open the door above me and climbed into my room.

Apart from that initial instance, the mirror was now the first thing I looked at when I entered my room. I looked disgruntled and untidy, my ponytail tangled with leaves, loose strands awry. *Jeez, it's not like I rolled on the grass or something.* I walked to my vanity desk, placed the camera in the drawer, and threw my hair over my shoulder to rid it of leaves. This was one disadvantage of having long hair.

For no reason, I glanced at the mirror and caught a glimpse of the thin, slithering scar on the back of my left shoulder. The result of an obscured barbed wire in a bush where my rabbit had been hiding, and I had carried this scar for many years now. While not large, the strange pearl-colour contrasted against my pale skin, making it noticeable. It didn't bother me because it was out of sight, anyway.

The mirror reflected my dad's head popping out of the gap in the floor. I turned and smiled. When he reached the landing, he stood akimbo and peered around the room. Feigning approval, he nodded.

"Well, your room is clean enough. Now… If I remember correctly…" he rubbed his bearded chin and frowned at the floor, "This ball requires a dress." He smiled and winked. "Let's go get yours."

That explained the keys in his hand. I laughed and shook my head.

"We can't leave now. Mom's making lunch."

He rolled his eyes and beckoned me to come as he turned.

"When did you get so mature and boring?" his voice was crisp and echoed in the narrow space, "It's just sandwiches. It's not like they'll get cold. We'll sneak out." He probably had her go-ahead.

When we reached the curve of the main stairs, he pressed his index finger to his mouth. I nodded and pursed my lips to keep myself from laughing. We snuck down the stairs and out of the front door. When we stepped onto the porch, we jogged towards the car in exhilarated mischief. It turned into a suppressed race as the two of us tried to out-walk-jog each other. I wondered what my mom would have thought if she saw us.

Hurried, we got into the car and burst out laughing. He put the keys in the ignition, cringing as the engine roared to life. The wheels spun as he tried to get away as fast as possible. I grabbed hold of anything I could grasp as rocks and grass flew everywhere, and he raced into the forest. Deep within the trees, he slowed down and acted as though nothing had happened.

"You see? That wasn't too dangerous, was it?" his voice was even.

"No, not at all. Well, except for some collateral damages like… oh, I don't know… my *neck*," I joked while rubbing it.

"Well, you see? Now there's a good reason we must go into town. I had a premonition."

"Ah, yes. Those are undeniable."

"I've taught you well."

"Yes, you have, Sensei."

We could banter for hours. When I was much younger, we acted out entire stories, creating props and clothes out of old plastic bags, fabric and boxes. Of course, I was a princess. He would be an evil king or monster, eventually destroyed by my *'perfect goodness'*. Andrew found it too awkward to join in. For some reason, he couldn't quite grasp the idea of pretence. Maybe he was just too young. He couldn't find enjoyment in pretending along with us. Luckily, he didn't do too badly when he went to school. My dad had home-schooled me for a few years between the ages of six and thirteen, though not in succession. The school would give permission when things were acute, but once I had a semblance of control again, I'd return.

Anna never asked about it. She chose the easier way: ignorance. I'd test the waters driven by my great need to share my burden, but I had the impression she was unwilling to go there. She was my only friend, and to have lost her because of something I couldn't help would've been detrimental to my young and needy heart. So, I had to master my soul—tame my child's heart's desire to have many friends and to be accepted because of my insecurities about who and what I was. I remembered playing on the carpet in front of the TV once, and a programme about space had been on. They'd shown a supernova or a nebula; I couldn't remember which one. I remember the vivid moving colours of particles and energy and thought that if I had to describe how my gift looked, that would be it. A cloudy mass of rainbow colours and power that was beautiful and terrifying all at once, not unlike the strange world when it came over me. *The Shift* always became more intense when I was miserable and lonely. Maybe it was tied to vulnerability. The music consumed me, incinerating the paper walls I had meticulously pasted as a façade. If I'd learned one thing from watching people, it was this: behind closed doors we were all the weird, uncool kid. As soon as that realisation had sunk in, I was okay.

"You're not supposed to think so hard until classes start. Spare your brain."

I grinned at him. Trying to hide anything from him was useless.

"Oh, I think I have some brainpower to spare for insignificant mind tortures."

He stayed silent, which caused a childlike discomfort to rise somewhere between my heart and stomach. Maybe I shouldn't have used 'torture'.

"Ah, don't we all."

At that, the tightened knot in my chest loosened.

The dense, tall trees made seeing the lake, or much of anything else, impossible. We soon passed the road we first came in with, but I only just recognised it as we drove past the T-junction, hidden as it was. I got to thinking…

"I guess you'll be the right person to ask about the town's history?" He got that knowing smirk he always did when he couldn't wait to share his knowledge.

"Some might argue that fact, But I know some of it. It's an old town, so there are a lot of variations. This area belonged to a duke, one that history has little to no record of. So, it's a bit shrouded in mystery.

Anyway, he had a beautiful daughter betrothed to another noble, as was customary. But one day, a young man filled with wanderlust happened upon her while exploring the world. Of course, her otherworldly beauty utterly bewitched him. They say she had white gold hair, skin like snow and dark brown eyes. She too could not stop herself from falling for him and succumbed to her desire for him; his vigour and the fire that burned in his soul. Their love was akin to Romeo and Juliet, passionate and short-lived. Although, it wasn't death that separated them, but he who left, presumably thinking it the more honourable thing to do because she was betrothed. And so was he.

She struggled to hide her broken heart, which prompted her parents to send her to their country home for a time. They thought she was going through a low season and needed a change of scenery. She had to travel by ship across a vast distance and would not return until the day before her wedding. Not long after arriving, she realised she was pregnant and kept it a secret. Only her chaperone remained unfooled but kept it to herself, and at the birth, they discovered it was twins. She bore two baby boys but unfortunately lost her life.

As her confidant, she instructed her chaperone to keep the secret and to ensure their adoption into a suitable home. She didn't want to dishonour her parents with the truth. The chaperone found the babies a home before the girl's parents arrived for the burial. Her persuasions were weak, though, and caused the twins to be separated into different towns.

The story's most tragic part was that the young man who stole the young lady's heart had been her betrothed. Unaware of this, the chaperon lived in the torturous pit of her secret, unsure whether to tell, watching as kingdoms fell because of the unforeseen death and torn alliances. The painful reminder led them to forsake the cherished country house.

The chaperone returned in old age to find the two boys, now men, and tell them the truth about their heritage. Her regret was heavy and multiplied when she could not find the men nor a trace of their adopted families. Discouraged, she returned to the country house, where she intended to cast off her breath on the grave of her keep.

When she arrived, she was surprised to discover the town had transformed from just a road with an inn to a bustling hub with a quarry and many other industries. It had become a proper town with the manor house no longer abandoned. She had received no word about the property being bought or revisited. It was supposed to have been a proverbially sealed tomb. Two men came out of the forest and approached her. At first sight, she knew they were brothers. They were *the* brothers." He gazed out the window as if he saw everything playing out before him. I frowned at him. The story seemed somehow familiar to me, and saddened me like it was a trodden path.

"Is it our house?" I whispered. He was quiet for a moment and then turned to me, smiling.

"Yes."

Ice ran over my skin; hair rose all over my body.

"Why does this story sound familiar to me?" *It had made me feel that way before.*

He frowned at the road and took long to respond.

"Well, I told it to you many times when you were little. I mean, the house runs in the family, and it's an interesting story. Who could've guessed we'd be part of the story one day?"

A thrill ran down my spine again. It shouldn't have felt peculiarly portentous—being a family story—but it did. Which meant, to some extent, we were royalty, if only by distant blood.

"What happened next? After she saw them. How did she know it was them? How did they find each other?"

Dad took a deep breath and pulled a face.

"That's where things aren't so clear. The story goes both men kept hearing rumours of exploits by someone who looked exactly like them, as their eyes and features were distinct. However, they knew full well it couldn't be them in those specific cases. You see, they were identical twins but for one difference: they were mirror twins with heterochromia in their eyes, one icy grey, the other hazel. However, as mirror images, one had their grey eye on the left while the other had it on the right. They eventually met; and one could hardly dispute that they were twins. How they came back, no one knows. They followed rumours and industries and found the house abandoned. As for what happened after the chaperone spilt the beans; she wrote a letter to the queen, widowed and old, confessing everything. But we don't know what happened after that. But of course, you and your mom are here, which means the bloodline didn't die out, and the brothers obtained legal ownership of the house. I don't know which bloodline dried up in the end."

What an unpleasant thought; so much history just for a bloodline to end.

We drove down the wide pale grey road for about another kilometre when it transitioned into cobblestone. The stones were square and neat, smooth, salt pink. I doubted they were original. The wild impeding cloak of the forest encroached upon the town, but the trees thinned out; the flora more contained and groomed. A stone bridge lay ahead, and on either side of it stood two giant reddish statues that stared down at the road like twin Michelangelo's David's turned into sombre judges. The bridge was too narrow for two cars to cross, and we waited our turn to cross over the bright blue waters of the canal that lured the lake's waters off course. Two people leisurely rowed a boat up the canal. The canal was about the width of three cars, bumper to bumper.

Beyond the bridge, the road widened once more, but not designed to accommodate modern cars, the surrounding buildings restricted its width. A road that followed the canal curve crossed the main road we were driving on. On either corner were tall buildings made of the same reddish stones. We went uphill, and the tall buildings with climbing plants on the walls and small balconies induced vertigo after a few moments, so I looked down at my lap for a break. Such a strange new world.

The buildings atop the hill lost their height, with only a couple of single-storey structures remaining. The wide left sidewalk transitioned into a piazza with cafés, shops, and animated characters that fit in a movie scene.

One of these characters, in particular, drew my attention. The old man with sun-weathered skin crouched down to feed the pigeons on the ground. They weren't the morbid blue-grey I was used to, but snowy white. He sat down on a weathered bench and opened a case I hadn't noticed he had with him. A bruised saxophone emerged, clasped between old hands.

He played without pause. Though the sound was faint through the window, my senses shifted momentarily, and I shook it away. My dad sighed and squeezed my knee.

"You okay?" A redundant question, he knew.

"Yes."

It was difficult for him, not knowing what my *condition* was about. I saw his frustration grow on more than one occasion. Despite the frustration it caused him, he became enamoured and willingly beguiled when I played music for him.

"Oh, here's a spot," he declared, breaking my reverie as he swerved into a parking.

"Do you know where the place is?"

He frowned at me. "No, I don't. I thought we'd wander around aimlessly until someone took pity on us and gave us a dress. I thought that would be a fun thing to do."

Rolling my eyes, I got out.

"Don't sass me, mister I-often-forget-I-need-to-know-where-I'm-going."

He pulled a face and walked into a narrow stone-faced alley, confident. I followed him up to a wide patterned glass door a few strides along and he opened it. A black sign in elegant gold script swung above the door. *Beatrice's.* Fancy. My dad's confidence surprised me as he walked in like he had been there a hundred times. A short corridor with a wooden floor and blue Persian carpet lay behind the door, ending with a tainted brown glass door. Upon entering, a bell above the door chimed. I needed a moment to absorb the ballet-studio appearance of the large room filled with beautiful clothes and dresses on golden hangers. No one was at the desk.

A halo of light flowed through the angled glass roof, highlighted by the mirror-flanked walls and polished floor of the room. The musky scent of polish still hung in the air, along with the classical sound of piano music in surround sound.

I was so fixated on the room I didn't notice Dad had moved to the waiting corner on the left, a chic upholstered sitting area. He sat down and cleared his throat, implying I should stop gaping like I wasn't used to these types of shops, but I wasn't. I approached a cream-coloured chair and sat down, feeling like I'll be scolded for doing so imminently. Dad got hold of some lady's magazine, which he pretended to find interesting. The model on the front page looked like she had extra joints and wore a weird hat. '*Hatters Digest*'. Peculiar.

"Wow," I breathed as I absorbed the full beauty and intricacies of the room. Dad didn't lift his head and kept paging through the magazine.

"Uh-huh."

The far-back door flew open—I jumped from the chair, nearly falling off. A tall and voluptuous woman emerged, displaying a cover girl's smile. Beatrice, I assumed. She posed an intimidating impression, as if she wanted to place me on a stage before a crowd, put a spotlight on me, and yell, '*Look at her*'. My hands tightened around the armrests as she approached.

"Ah! I didn't hear you come in!"

Her eyes locked on me, and she walked straight up to me like a missile. A sudden sense of entrapment sprang through me; a part of me wanted to flinch or run away. I recalled my manners and stood up, giving an awkward smile, self-conscious of my dangling arms.

"Oh my! You must be Josilyn. Your mother was right; just look at those eyes; even bluer than I imagined!" She exclaimed in a deep operatic voice, collecting me into an enveloping, plump hug. *Way too tight.* After a few seconds that felt like an eternity, she pulled away and pinched my chin between two thick fingers, scrutinising me.

"Such a peculiar, innocent beauty. And yet…" she trailed off in thought, then snapped back, took my hand, and pulled me along. She was strong. I stared back at my dad with gigantic eyes, a smirk painted on his face, pretending to 'read'. Her description of 'peculiar, innocent beauty' left me confused. I'd always thought my face was childlike, too pouty, too rounded with a pointed chin. My eyes were big, and I seemed either perpetually surprised or almost asleep, dreamy. She towed me to the door she came out of earlier, her hand cold and clammy around mine. Her dark brown hair, cut into an immaculate Chinese bob, moved like satin through the air. Her dress was a vintage button-up, knee-high, and body-hugging silk. The colour was light buttermilk with a darker shade damask pattern and fit her full hourglass figure well.

A spacious dressing room awaited behind the door, with six cubicles—three on each side. Golden ropes pulled aside the thick brown velvet curtains with large golden tassels, a skylight scattering light from above. *Lots of lights.*

"Wait here for a second, Pumpkin," she commanded, disappearing behind a door that seemed too small for her. In the awkward silence, I stood and listened to the sound of plastic being ripped. I didn't know what to do with myself.

She reappeared.

"Here it is."

She ceremoniously spread the champagne creation open against her chest, revealing the dreamy, beautiful dress in its full glory. My breath caught. Like an urge, I stepped forward to touch the big, flowy skirt. The layers of tulle were thick and luxurious and soft between my fingers. The shades varied among them. Peeping out beneath all the tulle was golden satin. The bodice was a full-on corset with exquisite strings, ribbons and lace, some of subtle gold, others of light coffee. Its structured lines gave it a modern flair, emphasising the female form, even off the body. The tulle puffy bishops' sleeves were off the shoulder. My tongue dried from gaping.

"Well, staring is rude, isn't it?! Go try her on so I can see if she fits!" I looked up at her, the cold air in my widened eyes. I didn't know how on earth I'd put it on? She guessed my thoughts.

"Oh, don't worry about the corset. It's quite easy to put on yourself." I took the two-arms-full dress into the cubicle, surprised to find it roomy with large mirrors on the three walls. The side mirrors could rotate, providing a view from all angles. I had a thorough dislike of dressing rooms. No matter how good I felt that day, it always made me look like ugly melted ice cream. I avoided looking as I got dressed, which was surprisingly easy. The bodice had faux buttons at the back but fastened with a hidden zip. I couldn't secure the clips myself, but that wasn't a problem. Side lacing on the bodice allowed for dress tightening when required. I rose to my toes and stepped back to look in the mirror.

Breath left my lungs, and my eyebrows shot up. I felt like I was having an out-of-body experience, watching someone else in the mirror. I couldn't believe the dress on me—a dress for movies and runways, not an obscure ball in an unknown town, *not* for a small person.

The tulle also covered the bodice, encrusted with vintage gold beads in detailed swirls on the torso. It draped off the shoulders like a delicate, soft mist. The neckline was heart-shaped and much lower than I was used to. The corset amplified the exposure. My shoulders slumped, somewhat trying to hide.

"Well, what's happening in there? Are you getting on alright?" She had an edge to her voice. I had forgotten about her. I moved the heavy curtain away and lifted the front of the skirt, rising to my toes. With it still spread across the floor like a fantasy robe, I stepped out.

Awe filled her gaze as she devoured me from head to toe, like I was a revelatory éclair to be consumed. My shoulders rounded even more. Her eyes changed, and she pushed me back through the door, into the hall where my dad waited. I nearly dug my heels into the floor, but I'm pretty sure it wouldn't have helped. She stopped and squared me up in my dad's direction. She stepped to the side and displayed me to him as a magician would their prestige. He looked over his magazine and lowered it without taking his eyes off me. His eyebrows lifted. She didn't seem to appreciate his delayed reaction because she gave an exacerbated sigh and took me by the shoulders, bodily rotating me towards a large mirror. Her face beamed—understandably so, seeing the dress in the mirror again.

"I'm speechless." My voice was uneven. Her face scrunched into an even greater smile, and she squeezed my shoulders. Dad stood staring at me with a strange twitch of his eyebrows.

"There's more," she walked to the counter, picked up a wooden box, and returned. "Open it."

Uncomfortable, I opened the lid as she held the box out to me. My jaw dropped. I couldn't keep my greedy hands from picking up the stunning mask. Gold and coffee lace covered the soft champagne mask, with intricate patterns of tiny pearls and vintage golden beads, and coffee-coloured feathers blended in.

"Wow. This is stunning. I've never seen anything like it. Thank you so much."

"No, thank *you*! I've been doing this for years, but I've never had the opportunity to give this one to someone. It inspired the dress. I'm glad you like them both."

"I *love* them both, thank you."

My dad appeared close by, watching us.

"That's quite a dress, Honey. You look ravaging," he frowned, "I'm not sure how I feel about that." Beatrice laughed in high spirits.

"Oh, the sooner you accept the inevitable, the better!"

Shy, I smiled at him but couldn't hold eye contact for long. My stomach twisted, though I wasn't sure why.

"Evelyn has already sorted out the payment, so let me just place that in its box and then you're good to go." She announced with a satisfied smile.

Four eyes watched as I walked back, but it felt like a thousand. I found my hands trembling as I took the dress off. The last few weeks felt like a mystical story, like I'd stumbled into a fairy-tale world. The house, the forest, and the dress were all surreal, but somehow it left me feeling uneasy. Fairy tales were dark in general.

Beatrice stood waiting outside the cubicle when I stepped out. She gave me a look and disappeared behind the small door again. I wondered what was behind it. Perhaps a legion of small elves crafting magical dresses. She reappeared with an enormous matte black box, her name written in gold. I thought to take it, but she walked past me into the large hall. She pushed it into my dad's arms. Bewildered, he stared at her. You'd think she'd handed him a bull's head or something.

"Enjoy the moment, my dear! I'll be looking for you come Friday night. Goodbye," she said and retreated into that mysterious backdoor unceremoniously.

We stared after her for a second and then at each other, wide-eyed. I opened the doors for Dad, and we left. Outside, eyes gawked at the enormous box as we walked to the car, and I was glad I was not the one carrying it. Dad nearly bumped into someone and dropped the box right by the car. Eyes made me nervous, but we reached the car soon. A little girl stared at me while I waited for the car to unlock. I smiled at her, and she blushed and hid behind her mother.

Every time I surveyed the town, I uncovered a new marvel. The stone and cast-iron balconies on higher floors, the moss and climbing vines clung to the stone walls of alleys and the fascinating people looked nothing like I was used to. What seemed like a perpetual saturation filter tinted the town, enhancing the contrast between the vivid green of nature and the reddish masonry architecture, making the colours pop even more.

Unable to do a U-turn due to the increased traffic, we drove around the block. I didn't mind; it all being so beautiful. The forest seemed denser and engulfed us as we drove back, making my dad and I think we'd taken the wrong turn, despite there being no turnoffs—just a single winding road all the way home.

We drove through the arch and saw Andrew on the porch steps, chin on his knees. He saw us and jumped up, running into the house.

"Uh oh. Looks like you're in trouble," Dad sighed.

"*Me?*"

"Yes. You fickle child." He kept a straight face, but I burst out laughing.

We got out and I beat my dad to the box. Carrying it from here was only fair, since it *was* mine, after all. When I reached the front door, I slowed down to listen if I could hear my mom.

"I can't hear them. Where do you think they are?" I turned around, but evidently, I was talking to myself, as my dad was nowhere to be seen. Probably hiding. I shook my head and snuck into the house, tiptoeing to the stairs. This was, of course, all an act; we weren't hot-tempered people. I didn't hear anyone as I ascended to my room. My eyes darted to my mirror when I stepped onto the landing. It wobbled as if someone had shoved it. The hairs on my arms stood on end, and the box fell from my hands, the dress spilling onto the floor like a golden river. I stared at the mirror, bewildered and unsettled. The room was empty, with no breeze strong enough to affect something stuck to a wall. I took a hesitant step towards it, and it stopped moving right away, and so did I. I felt my heart beating in my neck and the oxygen rushing to my head. The silence was thick and solid, apart from my heart. Unblinking, I stared, waiting to see if it would move again, but it didn't. I took another tentative step. It had certainly moved. Unless someone had snuck mushrooms into my breakfast.

Confusion contoured my face as it became a mirror in my psyche again. I reached out to touch the frame and wiggled it with increasing force. It didn't budge, not even a little—rock solid. The frame was, without a doubt, affixed securely to the wall. Was my mind playing tricks on me?

"Joseph?!" Mom called from below, and I jumped at the sudden interruption. Eyeing the mirror, I descended my steps just in time to see my dad hastening to their room, but when I followed him, he turned into the left corridor.

"Dad?" I followed him to see what he was up to. He rushed into his study on the right side. Faint footsteps grew clearer and drew my attention. Mom looked at me when she reached the landing.

"Where did he go?" I understood. I hesitated a second, almost looking at the study, then lifted my shoulders.

"Don't know." Unconvincing. Sceptical, she peered at me, but then walked to the study like a mind-reading missile. I was that obvious, it seemed. I followed her. My dad stood behind the door and looked at her with big, innocent eyes.

"I'm pleading not guilty. She made me do it!" Mom and I stared at him in surprise, not knowing what to make of it, and then burst into laughter. What a traitor!

"Don't be silly; I just want to know if you got the extra lanterns for the forest?" He relaxed his posture and straightened up with deviance.

"I knew that. Yes, I just placed them under the canopy. Have the decorators said anything about their whereabouts?"

"They called about five minutes ago; they will be here shortly. The road was quiet, so they're a bit early."

"Fascinating. Should I bring the lanterns in?"
She answered in the affirmative, and he passed us. She lingered.

"So, do you like the dress?"

"Yes, it's stunning!" I remembered I had left it spilt on my floor. "Thank you for all your trouble, Mom. I appreciate it a lot. It's more than I could've ever asked for."

"No trouble, Honey. I enjoyed the thought of you in a dress like that." The roaring of a truck in the distance became noticeable.

"A truck? I didn't quite realise it's *this* big of a deal."
She looked at me and turned around, shrugging.

"You have no idea."

I didn't consider myself shy per se, but I had the urge to escape and retreated to my room. Gathering up the dress, I glanced at the mirror with suspicion. I opened my window and leaned forward to peer outside, a bird's-eye view, without having to deal with social awkwardness. The lawn turned into a busy gathering within minutes as the decorators unloaded. I should have guessed as much when I heard they would start today already.

The side of the truck had the words *"Mega Deco"* printed on it. About fifteen men emerged from behind it, carrying an immense bag.

"I'm hiding out with you, okay?" A jolt went through me when Andrew spoke behind me.

"Don't sneak up on me!" I shrieked, and he laughed, unfazed, as he came to my side, knees on the broad windowsill.

"So, it begins."

I pondered the statement, wondering what the future held.

"It has begun," I mimicked.

Chapter 3

Mom and I returned home from the hairdresser—a tiresome business. I had no idea what she used on my hair, but it ended up being almost jet-black. They did our makeup too, so we'd showered before we went. They gave me a gold and black smokey-eye look that made my eyes appear witchlike—*otherworldly*—if I had to say so myself. It freaked me out a little, and the beauticians kept talking about it.

We passed the arch into the clearing and caught the house in the final preparations stage. The enchantment surpassed its usual level: lanterns decorated the left side of the stone road up to the house, hedging it off, and flower petals of various sorts and colours lay strewn on the lawn. A blood-red Capri marquee draped in fairy lights occupied the lawn, the floor a temporary wooden deck that held the decadent buffet. I heard the caterers talk about truffle-buttered roasted potatoes and crumbed mushrooms, and my mouth watered just thinking about it. Red mosquito nets hung on the sides to keep insects out. A live orchestra would occupy our ballroom, which would host dancing.

The full magnitude of the evening hit me. All the red made my heart speed up. It looked dramatic against the backdrop of the old mansion and a dormant volcano.

Fairy lights adorned the pillars and balustrades of the porch, no corner left in darkness. All the lights in the house were on—including my room—though it wasn't dark yet, and it gave the house a sense of liveliness instead of the usual tranquil silence. I felt uneasy at the idea of strangers in my room—unfamiliar, having so many people in my space.

"It took longer than I expected. We need to get dressed right away; guests will start arriving in about thirty minutes, maybe sooner," Mom fretted, darting out of the car. Our car would be out of sight, behind the gazebo next to the kitchen. Mom went through the kitchen, but I went around front. The ballroom chandeliers were on, the orchestra on their temporary stage against the large concave bay window overlooking the forest.

The fairy lights with red gauze petals woven through the balustrades looked like flowers. Outside the front door, a waitress poured champagne into rows of glasses. Like the rest of them, she wore a forest green 17th-century French-inspired suit. She smiled when I came up the stairs. On the porch and all over the house were bouquets of red, blue, and purple flowers—roses and lilies—in pewter and vintage gold vases. I had never seen a blue lily before, but it just upgraded to my new favourite flower. The ballroom buzzed with activity as people walked back and forth. I heard the masters of ceremonies talk non-distinctly as it echoed.

When I reached my room, a man standing at my desk startled me. I stopped in my tracks. With his back turned towards me, he just stood there, frozen. He evidently didn't hear me come in. He wore a black suit with no mask, his hair a voluminous honey blonde. Guests weren't supposed to be here yet. I didn't want to be rude, so I stood there staring at him. He grew aware of me and turned around. I was surprised to find him not much older than me. He met my gaze, and his absent expression turned to a frown as he looked at me.

"Oh, I'm sorry. I was…" he looked at the ground, perplexed, "doing last checks. I'll be on my way." He strode towards me—to the stairs—and his amber eyes, for a moment, locked with mine. Something about it seemed brazen, and I felt my cheeks flush. I took a step further away to let him pass, his movement liquid and slow. He descended the stairs in no hurry.

"Would you please close the door below?" He turned and looked up at me with large, enchanted eyes. It startled me, and I felt my heart swell.

"Of course." He closed the flap on himself, and I stared at it for a while, replaying the unexpected exchange. My cheeks glowed. One disadvantage of the room: having an awkward trapdoor as the only entry point. I stooped and slid the chain lock into place. Having someone come in while I was getting dressed would be the worst.

The windowsills had vintage lanterns on plates. My desk and the surrounding floor were adorned with glass vases showcasing elegant, deep purple lilies. The mirror had also gained an array of fairy lights on its frame. I wondered if *he* had done that. I suddenly felt uneasy in my room.

After retrieving my dress from the wardrobe, I set it on the bed, along with the mask. I stared at the duo for a bit, in sheer disbelief that it was my shell for the resplendent evening.

Just as I finished putting on and fastening the dress, a knock came from the floor. I unlocked the door, and my mom emerged looking ravishing in a fitted satin, king-blue dress. I had never seen her in a formal dress before, or so well put together. Her eyes grew large when she saw me.

"Mom! You look absolutely stunning! That is definitely your colour!" Her cheeks flushed, and she ironed the dress with her palms.

"Thank you. Your father deserves the credit. But Honey, you look… so, *so* beautiful! I almost want to cry."

She helped fasten and adjust the bodice until it formed against my body like paint. She gave me an antique-looking golden ring dressed with a single, oval-shaped garnet that looked like solidified blood. "Wow, it's beautiful. Thanks Mom, I love it." I gushed and gave her a warm hug. The ring went well with my dress and the colour scheme of the evening.

"I saw it in an antique shop in town, and I had the impulse to get it for you. I thought you'd like it," she said with a smile, "Finish up and get downstairs. We can't be late." She took her leave as arriving cars whirred outside, signalling the first guests.

I donned the mask, which worked like spectacles. My half-up, half-down hair concealed the curved golden stems. I looked in the mirror for the complete image—decorated room and all. It didn't look like me in the reflection. I danced around and watched my dress sway—quite a sight, though I felt disconnected from myself. It could've been a dramatic oil painting.

I looked at my back and saw my scar showed. For some reason, I felt self-conscious about it, but couldn't do much. As I regarded myself in the mirror, a sense of unease pressed into me, which made me escape the room. Fairy lights also lined the narrow stairs now. The thrum of many people in the foyer reached me, and I grew nervous about making my entrance. It felt like a movie cliché. To my great relief, I attracted little attention as I descended.

I was halfway down the staircase when the pianist commenced their arrangement in the ballroom; Chopin's Nocturne in C# minor. I have always loved the composition. *Dramatic. Melancholic. Passionate.* My senses rushed like temperamental waves, and I buckled against the balustrade, clenching my eyes shut. I heard the alarm in someone's voice on the ground floor when they asked if I was okay. The yellow mist of their voice curled up towards me in wisps, then faded. I nodded and forced a smile, taking a deep breath as I opened my eyes. Supporting myself on the balustrade, I continued the descent. Below, people received champagne at the front door and entered the ballroom, parlour, or stayed in the foyer, oblivious to me. The only exception—the man in my room from earlier. He looked at me with intention when I reached the foyer floor, but I chose not to engage and wandered onto the porch. Had he been waiting for me to come out? I received a couple of glances from behind masked faces and resigned to look at my feet as I walked to the gazebo.

Utilising the valet services, the cars would pull up between the porch and the marquee to drop off their occupants, then circle the tent in a clockwise manner before finally exiting the clearing. A stop-and-go operational at the arch. They used a semi-open field one kilometre away for parking. The cars ranged from Mercedes and BMWs to Porsches and Audis to plain old kombis holding multiple people, all in impeccable garb and masked up.

"There's a lot of people tonight." Andrew stood under the gazebo; I walked over to him. He looked adorable in his black suit and white ruffled collar. His strange black harlequin mask covered the upper part of his face. The eyes slanted upwards in an awkward manner, with splashes of bright blue and white that contrasted against his light brown, wavy hair. The four of us were all brunettes. My mom's and mine were an almost black-brown, and my dad's was the same as Andrew's, though the grey was taking over.

"Yeah. We should have expected as much, though I didn't. But yes, there is."
He bit his lip, "So, I guess there won't be kids my age coming then."

"You never know." I doubted there would be. "Why have I seen so little of you these past few days? You only come out of the forest to eat and sleep…" I nudged him. He was almost my height—not much of an accomplishment—but if Dad's height was any indication, he would tower over me in a couple of years.

He stared at his shoes, twisting and turning his feet.

"I like the trees. It's so strange and green, so much different from Weatonburg," He turned and gestured to the surroundings.

Rich orange light washed over his mask. *Sunset.* The rolling clouds were bundled roseate scarves dipped in blood and set on fire; the light breeze made them sway around like dancing flames. My breath caught. The beauty stung my eyes. I had never seen such an intense sunset, and the bulging, rolling clouds awakened a foreboding tug inside me.

"Are you ready for Monday?" Andrew pulled me from my reverie. Reluctant to shift my gaze away from the clouds, I lingered.

"I'm… uncertain. Everything's different now. I mean, I'm thrilled I'm done with school finally, but I fear the unknown that lies ahead. I don't know what to expect."

"It's not like they can teach you anything, really. I don't know why you're even bothering." He shrugged and flipped a curl trailing down my back. I ruffled up his hair. Not that it was significantly tidy. We talked some more as all the guests arrived. The orchestra began playing Arvo Pärt, Fratres.

"We should go in. Formalities will begin soon." Andrew walked before me, and I glanced back as I let others walk in. Twilight had fallen, and only a few cars came up the road. All the lights were coming into their justice. I lost myself again, and when I came to, I was strolling towards the ballroom with a champagne glass in my hand. I didn't drink alcohol because it didn't mix well with my 'constitution'. Only a few people remained in the foyer and parlour. Most had gone into the ballroom, and I hesitated at the door. The ballroom seemed like a time capsule tonight, the chestnut floor laden with spectres of a bygone age. Above, the coved ceiling was coffered and held two vast golden chandeliers. The far wall was a bulbous concave window, where the orchestra's stage stood. Steps to the hallway were to the left of the stage, closest to the kitchen, where servers emerged with canapes. The room murmured with conversations, and the masks gave the crowd a sinister and imposing air.

I took a breath and descended the six steps into the crowd. The women's dresses were all exquisite, so I didn't stand out too much. As a waiter passed by with a tray, I placed the full glass of champagne on it. He didn't walk far before another guest snagged it. I moved closer to the stage as the masters of ceremonies ascended and grabbed the mic. I wondered if any of the orchestra members were students at the university, too.

The welcome address included expressions of appreciation and gratitude towards all those in attendance, some of high importance judging by the crowd's reaction to their names. In addition, they shared feedback on the donated sum and presented a comprehensive breakdown of the designated uses. They mentioned the waiters would replenish the outside buffet throughout the evening and for dancing guidance to follow the appointed aides. With that, the dance floor was opened. Everyone made space in the middle for the demonstration by five couples. When they stood across from one another, the orchestra began. I toppled inwards and looked down. Around me, the gowns were glowing and misty, and I saw the rhythmic music waves sway the mist. I took deep breaths until the gowns appeared normal and the floor seemed like wood again, not water. Finally, I could look up and watch the dance. It looked spectacular only because of the swaying dresses and music, as it consisted of simple turns and walks. I reckoned I'd be able to do it. Others were joining in or even doing their own thing further away. Laughter could be heard everywhere, and the energy was lime green. I couldn't help smiling. People gathered in groups to talk or filtered out of the ballroom, but I quite enjoyed the vibrancy and stood there watching. Mom and Dad were dancing on the other side. They looked happy.

I felt a whisper next to my ear and cringed, but no one was close enough to have done it. A girl from a distance away looked at me, and when I made eye contact, she smiled and gave a little wave. I smiled and nodded to her. *Weird.* I felt uneasy and walked around. Mom and Dad passed close by, and when Mom saw me, she smiled even wider. My senses buckled in on themselves, and my knees almost did too. I reached into space to grab something to support myself with but came up empty-handed, so I stood there wobbling.

I felt my hand being taken—pulled to the centre of the room. The shock of it settled my senses back into order, and when I looked up, I saw a dancing aide. Before I could protest, he had me hopping and turning. A subtle pleasure, I found, and I soon enjoyed myself as I was passed along to other partners and crossed with other women. More guests were being dragged in to take part, while others—confident now—joined of their own volition. The girl who had waved to me earlier crossed me a few times. The music slowed, and the crowd came to a respite. Everyone was smiling, a peculiar bond threaded between the crowd, and strangers felt like friends. Summer by Vivaldi began, and the dancing started again.

I bobbed and moved through multiple dancing partners when the last high-paced segment approached. My partner spun me around and let go just as the high pace began and the room blurred. I wasn't sure where I was when *he* took hold of me, pulling me close, closer than any previous partner, and I realised how warm his hands were. He was taller than I'd thought. We were going off script, weaving through everyone there, spinning, spinning, spinning, bodies together, bodies apart, until I felt my stomach turning from exhilaration. I was a puppet in his arms, and though I didn't know what I was doing, he was in absolute control. He lifted me into the air by the waist as we spun, and I put my hands on his shoulders, looking down into his uplifted face. Although he wore a simply shaped red mask with embossing, I recognised those eyes. He put me down and, for the first time, spun me out to another partner. An intoxicating crescendo amplified by the boisterous laughter everywhere. While passing by others, I was searching for him. I caught sight of him again, looking at me as he turned another woman to her next partner, but someone passed him, and then he was gone. While I was searching for him again, he pulled me closer and looked down at me with a broad smile. I didn't know how he'd teleported from where he'd been, but I laughed. Without a doubt, one of the most exhilarating experiences of my life. He spun me by the hand, around and around, and I felt like I was floating. My senses were brimming against my skin, against every nerve, but they didn't shift. As the music softened, he pulled me to a stop, his eyes on me. For a moment, a shimmer of green flickered past them as he let go of me, backing away and bowing into the crowd, eyes bright and locked with mine. I searched for him, but he had disappeared like the mist again. Overheated from all the dancing and energy, I stepped outside.

The crisp air was refreshing, and the marquee looked spectacular with the lights and people around it. Inside, the buffet was a feast, with many people standing around, eating and laughing. I got a plate and stacked it with all the goodies—from sweet to savoury and anything else you might desire. I was enjoying a bite when I felt that burn of someone staring at me, but when I turned, only the tranquil sight of forest and the lake greeted me. My senses were out of whack. I had friendly conversations with a couple of people who saw me standing alone, while others made a comment in passing, but I'd admit I was looking for *him*. I didn't understand his role for the evening.

"Only *one* girl has a dress like that!" I heard someone exclaim close by. Beatrice. My heart sank a little. People were looking at me. She wore a white and emerald green mask with a wide green dress. She walked towards me with arms wide open. I felt a powerful urge to pretend I didn't see her and disappear. She sandwiched my face between her large, icy hands, turning it from this side to that like she was investigating an orb.

"Marvellous," she breathed and paused, "My… Your eyes could cut through souls. I dare say they're brighter than ever."

"Err," I started, completely embarrassed, "Th—thank you." I pulled my face away. To my relief, Mom emerged out of nowhere.

"Hello, Beatrice! I've been wondering where you were. How are you? Listen—thank you for this dress! It exceeded our expectations."

"Ah, Evelyn! I'm fantastic, darling. Oh, no problem at all. I must say, Josilyn is a jaw-dropper! Those *eyes* are bewitching. Those lips! Ah, and that tiny waist! I hope Joseph has a shotgun! You aren't in a desert land anymore, my dears. They will have to lock you up in your tower, Darling," She locked an invisible door and threw the key away.

Well, that escalated quickly. Though, Rapunzel was one of my favourite stories.

"Oh, excuse me, dears." She exited the conversation. I stared after her, stumped by her choppiness. I looked at my mom with wide eyes and started laughing. She did too.

"I saw you dancing, and I must admit I was a little surprised, but delighted!"

"Same to you. I don't think I've seen you with such a wide smile in my life."

"It's definitely the best time I've had in a long, long while." She returned inside with a plate of food for my dad, who she mentioned was engaged in a deep conversation with someone in the parlour. I accompanied her and asked if she'd seen Andrew, but she hadn't. I later found out he went to hide in his room, which, unlike mine, wasn't open to guests.

Dad was enjoying his company and appreciated the plate. He told me how beautiful I looked since it was the first time we had crossed paths since that morning. He, of course, also asked who the young man was I had danced with, and I could, in sincerity, tell him I didn't know. I hoped he might have known since he and Mom were involved with the planners. One master of ceremonies beckoned my mom out of the room, and I semi-followed them into the ballroom. They talked with animation about something, but I wasn't listening. I was looking for *him* again in the dancing crowd. But he wasn't there.

The MC went onto the stage and announced the orchestra would take a twenty-minute break. She encouraged guests to take advantage of the time to enjoy the buffet outside and provided information about which rooms were open to view and where the bathrooms were. Most of the people dispersed, and my mom came towards me. A plain-looking woman struggled through the crowd towards us—mousy hair styled in a short, curly bob and thick brown glasses over a brown lace eye mask. A yellow flower in her headband seemed too bright against her complexion and attire. Her simple brown dress had some beading. She moved with singular purpose, her eyes locked on me, making it clear we were the object of her desperate interest.

"Oh, excuse me," she started with a fragile voice, "I overheard someone call you Josilyn. You are the Greys, correct?" she inquired with expectancy.

I glanced at Mom for direction in this odd encounter. She was absentminded, it seemed.

"Yes, I am Josilyn Grey."

"Oh, my stars, what a day. That's amazing. It's such an honour and privilege to meet you, Josilyn. I've read about you." Her demeanour held a peculiarity. *Read about me?* I frowned, mystified. My eyes must've held hundreds of questions because, after an awkward few seconds, she continued.

"Oh, where are my manners… I'm referring to your anomalous musical aptitude," as if ashamed all of a sudden, she looked down, "I did my doctorate on savants, and I came across your name. Not that you're a savant; the paper merely mentioned you because you showed abnormal giftedness. I tried finding out more about you, but there was no more information available."

My hands trembled. As the shock set in, I forced myself to take a deep breath. I felt violated having this aspect of me, which had caused so much hurt, brought up so unrestrained. I was ill-prepared.

"I was not aware I was researchable nor that there were papers written about me," I answered coolly, my heart racing as if I had just sprinted miles. Feeling exposed, I wanted to hide or die, or both.

Shy, she smiled, reading my tone, "Generally not, no, but I had permission. I apologise if you feel I intruded—" but Mom stopped her mid-sentence.

"No, no need to apologise! It's quite alright. It sounds like an interesting thesis. Don't mind Josilyn; she is not used to people knowing who she is, that's all. We weren't aware there were records about her."

"I couldn't access any medical records, merely summaries and overviews. I only came across it because the word 'savant' was used in reporting that she isn't one, but displayed attributes that resembled a savant. The document described a few example tests performed to prove this."

I felt uncomfortable in my skin. *How ethical was it to just give out information like that?* An awkward silence permeated the air. Well, awkward in my opinion, but then Mom said what I dreaded she would. I didn't speak because I felt the emotion in my throat.

"Would you like her to play a song for you?" My head snapped to her, icy shock blasting through me. I was stunned. Mystified, I scrutinised Mom's face for any sign she was joking. I wanted her to look at me and see my incredulous eyes, but to no avail; her eyes stayed focused on the woman's face. I couldn't believe she was doing this to me. She had never understood.

The proposal surprised both the woman and myself, though our reasons were utterly dissimilar. I wanted to scream *"No!"* but was dissuaded by the awkward social dilemma that would ensue.

"Oh, thank you, but I don't want to cause discomfort," she vacillated, diverting her eyes to mine and showing that was untrue. I saw anticipation burning in them, green like greed, and eyes never lied. She made me feel guilty and uncomfortable, and seconds later, Mom gave me the Judas kiss.

"No, there's no discomfort. Josilyn lives for music. It's like breathing to her. And, of course, there aren't many her equal. It will be a great delight." She insisted.

Music was second nature to me—if not first—but playing a song about *someone* in the way intended now was always different. *Much* different. Imagine this: reading an explicitly vulnerable autobiography *and* writing an essay about it, all in less than a second—emotionally exhausting.

"Maybe I can do this another time, Mom? I don't want to overstep the formalities."

"Oh nonsense, it's our house, and the orchestra is on a break. There's barely anyone here."

"I'll get my cello," I gave in to defeat. Maybe if I took too long, the orchestra would be back.

"I don't think that's necessary," She steered me towards the podium where some orchestra members were standing around.

"Mom…" I pleaded. My throat constricted.

"Oh Honey, there's nothing to worry about. Honestly, I don't know what your problem is."

She didn't get it; the playing part was not my problem. I had played in front of many people before. But she wasn't asking me to play a composition; she was asking me to *create*. She couldn't even begin to imagine—to fathom—what it took from me and what it imprinted into me, especially with a stranger. I've only done it a few times with people I knew and trusted. My mom made her request to the MC she had spoken to, who looked at me with a fretful frown but nodded. She probably didn't know what to think or do.

Mom climbed onto the stage and addressed the cellist. A 4/4 cello. I hadn't played on a full-sized one before. Mine was smaller. I wished that would count as an excuse. My heart raced as I watched her talk to him and gesture to me. He, like everyone else who was rational in this situation, was perplexed.

The little woman was right behind me. Sure, she was small and timid, but another hue laced about her I couldn't place, which made my reluctance more severe. People could be cruel and selfish without realising it.

"All set, Josilyn." Mom was ecstatic. She loved it when I composed on the spot. It didn't happen often because I avoided it with vehemence.

Reluctant, I trudged up to the podium and claimed the cello and bow. It weighed much more than mine. I sat down and positioned it between my knees, leaning against my chest. I braced myself and plucked the four strings. They were slightly out of tune, but I played on scordatura notation anyway, so I adjusted them. I stroked over the strings with the bow a few times and adjusted the tension. The energy accumulated inside me like a storm—no escaping now. I closed my eyes, took one deep breath, and opened them again. The few people left in the room looked on with curiosity. I attempted one last shot to save myself,

"What should I play?"

"Oh, you know we want an improvised composition, Josilyn. Any musician can play a known song."

My heart pounded violently, and my stomach churned. I pursed my lips shut and restrained my words.

"Okay," I exhaled, my cheeks flushing. When I looked up, I saw *him* standing at the entrance, watching me. I shut him out.

"You can hum or sing any number of notes and she will carry it further. Go ahead." Mom announced. *Yeah, go ahead; ruin my evening.* The request flustered the woman, and she gaped at my mom, hand jolting to her mouth. I thought she knew how this worked.

"Oh, um, I really can't sing. She can play anything." She responded in jitters.

"That doesn't matter! You can drop a stick or move a chair, and she could play something with that as inspiration. Believe me, *any* amount of notes, whatever comes to mind."

We all know you'll do it eventually. I felt a little guilty over my antagonism but couldn't get myself to tame it. The woman looked around, seeming uncertain, and bit her lower lip. A moment later she expelled a nervous giggle and then uttered four perfect notes. I wasn't expecting that, to be honest. *Let's get this over with.* The storm built up inside me, and I felt the hairs rise over my body like frequency antennas.

I closed my eyes, humming the four notes to myself, repeating them over and over. I listened and watched as they arranged themselves and expanded into their own composition. Just like her, it had a dark tinge to it. At first, I had a sinking feeling, like the dark was pulling me in, but it subsided. I breathed, bracing for the wave to come; in and out…in and out… in.

My senses shifted, rolling around like a crashing wave inside me. The bow dragged over the strings, the vibrations quivering through my fingers and arms. All I could see, feel, hear, taste, and smell were the four notes that resonated through me. The *Pulse* clawed at the surface of my being, wanting to come out. It felt like trying to contain an explosion. The electric wave vibrated through my body and commenced its crawl up from my heels.

Her name was Miriam.
It crept into my ankles.

Her heartache was sticky black with grief, and my stomach convulsed with the metallic taste.

It reached my calves.

The hymn flowed through my chest like a light beacon; a sad, intense melody sending a singular thrill through me, opposite to the direction of the wave.

Her husband, Alvin, had torn her heart apart like tissue paper.
I felt the vibrations of the strings in the air as the rhythm intensified. The wave turned into a pulse and shot through my knees and thighs. I breathed against the anguish.

After twenty years of marriage, childless, he told her the previous week he didn't want her anymore.

It reached my stomach; the nausea was almost too much.
He told her it wasn't her fault, that he was an idealist, a dreamer, and they'd just grown apart.

A low, breaking sound escaped my mouth, and I held control like a bridle on a wild horse. I couldn't stop.

She begged him and told him she could change. That she would change for him. That they could make it work. She said losing him would break her. He was the only one she had. He was her world.

The *Pulse* spurted through my neck.
They had fought for such a long time. He packed his clothes to leave. She begged and pleaded, on her knees, crumbling. And as she crumbled, so did I. It surged into my head. A horrendous ache burst through my brain as my fingers slid over the strings without mercy.

He pulled her to her feet, calling her pathetic, and continued walking out. She grabbed his arm and clung to him. He turned and slapped her to the ground and yelled there was another; there'd been another for eight years.

My body went numb—*abrupt stop.*
My hand holding the bow fell, and it slid from my grasp, bouncing on the stage.

I breathed in and out, trying to calm the fire in my head.

My senses dragged back into position, and my hearing zoomed out. I opened my eyes and got a shock. The room, no longer empty, was as silent as the grave; not one breath, not one sound. They gawped at me. I looked down, my cheeks flushed. How awkward would it be if I got up and exited the room in such silence? My torture ceased, but a moment later when the entire room erupted into applause and shouts. I'll admit, I was relieved. Looking up at the sea of masks, I smiled.

I looked at Miriam. She stood silent, staring at me with saucer-sized eyes. Her hand covered her mouth, and her chest started jerking. She was crying. I felt my face contort in empathy, but she turned and disappeared into the crowd. I couldn't see her anymore. The orchestra members beamed as they came up the stairs. The cellist praised the composition and asked if I'd written it myself. Well, technically yes, but also no.

A look of genuine shock plastered Mom's face. It was a heart song I would've preferred not to do, but if I had to, it should've been private. I don't quite understand it, but all bodies are energy and frequency, which I picked up and read. I'm sure I could do something even without someone singing. It just helps with the channelling. Not that I wanted to practise the theory, but it was the only explanation for why I could see others' memories and feel their emotions. It had never been so overwhelming and painful before. Most often, it was petty problems, but everyone always thought theirs were the worst.

Mom met me when I descended.

"That was so moving, Hon. I hope there's a recording. You should notate it; it would be such a waste not to hear again." Unfortunately, it didn't work like that, because no song was ever the same after the first time. I stared at the floor, aware of a multitude of heavy gazes on me. My headache refused to be ignored any longer, and I winced.

"Do we still have the meds in the kitchen?" I slurred, my brows furrowed, trying to ease the internal pain.

"Are you alright?" She stroked my face. "You look pale." She exhaled sharply and pressed the back of her hand against my forehead. Her skin was cold. I removed her hand, nervous about the attention it might attract, and turned towards the kitchen.

"I'm fine. I felt it coming earlier tonight. It just chose the perfect time to arrive." Mustering a feeble smile, I pushed through the crowd, which parted to make way for me. Some tried to talk to me, but I ignored them. The headache didn't care for decorum. I wrestled my way to the cabinet through all the catering staff and waiters, feeling like an intruder. Popping two pills into my mouth, I guzzled water from the tap like an animal. Much to my relief, the number of people in the hallway was minimal, allowing me to smoothly traverse towards the foyer. It felt like half the length of an eternity away, my head splitting. The orchestra was playing again, an arrangement of Moonlight Sonata. Though I loved the piece, it made my head pulse to the beat. I rubbed my temples. Crossing the foyer to the stairs, I heard my name mentioned—my attention desired—but I kept walking. I couldn't care less if they thought me rude.

Mom fluttered at the front door. *Oh, no.* I didn't want her to fuss over me now. It hurt my head, but I walked even faster as I moved to the stairs.

"Oh my, how long have you been here? Why are you standing outside? Are you waiting for someone? Come in, come in!" she flitted back into the ballroom without noticing me. I noted the figure enter but didn't look because the *Pulse* burst through me, and I toppled against the balustrade again. Climbing the stairs posed a hazard. I steadied myself, feeling the guest's eyes on me, but I didn't provoke fate by looking to see who witnessed my vulnerable state.

The music faded with each step, but the beating in my head intensified. Only halfway up my steps did I hear the loud voices and laughter coming from my room.

I slumped against the wall and almost cried from the sheer pain and lack of peace. I uttered a loud groan, pulled a face, and turned around, defeated. Deep breath. Where could I go where it would be improbable for anyone to stumble across me? My mind flickered to the perfect place—quite sudden and clear for the state I was in—and I headed downstairs almost without having decided to do so. The pain pressed at the back of my neck and forehead.

Outside, many were enjoying the buffet and standing around the lawn. I slipped down the porch steps, passed the lanterns, heading to the left of the house.

I looked at the brim of the forest on the mountainside. The opening and path into the forest lay ahead. Lanterns traced the path, disappearing into the dense trees.

Maybe I shouldn't. I didn't want to come across an amorous couple, but I'd just look for another place if that happened. The pain made me drunk, and I inhaled deeply as the opening called to me. My high heels ploughed into the ground, so I took them off, my hands shaking. The grass was cool and soothed my feet. I wasn't even aware they'd been hurting. Each step produced a painful pounding in my head.

I reached the opening of the forest and hesitated, entering the woods at night. As I listened for voices, all I heard was the light breeze singing through the trees. I glanced back once before wandering forward along the lanterns.

Thick bushes hemmed in the forest path between the trees on both sides, forming a tall but narrow natural passageway. Two people could not walk abreast with ease. For some inexplicable reason, each step carried a deep sense of foreboding, embracing me like dark waters. It made me pause and look back. The lanterns were spaced sparingly along the way. In certain areas, darkness prevailed, save for a faint, sinister glow amid the trees. I searched for the source and found my answer in the full moon; the culprit painted the trees with a strange radiance. With all the other lights shining around the house, I hadn't noticed the full moon.

Up ahead, the path made a sharp turn towards the mountain—I couldn't see beyond it. Floodgates of adrenaline flowed through me as I approached and peeked around the curve. No one was there, but the sight nabbed the breath right from me.

The trees opened into a cosy, circular area, sheltered by the mountain face and trees. Thick growth covered the ground, so each step made a *squishing* sound. White, curved rock formations adorned the mountain face, and pale moonlight made them look like dried-out bones.

Mom had mentioned this place, but I hadn't had the chance to come here yet.

The soft murmur of flowing water became audible. What looked like black liquid dribbled from the top of a tall, white rock. It could be blood, could be water. I traced the stones, the volcano, upwards towards the open sky. No branches obscured the bright, starry cosmos. The night sky was so clear that if I reached out, I might scoop the stars from their home. I rarely looked up at night, fearing I would shift as I did. It happened once when I was young, and the sight and colours of the heavens were an overwhelming display that had nauseated me.

I reached the rocks, patted the surface to test its dryness, and sat down heavily, utterly exhausted. I removed the mask, not wanting any pressure on my sensitive head. The water flowed down right next to me into a small natural basin. I wondered why the water would be so dark. Cool under my fingers as I brushed the surface, it formed swirls and waves. The stars shone in the reflection and it looked like a piece of the sky entrapped on earth.

The gentle tingle of the water calmed me, and my headache faded. A light breeze emerged through the trees, caressing my skin, tugging at my hair, and brushing my dress against my ankles.

I closed my eyes and allowed the singing water and wind to soothe me. It was a sweet hymn and my eyes teared up. With the wind smelling of mint and looking like a blue nova, the ground buzzed like a thousand insects. The world had shifted around me, gushing luminous mist again.

My senses shifted; the *Pulse* began in my feet, sending a current through my veins. I found myself swept into a sea of a glowing bright world around me. The trees were vivid and clear, insects moved in harmony, and leaves sang. My head felt light, and I felt weightless, like I could float into the air at any moment. I was so content, so at home and elated, I parted my lips to join in the melody. But the sound choked in my throat.

A disharmonious interruption stopped the reverie. It sounded like a string snapping; my eyes shot open and my senses slinked back into place.

Petrified, my throat tightened. Was I hallucinating? A silhouette emerged from the mouth of the pathway, shrouded in darkness. All sound seeped away as if the forest itself had sworn an oath of silence.

Heart pounding wildly, I stared at the large, motionless shadow. Although it had the shape of a man, it was massive in stature. I didn't want to blink. Maybe my mind was playing tricks on me.

I exhaled sharply, as if someone had punched me in the stomach. The shadow glided forward like a ghost. A scream itched in my throat but couldn't escape. I *hoped* I was hallucinating.

"Have I frightened you?" a deep liquid voice slithered towards me from the dark, only slightly waking me from my stupor. "Forgive me; that was not my intention."

What *was* his intention, I wondered?

The shadow glided closer. My heart galloped out of my chest, but I couldn't move.

"I saw you on the stairs when I was in the foyer; you seemed ill, but I couldn't find you anywhere." With his last word, he stepped into the light of the moon and the lanterns. His entire face donned a plain but textured, expressionless black mask. It seemed moulded to his face, burned wood or black clay. With eyes shrouded in darkness, he stood there in silence for half a lifetime as my heart pounded in a wild frenzy of fear. When it had marinated well, he removed the mask.

He looked nothing like the monster my imagination had conjured in the waiting. He was even taller than it had seemed. Though fear had first blinded me to it, my attention was soon captured by his thick, tousled head of dark wine-red hair. Never in my life had I seen hair such a shade of red. It was a deep shade but unmistakably red, even in the dim light. The colour of passion, of danger, but the line between them seemed blurred. The colour made your heartbeat quicken with just a glimpse.

His face was striking—strong, with a chiselled angular jaw, an exquisite aquiline nose, and prominent cheekbones. Thick, dark brows. Despite his stunning features, it was not a face you'd find on a magazine cover. That would allude to a certain level of mortal hubris, for his beauty was a thing of terror, a thing of subtle, ancient horror. It churned my stomach, more terrifying at that moment than anything else. I had a strange compulsion to look away, as if gazing upon a godlike entity and it was sheer audacity to do so. Though I wanted to look away, I couldn't. There was something about him, a look, a glimmer, that divulged trouble followed in his wake.

"Your musical rendition ambushed me, and I was moved—compelled to meet the one who conjured a melodious spell such as no one ever has." His eloquence wooed me, captured me, as he glided closer and closer. Warm honey dripped from his voice as he spoke. His accent was unfamiliar.

I was caught in a trance. It dawned on me that perhaps I wasn't awake.

His attire, a three-piece suit, was all black, the vest buttoned up, but the shirt collar wasn't. The neckline dipped low, revealing a fine sliver of silver around his neck, the end concealed behind the vest. His warm, tanned complexion was in perfect harmony with his red hair. His countenance was confusing; strong and manly, yet with a false, almost boyish vulnerability trying to sell itself to the gullible. Me, in this case.

I was frozen and realised I hadn't said a word. He stopped, and a mischievous, crooked smile curved his full lips.

"Where are my manners?" His deep chuckle boomed. "I am Adrian."

"No surname?" I asked stupidly before thinking. *Of course, he had a surname.* Blood rushed to my cheeks. He found my question amusing, and a dark chuckle reverberated through the space between us, which seemed to shrink with each moment.

"No, just Adrian."

All I could do was stare at him blankly. I didn't know what to say, afraid I'd say something stupid again.

"Err." I stuttered. "He—hey, nice to meet you."

His presence was intoxicating, frightening, and *strong*—like a thing of substance. My senses were wary but seemed too shy to misbehave. I was uncomfortable, and I felt very, *very* small.

He stared at me, unblinking. The sclera below his irises was visible even from where I sat. He tilted his head in a strange way, almost pushing his head forward. I swore he sniffed the air. Ice trickled down my neck, and a mocking laugh heaved from his chest.

"Correct me if I am mistaken, but are you not supposed to provide your name in an introduction as well? Or has the code of conduct changed?" Stars were born in the darkness of his voice.

I gulped. *Why am I such an awkward idiot?*

"Josilyn," I cleared my throat. "I'm Josilyn Grey." What was it with my sudden obsession with surnames? I tried to pull myself together. Rising to my shaky feet, I deliberately pushed the fog from my head and my right hand forward to greet him. It might help shake the feeling of unease. My insides twisted as I neared him, and I swallowed as I stopped. Bright emerald eyes framed by dark lashes drifted down to my suspended hand without moving. He looked perplexed, as if he didn't understand what I meant to do.

We stood like that for what felt like minutes. I was mortified and wanted to die.

I was about to drop my hand in embarrassment when he took it with his left. *That's not how you shake hands.* His skin was ablaze. Deep-set almond-shaped eyes locked on mine as he bent lower, and kissed my hand. Electricity ran up my arm, my skin warm with the contact. I was very aware of his lips on my skin. I gaped at him, unable to utter a word. In some forsaken part of my mind, I wanted to pull my hand away but didn't, so it just lingered there, between his warm fingers, while his eyes kept me captive. He straightened up.

"Thrilled to meet you." His voice smouldered, a coy smile on his lips.

All the blood pooling in my cheeks left them scorched.

Seeming reluctant, he relinquished my hand, his touch lingering on my skin. He broke his gaze away to the rocks behind me. Every sense in me was aware of him and absolutely transfixed.

"Shall we?" He enticed and glided past me.

The strangest feeling—like my brain had died. First, I followed him with my eyes, portentously mesmerised by the strange man. Then, without my permission or instruction to do so, my feet moved after him. Why I followed him, I couldn't say. I wondered how old he was—usually, I was rather good at guessing such things, but now I was at a loss.

Gracefully, he sat down, and I awkwardly positioned myself to his right. I didn't want to sit so close, but for some reason, I did. He turned towards me with a brilliant smile.

"So, you are new." He stated.

"Uh, yeah, I am. Are you not?" I asked stupidly, once again. Of course, he was not, otherwise, he wouldn't have known *I* was. My cheeks burned even more. He noticed and smiled, but then stared past me with such intensity I almost turned around to see what he was looking at.

"No. By far, I am not." He seemed amused.

A strange vibe came from him. I pursed my lips, looked down at my hands cradled in my lap, and played with my ring.

He noticed.

"Where did you get that?"

I looked up, but when I saw the intensity with which he gazed at me, I promptly looked down again. *So strange.* My heart drummed louder and louder.

"It was a gift from my mother."

"Tell me. How long have you been composing?"

He didn't stick to one topic for long. His question sounded more like an order.

"Um, I have a unique gift that allows me to master any instrument in rapid time, instantly, actually. I've been playing cello since I was five years old, so fifteen years." Before I could decide what to say, I followed the order. I couldn't believe I had just said that. No one had ever extracted a sentence like that out of my mouth. He gazed at me in delighted surprise.

"Well, that is spectacular! What a beautiful memoir for a life; the master of music."

He awaited a response from me, it seemed, but I was incapable of giving it. I couldn't believe myself.

"Do you like Ostia so far?" The question was softer this time, and I felt more at ease as the bars around my throat broke.

"I love it here. It's so beautiful. The atmosphere is calm and peaceful—and inviting, like everyone has known you forever. But I can't help feeling there are many secrets hidden here." I didn't know why I said that. He was looking at me, and I tried to avoid his gaze, so I stared upward and looked at the full moon.

A frown puckered my skin as I looked up.

The moon was higher than I thought it would be. The full circle glowed like a golden pearl on the dark ocean floor.

"Wow," I trailed off. "Just look at that," I said, not to anyone specific. It went quiet for a beat, and I almost thought I was alone.

"I do not need to look up. I can see heavens reflected perfectly in your eyes," He stated matter-of-factly. My cheeks became inflamed, and I was grateful for the dark. I looked away over my shoulder. I thought the comment was unnecessary. If anyone else had said something like that, it would've sounded cheesy, but not coming from him.

"Your eyes are mesmeric, Josilyn. Forgive my boldness in saying so." He said almost shyly. *Almost.* He couldn't expect me to look at him after a comment like that, so I just smiled to myself. Mystified by this odd situation, I was clueless about how I should act.

"Your eyes… I am hovering above an iceberg forged from frozen stars, seeing how it submerges and melts into the dark ocean. The depth; immeasurable. No way of telling the amount of life crawling beneath the crystal surface."

The moment was too much, and I wanted to laugh, but it caught in my throat—no sound escaping. My face glowed.

"Uh, thank you." The laughter was evident in my voice, and I cleared my throat. He looked at me, blank-faced.

"Well, I am glad I amuse you," His tone was light, and he smiled. I was thankful he wasn't offended.

He looked up at the moon and gave a loud sigh.

"Sparks of light in the heaven shines; the worlds of the unknown hide behind the clouds descending from the darkened skies. No turning back when the wolves start to cry." He took a deep breath and looked at me.

"Did you come up with that just now?"

He winked at me.

"No. It's an old hymn from the local tribe. Translated, of course." He looked down and smiled as if just remembering something at that moment. It seemed like an odd hymn for a tribe to be singing. I abruptly rose to my feet with no conscious decision to do so and wandered around the open area.

I wondered why I was doing it.

He stood behind me, so close I could feel the proximity. I heard his constant breath and felt it on my neck, though faint and warm. Too warm.

I didn't know what was happening.

My heart hammered against my chest like it wanted to escape, and my palms were clammy as his warm breath reached my neck. Dread crawled under my skin and wound itself around my throat.

I couldn't move.

Something cold touched my shoulder where my scar was, but the trail it left was scorching. *Tracing my scar with his fingertip.*

Goosebumps rolled over my back.

"This is an interesting scar you have." He sounded distant. I cringed away from his touch and turned around to face him. The heat was still on my back and it spread like a wildfire; like liquid flowing over my skin.

Unnerved, I tried to calm myself. I couldn't read the situation and grabbed the first topic that came to mind trying to ground it.

"How old are you?" Something about him terrified me. I toiled for a piece of sanity and tried to sound grown-up, but my voice was weak.

He stared at me in amusement.

"What a strange question to ask." He paused, pondering, and his expression changed into one of wicked playfulness. It made me catch my breath.

"Why don't you guess my age, and I'll tell you when you get close." With the last word, he took a step towards me. I gave a step back. His smouldering, vivid green eyes pierced right through me. My breathing intensified, the adrenaline rushing through me. I had never seen eyes *that* green; they were wild and mischievous.

"Uh," I stuttered. "I can't really say. You look young but seem old. Thirty?" He looked older. Or younger? I just didn't know. He chuckled and gave a step closer.

"Cold."

I felt the urge to run but a yearning to stay. I gulped.

Younger or older?

"Twenty-eight?" I gave it a shot.

His full lips pulled into a crooked line.

"Warm."

My heart pounded in my ears. The whole scenario exuded and begot mischief.

"Twenty-four?" I breathed.

He slipped closer, standing against me, and gazed down into my eyes.

He was as tall as a tower.

"Flaming hot," he stated, his expression intense.

I didn't like what was happening. The energy bristled under my skin.

"Oh, I wasn't expecting you to be so young," I replied curtly, but my voice was rough. I wanted to stare at the ground but couldn't. He was standing too close.

He inhaled deeply, looked past me, and exhaled.

"It's been a pleasure talking to you, Josilyn." He drawled. "Unfortunately, I must leave you now. But I will see you again."

He made it sound like a promise.

He smiled down at me and then glided to the opening, disappearing into the shadows of the forest.

I stared at the opening for a long while, rubbing the back of my shoulder to ease the inflamed trail.

Delirious, I walked to the opening too. I was exhausted, and my feet dragged with each step. I didn't understand how I could suddenly be so tired. The path felt miles long. I stumbled forward, numb, and only realised where I was when my mother yelled at me.

"Josilyn! Where on *earth* have you been this entire time?! I couldn't find you anywhere! Do you have any idea what time it is?" She exclaimed, running towards me from the house.

I didn't understand why she was so upset. It seemed to me that I had been away for no more than half an hour, if not less. I stopped and stared at her in astonishment. The last couple of people were leaving with the valets. The marquee had already been disassembled.

"What time is it?" my voice was tight.

"2 a.m! I was worried about you. You didn't look well the last time I saw you."

An icy shiver ran through me. The entire evening had flashed right past me like it had spanned only a few seconds. I didn't know the exact time, but I couldn't have gone to the clearing later than 9 p.m.

"Sorry, Mom. I had no idea how long I'd been away. I just wanted some silence, and there was nowhere else I could go." I apologised as we walked up the steps.

Dazed and confused, I meandered off after we said goodnight, and to my surprise, I found myself in my room.

It felt like I was blacking out every few seconds.

I looked around aimlessly—the windows were open, but the fairy lights and all the other decorations were gone.

I fell onto the bed on my stomach, just wanting to rest for a little while. I would take my dress off later. But as soon as my head hit the mattress, I fell into a dreamless sleep.

~

At some hour in the night, I woke up to a delicate movement on my shoulder—like a feather over my bare back. Still half asleep, I opened my heavy lids, blinking sluggishly to orientate myself.

I hadn't moved an inch since I lay down. My brows furrowed, and I turned my head towards my shoulder.

Caught off guard, I stared at the giant butterfly with as much energy as I could muster. As soon as I saw it, it lifted off, hovering over me for a few seconds before swirling out of the window. I stared after it for a moment, but my head dropped back on the mattress and I fell into a comatose sleep.

Chapter 4

I groaned into consciousness, still lying on my stomach, body sore and stiff. It was a restless night, and I had a mess of strange dreams which didn't allow me to have restorative sleep. My neck hurt when I sat upright. The previous night rushed through my brain. The dress, the dancing, the food…*Adrian.* If I wasn't still wearing the dress, I might've thought it all a dream. I looked in the mirror. My smudged makeup had me looking like a dishevelled corpse bride.

"That's attractive."

The room was arctic, and outside, a mist wall enclosed the house. I couldn't see anything further than my window. Mist vapour rolled into my room, so I closed the windows. I stared into the fog, awed. It felt like being inside a cloud.

The bathroom plumbing was old, and whenever I showered, the pipes sang, making it difficult not to shift. It took concentration not to be pulled in. After the shower, I put on a long, casual black dress with tights, boots, and a blue sweater. I put the golden ring on a leather string from my art supplies and hung it around my neck. It sounded purple.

On my way down to the kitchen, I met my mom on the second-floor landing. She complimented my new accessory. She had a tray with cereal and coffee, and we went to the parlour next to my dad's study. Two ways existed to access the parlour: the first at the opposite end of the long hallway to where my hidden door was. That end had the sunroom stairs. The second was through the hallway opposite the silo, which led past Dad's study. I didn't understand it, but my stomach had a strange nervous energy when I saw her. I thought I might just be starving, and I devoured the food in an unusual, primal way. Her gaze was studious, and the energy built beneath my skin.

"Where did you say you were last night?" The energy below increased. My neck muscles tightened. Was she concerned or curious?

"Like I said last night, I had a headache and wanted some quiet." I shifted on the sofa.

"So, you were alone in the forest the whole time?" A deep, looming alarm inhabited her probe. *Adrian removing his mask.*

"No, I wasn't," I'd wanted to put her at ease, but regretted it, as it didn't change her tone at all.

"Who were you with then?" She could be quite neurotic on certain occasions. I opened my mouth, about to tell a blatant lie that it was the guy she had seen me dancing with earlier. But I wasn't a liar. I frowned. *Why would I want to do that?*

"A guest found me there, but we didn't talk much." I didn't understand my illusiveness.

"Does this guest have a name?"

"Um…" I was unwilling to say, which was silly. Though, what were the actual odds she knew enough people by name? "Adrian." I feigned boredom and gave a pretentious yawn as I stared at the balcony behind the sliding doors. My nerves were brittle. The encounter from the previous night gave me shivers.

"Hmm," she trailed off. "What does he look like?" I cleared my throat from its knot. I was eager for a change of topic.

"Red hair, really tall."

Her face lit up.

"Oh, I did see him! Black suit and mask? He was a little odd." She frowned. I stared at her, bewildered. At least I knew I didn't imagine him. The energy burst.

"You met him?" My tone was dangerously close to the fringe of hostility, but she was oblivious, and I was grateful. I took a deep breath, perturbed by the curious rage which simmered beneath my skin.

"Well, I didn't *meet* him. I was in the foyer, and he stood outside the front door like he was waiting for someone." My heart pounded louder and louder and my hands were clammy. Adrenaline ignited my nerves. I didn't understand my physiological reaction.

"Oh. He seemed good-mannered to me. Old school." I fought against my defensiveness. Saying anything else would have laid bare the internal brawl inside me. I felt overwhelmed by my peculiar emotions. I stopped myself from chewing my nails.

She received a call and dawdled to the sunroom stairs and went up. She liked the view, and the house didn't have another study. I heard a flush, and Andrew emerged after a moment, looking groggy. He sat next to me and drank the milk from the cereal bowl. I pondered my strange internal reaction to my mom and felt despair and shame over my unnatural, menacing feelings about her curiosity. We were talking about Andrew's plans for the day when my dad entered and frowned at me. We had a frowning stare-down, and I won.

"Don't you have an orientation to get to?" He asked, and I jumped to my feet.

"What's the time?"

"Well, it doesn't matter, clearly."

"Dad!" I hastened to the long hall and heard him say 9 a.m. when I was almost halfway to my stairs. I only had to be there by 10 a.m., but the fog would make driving hazardous. I gathered my stationery from the desk drawer, where I had shoved it before the ball. A breeze swept across my neck and gave me goosebumps. One window was ajar. I must not have closed it right. My dad stood leaning against the balustrade post when I got to the second floor.

"I'll take you. I don't want you driving in this fog." Smiling, I sighed my gratitude. Mom came down the hall, still on the phone. She held it away and whispered, *'Good luck'* with a quick hug. I might have her hair, but not her eyes. They were a deep, smouldering yellow-brown; dark moss stained with mud when she was angry. We made our way to the car via the kitchen, and the thick, icy fog wrapped around me like a suffocating scarf. The lack of visibility made it difficult to know which direction to walk in—I couldn't even see one foot ahead.

"How the heck are we supposed to drive through this?"

"The car has sensors." As if that was good enough to ease me. It wasn't. He wiped his glasses off in the car.

"Dad, seriously, though. I'm sure they'll understand if I can't be there. If they even notice."

"Oh, you're going, Missy. I'm so tired of all your excuses." I shook my head at his clowning. The sensors ended up helping a lot, and the fog thinned as we neared town. We drove over the bridge and turned right—where we had gone straight two days ago—and after a few blocks, exited the old town again via a bridge over the canal. The town looked eerie, shrouded in mist. We arrived at the university forty minutes after we left home, almost three times longer than usual, according to Dad. It was in the newer expansion of the town, the first building erected outside the original village. The regulations required any new buildings to adhere to the original architecture, so everything on the 'new' side still looked like the old town. Over the years, the university added a few satellite department buildings as its popularity grew. We drove up the driveway and it felt like we were approaching another mansion.

"This place is like a lucky packet; it's always throwing surprises at you." My dad commented. The fog had thinned out, making it possible to see the building. I squinted through the window and read the large, red copper words on the front face: *'University of Ostia, Main Building'*. The building was the expected reddish stones and had large wooden windows on all five floors. Its U-shape opened towards us, with a lush green lawn filling the gap. Large trees spotted the lawn, some with benches underneath. A collection of people stood outside under various banners. Dad pulled into a parking spot. I took a deep breath as I absorbed everything, realising the next chapter of my life lay here.

The driveway ended in a traffic-circle stone fountain. The entire scene had an old, haunted look to it, and yet held a certain beauty. I wondered how many students attended—and a sudden fear of getting lost there caught me.

I found the old building shrouded in light mist with the hoard of people waiting, disquieting. My heart squeezed itself, and I wanted to climb back into the car.

"Will you get on alright?" Dad asked.

"Uh," I stuttered. "Yeah, I guess. I'll be fine. It just feels like the Eighth Grade all over again." In Grade Eight, I had to return to school for the final time. I had dreaded that day. He looked up at the vast building.

"Do you want me to walk with you?"
I smiled.

"Thanks, Dad. But I think I've got this." I tried to reassure myself.

"Well, I'll leave you to it then," He squeezed my shoulders and let go. "Text me when you know what time you'll be done."

I watched him drive away until the car was out of sight. My pulse thrummed in my neck, and turning, I took a deep breath. Avoidance could only last so long. I searched the banners on the lawn and found the assembly point for my course. When I passed the fountain, my senses slopped around, causing me to pause.

"Hey! You there!" I heard in front of me, but somewhat certain it was not directed at me, I ignored it. Though it sounded like it was.

"Hello!" the voice chimed close to me. Oh no. I looked up, and there stood a girl with honey blonde curls bouncing just below her shoulders, wearing a green blazer and jeans. She gave off a sporty, or energetic air. Her smile was broader than average, lips blending into her almost tanned skin. Light freckles dusted her nose. I clenched my bag to my chest, unsure what to make of her.

"Yes, *you*!" she laughed. "I'm Laura." She grabbed my hand and shook it. I wondered at her curious familiarity with a perfect stranger. Or had we met somewhere? She made quite an impression. I racked my brain.

"You're Josilyn, right? Gosh, your eyes are electric!" Her eyes were the warmest brown I'd ever seen; golden, chocolaty, lioness eyes. I had a peculiar fear that this encounter would be a repeat of the one with Miriam, who'd known something about me she shouldn't have.

"Um, thank you. Yeah, I am. How did you know?"

"I was at the Masquerade yesterday. I was staring at you when you turned and looked directly at me. It was weird because I felt like you had caught me out, so I waved at you." This unashamed admission of her own exposure took me aback. She reminded me of Anna.

"I remember that." I smiled, feeling somewhat relieved.

"Yeah, your dress was gorgeous, and not many people have such a head of hair. So yes, I was shamelessly admiring your look. But then, of course, you ended up playing that incredible piece as well and, *man,* I made sure to find out who you were." Her entire face lit up when she smiled. "I actually looked for you after the performance to introduce myself, but you disappeared like a ghost." She laughed again.

I hovered.

"Oh, I'm sorry about that. I had a terrible headache, so I disappeared for the rest of the night."

She sympathised, and we kept talking until an announcement called for everyone to gather under their respective banners. I discovered Laura was also a first-year music student and played the piano. The facilitators were senior music students who talked us through all the details of our student cards, cafeteria options, and our schedule as first years. They showed us all the classrooms we would use and the practice rooms at our disposal. Laura and I talked at length about what it was like to live in a house like ours and my experience of Ostia so far. She—like myself with Weatonburg—knew no other life or place, as her family had been living in Ostia for generations. They were among the first families to settle here when the quarry opened. Which implied a high probability that her ancestors knew mine. My heart felt strange and comfortable—*happy*—being found by her.

The orientation ended at 3 p.m., and my dad came to pick me up. Laura waited with me, and I introduced them. He knew about her family, which was unexpected. I was unaware he knew so much about genealogies. They lived on the far side of town, where we hadn't been yet. We offered her a ride there, but she declined, saying she enjoyed walking, and would walk from her mom's work in the old town centre.

~

On Monday, I drove in with my mom, but I was almost late because she was. Laura waited for me on the lawn, and we ran to our first class, making it just in time. Throughout the day, I wanted to ask her about Adrian. He'd said he wasn't new to town, and her whole family had lived there since the beginning. Maybe they were in school together. But alas, I couldn't muster the courage. At lunch, while sitting on the main building's lawn, I asked about the other guy I had danced with at the ball. I had little to relay other than that he was blonde, tall, wore a red mask, and that he had potentially been on the decorating team. She remembered seeing him while we were dancing and had thought he was my boyfriend. I blushed at this.

We walked back to the main building for our final two classes. I glanced up and I saw Adrian's reflection in the mirrored front door, standing by the fountain. Whipping around, I startled Laura and my senses waddled, the grass tasted yellow. But he was not by the fountain. I scanned around in vain—he was nowhere to be seen. Taken aback, Laura asked why I looked so shocked. I brushed it off, saying I thought I saw something.

Our last class was in a satellite building, and Laura told me to save us seats, as she had some questions for the lecturer. Administration also informed us that one of our subjects had a substitute lecturer standing in while the professor was at a conference. I walked alone on cobbled walkways through the lofty buildings and noticed how different everything looked without company. I turned a corner and slammed into a body coming from the opposite direction. My senses shuffled, and I was semi-blinded for a hot second. I heard them yelp and books scattered on the cobblestones.

"I'm so sorry," I managed, swallowing down the embarrassment knot that had formed instantly and stooping to help pick up the books and papers. My brain didn't register any of the words spoken by the person who I'd crashed into, as if sound had become static. I straightened up to face the situation, my cheeks aflame.

I sucked in a breath.

Miriam. I wished I could Houdini out of existence for a second. She adjusted her thick glasses, ironing her faded brown check blazer and ankle-length skirt.

"Oh, how silly of me. That's the third time this week. They should put mirrors on the corners, or I should wear bells on my ankles." She didn't look at me, and I had the impression she didn't realise who I was. I offered her the books and notes in my hands.

"Oh, thank you, that's very nice—" she looked up, and clipped her last word. We stared at each other, neither of us equipped to handle the situation. Her eyes were wide behind the glasses, and she frowned.

"Do I know you?"

"I—we met at the ball briefly." I stuttered. She searched my face, seeming to struggle to identify me. I wore a mask at the ball, so I guess her lack of recognition wasn't so strange. Something like recognition slowly registered in her eyes. Her cheeks turned red, and she looked away.

"Oh… Right. I… don't know what got into me that night to approach you like that. I never drink, but I was having a glass of champagne, looking at the lake. The next moment, I stood in the ballroom listening to your… to your composition. It was so strange. It felt like I was dreaming, and my insides were vibrating—sorry, I don't know how to describe it. I'm rambling, but I've thought about it the past few days and felt bad for putting you on the spot like that. It's unlike me." She was being genuine. If anyone was going to understand what she said, it would be me. Smiling, I nodded.

"I understand and I hope you're okay now…" The question reached deeper than the surface, and something in her eyes told me she understood.

"Yes, well… What else can one do but mend?" She smiled weakly and moved past me with a goodbye nod. I let my breath out, unaware that I'd been holding it. I appreciated the apology, but found it worrisome that she had such a reaction to one glass.

After class, Laura waited with me for my mom. She wasn't answering her phone, and after an hour of waiting, I called my dad to come and fetch me. I told Laura I'd have to consider my options for transport, maybe get a waitressing job to buy myself a scooter or something. But ironically transport would also be my biggest problem if I found a job. She offered to have me stay over at her house if it came to it, and I almost cried at the kindness of it. I expressed my gratitude for the offer and said I would see how things go.

Good thing I'd asked Dad to come: Mom only got home at 7 p.m., after we had eaten and I was reviewing the day's work. She came to my room to apologise before heading to the sunroom to do admin.

Two days later, I was sitting on my bed, listening to music and doing homework when *the Shift* announced its presence in the form of goosebumps. I dropped my pen and closed my eyes. But it was only teasing me because nothing came—like a wave that looked like it would be huge when it broke but absorbed itself instead. *Weird.* I finished writing, took out my cello, and positioned myself in front of the mirror. I still had to practise. My gift didn't lend me supernatural strength and endurance. *The Shift* didn't always come when I played, nor did my senses always shuffle out of place. Sometimes it was because I got a fright or had intense emotions; other times, no proper explanation existed. But whether shifting or shuffling or neither, I was always in tune with the vibrations—like a different type of hearing. I practised some improvisations. The room's acoustics were impressive. Middle Eastern music attracted me more than Western, modern music. My compositions had Persian and Slavic influenced sounds. I liked dramatic and moving beginnings, painful build-ups that begged for a release with complex flips, turns and glissandi. When I looked up, disorientation washed over me, and I felt strange vertigo when I glanced in the mirror. My eyes must have been unfocused because, for a moment, the mirror seemed to move. I stared at it, but nothing happened. My eyes were playing tricks on me. I climbed into bed.

It was the night of the ball, and I was strolling down the hallway towards the foyer. My headache was gone, and I enjoyed the *Moonlight Sonata*. Guests greeted me, praising the composition I had played. I thanked them and moved to the stairs. When I touched the balustrade, I turned and looked at the front door. Adrian stood at the threshold, his eyes locked on me. He wore no mask and smiled when our eyes met, a shiver running down my arms. The guests moved around as if we weren't there. My chest heaved and my heart raced, but I didn't break eye contact.

"Come in," I heard myself say. He took my hand and kissed it, and when he stood up straight, we were in the forest. My hand burned where he'd touched me, equal parts pleasure and pain. His hands came up to my face, and he took my mask off. His mouth was serious, his green gaze weighty when he whispered,

"I see you."

Waking up with a start, my hand remained inflamed. I looked at it but couldn't see much, except that I was shaking. The darkness outside indicated ample night left for sleeping. I took a couple of focused breaths and willed myself back to sleep.

~

Mom was running late again, and Dad couldn't be without his car, so he drove me to class. On the way, I mentioned my plans to find a job and save up for my own transport. He supported the idea and suggested doing gigs for restaurants or events. For some reason, I hadn't thought of that.

Laura was sitting on the fountain waiting for me.

"You know, your house is cool and all, but sometimes I wished you lived in town."

I shrugged, and we walked to a satellite building. It was a class we hadn't had yet, History of Music— also an optional subject for other degrees. We entered the vast classroom, filling with students we hadn't yet seen. It looked like an amphitheatre with tiers of wooden desks. We preferred sitting in the middle, third row from the front. We scooted in and took out our notes and stationery. The seats were uncomfortable, the desks narrow.

So much talking buzzed around us we couldn't hear each other and, rather than scream, we kept quiet and looked around. After a few minutes, a tall, willowy man garbed in a black suit entered the room with a black leather briefcase. He didn't look around as he strode to the desk, placed his briefcase on it, and opened it with his long, slender hands. He looked kind of creepy, truth be told. His cheekbones were prominent, and his hair was short and pitch-black. The black suit and black hair against his bone-white skin created an unsettling contrast along with his gangly form. When the students noticed him, the room quieted.

He glided around the desk and looked up.

He lifted his hands and clapped twice, and a booming sound shuddered through the room. A jolt went through me as the energy wanted to bubble to the surface. I closed my eyes and took a deep breath as I felt the chair melt away for a second. I grasped the desk. Everyone became silent and stared at him.

"Music is a higher revelation than all wisdom and philosophy. It is the mediator between the spiritual and the sensual life, the one incorporeal entrance into the higher world of knowledge which comprehends mankind, but which mankind cannot comprehend." He stared at the floor. "Profound words by the legendary Ludwig van Beethoven." He paused and peered around the room. "But, to love your future, path, and destiny, you must embrace the trials of your past, error or success. I will teach you the trails famed men and women left throughout history. I'm Doctor Dagworth, and that is how you will address me." He stated with a bored tone, the room muted.

"Perhaps, in a few hundred years, some of you will be the subject of a history class. I'd guess not. So, do your best to leave a mark in this world. Otherwise, your existence will melt into oblivion, just like the billions before you." He drawled as if bored. "Unless, of course, that doesn't matter to you." He walked to the board, a graceful ghost, and took some chalk from the desk as he passed. *Cheery.* Laura and I looked at each other, pulling 'yikes' faces. He wrote his contact information and hours on the board. The side door opened, and someone came in. I was busy writing the details and didn't look up.

"Jeepers." Laura breathed next to me.

"Hmm?" I responded out of habit.

The room burst into laughter. The energy pricked at my skin, and I closed my eyes, taking deep breaths. This was the exact reason I never wanted to be late. If a room full of people had laughed at me, I would've turned around and never come back. I felt second-hand embarrassment for whoever it was. I heard the footfall on the wooden desk a level above me until it was behind me, where the undaunted latecomer found a seat.

"An example of how *not* to get noticed," Doctor Dagworth quipped as he glanced over his shoulder. A low, brief chuckle behind me was the sole response. The hairs on the back of my neck stood up for an instant. Laura wriggled in her seat.

Doctor Dagworth started his lecture, and I quite enjoyed his presentation style. He had a knack for portraying history as a fairy tale, using his voice as his instrument. It was easy to forget to take notes while listening, and I had to force myself to stay focused. But the overwhelming amount of information eventually caused my hand to cramp. I sat back for a break and flexed my hand.

I felt the air pull away from my hair, and I got goosebumps, a thrill running over my skin. Cringing forward, I looked back, and my heart bucked. Adrian's burning emerald eyes met mine. Something akin to fear pulsated through my veins. I snapped back to the front, my eyes huge. *Was I dreaming again?* A heatwave washed over my back, and I felt him lean closer. His hot breath was on my right ear.

"Hello, Miss Grey. Your fragrance is resplendent, rapturous as sorcery, and the shock on your face accentuates your eyes," he whispered. I wasn't wearing a fragrance. I turned back to him. *Big mistake.* His eyes were dipped in mischief, a wicked smile on his lips. He was wearing a fine-knitted, dark olive-green sweater.

"I—I," I stammered, but when it didn't come out right, I snapped back to the front, my cheeks flushing. My heart pulsed against my neck. In my peripheral vision, I saw Laura looking at me in and I pretended to be focused on the lecture. But I couldn't ignore the intense gaze of the emerald eyes boring into the back of my head. I fought with every fibre of my being to not surrender to human instinct and turn around. I clutched at my necklace. It felt like he was willing me to look at him, as if he was pushing his presence onto my skin, demanding not to be ignored. Try as I might, I didn't hear a lick of what Dagworth was saying.

"Hey, what's going on? Are you okay? Do you know him?" Laura whispered. Dazed, I stared at her, grateful for the break in intensity—a wave of fresh air diluting the fog in my mind. I was drifting into space, and she pulled me back into my body with a yank. I didn't know how to answer the first two questions.

"Uh," I stuttered like a fool. "We met at the ball." I felt so stupid, listening to my nervous words as if she was asking me questions that could land me in trouble. His eyes burned my cheeks, and I looked down at my notes. Laura slid closer, and I stared at her with wide eyes.

"What did he say?" She pushed, her eyebrows pulled together. I licked my lips out of reflex as if it would glue them together and I'd have an excuse not to answer.

"I'm not even sure." My voice was almost inaudible. She studied my face, and her head flashed to the back, and I turned too. Adrian leaned forward as if to share in our secrecy and looked at me with innocence shining like metal.

"I could repeat my words if that would please you?" he stated in a guiltless, balmy whisper, his innocent frown made my stomach turn in a strange way. We stared at him, and I looked at her. She studied him with the astonishment I knew well. He didn't look like the average man you saw day to day. I wondered what was going through her mind. He was so frank and intrusive.

"Please, do tell me what is so fascinating that the three of you would interrupt my lecture?" a menacing voice broke through the madness of our situation. It took me a second to realise it was Dagworth. My cheeks burned with embarrassment, and I felt detached from my body.

"I beg your pardon, Doctor," Adrian took control. His voice was a deep siren's call. The room fell silent. "It was not my intention to interrupt the reading. I merely inquired from the lovely lady if she might have an extra pencil I could borrow." He spoke with leisure, enunciating each word like a spell until they seemed heavy. Although he sounded painfully polite, something about his voice—something in the atmosphere—gave the impression something dark loomed in the shadows and shrunk the room into a claustrophobic hole. The room was silent as a tomb. The energy coiled inside me, and people shifted in their seats.

Dagworth paused—no, froze—and stared at Adrian blank-faced, his eyes empty. After an eternity passed and the discomfort distilled into a gel—not as thick, but still palpable—he blinked as if awakening from a daze.

"Uh," he started, his voice was feeble. "Okay. My apologies for the misinterpretation."

I was sure he was being sarcastic, but he turned and continued with the lecture as if nothing had happened. No one missed that, and whispers sprouted around the room but clipped when Dagworth glanced over his shoulder. *What just happened?* Maybe he got side-tracked. But the air felt thick and enclosing. I was not claustrophobic, but I was unnerved. Something hungry permeated the air and coveted attention, and when no one else paid it mind, the full weight rested on me alone. That, along with Adrian's heavy gaze, suffocated me. The air looked red, but I was the only one choking on it; the rest of the class moved on after a few seconds.

As soon as Dagworth dismissed us, I fled the room like a coiled spring. I couldn't breathe anymore. Laura called after me, but I darted out the door like a panicked animal, determined to get outside. After leaving the room, I felt Adrian's presence lingering close behind me, sticking to me like static electricity. *Was he following me?* The thought pushed me through the stampeding crowd. I kept glancing over my shoulder, but I didn't see him. *The Shift* was building up inside me. I questioned my sanity for feeling as though he was right there when he wasn't. Perhaps I was just not used to guys like that. Perhaps that's how *Ostian* men acted.

Laura still called to me from a distance as I escaped into the icy wind and paced away from the building. I welcomed the flow of fresh, cold air into my lungs and inhaled so deep and long I began coughing. A violent urge to escape broke through, and I hyperventilated. Just short of running, I moved to the edge of the lawn. The energy built up in my core determined to rage to the surface and overwhelm me with its power. My bag fell on the grass when I hunched over, my hands on my knees, taking deep, steadying breaths. I closed my eyes and tried to push the energy back. *Not now. Not now.* Everyone would see, and that would ruin my day. Then all of them would know I was a spazzing freak.

It came.

The electric *Pulse* bulged out of its fringes, flurrying my senses to the point of insanity. They didn't fall into an order as usual, even if it might not be the right one. No order. No stopping. They shuffled and roiled, tottering like shells in a storming sea, and it made me nauseous. Rolling. Rolling. I couldn't tell if I was standing upright or floating upside down in the ocean.

Desperate for control, I pressed my fingers into my temples; *hard.* To some extent, it worked. They slugged into the proper arrangement.

I had never experienced that level of intensity before.

The energy still brimmed beneath the surface. I burned my lungs with a deep breath, opened my eyes, and yanked my bag off the ground. I was angry and emotional and not even sure where I wanted to go. Eyes stared at me from fathomless faces, and my cheeks warmed.

A chaotic tango between fire and ice flared through my nervous system, sending me back to square one: pandemonium. My eyes snapped shut as the *Pulse* beat through me. Just once. My hair stood on end over my whole body. Adrian stood before me, too close and even more frighteningly tall than I remembered. The heat licked at me.

My eyes opened, his proximity became apparent, and an involuntary gasp escaped from me. Passers-by stared at us, but when they met his gaze, they looked away and walked faster. His attention zoomed in on me. I loathed the way he made my heart pound out of my chest. *What did he want from me?* Two inflamed emeralds set in an expressionless face looked down at me. My stomach twisted with unease. Out of place for the moment, he gave a broad grin. His white teeth glowed like something out of a TV commercial, just a lot scarier.

"You're a slippery little thing, aren't you?" he chuckled, "Just when I'm under the impression I've got your attention, you disappear on me." He shook his head as if disappointed. Or disapproved.

His tone wasn't helping me warm up to him. I was unsure why, but something inside wailed for me to run. I stared at him blankly. The energy rolled. A growing urge to scream scratched at my throat, but iron bars coiled around my neck and prevented me from doing just that. *It was so unlike me.*

He looked at the ring around my neck and cocked his head. The muscles in his jaw tightened. His eyes drifted to my jaw and locked onto it. It made me self-conscious. Unblinking, he lifted his enormous hand and stroked the edge of my jaw, his thumb trailing from my chin to my ear. A hair strand was stuck to my skin. His touch left a flaming path in its wake. I wanted to turn my face away but was physically unable. I trembled. *What the heck.*

He exhaled a harsh breath through his nose and dropped his hand to his side. The blood throbbed fiercely where he'd touched my face.

"Will you not favour me with your voice?" he sounded bored. He stared at my lips, willing them to open. I would hate to break it to him, but that really didn't help.

"I—I," I cleared my throat when I realised I was not getting anywhere. *Pull yourself together.* "I wanted fresh air. It was stuffy in there."

Quiet for a moment, he pondered my statement and nodded.

"May I offer you a ride home after class?" he volunteered. "Yours, naturally." He chuckled and flashed his brilliant smile. My heart dropped again. I wasn't sure what he meant, but I *was* sure I didn't want to know. I swallowed hard to clear my dry throat.

"Thank you, but my dad is picking me up." My voice had a nervous edge.

"Josilyn! We have, like, five minutes to get to class!" Laura yelled from the main building.

Adrian blocked my view of her, and I peeked around him. She stood a little way from the front door, hesitance exuding from her body. Behind her, I saw Adrian and I in the door's reflection, and I was wholly dwarfed. It was almost comical. And frightening.

When I looked up at him, he was rigid and frozen in place, his eyes fixed on the distance—irritation bright and clear on his face. I glanced over my shoulder but saw nothing out of the ordinary. *What was he looking at?*

"I have to go, sorry," I walked past him and felt colder the further I got from him. I watched him in the door's reflection. Warmth bloomed inside me when he glanced over his shoulder after a few seconds before walking to the parking lot.

I was unaware I had reached Laura. She gasped and almost dislocated my shoulder when she yanked me closer.

"Ow!" I wouldn't have guessed she had that sort of strength. She reached out and brushed my inflamed jaw. I pulled away, but she was undeterred.

"What happened to your face?" she exclaimed, her eyes large with horror. I stared at her blankly and touched my jaw too, but felt nothing strange.

"What do you mean?"

She pushed me in front of the door. A dark blue network of prominent veins stretched from my chin to my ear on the one side of my face. I sucked in a breath. It appeared as though poison coursed through me, and my blood was fighting to escape. Dazed and horrified, I touched my skin, and the burn soothed somewhat.

"I… don't know. It doesn't hurt. Maybe it's the light refraction and heat." She lifted an eyebrow.

"Yeah. Light refraction. Definitely." She turned and walked to the next class. The lecturer hadn't arrived yet, and the room was still buzzing.

"Are you okay, though? You looked a little freaked out back there. I got worried when you bailed."

I bit my lip.

"Got claustrophobic with all the people and wanted some fresh air."

"Ah, okay, I see." She paused, and for a moment, I thought I was safe, but I was mistaken. "Did the jumbo-sized, hot but creepy redhead get claustrophobic as well?" My nostrils flared, which was unlike me. I suppressed it.

"Um. I don't know, maybe," was all I managed, because halfway through, my voice sounded sharper than it should have for the question being answered. I didn't understand why I reacted like that when people brought him up. It wasn't like I had something to hide. On the contrary, I was glad she called me away. I think…

"So, what's his name, and what's his deal?"

I gave her a sharp look but realised it soon enough to divert my glare. What was with me?

"I don't know what his deal is. We haven't had much of a conversation," malice tinged my tone. I glanced away and forced myself to continue. "All I know is he isn't new, so he must have been living here a while." I didn't say his name.

She frowned. "If he was living in the woods, maybe. I mean, let's be frank; he makes quite the impression. So, I would've seen him or heard about him. Someone like that doesn't blend into their environment. He doesn't look eighteen, though. I wonder why he has classes with us."

Ostia wasn't that small, but she was right; no one would have overlooked him. My encounters with him were so strange that I wasn't surprised my brain got jumbled. Maybe I'd misunderstood him.

"What's his name again?"

"Adrian," I answered reluctantly, looking into space, feeling like I'd just lapped a massive secret.

"Hmm. And his surname?"

Ice kissed my neck as I recalled our weird conversation. He'd said he didn't have one.

"I don't know."

"Oh, okay. Well, I've definitely never heard of him."

As the lecture started, my mind was occupied with the appearance of my veins earlier. They went back to normal a few minutes into the class. I knew this because Laura kept staring at me and informed me when it was gone. She asked me if I had a condition she should know about in case of an emergency. I almost spluttered a laugh.

The following Tuesday, when we exited the building, the scent of petrichor carried on a breeze from the trees. Rain. The *Pulse* swerved through me. A light moth rain drizzled down. When Laura noticed the shiver running through me, she asked if I was cold. The earthy scent was intoxicating, and the drops on my face cold. I looked up at the sky and enjoyed the moment.

"I was thinking, maybe I can drop you off on Fridays, and then we can go hiking or just hang out?"

A warm feeling enveloped my heart, and I almost wanted to cry. Laura wanted to spend more time with me. By choice. How wonderful it was—to be chosen.

"Um, that sounds awesome. I've never hiked before. My dad wondered if there were any caves to explore?"

"Oh, there are a lot of caves in this area, for sure. But few are safe or open to the public. Most are on the other side of the volcano, which is a nature reserve for the tribe. They're pretty wild, so people don't go there. And there are wild animals too. Most of the hiking is done this side."

I shook my head and laughed, confronted by how different things were in Ostia. When she asked how the job hunting was going, I had to confess it wasn't going anywhere. The biggest hurdle was transport. My dad had become the designated driver since my mom always had something keeping her somehow. The rain was getting heavier just as Dad turned into the parking lot. I could barely discern our car through the sudden downpour. Laura hugged me and mentioned how the weather was perfect for hot chocolate and a book before we both hurried off. By the time I reached the car, the rain had soaked me through. The seat squelched as I slumped into it.

"Sorry about the seat." My brain short-circuited in its search function when I met my mom's face, taken aback.

"Mom?"

"I've been known to be one, yes." She reversed out.

The rain dissipated the closer we got to home, and when we exited the forest into the meadow, the sun broke through the clouds and the mist was gone. The grass was vibrant and glowed with humidity. I squinted.

The other car wasn't there.

"Where's Dad?"

"He said he had some business in town."

I saw grocery bags on the backseat, which I helped unload while Mom scolded me for trying to carry too many at once. As I steeled myself for the burdened trek up the steps, Andrew opened the kitchen door and came down to help, as if summoned.

"Hey, Buddy! What have you been up to all day?" School only started on the Monday. He seemed hesitant to answer—careful.

"I...was around the house. Just wandering, the usual," his tone was strange. Who was he trying to fool when we all knew he didn't wander usually?

"Okay? So, we're doing the mysterious thing? That works for me," I nudged him and he gave a sheepish grin. He went out to help Mom with the rest, and I unpacked the bags, waiting for her to tell me where she wanted everything. We were still adjusting to the new kitchen.

Once finished, I placed my bag in the downstairs parlour, lingering to admire the multiple bookcases filled with all manner of books. My gaze wandered to the sofas, to the green Chesterfield, which was my favourite. Two desks looked out of the window towards the opening in the forest. Anyone could've seen me walk there the night of the ball, I realised. I stared at the forest and the lake. Prior to my conversation with Laura about hiking, I had never ventured down to the water, but now I felt the urge to do so. I was wearing knitted sneakers, but doubted it would be a treacherous journey.

I approached the treeline, looking for an opening towards the lake. When I reached the brim of the forest, I saw an overgrown path a little further to the left. I wondered if anyone could see me from the house. The atmosphere changed noticeably inside the forest, alive with birds up high, the trees speckled with neon green moss and, in some places, yellow. The air pressed against me as I made my way down the path.

I reached the lake, my breath catching at the sight of the clear, blue water. The town on the other side looked like a medieval conjuring. A not-so-well-maintained pier lay at the end of the forest. It looked forgotten. I doubted my family knew about it—the potential excited me so much that it almost had me running back. But I spent a while sitting on the bank covered by undergrowth, watching the calm water, the rolling hills, and the forest. It was transcendental. The trees and plants on the bank were dense all along the shore, and I couldn't see much to my left or right. I fished out my phone, took some photos, and listened to music. Again, I thought how different my life was now, and I got the urge to share it with Anna. I called her, but it just rang. I took a picture of the lake and sent it to her.

After about forty minutes, the light had faded, and I became acutely aware that I was alone in a forest. My senses dipped, the lake now pitch-black and soundless. My heart raced, and I closed my eyes, goosebumps rolling over my skin. The taste of mushrooms stuck to my tongue. I took focused breaths, waiting for the goosebumps to subside. My senses slipped back into order, and I got up to go back. The *Shift* lingered close by as I hastened up the slope—a more strenuous journey than I'd expected. When I stepped into the clearing, the pressure lifted and I saw a bright blue, tiny car standing next to my dad's. It was the cutest car I'd ever seen, and I walked straight up to it. I didn't notice my dad sitting under the gazebo and got a fright when he spoke.

"What mischief were you up to in there?" My senses shuffled for a moment, and I put my hand to my heart.

"Don't scare me!" He came around and met me. "Whose car is this? It's the most adorable car ever."

"I think so too. Zastava 750."

"I don't know Zastava 750, but they have a bomb car." I looked at him, but I had an inkling of what was coming. He smiled with a mischievous glint in his eyes. My body didn't know how to react, but my eyes widened.

"No way, Dad! No freaking way! You're kidding me!" I tasted the exhilaration in my throat. I looked at it again, and tears burned my eyes. Before, it was cute and pretty, but now that it was *mine*, perfection increased a hundred-fold. My lips quivered as I looked at it.

"Guess I'll call you Zastava 750 from now on." My dad commented. I touched the low roof with immense affection and adoration. Tears flowed down my cheeks, and I swallowed back a knot in my throat.

"Dad," I went up to him and hugged him tightly, "This is the most perfect gift you've ever given me. I don't have the words to describe how thankful I am."

"This is more a gift to myself, to be honest. So I don't have to haul you around the whole time. It really cuts into productivity." We smiled at each other.

"And I knew if you started working in town, the suffering would double. And I wouldn't get much sleep. So, no. This is a selfish gift purely for my benefit." I shook my head and turned back to the car. *My car.* I opened the door, which made no sound, though I'd anticipated it to creak, and sat on the tan leather seat. My heart swelled inside my chest. The inside smelled of pineapple air deodorant. I put my hands on the thin steering wheel, covered with the same tan leather. The *Pulse* beat through me. I heard a faint *meow* from the back and turned, meeting green eyes that reminded me of Adrian. Instead, these eyes belonged to a fluffy white creature, sitting on the back seat like royalty. *Gorgeous.*

"Um, Dad, I think you may have gotten more than you were bargaining for."

"Nope," he tried to squeeze into the passenger seat. Comical. "Norwegian Forest Cat. She's part of the deal. Apparently, she goes wherever the car does." We stared at the white marshmallow, and she stared back with big green eyes, which were locked on mine.

"She's so beautiful. What is her name?"

He pondered a moment, and I wondered if he was trying to make up a story or if he was actually trying to remember.

"I think they said Trjetsi-tji. It's in the language of the natives, Nomratj, and I think it means sleeping snowball." I wondered if it ever snowed here. I'd never seen snow before.

"Yeah…I'm just going to call her Tji-Tji." He laughed, got out and stretched, cracking like a glow stick. Frankly, it surprised me he managed to get in at all. He guided me into starting the car, and I drove around the clearing. I was used to an automatic transmission, so the car jumped and stalled a few times, but I got the hang of it.

When Dad said we should probably head inside for dinner, I opened the backdoor and, with cautious care, wrapped my arms around Tji-Tji's soft body. To my surprise, she did this without struggling or scratching and snuggled into my neck, purring. I beamed at my dad. He smiled and shook his head.

"Looks like I got you two presents for the price of one." We walked to the kitchen.

"You're a loving thing, aren't you?" I whispered. She looked up at me like she understood. I had never seen an animal with such attentive eyes. I cooed at her the entire way to the kitchen.

"Aww!" Mom gasped when I entered. "Gorgeous!" Andrew came over to pat her head, which she readily received, and when Mom took her from me, she didn't object to this new development either.

"Tji-Tji. She has a lovely temperament," I stroked her tail.

"Oh yes. She's beautiful," She paused a moment, smiling. "Do you like the other gift too?"

"Mom, I don't have words. It's beautiful. Without a doubt, the best gift ever," I assured her. Well, with one exception to that statement…

"I'm glad you like it, Hon. I'm okay with Tji-Tji in your room if that's where you want her to sleep. We can get her a basket later. If you don't want her on the bed, you can put some old towels on the floor. Though I doubt she will sleep on it with such a spacious bed and so many cushions in the windows. The towels are in the cabinet under my bed." She walked to the stove with the cat in her arm, saying dinner would be ready in twenty minutes. Tji-Tji was so different from my idea of how cats behaved, but I was in no position to give opinions about animals. My parents' room was on the second floor of the silo, also flanked by windows. The sunset burned with a stunning display outside.

A gentle draught passed through my winding staircase as I ascended with two once-white towels, which I arranged into a nest on the windowsill behind my bed. I heard movement behind me, and I jumped. The *Pulse* burst through me. I breathed a sigh of relief when I saw Tji-Tji sitting on the bed, staring at me.

"Wow! You gave me a fright, Lady!" I scolded, catching my breath as I picked her up. My pulse was racing. She meowed meekly and placed a gentle paw on my cheek, licking my chin. Even to me, who didn't know cats well, that seemed peculiar. She made soft *meows* at me again and gazed out of the window.

"What is it?" I cooed. She kept staring outside and meowing. *Odd.*

On the way downstairs, still cuddling her, I realised I'd left the keys in the ignition. I thought to give her the scenic route, thinking of how she'd seemed to look at the sunset from my window. We went out the front door and I pointed out the forest path, telling her about all the views and how she'd enjoy the forest. After retrieving the keys, we stepped back onto the porch, where Tji-Tji fidgeted, twisting and turning in my arms, moaning.

"Shh, it's okay, girl," I tried to comfort her, but she continued squirming and whining.

I was still trying to soothe her when we entered the foyer.
I looked up and froze. My stomach dropped through the earth, and shock vibrated through my skin. The *Pulse* ripped through me. I gasped at the figure standing at the foot of the stairs.

Chapter 5

Tji-Tji scrambled and broke free from my arms, running into the hall. Adrian stared after her with an unreadable expression. What was he doing in my house?

His expression—or the lack thereof—frightened me, and I couldn't speak. After a moment, he composed himself and his mouth spread into a wide grin, losing his ghoulish nimbus. He had quite a smile, I had to admit. My heart sped up involuntarily. *Traitor.*

"Good evening, Josilyn," his voice smoked in my ears, rich like aged wine. A ritualistic drum fest played in my ears as my heart raced faster and faster. His lips distorted into a crooked grin.

Where was my voice? I gulped and stared at him like a witless mute. My cheeks burned. Why did I get like this when he was around? I had no control over my faculties. I clutched my necklace. How did he get here? No other cars were outside.

I must have blacked out because when I came to, he stood right in front of me, which seemed to be his thing. I staggered back.

He frowned, and he scrutinised my face.

"Have I frightened you?" he asked softly. The gentleness in his voice disarmed me and touched my heart. My cheeks burned. I didn't understand my emotions.

He didn't even know me. I breathed deeply, intoxicated by an intense aroma filling the air. It was unlike anything I had ever smelled. My nerves came alive, receptive and absorbent. My senses buckled.

Unable to control myself, I leaned closer, a moth to a flame. Warm blood spread through my cheeks when I realised what I was doing. What *was* I doing? I stepped back and tried clearing my head, but it didn't help much.

"Yes. I mean, no. I didn't see you when I came downstairs, and I wasn't expecting you here." The unsteadiness in my voice irritated me.

He smiled, his eyes sparkling with amusement, and he licked his lips. He had closed the distance I had created a moment before.

"Of course. Forgive my unannounced visit. I was in the vicinity and thought to come by," He for paused a moment, "I wanted to see you." His eyes sunk into me, pulled me in, and his smile hid mischief. My heart responded. The rush of adrenaline made me dizzy.

"Oh," I managed in a horrifyingly feeble voice. He cocked his head to the side, listening. I strained my ears, but if there was something to be heard, it eluded me.

"It's been a while since I last saw you on campus." Although I managed, I instantly regretted confessing that I had noticed his absence. A soft smile touched his eyes.

"I do not particularly enjoy spending my time sitting in a classroom. But there are exceptions." He gave me a meaningful look, and I could not keep eye contact. I found myself staring at the veins on his large hand. He flexed the one I was looking at as if he knew. My heart skipped a beat as he stepped closer and bent toward me. I froze like a statue. The scent in the air distilled and fogged my brain. Slow and deliberate, he brushed his cheek against mine and pressed his mouth to my ear.

Warm, so incredibly warm. What was he doing? The flames erupted on my skin. His warm glow flowed to me, and something brushed my neck. *Move,* I told myself; *move.* But I couldn't.

"I have found myself drawn to you with unexpected fury. You lure me like an unsuspecting moth to a vibrant web. I am Icarus, and you will be my burning demise." His voice was low and dark.

My heart fluttered madly in my chest, and the *Pulse* beat in my ears. I closed my eyes, forcing my senses to submit. I collected them somewhat, and when I opened my eyes, he had straightened up, looking down at me with a burning gaze and that wicked smile. He was aware of his effect on me; even worse, he was *enjoying* it.

Footsteps came down the hall, and I felt a sudden sense of guilt. My senses shuffled. Andrew. He stopped when he saw us and stared at Adrian with wide eyes.

"Andrew," I breathed, "Err—This is Adrian."
His eyes hopped between us.

"H—hey," he greeted uneasily, frowning at Adrian.

"Evening." I looked up at him and couldn't place his expression. An awkward silence thickened between us, and without saying a word, Andrew turned back into the hall and disappeared. He wasn't *that* shy.

"Sorry, I have no idea what that was about." Why was I apologising?

"Don't concern yourself. I understand."
The silence became tangible, and I stared at the floor, avoiding his gaze. A low, rumbling laugh bounced against the walls, and I looked up. He stood beside the stairs, hand on the post, gazing at me with amusement. I wasn't aware he had moved at all.

He bit his lip, straightened up, and came closer. When he stopped short in front of me, he gazed down, his heavy eyes locked onto mine—a smile forming on his lips. With the back of his hand, he stroked my cheek, a feather-light touch.

"I think I should take my leave now," he announced and glided past me.

I turned and followed him like I was under hypnosis. He ducked his head as he exited the foyer, the top of his head only just missing the door frame.

"How did you get here?" I heard myself say. I didn't want him to leave yet, I realised.

He was already on the grass, headed towards the stone pathway. He turned when I spoke, a broad smile on his lips as he walked backwards.

"I live close by," he answered in a light, happy tone.

That couldn't be. I stared at him and tried to remember if I had ever seen other houses. To my knowledge, there were none close by.

"What? Where do you live then?"
He halted and enjoyed my curiosity far too much.

"Why do you want to know?" The spark in his eyes made my pulse race.

I didn't like the way he reacted to my question; it made me feel foolish.

"I'm just curious." To avoid his eyes, I stared down at the steps before me. He chuckled, the sound even further away now.

"You know, Josilyn, curiosity killed the cat."
I looked up and could just barely discern the mischievous smile on his face.

"I'm not a cat."

My reply was dry and irritated. Eerie—observing my bodily reactions as if they were something separate from me, from my own mind. As if it were its own entity. He stopped, regarding me for a moment, and sighed.

"No…" he breathed. "You're a little dove."

He laughed and looked up at the sky, his laugh echoing through the trees. I scowled at him and folded my arms over my chest.

"I haven't seen any houses close by." I snapped, suddenly annoyed.

"Perhaps you were not paying attention. Until next time, Josilyn. Sweet dreams." He turned and slinked down the stone pathway.

He moved fast. I could not respond before he disappeared into the tree line.

"Bye." I breathed, though he wouldn't hear me.

Too long I stood there, gazing after him like an eternal statue. At some point, I snapped out of it and went back inside. Fatigue hit me like a brick wall as I entered the foyer. My vision blurred with vertigo, and I aimed for the kitchen down the hall, stumbling. I was in a daze, my feet too heavy to lift. The walls contorted around me. Mom gasped when I entered the kitchen. I struggled to keep my eyes open.

"Josilyn, what's wrong?" She grabbed my face and stroked my cheeks. "You look like ash! Where has all your blood gone? Sit down."

I drooped onto a chair just in time. She shoved a glass of juice into my hand and instructed me to drink it all. I clasped it with shaking hands and lifted it to my mouth. *So thirsty.* Guilt made its appearance once again, and I didn't want to look at her.

"What happened?" she asked, as I slurped the last few drops. I inhaled until my lungs burned, and life trickled back into my body. Oh, how fresh the air was.

"I'm not sure."

Andrew peeked into the room wide-eyed. His expression relieved, and he entered, his posture relaxing.

"Where's Adrian?" he sat down next to me. A chill ran through me. I didn't want Mom to know he'd been there. My eyes flashed to hers. She frowned at Andrew, but her gaze drifted to me.

"Adrian was here?"

The edge in her voice caught me off guard. I felt caught out and looked down, shuffling the glass around.

"Yeah, he was, but not for long. He just stopped by to say hello. I wasn't expecting him or anything," I explained. A thick silence took form, and I refused to look at her.

"Is that why you look like this? What did he do?" She asked the dreaded question, alarm prominent in her voice. I looked up, and a weak laugh escaped my mouth when I saw the worry in her eyes.

This was why I didn't want her to know. She always jumped to conclusions over even the smallest things.

"He didn't do anything, well, not intentionally. He just gave me a fright because I didn't expect him." *Don't think badly of him.*

"He gave me a fright, too," Andrew stated dryly. We looked at him.

"Oh, come on, he's gigantic! And scary, with the red hair and green eyes."

"Well, I'd like to meet him next time he comes around." She put a full plate before me and made sure I ate. When I was done, she asked Andrew to help me to my room. I protested I could quite get there myself, but when I stood up, my knees buckled, and I grabbed the counter. She gave me an 'oh really?' expression, and I set out toward my room, though my legs were heavy.

Tji-Tji appeared behind me and followed close behind. Wordlessly, Andrew stayed by my side as we went up the stairs to my room.

I yearned for my bed to relieve my legs, and plunged onto it almost too soon.

"Are you okay?" he sat down on the bed. His words sounded a little strange, but I knew my mind was the one at fault.

"Yeah, I'm fine. Don't know what's gotten into me," my words slurred as if my tongue were numb. Silence fermented.

"Adrian didn't do anything, did he?"
He sounded careful.

"No, don't be silly," I responded too fast. He said nothing as he sat with me for a long while before getting up.

"Okay then. Goodnight, Sis. Sweet dreams."
The two last words reminded me Adrian had said them earlier. A strange, looming feeling inside me grew about Adrian until it dominated my thoughts. Why did I react like I did when I was around him? I was not myself at all. The more confusing part was that I liked him, even though another part of me also feared him.

I put my pyjamas on sluggishly, my balance still off. An urge compelled me to open the curtains and the windows. No breeze came from outside; it was a peaceful night. Perhaps too quiet. The rising, waning moon gave the lake an eerie luminance, glowing like a pond of gold in otherwise blue darkness. I gazed at the calm water for a few minutes, but weariness overwhelmed me, and I fell onto my bed, where I tumbled into a deep sleep.

~

A blur of people rushed around the university halls at hyper speed. I panicked and tried without success to get out of the crowd. I glanced over my shoulder. Adrian was behind me, and I turned around. He towered over everyone around him and stood motionless in the middle of the hall. My insides turned and sank as he stared at me with a mocking smile. My breaths became too frequent. Something was wrong. No sound. The silence was numbing, and I turned, trying to run away from him, but my feet were glued to the floor. Panic rushed through me. Why couldn't I move? My legs were numb and heavy. Nervous, I peeked over my shoulder again. Adrian came closer at a constant speed, unaffected by the blurring movement around him. His features were no longer mocking. Expressionless, determined. Fear crept over me, and my heart hammered against my throat, but I kept trying to run away. The silence pounded and rang in my ears. Louder and louder. Lights faded. Darkness swallowed me.

~

A low, pulsating drone resonated through my room and woke me. I jolted upright, gasping for air. The curtains fluttered wildly, and a gust ripped through my hair, blinding me momentarily.

It stopped.

The curtains fell back into place.

I felt the droning vibrate through me, causing a queasy sensation to settle in the depths of my core. I found myself on my feet, driven by the adrenaline rush. My senses fell out of place, and I peered around the room, blindly trying to find the source. My ears steered me in a direction, and my eyes focused on the mirror. *No.* I held my breath. I hoped I was hallucinating. Maybe the juice Mom had given me last night had fermented.

Ripples ran over the mirror as if made of liquid silver. The oscillation stemmed from the middle—like a pebble dropped into a pond—holding a rhythmic pace with the low pulse.

This was a dream.

I hesitated, but stepped forward, anxiety punching my heart. The floor was extra cold underneath my feet.

What if it was a safety hazard? Were there earthquakes here? I reached the mirror and stared at the liquid. Nothing else in the room moved. Not an earthquake. A glimpse of something in the mirror caught my eye, and I leaned closer.

A butterfly was on the other side, flapping its wings. My breath caught, and I staggered back. I spun around, but no butterfly fluttered about the room. I put my hand over my mouth in case a scream slipped out. It had to be a dream. Or perhaps I was, at last, going crazy. My heart raced, but I gave a slow step forward.

It had definitely been a butterfly—the only visible thing amongst the still silver. Maybe there *was* a room back there after all.

I lifted my hand and edged towards the mirror. My nerves erupted as I got closer. The cool surface beneath my skin surprised me. A creepy feeling pulled on my insides as my finger submerged in the liquid. It reacted like water to my touch, forming tiny ripples around my finger. Excited, I pulled my finger out, expecting it to be covered in silver. It was not. My finger was gone; I couldn't see it at all. Ice ran down my back. I didn't feel any pain, but I was too frightened to investigate what had happened. Where the heck was my finger?

I shook my hand and rubbed it on my pants. Without looking at it again, I ran to my bed and pulled the pillow over my face, trying to drown out the beating sound.

What was happening? How could my finger just disappear? Squeezing my eyes shut, I hummed aloud, willing myself to fall asleep.

I woke up from my shoulder being shaken with urgency and, gasping, cringed back against the windowsill. Terrified, I raked the room.

My pulse raced, and I met my mom's shocked eyes. She gaped at me with hands surrendered in the air.

"Honey, it's just me! What's wrong?" She was alarmed.

My throat clammed shut with emotion. *Mirror.* My eyes flashed to it, but it remained motionless as it ought to. Mom turned around.

My hand!

I looked at it, and my finger was back. Wait; why would it be gone? Confused, I stared at my hand, trying to remember why I thought it would be gone. Mom talked in the background.

"I'm talking to you!" she grabbed my face with both her hands. "Hey, are you listening to me?"

I stared at her, but her words were gibberish to my brain.

"What time is it?" I managed. She frowned, but then looked at her watch.

"Err, it's almost eight-thirty."

I jumped out of bed.

"Mom, I have to be at class by nine!" She didn't respond. I moved so fast it made me dizzy and I grabbed the first thing I laid hands on in my closet.

"Well, Honey, you pulled your pillow over your ears and couldn't hear the alarm an hour ago when everyone else could. Calm down. There's enough time." She left.

Oh no. She kept her cool, but I could hear my unwonted aggressive tone hurt her. I paused and stared at the trapdoor.

Humiliation wrapped around me for my childish reaction, my face glowing.

After a shower and re-selecting an outfit, I ate from the tray Mom had brought up. It made me feel even worse. I wanted to avoid her, so I snuck down the stairs and through the foyer. My bag was in the parlour. I got a fright when my dad spoke. He was sitting on the sofa.

"Where are you running off to?" he asked in his slow, usual voice. He had no idea I was feeling guilty, but I still found it difficult to look him in the eyes.

"Hey," my voice broke, and I cleared it. "I'm late—need to leave." I grabbed my bag and walked—nay, ran—out. At least I had avoided his eyes.

"Haven't you forgotten something?"

I turned around, and he jiggled my keys between two fingers. I was sure I'd put it in my bag. He threw the keys, and I caught them. A small flashlight hung from the ring, which hadn't been there last night.

"Thanks, Dad." I hovered.

"Pleasure, Honey. Please, drive safe." I gave him a tight-lipped smile. An unusual feeling was growing inside me, making me uneasy.

Semi-tranced, I walked to my car, got in and started the ignition. It made quite a ruckus for such a compact car. I turned and drove to the stone arch, which played doorman to the forest.

I wasn't an aggressive person, and I never snapped at my mom. Never. Rage brewed inside me, an alien sensation to me. I didn't have control of my emotions anymore. They were confused and rebelled against me. I had never felt so messed up.

As I raced down the ancient road, my eyes grew warm and spilt over. Not a wise idea. I collected myself and eased off the pedal, stopping in the middle of the road. No one drove there except us. My eyes blurred, and I closed them as my senses shifted. I reached for the ring around my neck, but it wasn't there. *Breathe.* I rubbed my sleeve over my eyes and continued driving.

I couldn't stop thinking about Adrian. Each time I did, my stomach twisted into a knot. Something gave me the distinct notion he was at the centre of my emotions' rebellion. I knew thinking that was foolish; no one could make me feel anything I didn't allow myself to feel. But that meant I *wanted* to feel the way I did, a notion I resented.

He said he lived nearby, so I examined the forest for another turnoff, but none came.

Within a few minutes, I exited the forest onto the main road. I drove too fast again and eased off the pedal.

Another coincidental curiosity struck me; each time I interacted with Adrian, I felt exhausted after he left. I was always on my guard and frightened, but somehow also drawn to him. It felt wrong to confess, but he lured me in the same way he so explicitly expressed I affected him. His actions were so strange, but somehow, it was like my body suffered from withdrawal each time he left. Or perhaps it was a stress release, I wasn't certain.

I arrived at the university, unnerved by the realisation that I had driven there without paying attention, considering it was my first time driving there alone. With the engine still running, I parked the car, my thoughts adrift. I had grown familiar with not having control of my senses—and sometimes my emotions, because it came with the territory—but this was not the same. This was so far out of my tier that it bordered on the absurd. It felt like he was rewiring my already messed-up brain.

A tap on my window made me jump, almost hitting my head against the ceiling. Laura stood beside my car, her mouth and eyes wide as she made wild gestures.

I turned my face away, wiped my eyes with my sleeve, and grabbed my bag from the seat.

"Oh, my goodness, Josilyn! Where did this come from? I thought you haven't looked for a job yet?" Her excitement reignited my own, and I smiled.

"Yeah, looks like that won't be necessary. My dad surprised me yesterday; said it would be even worse for him if I got a job." She laughed.

"Well, he's not wrong. I love vintage cars, and this one suits you. It's so tiny! Wait, aren't you going to lock it?" I smiled sheepishly, turned back, and did so. We talked about the world of opportunity that had opened as we walked to class. Dagworth was presenting a demonstration by a master's degree student he tutored. I was nervous when Laura told me this. A performance would place me in a tight spot. I couldn't control how and when my senses reacted to the music, but today the little control I usually had was wholly absent. I asked her which instrument to prepare myself. A piano, she excitedly announced—her major. I had never played one before. She'd been playing for ten years but mentioned she'd hated it when she started, which took me by surprise. I couldn't imagine anyone hating an instrument. That was like hating music, which was like treason to your soul. I reacted out loud before I could stop myself. She stayed quiet for a moment and gazed away. It looked like she was deep in thought. Maybe it was a sensitive subject.

"My mother isn't musical at all, so she forced me to become what could never be," she drawled, pausing a moment. She shrugged and continued. "I guess she succeeded." A wide smile spread over her mouth, and the sparkle returned to her eyes as she looked at me. She didn't seem bitter or upset, and her excitement about the performance indicated that, what might have started with negativity, had morphed into something good.

The presentation was in the auditorium, and we made our way into the main building. I glimpsed something maroon in my peripheral vision, and my eyes darted there, my heart racing. Someone's hat. How delirious had I become? I couldn't contain the hysterical giggle that escaped my mouth. Laura asked what I was laughing about, and I said I thought I saw something. Deadpan, she quipped that I saw weird things a lot. I laughed.

Dagworth stood by the black piano, his prodigy with him. They were in intense discussion. He could have been Dagworth's son; both had the same strange aura and bony features.

We found seats right at the front, and I entertained myself by watching the two men interact, studying the prodigy's affectations. They could almost have passed as authentic, but something about him was off-putting, but I didn't know what.

Dagworth stepped forward and looked around the room, which had filled up.

"Morning, students. This is one of our most advanced and decorated students who will perform a piece for an upcoming examination. I have uploaded an assignment on the website. You'll have the rest of this class to work on it after the performance. It's my privilege to introduce

Brinelle Aguillard," he swept his arm in Brinelle's direction and stepped back as he clapped, followed by the rest of the room.

Brinelle came forward and gave a stiff bow. He retreated to the piano and sat down gracefully. A show dog on display came to mind.

"The assigned piece is Rachmaninoff's prelude in G-minor, Opus 23 number 5," Dagworth stated proudly and stood by the piano.

Brinelle looked up at him, and they nodded. His jaw flexed in preparation, and his fingers found their place on the keys. I took a deep breath.

He blasted off with the intense piece, and the sudden music slammed into me like a battering ram. The air left my lungs, and the *Pulse* spluttered through me. I closed my eyes but saw the music bounce off the walls. The fast rhythm caused my skin to pound and my eyes to sing. A bouncing sensation moved through my body, and I couldn't contain it. The melody captured my pulse and dragged it along as it raced. A smile tugged at my mouth, reeled defenceless against the melody, my head weightless as it swayed.

An impetuous, echoing screech cut off my euphoria, and my eyes shot open. My senses snapped back to repugnant lucidity.

Brinelle's fingers continued to slide over the keys.

No one else seemed to have noticed the interruption, but something was definitely out of place. How did they not hear it? It sounded terrible. I looked around the room. *No one?* Laura looked at me, her eyes framed with question marks.

"What?" she leaned closer.

"Didn't you hear that?"

"Hear what?"

"I heard something…off."

She cocked an eyebrow.

"Maybe you're not used to Rachmaninoff's style, but I've never heard anyone play it so well." Adoration filled her voice.

I knew what I had heard, and it broke the harmony like a jagged thump. It seemed a better choice not to push the matter. I didn't want it to unearth something I preferred buried.

"Oh, okay," I sighed and continued watching Brinelle play the piece. It was indeed breathtaking, but the noise had bothered me so much, it prevented me from getting lost in the music again.

He finished, and the entire room applauded. He got up and bowed with a wide grin, revealing deep dimples. We caught each other's gaze for a second, and I looked away when I became flushed. Why did he look at me? He couldn't have heard us. Even though the possibility was absurd, my stomach clenched.

After Dagworth dismissed us, they walked out, and he appraised and congratulated Brinelle, who seemed timid. Not the way you would be when you couldn't take a compliment; the way you would be if you expected a scolding instead.

The students swarmed into motion with cheerful conversations at the prospect of no lecture.

"Wow, that was amazing. I can only hope to play like that one day," Laura trailed off, mentioning some printing she had to do and asked if I would join. I wasn't *not* listening, but her words travelled straight to the back of my head, my eyes fixed, glued to the piano.

"I'll meet you after," I responded distantly and approached the piano. All my life, I'd never been alone in a room with one. Its pull magnetic. Then again, all instruments were.

"Why do I get the impression you're not used to pianos?"

"I'm not. Weatonburg is rural; not exactly the place fine music and instruments are common," my voice was almost inaudible.

My parents discovered my gift for music by accident. Dad's one client had gifted him a cello for helping him out with a major audit deadline when he was still a clerk. He had someone come over for the cello's maintenance, since it wasn't being used. The man left it on the couch, and when I entered the room, I couldn't resist it. It drew me in, called me like a siren. I was young and small but positioned it intuitively and plucked the strings. That's when the *Pulse* took me the first time. I did independent examinations, and my parents opted to keep my ability a secret, which implied keeping me away from other instruments. I think it was to protect me, as it came with other oddities.

Laura said I probably wanted to feel the keys under my fingers, like most people did, and then left.

Hesitant, I caressed the keys with my fingertips and sat down. It felt weird.

My senses had shifted before the cello incident too, but my parents weren't aware. How would I have explained that everything around me created music and blasted light? I was barely five, and when I opened my eyes, my parents and the man were gaping at me.

My heart sped up, and I pressed down on one key, savouring the quick impulse that went through me. I placed my foot on the pedal and held it down as I pressed the key again.

The *Pulse* grabbed me and lingered as the note resonated through the air. *Different.* I stretched my fingers and positioned them as far away from each other as possible. My foot pushed down on the pedal, and I pressed the two keys. They rang through my skin and my eyes watered. I opened them and looked down, pressed down, and stroked my hand over all the keys. Electric blue mist swirled up like fog from the lake on a frosty morning. That didn't happen with my cello.

I closed my eyes and pressed each key, swirling it around in my mouth like wine so I could get a sense of each one.

The note I was looking for lit up and the entire song burned into me. The sensation was explosive, and I lifted my fingers for a moment. *Wow.* I hadn't experienced that in a while. In anticipation, the *Pulse* gathered around me like a terrifying whirlwind.

My hands scattered over the keys, pressing down hard. Fingers ached; my arms jerked from this side to that. The melody's rhythm dragged my heart rate with it. A hot tear rolled down my cheek when my hands eased into the song's calmer portion.

An entire emotional spectrum spurted through me, more vivid than in a long, long time.

The pace built up again, and pain gathered in my joints until it became unbearable. A murderous headache crept into my brain.

Numbness overtook my skin and goosebumps arose. I approached the part where I had heard the jarring note and played another one.

Perfect.

I breezed into the end and dropped my hands into my lap. They pounded with warm cramps. I took a burning breath and opened my eyes, which were unfocused, the room a blurred mess. Someone was here. Panic jumped me, and I blinked to remove the fog from my eyes. *Oh no.* My heart sank when the cloud cleared, and I saw the flustered face staring at me.

Oh no.

Jumping up, I distanced myself from the piano. When I tried to say something, a mere faint creak escaped. I gathered myself after a few heavy breaths.

"I—I'm sorry, I was just curious."

The confusion hadn't drained from Brinelle's face. He didn't respond, but kept staring at me. My panic flourished. How was I going to explain?

I wished he would say something; anything. He straightened up, cleared his throat and licked his lips, composing his expression into a blank, but the curiosity still burned in his eyes. *And anger.*

"You were curious?" he spoke with an accent. His quaint mannerisms confused me. I didn't expect his cold, lifeless tone. "I'm eager to know what you were curious about." His words were teal-coloured.

Was he being sarcastic or not?

"Nothing extraordinary."

"Oh, on the contrary, I think it is very much extraordinary," I couldn't catch his tone through his accent, and his face wasn't giving me much to work with, either. I knew I had to get out of there.

"I have to go. Bye," I headed for the door, but he slid in front of me and blocked the way.

I stepped back and looked into his sneering face, his hands behind his back like an uptight waiter.

"Surely you weren't planning on leaving so soon. You didn't answer my question, and I would *very* much like you to," he stated coldly, a sneer curving his lips.

Anger brewed in my stomach. He chose the wrong morning to give me an attitude.

"I don't have an answer besides the fact that I was curious." I spat the words.

"Really? Hmm…" he trailed off, and I could feel it in my bones; he was about to rub me up the wrong way. "I could make you answer me. For instance, have you thought about one important question?" his smile slanted. "Are you in trouble?"

His threat settled. I expected more from a master's student. It was not a museum, and no notices said: *no first years are allowed to play.*

It wouldn't help to play coy. With what he had just seen me do, he could make life difficult for me. I didn't want a re-run of how things were in Weatonburg.

"Look, I just thought I heard something odd, but it was just me. Can I leave now?" My voice was much harsher than I intended.

He grinned and the unexpected, piquant alteration caught me off guard. *What the heck?* Something was wrong with this boy.

"You heard that?" his voice was flat. So, he was aware of his blunder.

"Um, yes."

"Stupendous… Not even Doctor Dagworth heard it," he paused and gazed into the distance. "I over-reached and pressed down the wrong key halfway," he was in deep thought.

Emotions ran wild inside me. I didn't know why.

"I have to go now," My voice was thick and unsettled.

The *Pulse* shot through me when he took a tight hold of my arm before I could pass him. What was his problem?

I glared at him, but he remained calm as he gazed at me with icy eyes.

"How did you hear it?" his tone was light but menacing.

My arm was going numb, and I jerked it from his hand. I had an impulse to slap him. Rage wrapped around my head like a garland of thorns.

"I have good hearing." That was all he was getting from me. He explored me, his eyes tracing up and down, up.

"Obviously. Let's stop this game. How long have you been playing the piano?"

I imagined what his face would look like if I told him this was the first time. A smile tugged at my lips. My level of stupidity was not *that* pronounced.

"I'm majoring in cello."

I moved towards the door.

"What's your name?"

At the doorway, I turned and glared at him. I had had just about enough of him.

"My name? My name is as irrelevant to you as your false and arrogant superiority is to me. Keep your snooty nose out of my business and rather spend your time practising. You need it," I left.

A smile pulled over my mouth. I had never been that rude before and I *really* enjoyed it. My blood boiled and anger trembled through me as I darted down the empty corridor. I was not sure if it was anger or not, but it was such a rush.

I worried he might follow me, and I wanted to disappear into a crowd. *Ladies' room.*

He couldn't follow me there.

I stopped.

Adrian stood in the foyer with his back to me. I was happy to see him, and my heart sped with exhilaration. The feeling caught me by surprise.

My eyes locked on him, and I took no notice of anyone else. I couldn't move, not away, not closer. His back was rigid and somewhat hunched, like he was about to pounce on something. He straightened up. I kept forgetting how tall he was.

He turned his head slowly in my direction, just enough for me to notice the contours of his flexed jaw. His body followed his head, and our eyes met. A warm smile formed on his lips, and I hated the fact that it stirred my insides. Concern took shape on his face. For a moment, I thought Brinelle was behind me and was about to turn around when I heard Laura's voice.

"There she is now!" Her nervous voice shrieked. My eyes drifted past Adrian. I could just see her standing behind him, but she looked agitated and shy when I saw her face.

Not taking any note of her, he glided towards me. Like with all our encounters, I wanted to move closer, but at the same time, wanted to move away.

I couldn't do either.

His expression remained unchanged, and I wondered if there was something on my face. I couldn't lift my hand to check. He reached me at an astounding speed. I wanted to say hey, but my breath left me when he pulled me closer and pressed me against his chest. It sent a shock wave through me. Not what I expected. I was not sure how I felt about it. He was always so intense, and I felt numb and warm. He was as hot as a fever.

"Are you alright? You look distressed," he breathed close to my ear with abyssal depth in his voice and let me go.

He placed his hands on either side of my head and gazed into my eyes with immense intent. It created an awkward placement, and his large hands made a flesh helmet around my head. The excruciating heat filtered through my brain and eased my forgotten headache. My cheeks flushed.

He held my gaze with consuming eyes. I tried to look away but couldn't. He looked right into my soul, and I felt naked—exposed. Against natural law, my heart rate dropped.

"Josilyn?" his voice was delicious molten chocolate. I wished I could respond.

I tried to regain my focus by blinking like a strobe light. *Snap out of it.* Laura was beside us, a safe distance away, and looking at me intently.

As difficult a task as it was, I pulled away from him and was glad that he allowed me to. Something told me I wouldn't be able to if he didn't want to let go. His arms dropped to his sides, and he glared away, frustration evident in his features.

"D—did you have fun on the piano?" Laura asked with a shaking voice as she stepped closer with hesitation. She threw a suspicious glance at Adrian and looked mildly frightened. Did something happen between them? I smiled, attempting to ease her, but in my peripheral vision, Adrian had my full attention.

"Yes, I did. Like I said, I haven't had the chance to play one before."

My instinct almost made me look at Adrian because I could have sworn I saw him stiffen. He had no reason to react that way; I was quite capable of keeping my own secret. Well, from *most* people…

She looked away, frowning, recalling the conversation.

"Oh yes, I remember you mentioned something like that."

"Well, I wanted to fool around, and while I was busy, Brinelle came in." Uncertain how much I should reveal, I stopped short.

Adrian's face slowly turned towards me. I had forgotten he knew much more than he should. More than *anyone* should.

"Oh wow, you met Brinelle? You're so lucky! He's gorgeous, don't you think? Is he nice? What did he say?" a smile spread over her face, her anxiety forgotten and usurped by excitement.

Her reaction surprised me because she didn't seem like the type who would be affected by something like this. I was most baffled that she thought he looked nice. Even with the first impression, my first assessment wasn't '*nice*'. A looming feeling inside told me I should be careful with what I said next. It unnerved me, thickening the agitation. Though I resisted, I couldn't control the impulse and glanced at Adrian— quickly looking away when I met his piercing, seeking eyes. The rigid lines of his face scared me.

"Um, he is…okay," I couldn't look her in the eyes. Were it different circumstances, I would have told her straight up what I thought about Brinelle, but somehow, I *knew* I should choose my words carefully.

The silence which followed felt wrong, and I looked at her. What I saw frightened me beyond description. Her expression was alien, a cocktail of disappointment and confusion warring, but I couldn't say for sure. It changed her face into someone I didn't know. Her eyes were unseeing and empty, noiseless as a dry pit. Was she deep in thought? She looked completely signed out.

"Laura?" my voice had a shade of hysteria. Her head slowly turned to me, but her eyes delayed the process, like a doll. A slight crease formed between her brows. Her eyes might have been directed at mine, but they weren't seeing anything.

"Yes?" she responded in an eerie, hollow voice. It had an odd, suave trill to it.

"Are you okay? What's going on? You're freaking me out." I put my hand on her shoulder. *Was I hallucinating?* Her skin felt warmer than usual. I hoped she hadn't come down with something. As if in slow motion, she looked down at my hand and then returned her eyes to mine. *Creepy.* Was she playing with me?

"Yes," she stated again. "What did Brinelle say to you?"

I frowned at her.

"What's gotten into you? He didn't say much. He asked what I was majoring in and my name. That's about it."

"Why do you seem exasperated after your encounter?"

Exasperated. An odd word for her to use. She had to be playing with me.

"I wasn't *exasperated.*"

She didn't buy it, and I didn't blame her. Her eyes unnerved me as she stared at me until I was very uncomfortable. She was not letting it go.

"Look, he was a bit pushy, slightly rude, and kind of threatened me. It just put me off a little." *I had said too much.* I felt strange for not giving the full extent of our encounter.

The crease between her brows disappeared, and the rest of her body relaxed. She blinked as if awakening, and I was relieved when her eyes filled with familiarity, even if they were foggy.

"What time is it?" She sounded tired and swayed a little.

A strange turn. I opened my mouth to speak, but Adrian spoke first. By some miracle, I had forgotten about him.

"Josilyn, I will take my leave now. Something has come up that I need to take care of swiftly. I'll see you soon."

He looked at me with intensity. His eyes harboured a chaotic storm, which his calm, warm smile belied. He lifted his hand, and for a moment, I thought he was about to touch my face, but instead he stroked my arm with the back of his hand instead. My skin ignited beneath my sleeve as I watched him walk in the direction I had just come from. *What was he up to?* He hadn't received a call or text.

I looked at the time.

"We have some time left until our next class," Laura's eyes locked on mine, and I was happy they seemed filled with life again, but they contained a mischievous glint. I hoped she wouldn't veer in the direction I suspected she wanted to.

"Do you have something to tell me?"

"No, I don't. Do you?" It sounded more menacing than I intended, and I bit my lip. Thankfully, she played dumb.

"Nope, I'm good, but are you sure? He materialised before me and asked where you were. I wasn't sure if you'd want me to share that info, so I pretended I didn't know, which he didn't much appreciate. He's pretty intense. I wonder if he has a sense of humour. But man… the pheromones when you made your appearance… I was practically electrocuted with the sparks between you and Spice Lord. What's up with his hair anyway?" I couldn't hold my composure, and I burst into laughter. It might just have been a bout of hysteria. I shook my head. How must I even begin to explain when I didn't understand anything at all?

"I… don't know what to tell you, to be honest. He is a little intense. He stopped by my house yesterday, which was weird. However, he didn't stay long."

"But do you like him?"

I hesitated, but answered before she mistook my lack of response as something else.

"I barely know him. We haven't even had a full conversation, I think."

"Wait, so—you *don't* like him then?" She pretended to be confused. I bit my tongue before I almost shushed her.

My heart raced, and my palms glowed hot when I glanced over my shoulder, worried he could hear us.

"I am… perplexed by him. He's not like anyone I've ever met, so that carries its own intrigue, but like I said: it's too soon to tell."

I remembered a moment from the day before when he'd said I lured him in. What was he implying?

"Well, in that case, I can definitely tell you the feelings of cautious neutrality aren't mutual. He is excruciatingly, terrifyingly attentive to you. It's like he adjusts himself to your every word. It's a little worrying, honestly. Like he scrutinises your every reaction," she paused. "How could you not have noticed the way he looks at you? I feel like I'm intruding on something just by standing with you, and to be honest, I get a weird vibe from him, like total psycho-lover vibes. As in, red flag, as in, his hair is the punchline."

"You're being silly, Laura. I've had so little to do with him; it would be absurd to think that he already has feelings for me *or* the reverse." I responded quickly, wanting to stop my mind from stepping over the line and also to avoid the *vibe* topic.

"Okay, fine. I'll pretend to be blind. But pay a little more attention next time. I'm convinced you'll understand my point. Just don't end up drowned in the lake."

I didn't think it was possible to pay more attention to him than I already was when he was around. Time stopped when he talked to me.

The thought of him finding anything in me worth liking had my mind racing with the possible Utopia—I hated it.

Self-esteem issues were something I had to deal with from childhood, but in those cases, I'd known what about me put people off. That I couldn't turn the *Shift* off at random was the sole reason for my immunity to their stares. Later, I realised that their non-acceptance was not my fault, nor could I be held responsible for their small-mindedness and prejudices.

However, I'd never had to deal with the opposite situation. It was a completely novel experience, which my brain struggled to process. As an observer from the outside, I had always thought it a wondrous enigma the way one soul was drawn to another with the inability to resist the gravity, the sheer force reeling them defenceless and vulnerable to that one person who might be unaware of their sudden power.

Of course, I had never fallen in love myself, which I was thankful for in some way. From what I had observed as an outsider, it seemed like an endless cycle of situations of use, misuse, deferred hope, hurt and suffering repeated over and over to the point of aggravated annoyance at their gullibility. I guess one could compare it to an atomic bomb: in the beginning, a lot of chemistry and fireworks, but when the dust settles, everything around you is destroyed and in ruin. When I inspected my actions and reactions over the past few days, I might have fallen into the same pit. *No, I couldn't.* I would not lose all my senses to that cryptic and alluring stranger weaving himself into my life like a spider. I knew better than that.

"Josilyn, hurry up!"

Laura's voice yanked me back to the present. I tried to absorb the information on the paper before me, but didn't quite succeed.

"What's this?"

"Some kind of survey. Just fill in and pass on, be quick."

I filled it in robotically and passed it on. Laura suggested we go to her favourite coffee shop for lunch after class. Apparently, it had a fantastic bakery with delicious pastries and gourmet sandwiches. My mouth watered at the thought of a fresh chocolate croissant.

The doors opened, and I jumped in my seat. Instead of the substitute lecturer we'd had before, a striking, beautiful woman of significant age glided into the room. Her thick salt-and-pepper braid trailed down to the small of her back and the network of wrinkles carved into her skin did nothing to diminish her beauty. She kneaded her fingers together, not uttering a word as she surveyed the room. Her presence was palpable—the room went silent as a grave. Her lips were full, her cheekbones high. When she spoke at last, it whirred in a deep, husky, accented voice that mesmerised all who heard. The *energy* bristled beneath my skin, my senses shifted, and the air was purple.

"I need not tell any of you bright young souls what importance music carries for humankind. Music has been the subliminal influence of many throughout the centuries. I do not take music lightly because it is not insubstantial. Writing music is an intimate process of pouring one's soul out for all to feel. I do not wish to make you just another number on my roster, and my need to see, to feel, who you are as individuals is immense. Thus, as an introduction, your first assignment will be to compose a song, a new one, conveying who you are. I want to hear what you're drawn to. The type of sounds and rhythms. What makes you tick, and what inspires you. Let me see, make me feel. You have until next Friday."

Next Friday? A wave of groans and gasps rippled through the room. In times like these, I was especially thankful for my gift.

"It might feel like short notice, I know. But don't overthink. It doesn't have to be perfect because neither are you," she gave a soft, knowing smile and rolled into her lecture about compositional basics. She had a compassionate way to her, which made it feel less intimidating, and it felt almost therapeutic, listening to her speak and her occasional soft smiles. When she dismissed the class, she casually added,

"Oh, would a Miss Grey come to see me, please?"

A chill ran down my back as I absorbed my last name. Her gaze fell on me, and Laura looked at me, too. Why would she want to see *me*? Adrenaline rushed through my veins. I didn't like this. Laura frowned at me, questioning, and I shrugged. A thought crossed my mind and boiled my blood.

Brinelle.

I thought he would let it go, but it seemed like he'd made good on his threat. Playing the piano couldn't have been that unacceptable; we're all musicians. Maybe he lied about something.

A series of possibilities flashed through my head as I skulked towards her, none of which I would have preferred. I looked up and met her soft and friendly expression, her dark brown eyes. That didn't fit with my expectations of a scolding at all. I opened my mouth to greet her, but couldn't recall how she had introduced herself.

"Hello, ma'am," I guessed was a safe substitute.

"Oh my, how silly of me. I've forgotten to introduce myself again, haven't I? I am Professor Giovaniello. You must be wondering why I want to talk to you, Josilyn."

It caught me off guard that she knew my name, although probably not unusual. She leaned back against the desk.

"As I told the class, I'm quite fond of my students and do not see them as just a name on a ledger. I do background checks as a rule, not an exception, with each new class group. Your records are quite vague. I couldn't find any music tutors, only your musical grade scores. Now, what *did* draw my attention, was the fact that you completed Grade Eight aged eleven. Which is—" her eyes widened, her hands gesturing grandeur as she looked at me in wonderment. "I won't interrogate you since there is no point, but however spectacular your gift is, I want to give you a warning, Josilyn," She paused and peered into my soul with her chocolate eyes. "Many indulging monsters roam the earth, scoping for prey, and they will stop at nothing to get what they want. Their lust for rank fuels them, driving them to new lows. I can feel you are something extraordinary. Choose your friends well. Miss Everdale is a wise choice, so far."

I couldn't locate any words when she finished talking. What was I supposed to think about that? It's not as if my gift could be utilised for world domination or a similar purpose. I cleared my throat before I could talk.

"Thank you, Professor. I appreciate your thoughtfulness." I offered a polite smile, and so did she, gazing at me for a long while.

"You're most welcome, Josilyn. Enjoy the rest of your day," she turned to the board, and I took the cue.

"Good day, Professor."

Laura waited right outside the classroom in agitated curiosity. I hoped she enjoyed disappointment.

"Well? What did she want?"

"She does background checks on everyone but couldn't get much information about me. Small town curse, I guess."

"What? You mean she knows *everyone* by name?" she uttered, shocked. Her face amused me.

"Yes, I guess so. She knew who you were as well. Maybe they have photos of us."

How else would she have known what I looked like?

"She knew who I was? That's creepy. Does she memorise every student's face and name in her class? Who does that? Seriously, get a hobby, woman."

"I think she's old school."

"Well yeah, she looks old."

"But still beautiful."

"Oh, no denying that. Imagine what she looked like when she was younger. Unfair."

We walked over the bridge to the town, through red cobbled streets and alleys. The sky was turning into a thick, sombre grey. The balconies above overflowed with vibrant flowers and lush plants. I wondered at how the town never lost its mystical air, and how I always felt like I was on holiday abroad.

We took our time walking, but heavy rain broke loose in torrents, and we sprang off running. After about a block, Laura pulled me into a decided direction and pushed open a door, and thrust me inside, closing it behind her. A cold gush of wind and water followed us into the warm interior. It was an amazing feeling, and the exhilaration of running in the rain made us burst into laughter, to the amusement of the slender, dark-skinned man standing by the counter. The way he looked at her made it clear she was a familiar face.

"Afternoon, ladies," he smiled heartily. Laura bounced to the counter. "Matthieu!"

"You're soaking my floor," he shook his head.

"Yeah, yeah. This is my friend, Josilyn."

"Hey," I greeted awkwardly.

"Hello, Josilyn. That is a beautiful name and, might I say, such beautiful eyes. Wow, forgive me if I offend you, but they almost look artificial." My cheeks flushed. "What can I do for you ladies today?"

"We'd both like a croissant. I want a number four filling, please. Which one do you want, Josilyn?"

"I'm sorry, ladies. We're all out. The next batch will be done in about an hour. We only have ciabatta's left."

"Oh no, Matt! How could you?!" she scolded teasingly, and my eyes swept over the menu. So many choices, most I had never heard of.

"I'm sorry, madam. Maybe if you stopped by more often, you would have better luck."

"Fine. I'll take the four on a ciabatta then."

"No deviation there. And you?" he asked me. I hadn't decided, but I wasn't picky.

"I think I'll try the seven, please."

"Good choice! I'll have it done in a bit. The backroom's fire is lit if you two wet puppies would like to warm up." he disappeared behind a door. I followed Laura through a narrow wooden door at the back, and entered a small, cosy room. A singular, medium-sized wooden table and a kindled fire in the hearth at the far back wall occupied the room. We threw our bags on the floor and went to the fire. The wet clothes were getting to me, so I was thankful for the heat on my skin.

"I can't get used to this town." I managed when the cold released my throat.

"Great, isn't it? Almost like all the greatest places in the world have been crammed into this little town." It did seem like that, yet it surprised me that few people knew about it. Perhaps it was just me. Laura asked me about the guy I had danced with at the ball and if I'd been able to figure out who he was. I had to confess; I had almost forgotten about him.

Matthieu brought our gourmet sandwiches with fries and salad and sat with us until the bell at the front rang. Although I tried to pay attention to the conversation, my mind wandered. Professor Giovaniello seemed familiar somehow, yet I couldn't place her. Someone with her striking beauty would have caught my attention. I would have remembered. Something in her eyes, something in her voice. It puzzled me. She hadn't been at the ball, surely? Otherwise, she would have said something about my performance. It made me curious.

"Laura, was Professor Giovaniello at the ball?" The rain had stopped, but the clouds loomed as we walked back.

"No, not that I can recall, but everyone was wearing a mask, so I can't say for sure. Oh, I almost forgot that I'm meeting my mom at work, so I'm turning off here. I'll see you tomorrow, though." She hugged me. It still felt a little weird, but I was getting used to it.

As we separated, I couldn't help but smile with contentment. For once, it felt like someone actually wanted me in their life. It was an elating feeling.

My car was one of only a few still at the faculty. Everyone wanted to get home as soon as possible, I guessed.

I plunged onto the wet front seat and groaned, looking at the gap above the driver's window. I was sure I hadn't opened any windows at all that morning. Sighing, I shook my head at myself, pulling a face. The damage was done.

My thoughts wandered as I reversed, but something slid onto my lap from the dashboard, and I slammed on the brakes.

Chapter

16

I stared at the object in my lap for a dragged-out moment—an envelope sealed with a red stamp. I turned the car off and picked it up.

My head and stomach spun. Who would break into my car and leave me this? My damp fingers trembled as I stroked its edges.

Adrian, I suspected.

I parted the wax from the paper, careful not to tear the envelope. Hands still shaking, I removed the handwritten letter from its nest and unfolded it. My eyes struggled to focus on the words, and for a moment, I thought the writing to be in a foreign language. The script was a fusion between sophisticated calligraphy and an inept child's hand.

Words took form and shaped into meaning.

Josilyn

My apologies for the abrupt departure. An unforeseen situation emerged that needed to be dealt with. It felt inappropriate to stop by your house once again. I apologise for that indiscretion as well—done out of desperation, as I have no other means to communicate with you. Pray, allow me the opportunity to atone for my series of missteps. If you are willing, meet me by the lake at your house tonight after twilight. If not, I shall find other means to amend. I hope to see you.

Yours, Adrian

Unexpected. My heart raced as I read the letter over and over. It felt like every fibre of his being was tattooed onto that letter. I could hear his voice in my head as I read it, as clearly as if he was sitting next to me in the car. My senses slipped off an edge, tumbling and turning.

As if in a dream, I had the sudden sensation of falling and grabbed the steering wheel, my breath wheezing. The car shook for a moment. A girl passing by came to a slurred stop and stared at me, looking alarmed. With a shaking hand, I signalled I was okay, while attempting a feeble smile. She frowned and hesitated, but continued walking. She glanced back, but I was soon forgotten when another student on a bike almost ran her over.

My sight tunnelled, and my senses slipped again; the electricity surged through me.

Something was very wrong. I was used to chaos in my head, but this—this was something different. A feral conflict raged inside me, and the gravity centre I usually grabbed at to equalise myself had shifted. I wanted to get home.

My shuddering hand pressed the key into the ignition, and my heart pushed itself up my throat. I turned the key, the engine coughing to life, and I backed out. My vision swam the entire drive through the town, and for once, I was thankful for the slow traffic. Out of necessity, my brain defaulted to autopilot.

Blurring green walls speeding by on either side snapped me back to manual control. Trees. I was alone on the road. The moment my consciousness returned, a clearance in the tree line appeared to my right, and my eyes stung with the lake's sudden brightness. It was a blistering blue today and reeled me in like a trance.

Nothing but blue. Only blue, and me, too.

The *Pulse* crashed over me like a tide, and I jerked the steering wheel. The car swerved, and I released the pedals. Every nerve inside me exploded with awakened energy. I didn't know what had taken hold of me. The best way to describe what I felt was the slow, excruciating deterioration of my psyche. My throat tightened and a deep heat gathered and burned in my eyes. I did not know how much time had passed before I took a deep breath and started the car again.

With fogged-up eyes, I drove into the clearing, noting both cars were gone. I thought my dad would be there.

As I got out of the car, the silence bombarded me, and I stopped in my tracks. Bewildered, I swept the surroundings. It shouldn't have been so quiet. Something was off. I ducked my head and skulked to the house, the silence ringing in my ears.

A single caw echoed through the forest. I pulled my bag closer to my chest as I stole a glance around me, but found nothing to see. No other sound came as the echo drifted into silence.

My hands shook as I grasped the door handle, opening it fast and pressing my back against the door after I shut it. My rapid pulse sent blood sloshing through my veins with such force that my head bobbed as I scanned the foyer. After a moment, I realised I hadn't breathed. The silent house became infinitely bigger and emptier, knowing I was alone… It brooded and plotted, a soundless eye, watching.

"Andrew?" I uttered with as much confidence and volume as I could muster. I gulped. No response came.

"Andrew?" I tried again.

A vibration rolled up my spine, and adrenaline spread through me like a drug. No physical reason manifested itself for my body to react in such a way. Which was arguably worse.

Something was inside the house. A presence.

I ran up the steps, unsure whether the footfall echoing through the empty house was mine or someone else's. The thought spurred me forward, quickening my pace. When I reached my hidden door, I yanked it open and threw it shut behind me. On my ascent, I almost lost my footing more than once on the narrow steps.

I was in my room. *Safe.*

I pushed the chaise over the trapdoor, and my imagination ripped open like a bag of rotten meat. *No. No-no-no.* I backed away and sat down on my bed, my hand crushing over my mouth. *Don't scream. Don't scream.*

Ice crawled over my skin like a legion of insects. I raked the room for something uninvited. Nothing was out of the ordinary. Except for the undertone of subliminal darkness. What had inhabited me? My sensory faculties staccato'd like electrons through a wet electric fence. Short pulses ripped through my body, and my muscles contracted with every shift. I needed to shed the paranoia.

My legs moved without my instruction. I removed my cello from its case and rested it against my chest. My hands shook as I tightened the bow. The cold wood against my burning skin calmed me. I hugged it to my body and drowned my eyes in darkness.

Energy spurts raged on inside me like a swarm of vengeful bees. The bow dragged over the strings, and I heaved as my arm vibrated. The *energy* was different. Scorching heat heaped up in my stomach, building like a detonated atom bomb. Silence rang in my ears, my eyes pounded…

The bomb exploded.

Heat stormed through my flesh, and my fingers burned over the strings. The melody it spat out was eerie—strange. My hairs stood on end.

What was I playing? It sounded nothing like me. Fire flowed into my arms and weighed them into the melody, reflecting its monstrous, disturbing beauty. It was the darkest composition I had ever allowed through me. And it was more beautiful and possessing than anything I had ever heard or played. It beckoned me deeper…*deeper.*

The bass delegated vibrations over my skin. My lips quivered. Images flashed behind my closed eyelids. I opened them, and the heat flowed out. Through the mistiness, I looked around.

The room was the same, but different. If I didn't know better, I would have said that night had gathered inside it. A strange gloom permeated the air. Energy radiated from each item and bounced off the walls. I saw music flow into everything, absorbed by all the radiant lights.

Whoom… Whoom… Whoom…

An unfamiliar, low drone interlaced with the music. I couldn't stop playing.

A weird sequence of notes caught my eye. They looked like soap tubes or bubbles. *What the…?* My eyes followed their path and stopped at the mirror.

I was going out of my mind. In the odd light—or consciousness— its appearance looked no longer like a mirror but a gigantic doorway. I couldn't see through to the other side, because thick swirling mist oozed from it, flowing towards me.

Ice penetrated my skin as the beckoning mist kissed it. I closed my eyes. *Ignore it. You're imagining it,* I told myself. *Ignore it.*

How long I played, I do not know, but I stopped when my fingers locked into spasms. I didn't move, not an inch. My arms ached, and lethargy settled on my psyche.

I clung to my cello, in dire need of the support. With closed eyes, I somehow dragged it onto the bed beside me and lay back. It didn't even take a second to fall asleep.

~

A gentle breeze caressed my cheeks and swayed loose hair over my face. My mind slipped from its unconscious state, but I couldn't open my eyes. The wheels started turning. I didn't understand what I'd seen earlier. Usually, when the *Pulse* hit me, it showed everything the way they ordinarily were, but in a different light, from a different perspective, or with a different lens. What had happened earlier made no sense.

My curiosity was sparked, but my mind was too numb for logical thought. My eyelids dragged open and peered in the direction the wind was coming from. It was almost sunset. If I wasn't so tired, it would have shocked me that I had dozed off for that long.

A window was agape, which I couldn't remember opening. I noticed my cello beside me. I put it back in the case and lumbered to the window with jelly legs.

Revitalising energy rushed through my veins with a shock. A large, vibrant blue butterfly sat on the windowsill. Unlike anything I'd ever seen. I froze, hardly breathing, and stared at it. It faced the woods, but when it felt my gaze, it turned. And looked right at me. *Was I even awake?*

This exchange lasted a moment before it launched up and hovered at eye level in front of me. Aggressive. Intrusive. I took a step back, but it came closer still.

Backing away accomplished nothing, and I stopped. The gentle vortices from its fluttering wings brushed against my cheeks and I carefully lifted my hand. It drifted down and settled there.

Unexpected.

My heart raced. Its tiny legs wrapped around my finger, tickling.

Careful not to frighten it, I angled forward, lifting my hand closer to my face. Even in the late afternoon gloom, the beauty of its bright blue wings with a narrow black rim was anything but dim. It seemed familiar somehow. Perhaps I had seen photos of it before. The behaviour seemed unusual to me, for an insect. Without warning, it lifted off, sending a jolt through me. It flew past my head and swirled into the room. I wheeled around and watched as it fluttered towards the mirror and hovered there.

It gave me the creeps.

It swivelled and bolted out of the window. I ran to the sill, observing until I couldn't see it in the darkening light anymore.

Adding that to my book of weird things I had experienced.

My tongue was stuck to the roof of my mouth. I pushed the chaise from the trapdoor but hesitated to open it. The fear from earlier licked my neck. What if there really was something? With a hammering heart, I opened the hatch and stared into the dark.

Just don't go there, Josilyn, I told myself. I took the first step. It required more control than expected to keep a steady pace down the icy steps.

The notion that I couldn't see around the corner made it much worse. I turned on all the lights as I went. The kitchen table had a note on it. No wonder I hadn't seen it when I got home. I checked my phone—dead.

The note was in Mom's handwriting. They couldn't reach me, but had to go to Fort Brau, the nearest city, and wouldn't be back until late. They'd taken both cars, as the one was giving trouble. The fridge had leftovers, but I wasn't that hungry.

My throat burned and constricted. I downed the water until I was nauseous and then had a coffee, which warmed me. I hadn't realised I was cold. As the last sip slid down my throat, I froze as it dawned on me.

Adrian.

I had forgotten about his invitation. I hadn't decided what I would do yet, but looking outside, I realised there wasn't much time left.

The sun had almost set, and the light was fading with each second. I had to decide. A book of thoughts flashed through my head, measuring, calculating, and considering.

Succumbing.

Without another thought, I rushed to the front door, threw it open, stepped into the fresh air, and hesitated. If I did this, there would be no turning back. I knew that. This would be it; the moment I would cherish or regret for years to come.

I took a deep breath and walked towards the luring trees. This was insane. I was about to enter a forest at night because a guy wanted to meet me at the lake. I shuddered, recalling Laura's plea that I do not end up drowned in the lake. Any person could see the trouble screaming from the page, but not me; oh *no*.

When I reached the treeline, I stopped. What kind of guy would tell a girl to meet him at the lake at night? Why didn't he come and meet me at my house? That would probably be awkward if I didn't want to go, but *still*. I guessed he knew about the jetty, and that this was where he wanted to meet.

The setting sun painted a gloomy orange glow on the trees and the ground, as if there was a fire close by. One burned in my heart.

The endeavour exhilarated me, and the measure of danger it carried tipped the scales. I walked down what I thought was the covered path to the jetty, but after a few metres, I couldn't distinguish a clear path anymore.

My unease grew thicker as I wandered. Despite the approaching darkness, it shouldn't have taken that long. The light faded and faded, and I couldn't see any opening ahead.

If I got lost, I would be alone in a forest at night, and Adrian would think I'd stood him up. Not that *that* was a huge thing weighed against the other, but still noteworthy.

Wait.

In my rush earlier, I had stuffed my car keys into my pocket. I extracted them and switched on the little torch attached to the ring. A sound of relief escaped my mouth, and I turned and shone the light around. I recognised nothing around me; the thick undergrowth had swallowed my tracks. I shook my head at my foolishness. Well, I guess I'd made the wrong choice.

"Idiot," I muttered. I took a deep breath. The surrounding terrain was flat, and I reckoned if I found the slope, ascended it, I'd get home. The lake, stone road, and our clearing formed a hedge around this area. If I kept to the right direction, that is. Which sounded simple, until I realised it wasn't. Panic crept closer by every minute as I stumbled around the forest, which looked the same no matter where I turned. I couldn't see far with the torch, but it gave me a slight sense of security. Until its light faded into oblivion.

"No!" I screamed. It drowned away, and the forest sank into an unnatural silence. I sucked in a breath and held it because my breathing seemed too loud. Icy spiders crawled over my skin as fear crept up on me from all directions. My mind played tricks on me.

Something moved to my left side and my head snapped there. My senses sharpened as the adrenaline rolled through my veins. My eyes were vigilant for any movement as my breathing sped up. Was that an animal?

I crouched down and pawed for anything weapon worthy. Something alien took a moment to register in my mind. Crawling under my touch. My lungs removed themselves from my chest with an aching blow.

I yanked my hand away, shaking off the crawling insects.

Hysteria boiled inside the cauldron of my psyche. The muscles in my throat contracted. A rustle behind me sent the *Pulse* through my nerves.

My surroundings lit up, and although the light should have been a good thing, it frightened me even more.

Black mist swirled past where I had sensed the movement, but all I saw was night. My heart throbbed in my neck like an African drum, resonating through the forest. What was that?

I sucked in a breath and tried to keep it steady, but it proved difficult. *This isn't real; you're just imagining it*, I told myself. I had to do something. Anything. I stumbled away, falling over roots and getting up again. I was making noise, and my breathing shallowed, my palms damp. Frozen, I stood listening like a frightened rabbit.

A twig crunched mere feet behind me. I turned to trembling stone.

It loomed behind me. Whatever it was, it was behind me. I didn't move; I didn't breathe. Its presence radiated towards me. The air was red.

"Who's there?" my voice broke. Dead silence lingered for an eternity.

"I've found you," a familiar abyssal voice reached me.

"Adrian?"

He didn't respond, but a rustling in the undergrowth came closer. What if it wasn't Adrian? Why didn't he say something? If he could see the horror gushing through my mind, he would have relieved the torturous silence. Cold sweat broke through my skin.

"Yes?" he spoke at last, and relief washed over me.

Yet not. My muscles remained locked.

"How—how did you find me?" I loosened myself and tried to turn around, but it wasn't necessary. He was right in front of me, where he hadn't been seconds ago. He caressed my cheek, igniting a burning trail on my skin.

My heart pounded so hard I feared it might explode. His body heat flowed over me, and I realised I was cold. He pulled me to him and pressed his nose to my ear.

The sudden warmth felt amazing, and I melted into him.

"I was anxious when you didn't arrive with the last light. I thought perhaps you'd decided not to come, so I went to your house to at least apologise for my indiscretions in person, regardless. But when I arrived, something was off. Your car was there, but you weren't. I needed to confirm you were not there, and I did not find you inside the house, which made me even more restless. The thought crossed my mind that perhaps you'd misunderstood and went to the opening where we first met, but you weren't there either. I was about to seek help when I heard you scream," he stopped. "It ripped through my ears. I came as fast as I could."

A pregnant silence descended as I absorbed the information. I hadn't heard him call out my name. Isn't that what you would do if you were searching for someone? And how had he done all that since the last light faded?

"I thought I should meet you at the jetty, but I got lost. And then my torch died. Which is why I screamed."

He took a deep breath. Whether out of relief or frustration, I couldn't say.

"It's an absolution that you weren't hurt, because when I heard you, I feared the worst. The images…" he paused. "I couldn't stop thinking about the tormenting guilt I would feel if something happened to you, and I didn't reach you in time." He sounded distraught, but a harshness stung beneath the surface. At least I was not the only one whose imagination had run amok.

"There was something here. It's fast. I thought I was imagining things, but now I'm not so sure."

I wondered if I should be bothered by him still holding me, but I couldn't muster any concern. A thought did cross my mind, though: I was alone with him, in a forest, in the dark. If he wanted to hurt me, I would be unable to defend myself. A woman's burden—seeing danger in every pause and silence.

He stopped stroking my hair, and his body froze against mine.

I pulled away and searched his face, but I couldn't distinguish his expression from his night-bathed face.

He repositioned his hands to cup my face. *Heat.* My breath left me, and my cheeks burned.

"Josilyn, you are safe with me. No erring harm will come to you while I'm close."

My heart skipped a beat when he said my name. *Erring harm* didn't sound right, though. Was the ambiguity placed there on purpose, or was my mind still playing games with me? He didn't allow me to ponder the thought.

"Now I can atone at last. Follow me." He let go of my face and took my hand, my heart fluttering as the electricity slithered up my arm. Normal electricity. No one had held my hand before. The heat was excruciating, but also pleasant. I bit my lip.

"Why are you always so warm?"

He turned to me, and even though it was dark, I could make out his warm smile.

"It's not me that's warm, but you that are cold. You should have brought a sweater."

Before I could say anything or breathe, for that matter, he abandoned my hand, took off his jacket and threw it over my shoulders. It caught me off guard, and awkwardly, I stood there, feeling its weight.

It was so incredibly, deliciously warm. Maybe it *was* just me who was cold. In all the hype and hysteria, I guessed I hadn't taken note of my somatic senses. My body might have been going into shock after the adrenaline overdose.

"Thank you."

He chuckled and took my hand again as we walked. It was a leather jacket, but I couldn't make out the colour. It smelled like the forest, only much more intense. Dark, earthy musk. Intoxicating. I inhaled deeply, until my lungs burned, thinking I could wear this until I drew my last breath.

He walked with precise movements, sidestepping obstacles in the path and tightening his grip on my hand when he anticipated I was about to stumble. A litotes sight; me beside him. I was not usually a clumsy person, but felt like a newborn giraffe beside him. A feeling I didn't like.

"How do you know where to walk?"

His chuckle was subdued.

"I have… good sight."

Abnormal, if you asked me. He didn't falter once in the dark.

"I hope you do not find it intrusive, but I found your mother's note. Forgive me for being frank, but it disturbs me they would leave you here alone—unattended."

If he knew what I had gone through that afternoon, he would have been even more disturbed. He slowed down and released my hand— hovering his near the small of my back.

His sudden proximity sent a charge and pheromone-induced hypnosis over me. The *Pulse* advanced like a ravenous wave, and I looked away, anticipating the blow. But it didn't come. This remissal befuddled me. *How odd.*

"My phone was dead… and it's not *that* bad. I'm not a child."

"There are vast collections of predators in this world, and *all* worlds, Josilyn." His stern reaction threw me off. Predators? All worlds?

"There are no predatory animals here, my mother—"

"I wasn't quite referring to animals," he interrupted.

What *did* he mean, then? Ice ran down my spine.

"What?"

"Here we are."

We left the forest, and my breath caught. A narrow, white pebble beach lay before us, a white rowboat beached at the water's lip.

A single lantern hung from each end, bobbing around to the gentle roll and casting dancing lights on the murky blue water. It was a dream. On the other side of the lake, the town's lights shone, and it looked like a medieval setting. Far to the left, I could just make the outline of a sailing yacht. It was magical, standing there on the shore, and the beauty stung my eyes.

"Wow…" I walked closer, the pebbles shifting beneath my shoes. "This is amazing, Adrian. but you didn't have to do this." A warm tingle ran down my spine when I said his name aloud.

He appeared beside me, and I jumped. I hadn't heard his footfall. Bemused, he stood smiling at me, both hands behind his back.

My cheeks burned when I caught sight of the bulging muscles under his long-sleeved shirt. It clung to him like liquid. *Oh my.* Diverting my eyes, I hoped he hadn't noticed.

"I know I didn't have to. I wanted to," he paused, a tiny and *very* sexy crease taking shape on his forehead. "You can swim, right?" Was he planning on innocently drowning me? When he looked at me like that, I'd willingly allow it. I stared up at him with saucepan-sized eyes. His lips curved into a wicked smile, but he didn't hold it for long before bursting into jovial laughter, much to my relief. I had been somewhat confident he was joking, but the possibility always existed that he wasn't. I shivered just thinking about swimming.

"I'm kidding! I would never do that to you," he struggled, still thick with laughter. It was the first time I'd seen this side of him. It was contagious, and my lips pulled into a smile.

He brushed my arm as he passed me. Despite the leather jacket, the touch sent a scintillating heat through me. My eyes followed him as he walked to the rowboat. He turned and, with a bow, motioned towards it.

"Madam?" his voice was alluring as ever, and his smile coloured with provocation. I hesitated for a moment, but it became impossible to resist him when he looked at me like that. I was at ease in his company for the first time I could recall. Rather ungracefully so, I teetered towards him on the pebbles.

I just hoped I didn't get motion sickness. When I reached the boat, he offered me his hand, and I took it, anticipating the heat, but not the thrill. Uncertain about how to go about boarding, I made an attempt, but failed gloriously. The boat was much higher than I'd thought and moved too much.

Well, that was embarrassing. I clasped the jacket to my chest.

In the next moment, concentrated heat spread through my waist and I was airborne. My legs turned into jelly as my feet touched the boat, and I plopped onto the seat. Adrian's hand was on the boat's edge, poised to jump. I grabbed hold of both sides, bracing for impact so I didn't go flying.

He jumped in, but the boat didn't even so much as rock. Was he a ghost? His movements might be light and swift, but it should have had *some* effect. Speechless, I stared at him as he took the oars and pushed the boat away from the shore. He was extraordinary. Heat leaked from my heart, and I crossed my arms, attempting to cover the vulnerable feeling that crept up on me as if I could force the emotions back inside.

The light from the lanterns draped his face and emphasised the perfect lines of his jaw and nose. I couldn't tear my gaze away. He must have felt it, and our eyes locked. One part of me wanted to look away but didn't. He looked at me for a long moment, his face unchanging, but then he smiled, a glint of mischief reflected in his eyes. My cheeks ignited.

"Do I have something on my face? Apart from your eyes, that is."

His frankness sent a shock through me, but I laughed. It felt odd to experience his humorous side, or perhaps it was the first time *I* was open to it.

"No, not at all," I sounded unintentionally lifeless.

"Then what's wrong?" he asked, tenderness weighing like an ocean in his tone, and I looked at him, surprised. I averted my gaze when I saw something in his had shifted. His eyes held deep, vast things I would rather not have pondered just that second.

"Nothing's wrong. You just seem different than before; lighter, in a way. Like some burden has been lifted from you." He puffed a short laugh.

"Well, not completely. But I am getting there, slowly."
Getting where, exactly? *Just ask Josilyn. He won't bite,* I coaxed myself.

"What's bothering you?"

He didn't answer, and I looked at him. He was gazing over the waters, deep in thought.

"Don't concern yourself with my minor setbacks," he sighed. "I'm someone who gets frustrated quickly if things don't go according to what I had reckoned. But don't hold that against me; I am also painfully patient."

Not to be melodramatic, but the way he said that sounded like there was a subliminal meaning behind it. I didn't know how to respond.

"I brought something," he folded over where he sat, his hands disappeared beneath his seat, emerging with a woven basket covered with a cloth. He held it out to me.

"I thought perhaps you would be hungry."
Feeling awkward, I lifted the cloth.

Croissants.
A hurricane of thoughts pummelled through my mind. There's no way he could've known about that morning. If it was not a coincidence, something was seriously bizarre.

An icy tongue pressed to the back of my neck, sending shivers through me.

"Th—thank you. I haven't had these in a while," I stammered, trying to mask my distress.

"Yes, I'm aware."
The hairs on my body stood upright. A confused panic infiltrated my mind like thick smoke inside a burning building. How would he have known? He seemed to pick up on my train of thought and reacted swiftly.

"Oh, of course, by chance, I overheard you and Laura talk this morning."

"Oh, okay." but it was not okay. "Wait a minute; we discussed it in class after you left. You weren't there."

He gazed away, frowning.

"I was there, but you didn't see me." His tone indicated the discussion was over. I didn't believe him. But what was the alternative? I'd seen him walk in the opposite direction when we went to class. Besides, if he *had* been in class, why didn't he say anything? I was sure I would have been aware of his presence in the room. I dropped the subject, against my better judgement.

He hadn't moved the basket, and I took a croissant. I *did* want one.

"I assumed you like chocolate?"

My heart froze. Had he followed us to the shop? On the edge of freaking out, I looked away; the chewing gave me an excuse not to talk. I nodded, my heart beating inside my throat.

The chocolate was more decadent than any I had ever tasted. Laura wasn't joking when she said they made the best.

"Yeah, me too," he concluded when I said nothing.
I felt myself relax, the tension releasing my muscles. Perhaps he chose chocolate because he liked it best. Soon, a comfortable silence reigned as we ate, and I couldn't resist taking another one. He didn't hold back either.

"So," he started when we were both done, "I'm interested to know why you decided to come here."

The question caught me off guard and I took a moment to formulate my response.

"Well, If I'm honest, before my parents accepted the house, I hadn't thought much about what I wanted to do after school. I just knew that I wanted to get away from Weatonburg. But something about Ostia appealed to me. Like it called me." Well, that was stupid. He leaned closer, interested. His eyes encouraged me to continue.

"I don't know. It sounds so silly to say it out loud."

"No, please continue," he urged me. I liked that he wanted to hear more, and my cheeks burned. But at the same time, I couldn't help wondering why. I bit down on my lip as if to prevent myself from saying something foolish. This drew his attention, and his eyes drifted to my mouth. A tingle ran down my back. Unnerved by his new focal point, I talked.

"Well, the town is beautiful and unique. I loved the forest, something I didn't know back home. The artistry and culture were attractive. And I mean, the house is a dream. This whole place is just like a siren song I couldn't ignore. It is everything Weatonburg wasn't. I recently discovered my dad had told me the town's story when I was very young. It must've imprinted on my psyche."

"Aurelia, yes. Tragic story." I frowned. Who was Aurelia?

"The Duchess, her name was Aurelia."

"I didn't know that was her name."

The jacket felt heavy on my shoulders. Thinking back to the previous topic, I realised how much happier I was in Ostia than I ever was in Weatonburg. This felt more like home, as strange as that seems.

Adrian's mouth shaped into a wide grin, which seemed a shade out of place for what I had just said. His expression shifted into something more serious. He leaned closer and placed a scorching palm on my knee.

Uh oh. The sheer intensity burning in his eyes startled me, but I found it impossible to look away.

"Seems like it's the will of the Fates to have you here, then," his voice dripped warm honey.

He had a habit of making me feel uncertain about how to respond, so I tried for a smile, my heart throbbing against my neck when he didn't break eye contact.

The world grew silent around us, as if I had become deaf. Something was about to happen, but I didn't know what. Panic swirled around in my head, but I was paralysed, which was disturbing. My senses dragged into disorder, and in the brief second they shifted, I didn't see Adrian opposite me, like he had been a moment before. Not in the conventional sense.

A concentrated black mist of wispy strips had replaced his body. I gasped at the sprightly sight, but it disappeared as quickly as it came. Had it been because it was night? I hadn't seen people in the dark when I'd shifted before. I didn't see people at all because I had trained myself to close my eyes or look away.

He broke his gaze with a sigh and an expression I couldn't place.

I hoped he didn't mistake the shift for something else. He wasn't aware of that part of me, and I didn't know if I wanted to tell him just yet.

I looked at him, nervous, as he peered over the black waters. The moon cast a faint glow over his face. Though not full, but it was still bright. He turned his head and looked at it too. The lake was mesmerising in the light.

"Oh, I've almost forgotten. I found something I thought you might like," he reached under his seat again. His efforts embarrassed me. No one had ever gone through so much trouble for me. For what reason was he doing it? He smiled and stretched out his hand. A small black box was cradled in the middle of his open palm. I felt awkward, but smiled, not knowing how to react. A warm smile met my gaze.

"Take it," a tender whisper. My heart squeezed. Reluctantly, I took it. The box wasn't that small; his hand was just massive.

I opened it with trembling hands, feeling the weight of his gaze. Nestled in royal blue tissue paper was the most beautiful charm bracelet I had ever seen. With a gasp, I looked up into his beautiful smile.

I lifted it into the light. The delicate silver chain was clear and almost translucent—like the one around his neck—and had exquisite charms such as music notes, crystals, cellos, and butterflies entwined around it. The butterflies were an interesting choice. Tiny pearls and crystals encrusted some charms, and they glistened in the lantern light. My heart squeezed. I'd seen nothing like it.

"Wow, this is… beyond beautiful. I… don't know what to say. You really shouldn't have." I didn't even want to know what it had cost him, and I couldn't accept it. Emotion was stuck in my throat.

"And you should know by this time I do things that seem unnecessary to you."

In a flash, he encircled my wrist and pulled it towards himself, fastening the bracelet without difficulty. I barely had time to blink or pull away before I realised I was wearing it. How had he managed to snatch it? It had been in my hand a second ago.

My heart sped up when he didn't let go of my wrist.

I stared at him, and he simply smiled, bemused. Well, I guess he was giving me no choice in the matter.

"Thank you very much. I love it," I hesitated. "This means a lot to me."

He lifted my hand and shook it around, the crystals reflecting light, and we laughed. It felt a little silly, him jiggling my arm like that.

"It's a perfect fit." His eyes burned into mine, and I shifted my gaze away. The heat from his hand already filtered through my skin, and I was acutely aware of his grip on my arm. He let go slowly, caressing my skin as he did. Leaning back, he breathed a sigh and peered over the water again.

I couldn't say for certain in the dim light, but it seemed like his lips were moving, as if speaking, though I couldn't hear anything. I squinted, trying to distinguish if I was imagining it, but they were—rapidly. Was he talking to himself? He stopped and breathed a frustrated sigh as he stared up at the moon.

"What's wrong?"

His body frozen into place, his eyes searched the sky, as if he hadn't heard me.

"Adrian?" I tried to get his attention. The way he acted was rather alarming. His posture relaxed, and he smiled warmly. His eyes melted me. *In that case, never mind then.*

"Everything is in order. My thoughts just roamed a little. Would you like another croissant?"

"No, thank you." He gazed at me, and he did so for a long while until I grew uncomfortable.

"What?" A stupid question, but I was desperate to change the atmosphere. He looked down, and a crooked smile formed on his lips. If I didn't know better, I would have mistaken him for being shy.

"I'm…" he paused and looked up at me. "I'm fascinated by you, Josilyn. You're an absolute breath of fresh air. Riddles and puzzles have always intrigued me. Your mind seems to be the most difficult labyrinth I've ever encountered. And, at the risk of sounding conceited, it's a genuine achievement to catch me unprepared, caught in a maze."

I felt the blood rush to my cheeks. I was a riddle? He took a deep breath, held it, and smiled at me with tenderness in his eyes.

"Thank you, but I think perhaps you are reading too much into me. There aren't many mysteries about me, and the biggest one, you already know about. On the contrary, I think *you* are the riddle here." I aimed to change the subject's focus.

He chuckled and leaned back against the boat.

"I might know of your gift, but I'm convinced I don't even know the half of it; perhaps neither do you." He continued before I could speak, "I'm the riddle? I am what I am; there is no riddle about that. But I'm curious, what do you find so abstruse about me?"

Surely, he must have been joking. *Nothing* about him was normal. But that was not something I could say to him. Where would I begin, anyway? His enormous size? The unusual way he spoke? His peculiar handwriting? The way he made me lose control of all my faculties in more ways than just emotions? The list was infinite.

"Well, isn't that the point of a riddle? To be difficult to explain? If I was able to say why you are puzzling, then, in fact, you are *not* difficult to fathom."

He pondered the statement for a moment.

"Just point."

"Thank you," I said, feeling good about the fact that I'd made him think. He looked at me with something in his eyes that caused a strange feeling to creep up on me.

Oh no, I hoped my gut was mistaken.

My heart rocketed. Swiftly, he closed the distance and cupped my face between his large hands as he crouched on his knees. I caught my breath. His movement had barely been noticeable.

My gut wasn't wrong.

What was I going to do? It was happening too fast. His face was no further than five inches from mine, hot breath ghosting against my face.

I felt like a mouse being cornered by a cat, hypnotised by his burning eyes. His gaze drifted down to my lips for a second, but returned to my eyes. He came closer. Panic shot through me.

The vocabularies of a thousand languages ran through my mind, but I was mute.

Oh no, oh no—not yet!

I could almost feel his lips on mine as my thoughts raged.

"Don't," I breathed, pleading, and pulled away. He stopped abruptly, not moving closer, not moving away.

I swallowed hard as I looked into his blazing green eyes. Our faces were way too close to be looking at him, but I didn't know what else I should do. I wanted to push him away, to create space, but I couldn't risk touching him. I realised then he never closed his eyes. *Strange.*

The lack of expression on his face frightened me a little, because I knew that whatever he decided to do next, I would have no power to oppose it.

His breathing seemed shallow as he kept looking at me for what seemed like an eternity, before he sighed and moved back to his seat. I couldn't manage to stifle my sigh of relief.

That was intense.

"Forgive me, Josilyn. I find it difficult to think straight, or at all, when I'm with you. You take the breath right out of me," he apologised in a low, raw whisper and paused a moment. "I think it will be prudent to take you home now."

I wanted to disagree, to stay with him longer, but I didn't want to confuse him with what could be perceived as mixed signals.

Why did he have to do that? Not that I *didn't* want him to kiss me; I just wasn't ready yet. It would have been my first kiss, after all.

"Okay," I acquiesced, almost inaudibly, and against my will.

He removed his gaze from mine and took a deep breath as he gripped the oars and turned the boat towards the shore.

He seemed sure which way to row, even in the relative darkness.

A pregnant silence hovered between us; the only sound that of the soft lapping water. I searched my mind for something to say, but found nothing. What mauled my mind was it didn't feel *right*, something he would not have wanted to hear. He didn't say anything either, and though I knew it shouldn't, it spiked my anxiety.

He didn't look at me once since he looked away. It made me feel I had offended him, or even worse, hurt him.

When we reached the pebbled beach, the boat was barely ashore when he jumped out.

I didn't want to vex him further and turned my back to attempt climbing out myself. The next thing I knew, his warm arm circled my waist again, his hand flat on my ribs, as he lifted me out of the boat. When my feet touched the ground, he pressed me against him and didn't let go for a few moments.

I guessed he wasn't as angry or offended as I'd thought. I could feel his heart beating, and had to force myself to not look up at him. That would be circumstantially unwise.

"Thank you," my voice was slightly strained. I felt awkward, almost guilty, though I didn't know why. His jacket on my shoulders worsened the feeling. It was not like I did anything *wrong*.

When he let me go, I was a bit stunned when I saw his warm smile.

"You're most welcome. Wouldn't want you to sprain your ankle," He paused. "We're not going through the forest again. There was no need for that in the first place. Perhaps I should've been more specific in my letter. We're near to the stone pathway."

"Oh, I didn't *realise*."

"It was my mistake. I neglected to mention it. I don't know where my head was."

He strolled in the opposite direction from where we'd approached earlier, but waited until I reached him before walking further.

Guiding me once again, his hand close to my back, I could feel the heat even though he did not touch me. He pulled me up a steep piece I was struggling with in the dark.

After only a few short feet through a thin strip of forest, we reached the road. He hadn't been kidding; it was much safer this way.

A bit disoriented, I started in a random direction, but he grabbed my hand and gently pulled me back.

My cheeks burned. Where was my head?

"This way," he chuckled. "You're not a night person at all, are you?" I didn't understand why, but I felt wary, like I was stepping on eggshells.

"No, but I don't know if there is any part of the day I'm effective."

Unlike most people, I had never been able to determine whether I was a '*night*' or a '*morning*' person.

"Hmm, I understand."

He hadn't released my hand, and I was becoming very much aware of it. He seemed unfazed by what had happened earlier, and I was unsure if that was a good or a bad thing. The entire situation was new and bizarre to me. I couldn't believe that he found anything interesting about me, yet here he was.

Sooner than I expected, I saw the house and was oddly sad about it. All the lights in the house were on; my parents must have been back. Oh wait, that had been me.

He surrendered my hand when we reached the porch steps and let me walk ahead. At the front door, I turned to say goodbye, but my eyes shut reflexively for a second, my senses shuffled, and the adrenaline spurted through me.

Adrian stood against me, looking down at me with blazing eyes. My heart dropped. Did he not hear me the first time? He moved even closer, crowding me in, and I tried to back away, but was trapped against the door.

I wanted to laugh, but also not.

"Josilyn, I don't mean to be a nuisance, but please, just tell me; the feelings I have for you, are they reciprocated to any degree, or am I riding a phantom horse?"

His tortured expression tugged at my heart, which threatened to burst out of my chest. My mouth was dry. No escaping now. Why was he in such a hurry? I had never had to deal with anything remotely as intense. In the second I blinked, my senses drifted apart, and a screech penetrated my ears, but only for a second. I cringed. What on earth was that?

Before I laid my heart down on the slaughter table, I looked around to ensure my parents weren't back yet. He seemed to read the thought.

"They're not here yet," he informed me, certain.

Unsettling: that he knew what I had thought. My teeth sank into my lip. And how could he be so certain, anyway?

"I—I don't know what to say." I extricated, weakly, and tried to move my face away, but he didn't allow it, shifting his to accommodate for my alteration.

"All I want is an answer, whatever it might be."

I couldn't believe I had to have this conversation now, and to be frank, I wasn't sure if I was ready for it just yet.

Sorting through my thoughts, I closed my eyes and took a deep breath. I might as well take a leap. What was the worst that could happen?

"Okay… I *do* have… feelings… for you, but I need time to understand what that means. Because I've never been in this situation, and honestly, it's freaking me out."

I couldn't believe I had just said that out loud. My face burned. He stayed quiet for a moment, eyes locked on mine, before a slight smile spread across his lips.

"That's enough for me. I will wait. As I said, I'm a patient man," he whispered and bent closer. I looked down, not wanting him to see my burning face.

My heart jumped when he slid his arms underneath mine and embraced me tightly, pulling me up so that I stood on my tiptoes. I found my arms wrapped around his neck. He didn't give up.

It was sweet, to be wanted.

Blood pounded in my neck, and I closed my eyes when I felt the *Pulse* coming. My senses shifted, but fell back into place abruptly when I felt his lips on my neck. He was testing my limits. I opened my eyes as the adrenaline kicked in. He showed no signs of desisting. Slowly, his mouth travelled down my throat, until he placed his nose in the hollow at the base of my neck. My heartbeat intensified. I was self-conscious when I swallowed.

My head was spinning, and my knees felt weak. I might have crumbled to the ground if he wasn't holding me up. Time was running out. I had to decide. By some miracle, I mustered the willpower to pull away. I was somewhat surprised when he let me, but when he stepped back, the frustration was evident on his face.

That was his own fault; he hadn't listened the first time. Fighting the yearning, I shrugged his jacket off and handed it back to him. The sudden cold was solid.

"Goodnight, Adrian," I greeted him curtly and turned for the door, still feeling the heat emanating from him.

My senses spluttered into disarray when he whirled me around and kissed me on the cheek before letting me go and stepping back.

"Goodnight, Josilyn," he mimicked in a more alluring way, but was already down the steps and walking into darkness before I could react.

I stared after him until there was nothing left to see.

It was better that way. If he had known how close I'd been to caving... My cheek burned with the touch of his lips, and any part of me that was in contact with him glowed, but my neck burned the worst. When I touched the area, my skin was hot to the touch.

As I blew out a breath, I opened the front door and headed for the kitchen. I remained perplexed about how he'd known my parents weren't home yet. I didn't know what one would call that. Intuition, perhaps? I had 'intuitions' others didn't have.

I downed three glasses of water before I quenched the thirst. When I stepped into the hall, the strange fear from the afternoon crawled over me again. Trying to ignore it, I forced myself to walk slower, but it felt like torture. Panic crept over me when I reached my steps.

I hadn't switched on my light. As if walking up a dark, winding staircase wasn't bad enough.

I swallowed hard and took the first step, and the next, debating whether it was better or worse that I had left the trapdoor open. Just as I placed my hands on the floor above, something brushed against my leg and swished into my room.

With a blood-curdling scream, I stumbled back, almost tumbling down the stairs.

When my back hit the opposite wall, I slid down, my hands clasped over my mouth. Hysteria pounced on me like a stalking predator.

I couldn't handle it. Tears burned my eyes before flowing. I tried not to squirm, but couldn't manage it.

It took everything I had not to scream when movement stirred in the hollow's darkness. I had to do something; I had to move.

My eyes flashed between the stairs and the opening. Whatever it was had to be staring at me. Just as I calculated my chances of escape, I saw it moving closer from my peripheral. My heart wrapped around my throat.

I slinked my gaze towards it. My mind couldn't process properly. I couldn't believe it.

Tji-Tji. She stopped. We stared at each other, and she *meowed.* I burst into wild laughter, a madman's laughter.

Poor thing, she must have been just as frightened as me. I smiled at her and patted the ground next to me.

"Come here, you," I cooed, and she ran to my side, rubbing her head against my hand. I picked her up, stroking her head. She placed her paw on my cheek, looking at me with her big green eyes. Her presence put me at ease, and I got up.

A knock on the front door echoed through the empty house. I froze.

Who on earth could that be? I wasn't expecting anyone tonight, and my parents hadn't mentioned anything. I hesitated, trying to decide whether to go down and look. Was it safe? Outside Surveillance cameras were going on my wish list.

Tji-Tji looked at me.

"You're not helping."

She meowed, and I breathed a sigh. Maybe it was important. Strange, they hadn't knocked again.

I was self-conscious when I descended the stairs. Anyone on the porch could see me through the large window flanking the door. It was dark out.

I squinted but couldn't see anything.

Tji-Tji became uneasy when I reached the door, and I secured the chain before opening it just a crack.

Adrian.

Frowning, I closed the door to unchain it.

He grinned when the door opened again. What was this fool doing here? In a flash, Tji-Tji lurched from my grip, screeching, and shot upstairs, leaving a stinging pain in my hand.

"Ow!"

I stared down at the scratch as the blood surfaced.

"Ouch," I breathed, looking up at Adrian, who was staring at my hand with a puzzled expression.

Had he never seen blood before?

"Hey, what's wrong?" I itched to stretch out my hand and touch him, but something stopped me.

A deep frown carved a line on his forehead as he looked up at me. Questions radiated from his eyes, but I didn't think they were directed at me.

"Nothing," he said, dull, dazed. "I—" he shook his head. "You dropped your keys in the forest, and I forgot to give them back."

It was unlike him, fumbling for words.

"I didn't even realise, thank you," my voice mimicked his, hollow. I had no idea what was going on. He stared at my hand again and slowly lifted his. I took the keys, not taking my eyes from his face, until I realised I had smeared blood on his hand.

"Oops, sorry about that, I'll get a tissue—" I was about to turn, but he stopped me.

"No, it's quite alright." His voice was meek, almost lifeless.

His eyes were now focused on my hand again, making me self-conscious. I lifted my hand to investigate. Blood trickled down my finger in three thin trails.

I didn't realise I was bleeding so much. When I looked at him again, shock ran through me to see a fine network of bluish veins form on his nostrils.

What the—?

I stared at him in alarm, but he kept his eyes fixed on my hand.

"Adrian! Are you okay? What's going on?" I panicked. He blinked rapidly and stared at me blankly.

"I'm fine. I think I must go now. Goodbye." His voice was toneless as he turned and walked away. I didn't know what to do, but didn't want to go outside. He was freaking me out a bit. Conflicted and confused, I stared after him until his outlines disappeared in the darkness.

For some reason, it bothered me that I had to close the door, as if breaking an invisible connection by closing it, and it was difficult not to cringe when I did so.

Why had the veins on his nose surfaced like that? I had seen nothing like it. Perhaps he suffered from momentary anaemia, which would mean he was squeamish. The blood must have caused it.

Blood.

I had forgotten about the scratches. It had stopped bleeding, but was quite a mess. I went to the guest bathroom to clean up. Tji-Tji had had quite a go at me. The aggression was so abnormal for her.

The wound burned as I held it under the running water. Fresh blood surfaced, flowing down my hand in different shades of red.

My mind wandered at the sight, the flowing blood resembling the fiery sunsets I'd grown used to, the dark flame of red hair I was becoming attached to, and the ardent touch I was growing shackled to.

I shook my head to rid myself of the thoughts while drying my hands. In the middle of the foyer, I stopped in my tracks. Motionless, I stood there.

A buzzing in my ears emerged after a second and vibrated through me. Such an instant thing that I stumbled forward and had to grasp the balustrade before plummeting to the floor, nausea thick in my throat.

I couldn't distinguish where it came from as I dragged myself up the stairs with great effort. I wanted to get to my room, but a shadow of misery and helplessness enveloped me as I stared up at the remaining stairs, which looked like they stretched up further and further with each step I managed.

My senses dragged into pandemonium and electric blasts surged through my bones, contracting my muscles, pulsating to the ferocious beat in the air. My foot caught on a step and, once again, the balustrade kept me from falling.

What was happening? I closed my eyes, but it didn't stop me from seeing. The house looked like a tornado had struck it, the staircase the sole remnant. Winds of black mist swirled around me, my hair yanked in all directions by the violent gust. *I must be dreaming.*

I braced myself, gathered every morsel of energy I could, and managed to close in on the landing, which seemed to hover in mid-air.

As I reached the last step, I turned around and collapsed, resting my head against the balustrade. Everything turned dead silent. My last thought was that, strangely, my senses hadn't shifted during this bizarre episode.

At some point, I woke up. Or at least, I thought I had. I felt trapped between a state of semi-consciousness and unconsciousness.

Everything around me was quiet and eerie. It hurt when I lifted my head from the post, and I wondered how long I had been out. I squinted, trying to weed out the mess in my head.

The house was different. Gloomy.

I took a deep breath and licked my dry lips. With both hands on the post, I pulled myself up, but froze halfway. I blinked, staring at my bracelet in confusion. It looked dull and worn, like a piece of scrap metal around my wrist. How could that be? It had been so bright and beautiful? A wave of sadness engrossed me. Filled with regret, I tried to touch it, but it split in two bracelets with a faint *crack*. I jumped and held it away from me.

A dark mist sprouted from it and flowed in sharp shreds towards my room. It was a messed-up dream, and my logic screamed that I should by no means follow it. My eyes traced its path, incredulous. Without deciding to, I rose and followed the fog into the opening.

As if hypnotised, I walked into the same dark room I'd been so frightened of earlier without the slightest bit of bother. Following a thread of black mist. Trouble screamed from far off.

Even in the dark, I somehow still saw the mist. Exhaustion pooled in my body.

I entered my room and became mystified. The mirror had turned back into the mist-filled doorway of earlier.

If this was not a dream, I hadn't felt my senses shift. Which meant anyone else would see the same thing if they were in the room.

But if I did *Shift*, it had never been so continuous, smooth and constant. The mist was different, too.

Rather than the greyish black from the afternoon, it was a bright, almost glowing ice blue, perfectly visible in the pitch blackness. As if it became aware of me, the doorway mist stretched into the room, like tentacles searching for something.

It looked like an octopus.

The mist of my bracelet swirled towards one tentacle and merged with it. An invisible force pulled my hand upwards. The other tentacles turned towards me.

I couldn't move. My throat turned into solid ice as they came closer and enclasped me.

My pulse sped up when I was pulled forward. A gentle but undeniable force. I tried to push back but stumbled forward when I could find no purchase.

What was going on? I was unable to make a sound, desperately trying to dig in my heels, but being dragged closer to the opening, regardless. As the panic bloomed, I harnessed all my strength to turn around, feeling the pressure on my stomach.

I must have looked like a madwoman, wrestling the air. I tried to bear forward, to anchor my feet to the smooth floor, but to no avail. The doorway was soon inches from my heels.

An unworldly, sucking scream tore the air behind me, resonating from the blackness.

It sounded like something hungry was behind the mist. I screamed too, but what came out was a muffled puff. I stared backwards in horror as I descended into the dark.

Chapter 7

I stood sheathed in mist. My heart pounded, wild, but I'd forgotten why. Like a dream that changed course halfway through. Sucking in a deep breath, I almost choked as the thick, wet vapour overwhelmed my lungs. I blinked, trying to see, but the mist was a wall. I waved my hand around and the fog swirled away a distance, but soon closed in again. No sound was audible, apart from the blood rushing in my ears. Was I awake? Cautious, I stepped forward and blinked as the mist precipitated on my eyelashes. I wiped it with the back of my hand, and a sudden burning made me look down. The three thin, red protruding lines threw me off for a moment. *A cat. My cat. T—. Tji-Tji?*

Like a reflex, I unclasped the bracelet from my wrist and dropped it, stepping back. I was unsure why, because it was just a charm bracelet—a beautiful charm bracelet. The memory of Adrian putting it on my wrist flashed through my head.

I heard—felt—something move behind me and spun around. As if sucked back, the fog rapidly pulled back and away from me, but revealed nothing. Wherever I turned, I was surrounded by darkness so complete that I felt blind.

When I turned again, I was at the second-floor landing looking down the foyer stairs, the lights on. The orchestra played in the ballroom.

It was the ball.

I looked down, gasping as I absorbed the blood-red tulle skirt of the dress on my body, shimmering like a wet sacrifice cascading around me. My eyes drifted down the stairs. At the bottom was the blonde-haired man from the ball, smiling up at me. Our eyes locked, and relief flooded my heart, and I smiled back. I placed my hand on the balustrade to begin the descent, but before I could take a step, he was in front of me. With a bow, he took my hand and kissed it. My cheeks burned, and I pulled my hand free, but not so it would be rude.

I had so many questions but failed to frame them. He stepped up to my level, shoulder to shoulder, though he was taller, our torsos to opposite sides. His golden eyes stayed on me, and I was transfixed by him and his comforting smile. He offered his arm.

"Have you seen the moon on the lake tonight? It's almost as beautiful as you." He said it with such self-assurance that I couldn't suppress a giggle as I accepted his arm.

I was so enraptured, I didn't realise we'd ascended my stairs until we reached the landing. We had met mere moments ago, right here, in my room. He escorted me to the window, my hand still around his arm. I could not stop looking at him, and I saw the moon glisten in his eyes as he peered outside. He looked at me.

"Look."

I tore my gaze away, looking to the window.

Mist lay over the forest and the lake, the moon casting a golden hue over it all. My breath caught. It was a painting grafted in gold dust and magic, sprinkled with dreams. Music started playing, but not from the orchestra. It was a melancholy song from my playlist. I didn't have time to think about where it came from before he turned to me and pulled me close, and we danced. My ear was against his chest, and we danced slowly.

It could've been a second; it could've been an eternity.

His heart thrummed faster than I expected, and I realised we had stopped moving. I pulled away to look at him, but found myself against the mirror. Disoriented, I turned around. He stood by the chaise, staring at me with a blank expression. My heart hammered in my chest. Something in the set of his jaw seemed *other* as he cocked his head to the side. Like a shadow sucked in by a vacuum—feet first, he disappeared into the darkness beneath my bed.

I woke up with a start and sat upright, wincing. I was on the floor. My right side, which I'd lain on, stung from the sudden motion. The bracelet lay splayed on the floor by my knee. My heart rose like a helium balloon in my throat as I stared at it wide-eyed, but I didn't know why. I looked up into the mirror. I looked like hell. Or something the cat had dragged from it. My gaze fell on my hand, where the three red lines blazed.

What happened? The last thing I remembered was washing the blood from my hands on the first floor. Now I'd woken up on my bedroom floor. The *Pulse* pounded through me like nausea, and I keeled forward, closing my eyes. A groan escaped my mouth, unsummoned. I sucked calming breaths until I felt it subside back into my marrow. With some hesitation, I picked up the bracelet and got up stiffly. A cold drop ran down my spine when I turned to the bed. I couldn't explain it, but it felt like something was staring at me from beneath it. My heart drummed against my neck until the blood sang in my ears. I heard only my rapid breathing as I sank to my knees, placed my hands on the ground, and leaned down. Wild energy pounded through me as I anticipated what could be lurking beneath. My palms were clammy on the wooden floor as I gazed into potential horrors.

I met green eyes.

My heart dropped. *Tji-Tji.*

Relieved, I expelled an iron-tinged breath and pressed my forehead against the floor. I heard a meow, and feet pitter-patter closer.

"You nearly killed me twice today. Do you know that?" My throat burned as she squeezed underneath my arm, licking my chin. I touched her soft fur and sat up, pressing her against my chest. She purred.

"Do you know why I was lying on the floor? Because I have no idea." She tapped her paw on my wrist and meowed again. I was unsure what to make of that, but exhaustion flooded over me without warning, and I almost fell asleep right there. It was 01:37 a.m. I had to be up in five hours.

I got into bed, Tji-Tji by my side, my senses shuffling as my head hit the pillow. The criss-cross canopy above me stretched into the heavens like a tunnel. I squeezed my eyes shut and turned on my side, scooping Tji-Tji closer. My head swam, and it felt like I was drifting into space. I opened my eyes and regretted it right away.

The tunnel above my bed inverted, and it felt like my bed opened and sagged into an abyss. I stared around me. Tji-Tji lay heedless as the bed swallowed us into utter darkness. I felt a falling sensation and shot upright.

My alarm went off.

It was 7 a.m.

My heart galloped, a wild thing inside my chest. The daylight was a shock after… *After*… what? I strained to remember the night before or what I had dreamt, but it was a locked-up vault. My senses keeled over, and I grasped the sheets, feeling like I was standing on a ship. After a few steadying breaths, I opened my eyes.

It was 7:17 a.m.

Dad was in the kitchen making coffee when I came down. A peanut butter and honey oatmeal bowl stood steaming on the counter.

"Mine?" I asked, my stomach churning. Did I eat last night?

"I remember you calling me Dad like it was yesterday." I rolled my eyes, went over, and hugged him.

"Good morning, *Dad*. Is this oatmeal mine to consume?"

"Why, of course. You know I can't stand the stuff." He hated oatmeal. My stomach gurgled loud enough that he cocked an eyebrow at me. I asked about their trip. They'd stayed much later than expected because the dealership didn't have the part, and they couldn't drive back safely without it.

"Hey, where were you last night?" He looked confused. My heart raced. I only went to the lake with Adrian, but they were away, so why would he ask that?

"What do you mean? I was here." I was here… *in the vicinity.*

"Did you fall asleep somewhere else?" A peculiar question.

"I…don't know how to answer that. I woke up in my bed this morning…" He frowned. "Uh… I'm not sure why that's so perplexing, Dad?" He shook his head.

"Maybe I was too tired. When we got home at around 10:30, all the lights were on, so I thought you might still be awake, but you weren't in your room when I went there. Your car was here, and your phone was on your bed, so I thought you were home but must have fallen asleep somewhere." He wasn't accusing me; he was genuinely confused. Ditto. I had no recollection of being somewhere else at that time. I shrugged. He mirrored it, took his coffee, and kissed me on the head before heading to the porch.

After finishing breakfast, I hopped into my car, the seat still a little damp from the rain and the open window the day before. As I entered the forest, I wracked my brain to figure out where I could've been after Adrian had left… and noticed the scars on my hand. I remembered Tji-Tji scratching me… and Adrian at the door. I remembered blood. Then I'd woken up.

I reached for my neck, for the ring, but it wasn't there. I forgot when last I'd worn it.

And then, as if my mind had been tugging at me the entire morning to reveal something, my thoughts dragged into order. Pieces came together like a magnetic puzzle. The previous night held a lot more detail than I could recollect just minutes earlier. My question was, why did I remember now? My heart fluttered when I recalled the things Adrian had told me and the things I had said in response. The almost-kiss. *Both*. My cheeks burned.

"Was I really that stupid?" I said out loud. Of course, I *liked* him. Much, much more than anything I'd ever felt for anyone. Much more than I had thought, and a great deal more than I was willing to admit. To him or myself.

It unnerved me that it had hit me so fast. Shouldn't it have taken longer for such feelings to develop?

Blue in my peripheral drew my attention, and I looked over as the lake came into view. My eyes searched and soon found the pebbled beach now fresh in my memory. Strange, how I had never noticed it before. For some reason, I was surprised that the boat was gone, but of course he wouldn't have left it there.

I still didn't know where he lived.

I held his face in my mind. As my thoughts swirled, remaining speculative about him and my feelings was ineffectual. He was quite beautiful. Well, maybe not *beautiful*. Beauty had the danger of shallowness to it, which was the farthest thing from him. He had an unconventional, uncommon beauty. It grew on you, almost too overpowering. As if you needed to build resilience to the exposure. That is, if staring at the sun could toughen your eyes. His features looked foreign, ambiguous, and I was convinced I'd never seen anyone that looked quite like him. An amalgamation of different beautiful features. Italian. Greek. Middle Eastern. Who knew?

I reached the town and the university turnoff soon. I must have been driving faster than I realised. Many parking spots were still open.

I found myself wishing Adrian would already be there. He had the habit of appearing out of thin air. My heart raced at the thought of seeing him within mere moments.

An unusual, sweet scent lingered in the air when I stepped outside. I guessed the trees were giving off the delightful, almost herby fragrance. My eyes were sensitive to the light, making me squint. A sudden gust flowed around me.

"Josilyn," I heard Adrian's voice and turned around; my heart burst in anticipation of meeting his green eyes. But he wasn't there. I looked around but couldn't see his auburn hair anywhere.

"Josilyn…" I heard it again, and this time, it sounded like it came from the fountain close by. I thought I saw someone on the other side, blocked by the water feature, and I crossed the road. Strange that I heard the voice through the rushing water. I made a quick three-sixty in case he was standing close by, but he wasn't.

Someone was sitting on the opposite edge of the fountain, and I moved around it, expecting it to be Adrian. But there was no one there. I didn't understand… I was sure I had seen someone. Baffled, I walked around the fountain, wondering if he might be messing with me. I heard him chuckle so close that I turned around, but again, he wasn't there.

"Where are you?" I asked aloud. Determined to prove my sanity, I walked up to the fountain, stepped onto the rim, and looked over the protrusion. Unless he was lying flat on the ground behind the edge, he wasn't there.

The *Pulse* shot through me, and a blue shock wave rippled out from me into the surroundings, my senses knocked into chaos. I realised I was one unstable step away from landing in the water. The water did not sound like a fountain, but like a massive waterfall, and when I looked down, it did look like a waterfall gushing into a dark depth. My heart raced as I stared down at the unfathomable drop. I squeezed my eyes shut and concentrated on slowing down my rapid breathing. I heard my name over the rushing sound, but it sounded faint. My knees felt weak, and with tentative care, I moved my foot backwards until I felt the edge at my heels. I gave a controlled step back down. The space between my feet leaving the platform and hitting the ground felt like an eternity.

"Josilyn," so close it felt like his lips were pressed against my ear, and I flinched when I felt a hand on my elbow.

Laura.

Clarity returned, as I met her frowning face, her hands in the air, palms towards me.

"Whoa, are you okay? It's a bit early in the morning for a swim in the fountain, don't you think?" She smiled, but I could see concern tinged around her eyes. I took a deep breath and cleared my throat, looking around me. A few curious eyes were on me, but I couldn't blame them. By pure chance, I looked up and saw what I thought was Professor Giovaniello looking down from a window.

"We'll be late for class, come on…" Cautious, Laura took me by the elbow and steered me towards the building. A switch flipped, and the energy seeped from me—I felt instant exhaustion. Unsure if I was even awake, I pinched myself.

"If you're not sure you're awake, you can look at your hands… If they look abnormal, you're probably dreaming." Her notice and remark were unexpected. I raised my hands. They looked fine, though they trembled. I lowered them with a nervous laugh and tried to make light of what I didn't understand myself.

"I don't think I slept well last night."

"That's what you get for going out partying without me."
Near the front door, she released my elbow, and I managed on my own. Once we sat down in class, I breathed relief; my legs weighed a tonne.

My mind must have gone into battery-saving mode because I came to a few classes later, sitting in Professor Giovaniello's classroom. The weight of someone's gaze pressed into my right cheek, and I looked up, locking eyes with a guy I had never noticed before. Brazen, he didn't flinch when our eyes met, even though I'd just caught him staring at me. Cheeks flushing red, I averted my gaze. I thought of Adrian, whom I hadn't seen at all. My phone vibrated, and I immediately checked it, half expecting it to be him. It took my eyes a few seconds to recognise "Anna" on the notification bar.

Professor Giovaniello emerged from the door, and I put my phone away. The magnitude of her beauty caught my breath. Her hair hung loose a few inches below her hips, a silver and black river. It looked so healthy and soft that I yearned to touch it. She looked straight at me and smiled.

"Good morning, children," her velvet voice oozed through the room like warm air on a cold evening. The whole room greeted her, not at all fazed by the diminutive noun she used.

Her full lips curved into a soft line. Something was different about her that I couldn't quite put my finger on.

"I forgot to introduce myself yesterday," she purred. "I guess I was just as eager as you for the free period." Laughter all round. She was a puppet master and holding us right at her fingertips. I realised the change which perplexed me had to do with her face, after scrutinising her as she spoke. Yesterday she'd looked almost ancient, but today she would pass for barely middle-aged.

It all felt like a staged production, where everyone did exactly what someone wanted them to do. *Strange.*

She started the lecture, and where my mind would have wandered, I found I *wanted* to pay attention, and I was not the exception. Not a single person was busy with something else. Though she talked about principles I'd mastered long ago, I found it difficult to even tear my eyes away for longer than a few clipped seconds.

The class continued in excessive peace. It felt supernatural. Did everyone just adore her?

She dismissed the class when she was done, and Laura leaned closer.

"That guy has been staring at you the entire class. He's cute… maybe we should go talk to him." I followed her gaze and met his eyes for a second time. He smiled a slow, crooked smile, which I returned with half-hearted equality before looking away. I noticed the professor looking at him, too. Was that a coincidence, or could she hear us?

"I don't think so. Maybe he was staring at you… Like you were staring at him."

"Are you calling me cock-eyed?"

"I mean, if the shoe fits…"

She clicked her tongue and gave me a playful shove and I stumbled— my side stinging. I gaped at her, and she expelled an unattractive but hilarious cackle. I shoved her back as a joke, except I underestimated my strength, and she nigh flew, grabbing the desk. Both shocked, we stared at each other.

"Sorry!" I hoped she wasn't angry.

"What the heck? You've got to ease off the steroids, bro." She laughed, putting her hand on her heart. Relief washed over me, and I laughed too.

We got our bags and headed out.

"Miss Grey?" It was the professor. We stopped. She looked even younger up close. She glanced at Laura, who quickly offered to wait outside.

"Yes?"

Her eyes flickered to someone behind me, and I turned. It was *that* guy. He looked at us both, smiled, and sauntered out. A small crease formed between her brows as her eyes followed him. For a moment, my vision was hazy, and the air looked reddish-purple. I rubbed my eyes.

"My apologies for calling you after class again. I'm just checking in to see if everything is alright. I saw you at the fountain this morning. You looked distressed."

So, it *had* been her. How could I explain what had happened there when I didn't quite understand it myself? I tried to make light of it.

"Oh, don't worry about that. Laura was just playing with me." I smiled, willing her to believe me and let it go. She smiled and nodded.

"Alright," she took a deep breath, "I won't hassle you further. I'll see you tomorrow."

Laura and I spent the rest of the day doing classwork. She teased me about the guy in class and then she asked me about the guy I'd danced with at the ball. A memory clawed at the surface of my mind but couldn't escape. I told her I didn't think I'd see him again. I noticed she didn't mention Adrian. That I hadn't seen him all day made my heart clench.

On my way home, I became more and more exhausted the closer I got. I reached for my necklace again, trying to remember the last time I'd worn it. When I saw the white beach, I wondered where Adrian was.

I wondered if it would be too forward to ask for his number the next time I saw him.

Both cars were gone when I arrived home. I headed straight up to my room to look for the necklace. I couldn't remember taking it off, and the thought of losing a gift from my mom disquieted me.

Tji-Tji met me on the second floor, ran to me, and I picked her up. When I reached the landing, she jumped from my arms and disappeared under the bed. I searched everywhere I could think of, even under the windowsill cushions, between my sheets, under the bed, the desk cabinets, and jacket pockets. I didn't find it. What I did find, was the bracelet Adrian had given me the night before, lying on the floor a distance away from the mirror. I paused, my pulse sped up as I looked at it, glistening on the floor, so out of place. It evoked emotions inside me I didn't quite understand. Was it because Adrian had given it to me?

The *Pulse* simmered and vibrated in the soles of my feet but didn't move up. I wiggled my toes and shook my feet like a cat with wet paws, but it didn't do much. *This is silly.*

Stepping forward, I picked it up. How had it ended up there? I put it on and went searching through the rest of the house. It wasn't in my parents' room, or any second-floor room. I couldn't imagine it being somewhere in the first-floor parlour or the kitchen. Maybe my car?

As I descended the stairs into the foyer, Chopin's nocturne number 20 in C# minor began to play. I gave another step, listening. Jovial voices echoed from the ballroom. I gave another step. My senses lilted, and I grasped the balustrade. For a moment, red tinged the air, and I noticed it was dark outside. I reached the last step and looked down. I was wearing my ball dress. A hand was offered to me, and I looked up into a red embossed mask and golden eyes. It was *him*. I took his hand and, smiling, he escorted me to the ballroom through the throng of masked guests. The music pulsed the air in red and dark blue tinges, swirling on the floor like mist on a bass speaker. His hand burned on mine as we descended the ballroom steps.

"What is your name?" I heard my raspy voice. He looked at me with a crooked smile. His eyes looked green in the strange light, and I blinked. A dancing aide took my hand and led me onto the dance floor as the dance began. It was a slower dance, but we still switched partners. I looked for him as I blurred through the crowd, but couldn't see him. The red mist in the room thickened.

He appeared before me and pulled me close. The heat of his hand on mine sent a shock through me as we wove through the crowd at a speed which made me lightheaded. We slowed down again, and he gave a step back. Someone passed between us, and when they moved away, Adrian stood before me. I gasped and blinked, but I was dancing with the gold-eyed stranger again. I looked up at his face, and he smiled down. My heart raved inside my chest while I looked around for the red hair. I suddenly felt strange in his arms, whatever his name was, while Adrian was around. I wasn't doing anything wrong, dancing with a stranger, so why did I feel guilty?

He lifted his arm and spun me around, and as I spun and looked at him, he changed. One rotation, he was the blonde stranger I'd met in my room. The next, it was Adrian turning me around. And then back again. My heart pumped violently, and I tried to stop, but the momentum was too much, and he was too strong. I looked away, distressed at the changing sight. The spinning stopped, and he pulled me closer again as we resumed our dance. I looked up at his golden eyes, investigating his features and blonde hair.

"What is your name?" The panic in my voice was raw. A warm smile curved his lips, and he continued our dance. In a tone that laughed, as if I was joking, answered,

"Adrian," and he morphed into him before my eyes.

"Hellooo? Anybody home?" My dad stood before me, waving his hand in front of my face. I gasped and fell back, sitting down on the step behind me.

"Whoa, kiddo! Are you alright?" He knelt at my side at once and checked me up and down. I looked around in utter bewilderment. We were in the foyer. It was light outside, and I was wearing the clothes I'd worn to class. My breath chased. He stroked my hair, trying to soothe me.

"Shh. It's okay, Honey, you're okay. You must've phased out. It's 5 p.m, on Thursday afternoon. You had an oatmeal and honey breakfast and went to class, and I don't think you've been home long." Rattled, I looked into his concerned eyes. I didn't understand what had just happened. But one thing was certain: I had not just "phased out".

"Control your breathing, Hon. You're going to make yourself sick." I tried slowing and controlling my breath. The *Pulse* spat through me, and I convulsed. My senses knocked over, and I heard a momentary screech. I grunted loudly, straining for it to stop. My head felt like it was splitting open. Dad was squeezing my hand and rubbing my back.

"Baby, come back. You can do it. You've done it before." Hot tears streamed down my cheeks. I dug my nails into the balustrade. The *Pulse* beat through me like a wave. I hit my thigh with my fist, as if that could stop it, and my dad grabbed my hand.

"No, don't hurt yourself. Come on." He pulled me up and held me as he walked me to the parlour. I heard him call my mom. Andrew came running, and my dad instructed him to make sugar water. I focused on my breathing and bright blue skies as my dad sat me down.

By the time Andrew came back, I was okay for the most part, but drained the glass anyway. After sitting for a few minutes, exhaustion pulled over me like a shroud. I fought to keep my eyes open. My dad saw me struggle and told me to sleep if I wanted, so I lay down on the couch and fell into a restless sleep. Mom woke me up with great gentleness, whispering and caressing my arm. I drifted back into consciousness. A food tray waited on the coffee table. They sat with me as I ate and kept the conversation light. They didn't ask me what'd happened, probably because they assumed it had been the normal glitch. I was glad though, because I was too confused to explain it. The more I thought about it, the less clear it became. I asked my mom if she'd seen my necklace, but she hadn't either.

After a lethargic shower, I crawled into bed with heavy bones, falling asleep as soon as my head hit the pillow. I dreamed of dancing with Adrian at the ball and meeting him in the forest later—in the normal dream way.

It felt like a truck had hit me when I woke up the following day. Getting to and through class without yawning and falling asleep was a vicious struggle. Laura joked about my new night-time habits, saying I must invite her with next time, unless it included a guy. I could see from her raised eyebrows she wondered if Adrian was involved. In a way, he was, but not the way she thought. I brushed those sentiments away, mentioning I hadn't seen him since Wednesday. It hurt a little, and I wondered if something was wrong, or maybe what I had said put him off. I tried rehashing Wednesday evening, but it was like a dream dreamt months ago.

No one else was home yet and, though I was exhausted, I fought against it. My sleep was already troubled, so snoozing the entire afternoon away wouldn't help. I opted for a shower instead, put on some music and steamed up the bathroom. It felt like a warm, atmospheric hug. I stood under the scorching downpour and relished the burn that left my skin red. I thought about Adrian's touch—equally searing, like a permanent fever.

The singing pipes became louder, and pulled me into its orchestra, my knees buckling. As the steam swirled around me, a memory emerged from the proverbial woods. I was standing… somewhere, surrounded by mist. I strained to unlock the rest of the impression. My heart fluttered, and I became uncomfortable as I stood there, naked. The steam turned from something comforting into something ominous with a flick of a switch. I turned off the water and got out, fanning my towel around so I could see anything hiding in the room, my heart rising in my throat. The memory itched at the back of my mind, but I couldn't quite unwrap it. I switched on the extractor fan, which did its job.

I approached my staircase with hesitation. Something about it gushed adrenaline through me. The trapdoor was open and my pulse speeding up as I went up just high enough to poke my head through. I looked around the room but noticed nothing strange. I turned on the steps and faced the mirror, which showed two wide eyes peeping from the hole. It could've been comical, were I in another state of mind.

I stared at the mirror, unblinking. A chill ran down my spine, and an involuntary shiver ran through my body. A whisper wrapped around me in the hollow.

"Josilyn?" I dropped my clothes, and they tumbled down the steps. My senses tumbled too, and I saw the muted sound waves drizzle down like a viscous mist. I picked up the fallen items, put them on the floor above me, and went downstairs. I wasn't sure who'd called me.

My dad stood below, leaning on the balustrade post with both hands. He smiled when I appeared.

"Good. I'm too lazy to climb stairs. Care to join me for coffee on the porch?"

We talked about his book research and my classes until Mom and Andrew came home. They sat with us for a while, but the conversation held little interest to Andrew, who set off into the forest; Mom cautioning him to be back before dark. Under her breath, she wondered aloud what he was doing in there. A little later, when she had gone to the kitchen, my dad noticed my bracelet.

"I haven't seen that before." He leaned closer to inspect it, and I held up my wrist.

"Yeah, it's new. I got it this week." I felt my throat constrict a little. A crease formed between his brows as he looked up at me.

"It's exquisite but formal compared to what you usually buy yourself." He baited me.

"It was a gift from a friend." My heart rate sped up. A frail image of Adrian on his knees on the boat flashed through my head. *Perhaps more than a friend.* My cheeks burned.

"A gift? That's thoughtful. Did she just feel like giving a gift, or did I forget something?" *She.* It made sense he'd think it was Laura. I hadn't mentioned anyone else. I hesitated. If I avoided correcting him, it would teeter close to lying.

"No, you didn't forget anything… I'm not sure why he gave it to me." My throat burned, and I watched the emotions run through his eyes as he absorbed the pronoun.

"He…" he repeated, a slight edge to his voice. "Will I be meeting him?" My heart dropped at the thought. I wasn't sure I was ready for that. I might implode.

"I don't know, I guess you will," was all I managed to squeeze out. He must've noticed my discomfort because he let the subject go, even though I could feel he wanted to ask more. I excused myself under the guise of helping Mom with dinner.

I spaced out and resurfaced, standing before the stove, poking chicken around in the pan, and Mom talking about an annoying tenant. The spatula dropped from my hand and splattered oil everywhere, but I picked it up and cleaned up. Mom was none the wiser. Sudden exhaustion folded over me like a heavy blanket, and I struggled to breathe. I took slow, steady breaths and willed myself to stay awake, at least until after dinner.

Afterwards, ascending the main stairs took much effort, and I paused halfway up, clutching the balustrade like life support. Dad crossed the foyer towards the parlour and noticed.

"Are you okay up there?"

"Yes, just exhausted." I smiled and went up.

I walked into the hollow, dreading the stairs ahead.

It was dark when I woke up on a sofa in the second-floor parlour. Disoriented, I hoisted myself up on my elbows. A blanket covered me, and I was still wearing what I had on after the shower. The curtains were drawn shut, limiting visibility. What happened? I sat up and waited for my eyes to adjust to the dark. I wasn't familiar enough with the room to know my way about, sightless. My heart rate steadily rose. I spread my hands open before me and could just make them out. They seemed normal enough. The sofa creaked as I wriggled closer to the edge, and I heard a loud grunt nearby. The fright was momentary; I knew the source. My dad's movement increased, and I saw his dark shape sit up.

"Hey, kid. You awake?" His voice was thick with sleep. He fumbled around on the coffee table, and the light went on. We cringed from the sudden illumination, and my senses dipped; the light waves streamed around like confetti. It reset after a lethargic moment. Dad pinched his nose bridge, put his glasses on, and looked at me.

"What's going on?" I whispered.

"I camped out with the specific hope you'd tell *me*."

"What time is it?" He looked at his watch, straining to focus.

"It's 02:37 a.m., Saturday."

"Why are we here?"

"An existential question perhaps better suited for another time." He sighed, "But if you mean why are we sleeping on the couch… You went up, and I saw you on the stairs. I'm unsure if you remember. A little later, Andrew called me. He was pretty spooked. You were teetering at the edge of the top step on the second floor, and you were unresponsive. He thought you were joking around with him, but you were burning up when he touched your arm. So, he called me. Your eyes were open, but you didn't react. I've heard you shouldn't wake someone up while they are sleepwalking, which is what I assumed you were doing. We didn't want you toppling down the stairs, so we escorted you to the couch, and I'm here to keep an eye on you."

"Sleepwalking?" I thought back, trying to remember anything after stepping into the hollow, but there was nothing. I ceased to exist at that moment. It freaked me out, not knowing what I'd done.

"Yep. You have two options. Either we spend the rest of the night here, or I lock you in your room, so you don't fall down the stairs." Both tempting options.

"I think you'll sleep better without being on high alert for me getting up and wandering to stairs to throw myself from."

He escorted me up and waited below the trapdoor until I'd finished putting on my pyjamas with dumb fingers. I ensured my phone was in my room, and he instructed me to lock the trapdoor, hide the key somewhere tricky, and put the sill cushions on the floor. After confirming I had done so, he left.

I woke up at 10 a.m. feeling like I hadn't slept at all, but I couldn't stay in bed the whole day. Catching up with some class work, emphasising Friday's classes, was a massive struggle. I thought a walk outside would get the blood flowing, but my dad was wary of me going off alone. He was afraid I'd fall asleep under a tree somewhere, but I told him I'd be fine and wandered down the stone road. The beach Adrian had taken me to lay below, and I gazed at it a while, trying to remember the night that felt like another lifetime. I found myself wondering if Adrian even existed. Where had he disappeared to? When I walked further down the winding road, I felt uneasy. My senses twisted, and the *Pulse* rushed through me, and I bent over, hands on my knees. A screech ripped through the forest, and when I looked around, everything glowed with ultraviolence, purples, and blues. I covered my ears with my hands, but the screech wasn't just auditory. As I faced the house, I observed a sound wave pulse originating from that direction. I closed my eyes, trying to control my breathing, and walked back. Even though my eyes were closed, I still saw the sound waves with each step I took.

Dad found me dozing off in the hammock under the gazebo. Rain clouds had thickened in the sky, and the first few drops were falling. The whole day passed like a fever dream, and by around 9 p.m., my dad escorted me to my room to ensure I reached it this time.

Daylight spilt through the windows, the sky blue and clear. A light breeze swayed the curtains, carrying a fresh, earthy scent on its flanks. Seated on my bed, I finished up the last task on my to-do list. I hadn't played cello for a few days and knew my fingers would come at me with a vengeance the longer I postponed.

I arranged the chair to face the mirror, sat down in position with my cello, and did some warmups. My fingertips stung, as anticipated, but

I pushed through, evolving it into a simple melody. Movement caught my eye, and I looked up into the mirror as a ripple ran through the silver surface. I stopped playing, my heart thumping against my neck. It didn't move again, and I wondered if it had been a trick of the light. I turned my seat around to face my bed and continued playing. After a few minutes, a whisper caressed the back of my neck, sending a shiver down my arms, but I ignored it and focused on the improvisation I was experimenting with. I made myself focus on the slides, climbs and turns, but I noticed the air shift behind me.

The trapdoor creaked and stole my focus as it lifted. I was expecting my dad. I did not expect red hair. As Adrian emerged, I shot up from the chair, and he turned to me with a crooked smile. He was inside my house. He was in my *room*.

"Adrian." I breathed, my heart hammering against my chest. Without a thought, I put my cello against the chaise and caught myself almost running to him. A wicked smile curved his lips. My thoughts went wild. "You can't be in here; my parents will flip. How did you even know where my room was?" I walked right up to him and pushed against his chest, willing him back down the stairs. A hidden compartment in my brain was quite aware of my hands on him and how bold I was being. The panic surpassed the awkwardness. He gave a lazy step back and then locked into place like a tower. I looked up at him, and my heart skipped a beat. His molten eyes penetrated right into my soul.

"I'm not going anywhere, Josilyn." The softness and determination in that sentence completely disarmed me, and my heart felt warm and large. My cheeks flushed red, and I removed my hands from him, my palms warm from the contact. I took a step back and didn't know what to do with my dangling arms.

"How did you know this was my room? The house is enormous." Without breaking eye contact, he stooped, closed the trapdoor, and came back up slowly. My heart went wild.

"I followed the music, of course." He had something in his other hand, I noticed for the first time. It was a violin case. No, a viola.

"What's that?" I don't know why I asked. He smiled, brushing my arm as he walked past, and put the case on my bed.

"I thought we could play together." He removed something from the case that looked like a crossbow.

"Electric," I said out loud. I'd never seen an electric viola before. It looked like a weapon. He offered it to me like one would offer a sword.

"Electric has a certain… spark, which I prefer above traditional." He smiled as I took it from him. He chuckled. "I guess you can play it now." I looked up into his mischievous eyes.

"Not quite…" I found it strange that I hadn't shifted. If I had, the answer would've been yes. But maybe it was better this way. My psyche didn't need any more exhaustion. "It's beautiful." I handed it back, and he smiled. The prospect of playing with him sent a thrill through me.

"I was wondering what you played." I took my cello and sat down on the chair again. "What did you have in mind?"

"I'll lead. You fill in." His eyes danced as he positioned the viola and placed the bow on the strings. He dragged it over the open D string. It was a little rough, but it worked with the rock vibe. I was pretty impressed with his playing. He looked comfortable and natural, like it was routine. I listened as he played and accompanied him. It was a strange sensation, synchronising with someone with no sheet music, to improvise a composition without any previous duets, and above all, as my "natural" self because I wasn't using my gift at all.

It twisted and shifted into a high-paced, intense, dark Persian rock storm. My heart soared, the ecstasy distilled in my blood until I felt like I would float. A breeze touched my back as we played, and my mind took note. Adrian's eyes, for a moment, drifted behind me, before locking with me again. Something felt strange. I looked up at him, both still playing, eyes locked, and it felt like I was moving backwards, my chair gliding on a frictionless surface. My bow slipped on a string and distorted.

I stopped playing, turned around, and gasped. The pitch-black doorway syphoned me in—a feather in a vacuum's way. I wanted to jump from the chair, but my legs were immobile. My heart raged against my chest and a scream itched in my throat, but nothing came out.

Somehow, through sheer force of will, I threw myself from the chair.

~

Laura found me sitting in my car before class, staring into nothing. When I looked in the mirror that morning, I'd found a massive bruise on my right, my upper thigh, hip, and back, but I couldn't recall what had caused it. When she knocked on my window, I jumped, my senses toppling, but not enough to cause the usual distortion. I got out.

"You almost gave me a heart attack just now." The sky was dark like it had been the past few days. I was aware of yelling somewhere in the distance.

"I mean, maybe you needed the wake-up call. You look like you haven't slept." The adrenaline did wake me up from the numbness I had felt the past few days.

"I feel like I haven't either."

"Yeah, I particularly like the corpse bride aesthetic of the dark circles around your eyes and existential dread inside them."
I nodded as we walked toward the building.
"Thanks. I got up early to get the makeup just right."

"Great, but I think you could've spent the time better. By sleeping, for instance."

"Thank you, I'll bear that in mind for tomorrow." My dad had found me wandering around the house again the night before.

The screaming got louder. Small crowds gathered on the lawn, more than usual, avoiding entering the building. I soon understood why.

An old man garbed in dirty, torn rags stood by the front door, yelling. He held up a piece of cardboard, on which was scrawled in what looked like burned chalk: *"Purgatory is coming"*.

It was unnerving. A part of me wanted to avoid him, and another wanted to stare. Some laughter buzzed around us, probably a device born from discomfort. His beard was stained yellow, and shoulder-length, knotted grey hair coiled from a dirty, tattered beanie. But these things didn't keep my mind long. His eyes, white as bones, had no pupils. Was that even possible? I had never seen blind eyes like that. Had he ever seen, or was he born like that? I wondered at the wicked cards life must've dealt him.

He stared out wildly into nowhere and bellowed in a raspy, soul-scratching voice.

"The horrors will know no end… You will beg for death, but you will not find it! Cease your foolish ways! Mercy's cup has run dry, but your tears never will!" He repeated this over and over again. Something in the timbre of his voice disturbed me, and I wanted to remove myself as quickly as possible. I looked at Laura and saw she, too, felt uncomfortable. It was unclear what he expected from us, the audience… No instructions, just fire and brimstone. We would have to pass him, eventually. Our classes would soon start, and he didn't look like he was going anywhere soon. Someone asked where campus security was. We cautioned closer, trying to go unnoticed, but someone shoved past me and propelled me right into the old man. My senses shook, and I scrambled to regain my balance and escape, but he grabbed my shoulders, his fingers digging into my skin.

"Hey, watch it, you idiot!" I heard Laura yell after the guy who'd shoved me. It sounded like she wanted to chase him down and tackle him.

The old man's eyes were wide and wild.

"Sorr—" He interrupted my apology, his mouth falling open, and I felt the odorous breath on my skin. I tried to pull away but couldn't.

"Let go of me." My voice was small. His blind eyes darted from side to side as if images were flashing before him. His voice was almost inaudible, but distinctly desperate and… scared.

He spoke in short, rushed bursts.

"It's here," he panted, hyperventilating. "Beware—the pathfinder. They've come."

Just as Laura was about to insert herself into our entanglement, demanding he release me, he let go and stormed off. We looked at each other, my shock mirrored on her face. She put her hands on my shoulder, as he had done, except a lot gentler.

"Are you alright?" Concern radiated from her eyes.

"No, but I will be." I felt shaken. Being seized and having ominous things whispered to me was the last thing I needed.

Her eyes blazed with anger, and she stepped away.

"I'm going to punch that guy in the throat when I see him again. What a selfish douchebag." Her righteous anger made me feel a little better, I would admit. We reached our class just in time.

"Did you hear what he said?" I whispered to Laura. I just wanted it out of my head.

"No, I was etching that bastard's face into my mind, so I know who to punch. But please don't worry about what he said… whatever it was, it's probably a bunch of nonsense. Just let it go, Josilyn." The whole ordeal had left me feeling icky on the inside. When Dagworth entered, I was thankful for the distraction

~

I woke up just before 6 a.m. on Friday, disoriented and confused, as I'd been the entire week. I shot upright, and my eyes darted to the mirror, but was unsure what I expected. The last depot of images and impulses faded into oblivion. I saw an odd reflection. It looked like someone was sleeping on the chaise. I moved to get up and noticed I was wearing the previous day's clothes.

"Are you awake?" My dad whispered. As a precaution, I looked at my hands.

"Yes." He sat up and looked at me. It was still quite dark, and I couldn't see much. "Why did you sleep on my chaise, Dad?" He put his feet on the floor, back towards me, and stayed quiet for a moment.

"Let's get some coffee." Something about the way he said it sent a chill down my spine. I winced from the bruise on my side when I got up.

"You okay?"

"M-hmm."

He made the coffee in silence, and I made myself some oatmeal.

"How are you doing, Honey?" He asked after he put my mug on the counter. My heart raced. No use lying; he'd found me sleepwalking multiple times throughout the week and I looked like hell most days.

"I'm tired." I gave him a wan smile.

"Was the move hard for you? I know this is quite different from what you were used to."

"No! I mean, it is a lot of change, but I'd still rather be here than back there."

He nodded.

"Do you have too much pressure with your studies? Do you feel out of your depth?"

I almost laughed, but stopped myself.

"No, not at all. It's great. I enjoy being around musicians and living in such a beautiful town. It's more exciting than stressful."

"Alright," he took a deep breath and looked at me seriously, "Has anything happened that you might... not want to talk about? It's okay if you prefer not to tell me, but I think it would be good to talk to someone. I can ask around for recommendations."

I blinked at him. Was he suggesting a psychologist? I couldn't suppress a nervous giggle.

"Uh, no, Dad. Nothing traumatising has happened." I thought back on the crazy old man earlier in the week, but that didn't count. Adrian's face flashed through my mind, but though feelings could be frightening, it would be unfair to attribute the week's goings on to him. I took a deep breath. "Look, I know you're trying to figure out what's going on, but there's nothing I can think of. I'm not unhappy otherwise. My dreams are just super vivid since we moved here. Maybe I just need to exercise."

He sighed.

"Look, Honey, I'll be very frank; you're freaking me out a little, and your mom is very worried, especially after last night." He paused and gave me a pointed look. I stared back at him, questioning. I recalled nothing from the previous night. "It seems you don't remember last night, which is even more disturbing. When I went to check that you'd locked your trapdoor, I found you lying against the mirror. You were unreactive when I tried waking you. Your eyes were open, and vacant as you stared at nothing. Your pupils were so dilated that there was no blue." His voice caught with the last word, and he took a deep breath to calm himself. I couldn't blame him for being worried. That would've freaked me out, too.

"I'm sorry, Dad." I felt so bad for putting him through that.

"You're not doing it on purpose. But I can't let you go on like this. I've booked a doctor's appointment for this morning. I'll go with you." My heart dipped. Seeing a doctor felt extreme, but if it gave my dad peace of mind, I would cede. With the matter settled, we finished our coffee in silence.

I couldn't recall if I'd showered the previous night, so I went upstairs to prepare and message Laura that I would miss class. A shudder ran through me at my reflection in the bathroom mirror. I looked deranged. My knotted, blackish mess of hair against my pale, worn complexion had me looking like I had stumbled from a bad horror movie. The warm water felt good—soothing—and

I stood under the pouring water for a long while, not thinking. My body was exhausted, like it was fighting a subconscious battle.

A knock came from the door.

"Honey, you'll have to finish up." The water muffled my dad's voice. Reluctant, I got out and put on the random items I had picked out. Tji-Tji was waiting outside the door. I hadn't seen her for a while and picked her up for a hug. She was so soft and cuddly. I remembered her scratching me and looked at the scars on my hand. Why did she do that?

I was unsure how my day would work out, so I still took my bag, which felt like it weighed a hundred pounds.

Before I left my room, I found myself staring at the mirror, fascinated and hypnotised. When my dad called me from the hollow, I forced myself to break free. I was baffled. My nightmares all felt so real, but no matter how hard I tried, they slipped away from me. The sole remnant in my memory was the vivid fear, but not *why* I'd felt it.

Dark grey clouds stained the otherwise icy blue sky, and the green of the lawn and trees almost blinded me. My dad tried to drive, but his height made it difficult to operate the car while squeezed into the small space. Thus, the responsibility fell on me, the mentally incapacitated individual going to the doctor for falling asleep at random.

The practice was in the old town, a few blocks from the boutique. We soon experienced the advantage of having a tiny car when it fit into a spot no other car would've. A message came through on my phone. Laura.

> Is everything okay, though? Please let me know what the doctor says. I'm glad you're going.

With my dad beside me, I completed the forms. I'd had to do this quite a bit throughout my lifetime, so I had the gist. Dad stayed in the waiting room when I went in.

Doctor Lambert was in his late forties, quite docile and smiley. His hands were cold, and his office smelled of too-strong mints, which he was sucking and chewing throughout the consultation. He took all my vitals and asked if I'd always had low blood pressure. I had. My reflexes were sluggish, and my breathing rate low. When he asked about the reason for my visit, I told him in broad strokes: the sleepwalking, the brain fog, the moments of disassociating, my memory and focus being almost non-existent. He turned the light off and checked my eyes. My pupil stability was off, whatever that meant.

It was unsurprising when he informed me I was sleep-deprived and that we'd have to monitor my sleepwalking. I told him about my nightmares but didn't elaborate because I didn't want to open a can of worms. He said if the sleepwalking and nightmares persisted, I should consider seeing a psychiatrist because it sounded like I might be veering into sleeping disorder territory. However, as a start, I should minimise stressors, get some exercise and sleep as much as I could. He recommended I skip class that day. I was given powerful sleeping pills and instructed to take only half a tablet before bed, as a full one could easily incapacitate someone my size until Sunday. He was about to write me a referral letter, in case the symptoms continued.

"That won't be necessary. I know one. We didn't think it was necessary for that route from the get-go." Thoughts mulled behind his glasses, but if he had questions, he kept them to himself, and nodding, added that I could just call his practice if I changed my mind.

I'd seen a few GPs growing up, none of which knew what was going on with me. Of course, I'd been young, so I'd withheld no details from them. I'll never forget how one had looked at me after I'd described the things I saw. He'd arranged an appointment with a psychiatrist who, after examining me, told me of someone he knew who might be better suited for my specific spectrum of oddities. Doctor Nishati was, indeed, far better suited to help me. He had begun his career not as a doctor but as a physicist with a focus on quantum mechanics. I had no bad memories of him, but thinking about him reminded me of how far from normal I was. He'd known I was not just psychotic or schizophrenic, and he'd been intrigued to hear what I saw and experienced. Over time, he had explained his theories and how I tied into them. From a theoretical viewpoint, all matter, alive or inanimate, has a type of *personality*. Or something to that effect. All matter produced an energy pulse, though not visible or tangible in our dimension. He believed they were separated into another dimension, yet still connected. It was a foreign concept, which I hadn't thought about for a while. According to him, the human heart's energy pulse influenced its surroundings for a few kilometres. I was unsure what the *'influence'* entailed. He'd theorised I had somehow found a *'glitch'* in the dimensions and was observing the energy pulses of all matter around me. A wild idea, but it made sense in a way. Of course, he'd run a few tests on me, the results of which had supported his theory.

Dad sat outside in the piazza at a cafe, drinking coffee and eating a scone. Deep in thought, he only noticed me when I pulled out the chair to join him.

"Excuse me Miss, this chair is taken." I sat down and looked at him. My side hurt, and I bit my lip so he wouldn't see me cringe.

"So, what's happening? Are you turning into a werewolf or something?"

I chuckled and shook my head.

"Nothing that exciting, I'm afraid. Just standard sleep deprivation." Well, maybe not standard. "He gave me sleeping pills and recommended I skip class today. I have a note in case that's an issue, but I have no compulsory items today. Not that I'm aware of, anyway." I got my phone out and updated Laura. She messaged back saying she had told me to cut back on my nocturnal activities and look where not listening had landed me. I smiled.

"Sleep deprivation. What about your nightmares?" My heart jumped a little.

"He said if it persists, I should see a psychiatrist," I hesitated the rest on my tongue, "I could be veering into sleeping disorder territory." He pressed his lips into an awkward smile and nodded.

"I see."

"Are you coming home with me?" I asked after he'd paid, and we were walking to the car.

"Um, would you drop me off at the library on your way? Do you feel up to driving home alone?"

"No, I'm good. I'll go slow."

The library was outside the old town, a little further than the university. As I drove past the building in the distance, I thought of Adrian again, my heart speeding up. I longed to see him, even just a glimpse. The last time I'd seen him had been the previous week on the boat. Was it the previous week?

"Dad, have you ever heard a myth about pathfinders? I think it has something to do with an apocalypse." He looked at me, an eyebrow cocked.

"I'm a little surprised. It's not a well-known legend. In fact, I doubt you'll find anything about it. The legend goes that anyone with misguided intentions will inadvertently cause the apocalypse. They will have no idea what the consequences of their actions will be. The unwitting culprits are called the '*Riders of the Apocalypse*', though it won't necessarily be more than one. Pathfinders can be anything which catalyses the onset of the apocalypse. It could be one decision someone makes to cause their path to slip. A butterfly effect if you will. That's it. You won't find anything more."

Beware the pathfinder, he had said. *They've come.*

We drove down a tree-lined road and at a T-junction, took a left turn into the library lot. The gigantic building was of a similar style to the town, except for the massive columns on the building façade, making it look like an ancient temple.

"What's going on here?" My dad voiced. Only then did I register the droves of people in front of the building and the police cars present.

Chapter 8

I parked as close as possible, and as we neared the scene, the shouts crystallised into questions amid a frenzy of flashing cameras.

"We're not getting anywhere like this. One at a time, please," a man with buzzed grey hair and a starkly lined mouth standing on the elevated porch instructed. He stood tall and straight, with an authoritative air about him. Hands flew up and blocked him from view.

"That's the mayor," Dad whispered. I wondered for a moment if this was why he wanted to come, but he looked as surprised as me. We seemed to have stumbled onto an important press conference.

"You over there, with the weird tie."

"Mayor, what's caused this migration? Will they die?"

Migration? Die?

"We're investigating, but have no firm answers at this stage. Everyone is stunned by this. As far as we can tell, this is unnatural. You." He pointed at the next questioner.

"What precautions are being taken to prevent extinction?"

"We are busy with preservation measures, but recapture is difficult because they are delicate. Fortunately, researchers on the other side have found a remnant colony. Not all is lost, though this could be a massive blow to their numbers."

"They're delicate yet travelled over an ocean and survived. How is that possible?"

Crossed an ocean? Birds?

"What are they talking about?" I whispered to my dad, who only shrugged.

"We don't have answers at this stage. We suspect they landed on a ship and spread when it docked this side. That's only a theory. Mercifully, we are quite similar to their natural habitat. We can't tell how old they are yet, but their lifespan appears to have increased. UNEP is aiding the investigation. This is all we can disclose at this stage, so I call this meeting to an end."

He turned and walked into the building. The crowd disapproved and buzzed to life, screaming questions that went unanswered. The UN was helping? Sounded serious. Police blocked the steps to the sizeable front door the mayor had disappeared through.

"What do you want to do? Doesn't look like you'll get access to the library." I asked Dad. He shifted around as he investigated the scene.

"I think I'll linger a while. Worst case, I'll read and wait for your mom. You can go home, don't worry about me." I stayed.

The crowd dispersed after a while. A policeman kept his eye on us and came closer when we approached the steps.

"Sorry, sir, the press-conference is over." He held up a hand, which I found irritating.

"I'm here for the library. When will it re-open?" The young officer appeared a little taken aback and asked us to wait as he ran up the stairs and slipped inside. He returned soon. "The library is open; you can go ahead, sir." He smiled and let us pass. Through a window, I saw the mayor looking at us. The ordeal intrigued me and I wanted to know what had migrated. We entered the large, high-ceilinged antique athenaeum. The bookcases were dark wood and reached the wooden roof. The floor was dark wood too, with a massive yellow and blue Persian carpet at the entrance. It looked more like a museum than a library.

"Joseph. Didn't expect you." The mayor came closer and shook my dad's hand, then mine. "Hi, I don't think we've met, but I saw you at the ball. Josilyn, is it?" I was taken by surprise, but his face seemed familiar. I confirmed my identity, and he introduced himself as Hector.

"Not to pry, but what's going on?" my dad asked. Hector sighed and shook his head.

"The *Morpho Peleides* butterfly—discovered a considerable horde in the district. We have no clue how they arrived here. They could have flown, or maybe a black-market trade went awry. We're investigating. We only discovered it a few days ago."

My senses shifted but quickly normalised. A frown formed on my dad's forehead, and he blinked as if the information didn't compute.

"You see the dilemma? Everyone is baffled."

"Quite a mystery indeed."
I lingered, watching my dad absorb the information.

"Indeed. The natives on the other side are grieving. They're very superstitious with their mystical beliefs about the butterfly, and now it's leaving… You can imagine the chaos. They're saying it's the end of the world." A chill ran down my spine because we had just discussed the apocalypse. My heart drummed faster. And as they talked on, my mind checked out—I wandered about. A large wooden frame on the wall drew me in. It resembled a map or an aerial photo, but the landscape's shape looked strange, as if drawn from an odd perspective. Curious, I walked closer. The map was about as long and wide as a standard door. As I studied the heavy wooden frame, the golden words at the bottom caught my attention: '*Zerezin Mountain, 'The Crescent', Ostia region, 1859*'. It felt weird, history captured inside a frame. The Crescent. It was an appropriate name for the crescent-shaped volcano half surrounding the lake and town like a crescent moon. The lake's water was bright blue on the map, too. Our house was also depicted on the map, though small.

"Honey?"

I turned at my dad's voice. From the way they were both looking at me, I had the sense he had been trying to catch my attention for a while. Sheepish, I smiled, my cheeks flushing with embarrassment.

"Sorry."

He told me to go home—Mom would pick him up. So, I said my goodbyes and left. A few policemen, still stationed outside, watched me as I walked to the car. I almost forgot how to walk and clicked my tongue when I realised the car was still unlocked. I really had to stop doing that.

It was difficult to focus on driving, I had to admit. When I hit the main road, my mind switched to autopilot. I was more exhausted than I'd realised, and as I turned onto the winding road, I struggled to keep my eyes open.

A thought seeped into my consciousness. It will be at least another three days until I see Adrian. I missed him and wished I could see him.

I missed him.

A shiver ran through me. What a strange feeling. What would Laura tell him if he asked about me? "She looked like hell the whole week and went to the doctor. She's sleep-deprived and won't come in today." No matter how it's phrased, it wouldn't sound good. What would he make of it?

When I refocused, I felt disoriented, having already reached the piece of forest bordering the lake. The water was a sombre shade of grey today instead of the usual blue, reflecting the mountain like a mirror. The map came to mind, the perfect, smooth curve around the lake. I found it difficult to look away until it disappeared behind the thick trees as the forest swallowed me.

As I drew closer, I thought about what I would do now. It was still morning, and I'd have the house to myself until late afternoon, but I wasn't in the mood for anything specific, not even sleeping. An undertone of irritation simmered beneath my consciousness, though I couldn't identify the cause. I passed through the stone arch into the clearing. The day was beautiful, with light clouds overhead and the perfect temperature. Not hot. Not cold.

I reversed my car into the usual spot, now facing the lake. From this vantage point, the town was visible on the other side. I sat in the car, absorbing the virid scene and the fairy-tale setting that I now call home and I wanted to pinch myself. Sometimes I expected to wake up back in Weatonburg, passed out on my floor from the heat. I wondered for the first time: what did my ancestor, the noblewoman, think about this place? Was it a fairy tale to her, despite the sad circumstances of her stay, or was she used to beauty like this? I stepped out and inhaled the fresh scent permeating the air. My senses folded, and I buckled against the car. I shook my head and sighed. A magpie's song echoed nearby. I climbed onto the Zastava's bonnet and sat right in the middle, so I wouldn't roll off. I kept sliding a little.

I retrieved my phone to take a picture and checked if I had any messages. An unopened email lay in my inbox from the GP, which got me thinking. I scrolled through my contacts and found myself staring at the number. On impulse, I pushed the dial button and put the phone to my ear, my heart racing.

The line connected—a brief silence. "Hello?" The tone uncertain.

I fumbled. "Err, hello. Sorry for calling. I'm… not… I didn't think this through." The blood rushed through my head. Although I felt the sudden urge to hang up, I knew that would just be rude. I hadn't talked to Doctor Nishati in over six years. I was surprised the number was still active.

"It's okay, Josilyn. You wouldn't have called if there wasn't something going on. When I gave you this number, I said you could call whenever you need to. I'm glad you did." My eyes burned, and I bit my lip. I swallowed the lump in my throat and stayed quiet for a while, not trusting my voice. He spoke again.

"Are you still living in Weatonburg?" I cleared my throat and informed him we had moved and that I was attending university now. He was delighted I was continuing with music. After a while of small talk, he steered the conversation to my shifts, wondering whether the new environment had affected them. It was difficult, but I was honest about how they'd become more intense, teetering into hallucinations that blurred with my dreams. He always had this sympathetic way about him that made me feel safe and comfortable sharing, and I told him about the sleepwalking, my throat tightening. The sleeping pills, and the GP's opinion that I should see a psychiatrist if the sleep-deprivation continued. About my dad finding me on the floor, my intense nightmares I couldn't recall afterwards. The fear that simmered like an afterburn. How everything seemed blurred and locked up in the back of my mind.

I heard him writing, mumbling under his breath, "Amnesia, REM Sleep Behaviour Disorder, hypnogogic hallucinations, sleep paralysis… parasomnia…"

I'd never heard of most of those. It felt strange to examine my sleep patterns with him. Upon hearing the name of the sleeping pills, he confirmed it would've been his first choice too.

"So, from what you're telling me, you're displaying a combination of sleeping disorders. First, sleepwalking, which is odd because it's uncommon in adults, especially developing it this late. Most sufferers can remember their midnight adventures, which you don't. Second, REM Sleep Behaviour Disorder symptoms, where you get up and react to your dreams. Third, sleeping paralysis, which explains the memories of intense fear and hallucinations. But one cannot move during such episodes, hence the name. You also mentioned hallucinating while awake. We can monitor this, but parasomnia caused by sleep deprivation sounds like the diagnosis I'd gravitate towards."

My heart dropped. I protested, saying that the night excursions caused the sleep deprivation, not the other way around. He said it could be either way and repeated the GP's instruction to get rest and reduce stress. He thought it would be interesting to observe how *my* mind reacted to a sleep disorder, as my condition would likely cause it to manifest differently. We talked some more, he told me to keep him posted, and we said goodbye. Sighing, I watched the wind sway through the trees before walking around to the front door. I preferred that entrance because the foyer was so regal. I must confess, hearing the diagnosis from Nishati had lifted a burden from my shoulders and given me a lot more clarity.

Something shifted inside me, and a sudden euphoria flushed through my body. I opened the front doors and left them open as I turned into the parlour. Sunlight streamed through the windows, making the room look like a bibliophile's fantasy. Years had passed since I last indulged in anything non-academic to read. I wasn't a reader, but my mom and dad had quite the collection. I perused the spines on the shelves, hoping one would entice me.

'*Butterfly Encyclopaedia: Myths & Facts*' caught my attention.

Strange how you never noticed something until it unlocked somewhere inside your brain, then you saw it everywhere. It resided on the second-highest shelf, and I used the dark wooden ladder to reach it. It was difficult to extract, squeezed between its neighbours, and heavier than expected. I wondered if it had pictures of the *Morpho Peleides* they were talking about at the library.

I settled on the dark green Chesterfield sofa. The first few pages were quite dull; twenty-four thousand species, life cycle… *blah blah*. Luckily, the exciting stuff followed this introduction: myths and lore.

Greek mythology portrayed the daemon Thanatos as a young child holding a butterfly. The Greek word for butterfly was the same as soul or life, but, ironically, Thanatos was the personification of death. Children represented innocence, but here one was the harbinger of death. He was not a well-known figure in Greek mythology, with little said about him apart from being the twin brother of Sleep, the sons of Night and Darkness.

My stomach twisted just imagining butterflies migrated here because of a Greek god who had a twin called Sleep. A discomforting thought. Most mythologies contained some variation of butterflies representing the human soul. I didn't know this, but flames also drew them, like a moth. Certain tribes drew the parallel that so, too, our souls were drawn to heaven. The butterfly, both beautiful and fragile, shared these traits with the soul. I read on through legends, becoming bored before remembering my initial purpose. I was about to page to the index when a ghost-like butterfly drew my attention, and I read the little extract.

Dreams are exerted by the Soul Butterfly, which wanders around peoples' minds to find its own peace… The Soul Butterfly was described as an entity.

I flipped back to the index, found the name, and turned to a page adorned with six pictures. My eyes zoomed in on a shade of blue, so pure and beautiful—resplendent.

I read the description three times before the words sunk in. *Morpho Peleides.* Stunned, I turned the pages back and forth to look at the other *Morpho* species, and the *Morpho Didius* caught my eye. Although they hadn't been mentioned at the library, I was sure I had seen one before.

I lay back and stared at the beautiful creatures.

When I woke up, the book was resting on my face. I sat up—eyes heavy. The clock on the wall showed 1:39 p.m. I estimated I arrived home at around 11 a.m. Hunger squeezed my stomach, and I was happy to find leftovers from supper.

I wandered down the hall, aimless and unsure of what to do with myself. I stood staring out the front door. Wispy clouds threw slight shadows that danced like waves on the grass. I fished my knotted earphones from my bag in the parlour and went outside, planning to lie on the grass and enjoy the weather. I had never done so, and the impending novel experience was exhilarating. As I lay down, I grimaced from the bruise on my side, which had begun to yellow. I stuffed my hair under my neck so the grass wouldn't poke me. I found the song on my mind, maxed the volume, and pressed play. My senses shifted, and it felt good, like stretching a muscle that had been forced to stay in one position for too long. Goosebumps ran over my skin, fluorescent colours shone around me, and I breathed the sound of music.

The next song was a gothic rock favourite, and I sang along at the top of my lungs. They had the perfect dark and epic rock harmony that scratched my brain. Sometimes bands tried too hard and ended up being corny and overly theatrical, but this band was acquitted of that sin. I looped the song a few times before letting the playlist shuffle. Shade and light danced over my closed eyelids as clouds shifted overhead.

A dark, thick shadow passed over my face, its consistency scratched a part of my brain that others hadn't. I opened my eyes to the now darkened clouds, though the sharpness of the refracted light stung them. I was about to close them again when something in my peripheral vision caught my attention, and I stiffened. My heart rate climbed. I wanted to look at my hands but was too scared to move. Something big lay on the grass a few feet away, but I couldn't distinguish enough detail to recognise a shape. My hands were on my chest, and as subtly as I could manage, I pinched myself. It hurt enough to confirm that I was awake.

The loud music now tormented me, robbing my sense of hearing—a survival instinct often taken for granted. Mom said wild animals didn't come here. I hoped she was right.

Unable to fight the compulsion any longer, I turned my head. Blood rushed through me, hot and dangerous. My heart skipped a beat.

"Adrian," I breathed, as if punched. He was leaning on one elbow, body angled towards me, gazing at me with a bemused smile. His eyes sparkled.

I wanted to pinch myself again. I couldn't believe he was there. As I sat up, I took the earphones out.

"Josilyn." Endorphins flooded my veins. Just like the first time I saw him, his beauty hit me like a bomb. *Like a bomb*. My face lit up like a beacon. He'd been gone so long, maybe his feelings for me had changed in the meantime. I didn't give him much hope, so it would be fair. I composed myself—or as my dad would say, 'pulled myselves towards myself'—and lay back down, staring at the sky.

"It's rude to stare." The rawness in my voice left me queasy.

"My mistake," his dark voice slid into my lungs and unfurled, a shock to my sobered senses. "I was under the impression you were giving a show since I could hear you down by the lake." Light tones wove through his voice, and I knew he was smiling. I couldn't help myself. As I turned to face him again, my cheeks burned at the sight of his radiant smile. I loved that smile. My heart skipped a beat, and I smiled too, giddy at the sight of him. I diverted my eyes to the sky, embarrassed at my reaction. And he'd heard me sing. I hoped I sounded alright. Was this normal? I didn't know. I knew I could sing, so my self-doubt was illogical.

He found this all amusing and chuckled. Something in its registry was altered, and I looked at him again. He was now only two feet away. He had moved closer without me realising. My heart dipped before galloping like a wild horse. His proximity caused blood to rush through my body as the heat radiated from him. A dark musk scent washed over me, and I closed my eyes briefly from the sensory overwhelm, my senses hanging on a precipice. His lips curved into a wicked smile as these thoughts mulled over in my mind.

"You have a lovely voice." His words were a warm blanket.

"How long have you been lying here?" My airway was tight. He inhaled deeply, and I swore I could feel air flow over me towards him.

Goosebumps.

"I entered the clearing as you lay down. You may do the math if you'd like."

A shiver ran through me. From the number of songs I'd listened to, that would be about forty minutes ago. Had he been silently staring at me the whole time? I thought my embarrassment had reached its saturation point, but I was mistaken. My head was about to burst from too much blood. I shook my head and pursed my lips. I wasn't going to say anything further, though I ached to ask where he had been for the last ten days. It became apparent I didn't have the nerve to ask for his number. I wasn't sure where we stood now, after our last conversation. A million thoughts, but no words.

Silence lingered.

He caved. My heart warmed in a more literal sense than I could explain.

"I was eager to see you, but you were not in class." He paused, waiting for me to speak, but I did not. "Laura mentioned you'd not be in today but wouldn't elaborate. It was quite troubling if I'm being truthful.

And I was unwilling to let another day pass without seeing you. I soaked up the opportunity to watch you enjoy yourself."

What was it about his voice that made my entire being react? He was a siren, and I—bewitched by the song that lured me to my death. Unable to resist anymore, I looked at him. His eyes were intolerably tender, and my insides melted. I wanted to throw myself at him, ease the concern lurking in the depths of his eyes. I couldn't look at him anymore and shifted my eyes to the house. He drew me like a magnet, and it took physical restraint not to look at him.

"I went to the doctor. I've had some sleeping problems which worried my dad," that was all I wanted to say, but realised if I stopped, I'd have to look at him. "The doctor booked me off so I can rest because I'm sleep-deprived."

He didn't react, and after a long silence, I grew uncomfortable and dared to look at him again—a *big* mistake.

He bit his lip and studied my face with a worried expression, searching for more than I was giving. His concern touched me—stirred something deep inside me.

"It's not *that* bad." My voice was hoarse. He avoided *my* eyes this time, and it felt like punishment. Was that how he felt when I did the same?

"It's no mild matter when a doctor diagnoses you with sleep deprivation three weeks into your semester," he paused and casually took my hand from where it rested on my stomach. I inhaled sharply. Fire and ice erupted through my veins; ice because it was unexpected, fire because somehow his hand was warmer than I remembered. Seeming lost in thought, he played with my hand.

"What sleeping problems do you have?" He looked at me again. It felt like taking a breath after a long time underwater. It was an intimate paradox—relief that he looked at me but agitated because he was now holding my hand while doing so. My heart swelled. His eyes held no falsehood and gave nothing away. But why was I guarded?

I had to revise my English vocabulary to speak, but struggled to hide my shaky voice. He must have thought me foolish.

"Um –paranormia, or some—"

"Parasomnia," he corrected gently and continued playing with my hand. Distracting. I couldn't look away from him. How did he know that term?

"Yes. Although, he said I have a weird combination of a few. Some don't make sense." My thoughts drifted to the conversation with Nishati, but my mind was foggy, and I struggled to recall it.

Though I managed to refocus, I soon fell back into chaos. His face was only a few inches from mine, and my heartbeat was erratic, but I couldn't tell if he had come closer or had pulled me closer.

I was unsure how far I was from falling off the edge. His emerald eyes torched my skin. Too green. Too deep. Their abyssal quality swallowed me whole. He whispered as his gaze drifted from my eyes to my lips and back again.

Stop that, my psyche screamed.

"Which did he mention?" His voice was hoarse. I knew I didn't have the strength, but I had to stop this. My breathing sped up, and I bit down on my cheek and, with my free hand, pressed my thumbnail into my index finger; my lips were a no-go. I was caught in his web. I tried to clear my throat. Why couldn't I succumb? I feared what I didn't know.

"Um, sleepwalking, paralysis, nightmares," my words stumbled out incoherently as his gaze locked on my lips, and he came closer.

Oh no. I couldn't move. If my heart beat any faster, it would rival the performance of a fourteen-cylinder engine throbbing in my neck.

"What do you see?" His whisper was barely audible, his breath on my skin, his eyes fixed on my lips.

How did he expect me to make any sense now? It was difficult to speak. What did I see…? What were we talking about? An image flashed through my head, but it made little sense.

"Err, nightmare, lots of mist."

"Mist," he repeated, distant, "Interesting." He didn't seem all that interested. Not in what I had said, anyway. My gut twisted, and I felt something coming. He released my hand and trailed his fingers up my arm, over my shoulder, up my throat, and held my chin with his large hand, thumb on one side, the rest on the other. A blazing path flowed in the wake of his touch. His lips moved like he was murmuring under his breath.

I wanted to pull away but couldn't. The rest of my skin felt eerily naked without his touch. I could stay suspended in this moment for eternity; it was all that mattered.

He leaned closer and kissed my cheek. I closed my eyes as my senses fell. In a heartbeat, he retreated, and I opened my eyes. With one lithe movement, he stood and held out his hand. The sudden change of course took me by surprise, and I stared at him. Just as I thought I saw irritation on his face, he sighed and smiled. I must have seemed dull-witted, but I was confused and notably dazed. Not quite how I saw it going.

Strange, to realise I was a little disappointed, which was something to chew on. I gave him my hand and flew as he pulled me up, crashing against his chest. The breath knocked from me, my side stung, and I cringed. His chest vibrated as he laughed.

My heart fluttered from the adrenaline and pain. I was glad he didn't notice the latter because I didn't want him to let me go. As if we were dancing, he turned, walked us to the house, and lifted me onto the steps. His laughter died down, and he pressed his mouth to my ear.

"You're as light as a feather. I should stuff you with croissants more often."

His breath was hot in my ear, and I tried to gain control by pulling away, but to no avail—caught in the iron circle of his arms. His smell intoxicated me, and his body heat against me sent my pulse soaring. He laughed darkly. And it would have disturbed me if the thrumming of his heart didn't preoccupy me. It was beating like mad. He interrupted the distraction by bending low and pressing his lips to the base of my neck. I pulled away slightly from the shock.

"Don't run away from me," he whispered wickedly, his warm breath spilling over my skin. My heart convulsed. He held me tighter, and my side felt it, but I refused to say anything. He inhaled, leaving a tingling sensation on my skin. His hands ran down my arms, and releasing me, took my hand. I was dazed and disoriented, off-balance. My head swam. He ascended the stairs, my hand in his, and I followed as he led me into the house.

For the briefest moment, my mind found a gate back to reality, and I heard a car's distant roar. But I couldn't dwell on it long. He turned into the parlour and sat me down on the Chesterfield, picking up the encyclopaedia from where it lay open. I cringed from the pain and hoped it would go unnoticed. He closed the large book with one hand and put it on the coffee table. I half expected he would sit beside me, but he didn't, and I frowned at him without realising. He sauntered to a single-seater, plopped down, sighed, and smiled at me. The distance between us left me feeling naked and cold, and I blushed at the thought.

Mischief danced under his heavy eyebrows, his crooked smile pulling his cheek up.

"I don't aspire to be disrespectful the first time I meet your parents." His eyes were soft. I was confused. How would he know when he'd be meeting them? A car came to a halt outside, and the engine cut off. Doors opened and closed, and everything fell into place. The car I had heard. Mouthed agape, I looked at him.

"How did you hear them?" It explained why things ended as they did, but he must've heard the car long before me. He shook his head and chuckled.

"Perhaps you should go easy on the volume when listening to music. Anyone could have heard the engine from miles away."

The reminder of the earlier ordeal caused my cheeks to flush. I had phenomenal hearing. Voices approached, and as they stepped onto the porch, they burst into laughter. I was unprepared. Panic surfaced. What was I supposed to introduce him as?

It felt so official. So suddenly *real*. What if he was just a figment of my imagination? My heart pounded. I stared at the doorway, fidgeting with my nails. My heartbeat vibrated in my eyeballs. They would step inside any second and either confirm or debunk my sanity. Did Adrian know how anxious I was? I turned to him and jumped. He was sitting right next to me. I clutched my chest. Smiling softly, he raised his hand and delicately ran the tips of his fingers over my cheek before dropping his hand. Though he scarcely touched me, and the blazing trail faded after a second, it reassured me—brief as it was.

His eyes drifted to the door, pulling me right back to my current reality, and I shot up. My chest felt tight; I couldn't handle it. Adrian stood next to me and gently pressed his lips to my ear. What was he thinking?!

"Calm down," he whispered, and stepped away. I realised my hand had stretched out to him, and I pulled it behind my back. My heartbeat slowed. Mom was the first through the door. I felt nauseous, like all my veins were about to burst. She didn't notice us and walked past towards the hallway. My dad followed.

He noticed.

He stopped at the stairs, his eyes flowing between us before his gaze lingered on Adrian, assessing, measuring. I wished I could talk, but my throat closed up. What I suspected was a guilty and awkward smile pulled over my lips. I wanted to die.

"Evelyn?" he called, without volume, looking away, or a smile. He seemed to recollect himself, and a slow smile formed as he approached. Adrian closed the distance, holding out his hand. They shook, and a subtle jolt went through my dad's arm. So, he did exist.

"Good afternoon, Sir. I am Adrian. I met Josilyn at the ball, but I don't think we've had the pleasure." He was smooth, calm, and hypnotic. My senses dipped at his voice; the air tinged red. Everything smoothed out, the entire room at his command. Dad had a perplexed expression.

"Err, hello. No, I don't believe we have. I'm Joseph," My mom appeared. "And this is my wife, Evelyn. Honey, this is Adrian." My dad folded his arm around her, a frown cutting deep into his forehead. Adrian nodded.

"Hello. I think we exchanged brief words at the ball."

"Uh, oh… Yes, yes, I think I remember. Your hair is hard to miss. You were waiting at the front door?" He chuckled.

"Yes, that was me."

Hypnosis.

They stared at him with clouded eyes, like they were looking but not quite seeing. *Eerie.* I began doubting his existence again—looked at my hands. Baffled, I stared up at him, and he looked down at me. He smiled. My nerves cooled as he held my gaze. Many words tumbled behind his eyes.

"Well, would you like something to drink? I was just about to brew some coffee?" Mom interrupted the silent exchange. Adrian's gaze broke away, and I felt exposed. It felt like we were alone in the room. I couldn't believe I had let go like that right in front of them. I crossed my arms and stared out the window.

"No, thank you. I have to be on my way," he paused, and I felt him look at me. "Regrettably."

He was? My heart sank, but I forced myself not to look at him. I hadn't expected him to leave already.

"I dropped by on my way home to give Josilyn her class notes." I loved the way he said my name, and a thrill ran down my spine. It felt like he was casting a spell. The thought of him leaving saddened me. His visits were always so short.

"Ah, well, that's too bad. Very nice of you about the notes. But I expect you to stay longer next time. And to come by more often. We haven't met Josilyn's friends yet." my mom echoed my thoughts. I looked up at him. His smile was charming, working the crowd.

"That is my intent."

Though I yearned to hear that, my heart jumped. I didn't want us to be too obvious. If my throat was thawed, I might have screamed it out. I still felt uneasy, but it was unnecessary; Adrian played right into their books. Or perhaps it was the other way around. He reached into his dark jeans' back pocket, revealing a thick, folded wad of papers, and handed it to me. I was a little surprised that he indeed had notes for me because I assumed his comment was a red herring. If only I had a valid excuse to make him stay.

"Thanks," my voice sounded weak.

"Well, it was nice finally meeting you, Adrian! But since you're off, you'll have to excuse me," my mom gushed and fluttered off. *'Finally'* meet him? My cheeks burned.

"Yes, I'm glad to have met you," my dad added.

"Likewise, have a lovely evening," Adrian responded, and they retreated towards the kitchen. He followed them from the room, and like a shadow, I followed close behind. I ached inside, but I held my tongue.

He stopped and turned around at the front door, a mischievous smile on his face.

"See, that wasn't too bad." His eyes danced. "Goodbye, Josilyn. I'll see you soon." His voice was liquid gold. A large knot formed in my throat.

"I guess…" I smiled. "See you." It sounded even feebler than expected. I wanted him to stay but didn't know how to say it. He came closer and hugged me, but it lasted only a short moment—not even long enough to feel his heat. His scent washed over me, and I wanted to press my nose to his skin.

"Open it." He whispered against my hair, then turned around and walked away. He didn't give me a chance to say goodbye. I gazed after him, disappointed, and he half-turned, shooing me inside. That wicked smile was still there. What was he up to? I turned and threw the door shut behind me, annoyed. A gust ripped through my hair with unexpected fervour, and I turned around, surprised. I didn't push it that hard. The door was shut.

I opened the folded papers he'd given me. The first page had a written note. My mind took a moment to comprehend.

This is just a prop. I do have your class notes, but I've kept them from you for now. That gives me an excuse to bother you again this weekend.

See you soon

Adrian

At least I had another note from him to keep.

My dad appeared from the hall, his yellow footsteps registering and rolling over the ground towards me. I caught my breath, almost fumbling the note.

"Sorry kid, didn't mean to give you a fright."

My heart was racing, and I inhaled a calming breath, smiling and waving a dismissive hand.

"Coffee?" He cocked an eyebrow, as if he'd just suggested something ominous. With all the adrenaline coursing through me, I didn't need caffeine on top of that.

"Hot chocolate. I'm just going to put my bag in my room first." A long way to walk just to put my bag down, but I needed a moment after what had happened.

A song from earlier popped into my head, and I sang along as I climbed the stairs. The air was chill in the hollow.

I put my bag on the windowsill and unfolded the note again. The other papers were sheet music, and I listened as my mind played the notes. Why had he given me the sheet music? Something in my peripheral vision caught my eye. My senses drifted, and I closed my eyes. A mess of thoughts slurred through my head. I was hallucinating. When my senses were in order, I opened my eyes.

I was not hallucinating. Adrian stood at the foot of my bed with that wicked, lovely smile. I stared at him in pure astonishment, my heart racing. How in physics' name did he get in here? I wondered if there was a secret entrance that only he knew about. I opened my mouth to speak, but nothing came out. He turned to the mirror, appraising it.

"This is a beautiful relic."

"How did you get in here?" my voice uncoiled, hollow with shock. What if someone came up? The thought released panic, and I stared towards the steps. No sound was audible, and my gaze darted back to him.

He stood right before me, and I stumbled back, gasping. My heart sped up, and I absorbed his provocative smile as the waves of his scent hit me. He numbed my senses and yet ignited them simultaneously.

"How do you *do* that?" I almost yelled, but checked myself. His smile broadened, and he gazed over my head at the window with a deep, strange chuckled.

"I have my ways." His smile faltered. "I've forgotten something." His eyes were focused. Something obscured in his voice had me on edge.

"What?" I could barely hear the word. He sighed and looked at me, his eyes a raging inferno. My heart contracted. All amusement was replaced with burning intensity. No one had ever looked at me like that before, not even him.

I knew. My breaths were shallow.

He slid closer still. I backed away. His lips twisted into a smile, and he kept closing in. Each step he gave was mirrored by mine.

My heart raced, blood rushing to my cheeks. My legs hit the windowsill. Trapped.

His eyebrows raised as if asking, '*So, what now?*' I trembled. His smiled turned triumphant as he gave his last step, closing the distance. Was he insane? My dad could walk in any second. The thought didn't last long. His aroma whelmed me, the heat thickening the scent.

With slow movements, he placed his hands on the windowsill on either side of me. I felt his arms against mine. I wanted to look away, but could only look up at him. The intensity in his eyes engulfed me. He bowed his head closer, and my blood simmered.

"Don't run away from me," he whispered. A billion thoughts clogged my mind. My breathing was shallow and fast. Even if I wanted to, and I didn't, I would be unable to run. He lifted his hand and lightly brushed my lower lip with his thumb. The blood prickled under his warm touch.

It felt alien and intrusive. I wanted to escape the intensity, but his eyes pinned me down, incinerating my defences. He leaned in closer, his eyes hypnotic, his pupils large and inviting, black holes that swallowed me. My heart swelled. His arm circled me, his hand finding the small of my back, and he pulled me closer to him. His hand was so big it inflamed my entire lower back. I felt his warm breath flow lower and lower.

I stopped thinking.

He traced his nose down the bridge of mine and hovered a moment before pressing his flaming lips against mine; a deep breath escaped his lungs as he held the kiss. My lips tingled, and my lungs burned. Electricity buzzed beneath my skin; the *Pulse* eddied beneath my feet. The blood flowed through my neck to my lips and every part of my skin he touched. My eyes burned. He paused but stayed his lips. His hand moved up my back and pressed me to him as his lips moved again, slow, against mine. I didn't know what I was doing, but I followed his lead. It felt as easy as breathing, kissing him, and I melted into him. My head spun in ways I never knew were possible, and my senses burst out of place. Energy surges spat through my nerve endings and, combined with the heat; it became unbearable.

His lips became more urgent on mine as he pressed me against him with such force that I could barely breathe. It didn't matter. His hands moved over my back and shoulders, squeezing down my arms, and clasped around my wrists, lifting them behind his neck. He encircled my waist and lifted me onto my tiptoes. I found myself twisting my fingers through his silky, soft hair and pulling him closer. The heat burned through to my marrow straight into my soul. I could taste his earthy, dark scent. My blood went insane, boiling in my veins.

Without warning, he gently pulled away, and it took my all to let him. He pressed his forehead against mine before straightening up. My eyes were still closed, and I heard him blow out a breath. I could hardly breathe myself. I felt heat come closer again, and he kissed my eyes and trailed his lips up to my head, and inhaled, his nose pressed to my hair.

"Ahh," he sighed, holding me tight. "I have to go." A slow whisper, reluctance staining his voice. My eyes flashed open and met his; fuming and alive.

"They'll see you," that was not what I wanted to say, but it seemed less pathetic. What I wanted to say was: *"You can't leave. I don't want you to."* He was either oblivious to what my eyes screamed or ignoring it.

"They won't." A dark laugh reverberated from his chest. "And I think it would be prudent to wait a few minutes before you go downstairs." That wickedly amused smile shaped his lips again. It always seemed like he was hiding something and found joy in confusing me.

"What? why?" My voice was hoarse; his eyes melted.

"Trust me, okay?" His voice was impossibly tender, and I could not protest. He stroked my hair, looking over my face as if memorising it, and bowed his head down, giving me a clipped peck on my lips. Such a contrast from what happened seconds before. He let me go, and it felt cold without him close. Goosebumps ran down my spine.

"Goodbye, my Josilyn." He smiled, affection beaming from his eyes, and disappeared beneath the trapdoor. Feeling abandoned, I looked down, listening for any sounds from below—but none came. I wondered how long it would take him to slip out of the house. If he managed it, I would be thoroughly impressed, even more than I already was. I turned to look out the window and gasped aloud. He was already outside, gazing up as he walked backwards. He saw me looking at him and bowed, a jovial expression on his face.

I caught my breath. He whirled around and glided into the forest like an apparition.

As he disappeared, reality descended upon me. What had happened moments ago suddenly felt obscene, and I blushed thinking about it. I touched my lips. They were warm. Dazed, I turned around. My eyes caught my reflection in the mirror. Why did he say I should wait a while? I walked closer to investigate. I was lightheaded, almost—

My throat slammed shut in horror. A visible dark blue vein network branched over every inch of me, as if my skin was translucent. Aghast, I stared at myself and then checked my hands. They were fine. I touched my face, my arms; I was on fire. Responsive to being noticed, the blood rushed under my skin. My breaths were shallow, and I backed away from the mirror. When my calves hit the chaise, I sat, not taking my eyes off my reflection. It looked horrible and disturbing, but I felt fine. A little heady, maybe. What was going on? I stared at myself until the veins disappeared.

How long I sat there, I don't know, but I jumped when my dad called from the hollow. I double-checked myself in the mirror before heading down, feeling shaky. I was on edge and feared my dad would notice my emotional state. He handed me the cup. I braced myself, thinking he would ask about Adrian, but he didn't—only if I was still joining. I felt guilty that Adrian had snuck into my room and kissed me.

We joined my mom and Andrew in the second-floor parlour. It unnerved me even more, realising they were so close while Adrian had snuck past them. I swallowed the lump in my throat and asked my dad if the library visit was successful, but apparently it wasn't. He had filled Mom and Andrew in on my doctor's visit and the diagnosis of sleep deprivation. We talked about the medication I received and the option of visiting a psychiatrist if the problem persisted. I did not tell them I had called Nishati.

"Adrian is quite an attractive man, Josilyn," Mom commented innocently, filled with insinuations. My cheeks burned.

"Uh, yeah, he is." It felt uncomfortable saying that aloud.

"How old is he? He doesn't look first year." She was frowning now. He did not look 18, no.

"I think he said twenty-four."

"Twenty-four?" my dad seemed taken aback. "I thought he was older. How come he's in the same class as you?"

"Well, Josilyn is twenty, honey. Not everyone starts studying at eighteen." My dad nodded. Andrew quipped he was glad he'd missed him. When Mom asked why, he said Adrian was 'scary-looking'.

"He does have a presence, I'll admit. But I found him well-mannered and charming when we exchanged words at the ball. And I like the way he looks at you, Josilyn." This last part she said with a pointed smile. I looked away, sure my face was scarlet red. So much for my hopes of staying under the radar.

"By when must you take your meds?" My dad came to the rescue.

"Well, it can knock me out for eight to twelve hours, so it depends on when I want to wake up. But I was thinking about going to bed right after this." I lifted my mug. "I ate at around three, so I'm not hungry." All I wanted was to be alone, let my thoughts roam free, and process everything. I longed for Adrian's company. We'd only had a few stolen moments. Mom startled me when she reached over and took my empty cup. I hadn't realised I had finished the hot chocolate. She kissed my forehead.

"Goodnight, Hon. I hope you get some proper rest tonight." Andrew followed her out of the room, but my dad stayed. I shot up.

"Night, Dad. I'll barricade myself, just in case." I turned to the hallway.

"Josilyn?" There it was. Reluctant, I turned back.

"Yeah?"

"Did Adrian give you that fancy bracelet?"

"Yeah…"

He pursed his lips and nodded.

"I see… Well, this is a new territory for us all, so bear with me. It was inevitable, moving to a new place and you meeting new people. He seems alright. I did get a bit of a fright… he looks closer to thirty. I'm glad he isn't but try taking it slow? Rushing gets you hurt, and I don't want you going through that pain if it can be prevented." I waited for more, but that was it. My cheeks burned. He was right, this was a first, and it made me feel a little better when he looked as unsure as I felt.

"I know… I'll do my best." I was already failing.

"Alright," he stepped closer and hugged me, "Now, go medicate yourself for all our sanity's sake, please." I giggled and left.

I was relieved the conversation turned out less horrible than expected, but still wanted to get to my room. When I did, an unease licked at my neck. Being there reminded me of earlier. The kiss… the… veins. I walked to the mirror, paranoid they may have returned. To my relief, my skin was still clear, but as I stood there staring, other things became clear too. A memory surfaced like a drowned thing.

I backed away.

The night Adrian took me out on the boat. For ten days now, I couldn't remember anything about the dreams I'd had after he'd left. But after he asked me about them that afternoon, I remembered—albeit a small, incoherent detail.

My senses tumbled, a haphazard blur as the room moved around and over me, tasting purple and red, and I remembered.

Everything.

Mist pulling me into the dark mirror passage. Adrian inside my room the night of the ball. Adrian inside my room, playing the viola. Mist. So much mist.

My heart hammered against my throat, and I tasted blood in my sped-up breaths. I looked at my hands. *They were just dreams*, I told myself. I have a sleeping disorder. It made sense that I dreamt of Adrian and the ball.

I shook myself and rushed to my bag for the bottle of pills, nearly spilling the content over the floor. I gulped the tablet down, pulled on my pyjamas, and slipped into bed, unsure how the medication would affect me. Every dream I'd had flashed before me, seared into my eyes, and I squeezed them shut, humming aloud. *I didn't want to see. I didn't want to see.*

It freaked me out.

I froze.

I had swallowed a whole pill.

My eyes flashed open, and I pushed myself up. Horrified, I stared at the bottle. I couldn't reverse my stupidity. Even as I wanted to panic, I felt my body shutting down, my consciousness seeping away, and everything drained from my mind. I sagged back on the pillow. Was it supposed to be so…so…fas—…?

Dreams came. But they weren't dreams. I stumbled into a parade of my recent experiences and memories, all in the most vivid detail, like living it again. But someone had pressed fast-forward. They came in chronological order, only slowing with Adrian's kiss, and then it stopped.

Nothing but darkness accompanied me in that void.

A drumbeat echoed inside the void surrounding me, and my consciousness crawled up to the surface. I knew it in my bones; another nightmare was imminent. I refused to open my eyes. It couldn't be real; I'd taken a whole pill.

Boom. Boom. Boom.

The rhythmic pounding rolled on until I was convinced that I was awake, but my eyelids were heavy. I wasn't supposed to wake up.

Boom. Boom. Boom.

The beat was deep and low, an African drum that vibrated through my stomach. As I lay there, anticipating the hallucinations, a thought seeped into my consciousness. If it was just a dream, what was the worst that could happen if I let it play out? The idea released adrenaline through me, and my heart rate climbed. Reluctantly, I forced my heavy eyelids open. The thrum continued. My senses dragged out of place and returned, just to fall out again. *On, off, on, off.* Jerking, I escaped the bed. I knew where the sound came from and didn't bother looking at the mirror.

It differed from the previous time. My inner voice and body screamed at me in anguish not to carry on. My reactions were bizarrely real, my breathing shallow. I turned around from the window. My senses didn't roil. Though I'd expected them to dissolve into chaos, they were calm as a breeze. Instead of a dark doorway, my mirror was a strange vibrating liquid silver. Each beat sent shockwaves through the surface. I'd dreamt this before. I'd never had a dream repeated so vividly.

Wary, I approached the liquid wall. The wooden floor was cold under my bare feet. My nerves exploded with anxiety as I stopped in front of the moving mass. What if I was comatose? What if my mind had finally broken? I shook my head, refusing to entertain the thoughts. Because even if it were true, what else could I do? I wanted to know what was behind this thing that had beckoned me from the first. My heart yammered against my throat as I reached out my hand.

The silver was as cool as I remembered. A nervous smile curved my lips, relieved I was still alive. It looked like mercury. I swirled my fingers over the liquid surface, mesmerised by the beautiful waves and patterns. The drumming grew louder, as if suddenly more urgent.

I hesitated, calculated.

Cautious, I pushed my hand in. It was like pressing through jelly. I winced in expectation of what I might encounter, but there was nothing, just air.

I submerged deeper until it reached to my elbow. Watching my arm disappear was strange, especially knowing it would be gone when I pulled it out. The obvious conclusion was not to do that, then. I wiggled my fingers but felt nothing at all. My eyes caught something on the other side, and I leaned closer.

Butterfly.

I didn't feel as shocked as the first time. This time it hovered, waiting. If I could see it, where was my hand? I moved my arm around; still nothing. I pulled in a deep breath, shut my eyes, and stepped into the liquid. It brushed over my skin as I moved through. Ecstasy engulfed me as I took two steps and halted. An unknown world flashed through my imagination. What would I see? The possibilities were endless and terrifying. I used my available senses first, which hadn't shifted. I struggled to hear clearly because there was a noise which made no sense. It couldn't be right. Then came the scent. A fresh and earthy fragrance swirled in my nose, my lungs swelling. Ice coursed through my veins.

I opened my eyes and gasped.

Chapter

I once heard dreams were a recurrence of things experienced before. I knew now that couldn't be more wrong. All my life, I had seen nothing close to what I beheld now. Something beyond mortal imagination. The smells and sounds made sense now.

I gazed upon an ancient forest illuminated softly by a dim light source I couldn't place. If this was a dream, I had one heck of an imagination. Tiny sparks rose from the trees, scattering across the sky without fading or dying out. Mesmerised, I gaped at the light show. When I looked down, my body was visible, with no trace of the liquid silver. I returned my gaze to the timeless greenhouse before me and was about to take a step when the butterfly blocked my way. My breath caught. It looked about as big as two open hands, its colours a gorgeous midnight purple and royal blue.

As I admired it, I wondered why it kept hovering right there, the fluttering wings sending gentle currents of air over my cheeks. I stepped around it, eager to explore.

I flinched as my bare feet touched the cold stone and found it strange that I had a sense of touch in a dream. A white stone road lay straight before me, sloping down slightly. It was too dark ahead to see where it led. Dark spots patched the stones, and I knelt to inspect it. Moss, damp and soft under my fingers.

It hit me: I was standing in the middle of a road, surrounded by a forest, at night. An ominous stage, even for a dream. Insects buzzed around me, and as I straightened, my gaze travelled towards the darkness of the trees bordering the road. The branches looked like cloaks, giving them a ghostly nimbus. Uncanny then, that I yearned to touch them.

The tiny lights flowed through the trees to my left and seemed to beckon me. Just as I gave a step, the butterfly skittered in front of me again, and I halted. I waved it away, and the air swirled it away in dramatic circles. When it stabilised, it seemed to stare at me and kept its distance.

I padded closer to the trees, shivers running through me with each step as I surveyed around me. My back faced the other side of the forest now, and I tried to stay calm. At the edge of the road, I hesitated, unsure now. The trees were a little further away, down a slope.

A light speck settled on a nearby tree. So close. Curious, my heart beating wildly, I took the first step. The undergrowth scrunched, and I hesitated before the second step. My heart pumped faster.

Twigs snapped under my feet, and I peered around me nervously. Beyond the trees—only darkness. The tension lodged in my back like a knife, but I blew out a breath and turned back. The trunk was close, and I bent forward. My brain took a moment to register: firefly.

The forest dripped on my tongue as my jaw dropped. It was so bright that I could hardly believe it was an insect. Awed, I drew closer, but it took off into the air, whirling upwards, higher and higher. The presence of stars in the sky, despite my being within a mountain, startled me. Dreams often made no sense. The stars seemed closer than usual, but dimmer, like their light was dying.

The leaves looked plush and thick. Though I wanted to touch them, it felt somehow forbidden. As I was about to touch them, the butterfly swooped onto my hand, its wings thrashing violently.

"What?" I whispered, frustrated. My irritation abated when the trees on the other side of the road suddenly shuddered. Fear struck my heart like an icy arrow. From the sound of the motion, it had to be huge, and coming closer.

Run.

I ran, unable to take my eyes from the area it had come from. As I reached the white road, my foot snagged, and I went down hard on one knee. *Get up, get up.* Heart raging against my ribcage, I stumbled back up and then ran.

Ahead I saw only a smooth wall, ferns creeping over the surface where my mirror should be. *No.* The movement amongst the trees followed me. I whirled around, fear pulsing, anticipating a visual horror—saw nothing. I wasn't sure if that was better or worse. Helpless hysteria overtook me, and I banged on the wall with clenched fists.

"No! Open!" Intended as a scream but came out as a choked whisper. *Please, please, just open!* Fists numbed, I was crazed and nauseated.

The rustling stopped.

It was behind me; I knew it. Whatever it was had reached the road and was stalking towards me. I would have screamed, but unshed tears blocked my throat. My hands ached.

A slow thudding footfall on the stone. Four-legged. With every fibre of my being, I fought the instinct to turn and look. *Don't.* Closer. Only metres away. I felt it. A fresh wave of panic crashed over me, causing my teeth to chatter, and I banged harder. To my dismay, the thudding sped up. My resolve evaporated, and I turned my head. Everything inside me shook as I scanned the road.

I couldn't…

The wall dematerialised beneath my hands, and I crashed forward. The air felt weird as I fell; too thick. Adrenaline pushed me up off the floor as soon as I made impact, ready to defend myself, even if I was oblivious against what. I was like a blind, crazed animal. Glass broke.

I turned to the mirror, and it wobbled. I frowned. My throat was rough, singed with blood. The mirror stilled, but I riled. My senses shifted, surprising me, but only for a moment.

I clenched my aching fists. *What if it followed me?* Minutes passed—or what felt like minutes—and I waited. Nothing happened.

As I stared into the mirror, waiting, I noticed something… amiss. Every detail of the room, including the broken glass from my bedside table, was perfectly reflected. Everything–except me. I was not there. Not at all.

Dazed, I lifted my hands—nothing. Was I dead? My mind was fracturing in real time, and my hand flew to my face. Relief washed over me when I touched my cold skin. What a messed-up dream. It felt too real.

Exhaustion descended upon me like a wet blanket. I'd had dreams where I was too tired to open my eyes in stressful situations. I struggled to stand and stumbled towards the bed with heavy feet. Last time, my finger reappeared the following day. Why did I remember that now?

I felt drugged. Why was there always a twist? My head plunged into the pillow, and I closed my eyes with a sigh.

Faint *swishing* as I floated back into consciousness. It sounded like sweeping. My eyelids were heavy, and I felt spent, like I hadn't slept at all.

My eyes opened to the sight of Dad knelt on the floor, sweeping broken glass into a scoop. *Glass?* He must've dropped something. I yawned and stretched my limbs. Pain throbbed in my knee, and my body felt stiff. Tji-Tji meowed, and I eagerly pulled her into my arms. I was still dazed. The swishing stopped.

"Sorry, Honey. I tried to be quiet. Didn't want you to cut yourself when you got up." A frown formed. "I thought you'd be out like a light."

I had taken a whole pill, I remembered.

"No, it's okay. I guess it's about time I wake up." Probably Saturday afternoon. Maybe even Sunday morning. His frown deepened as he regarded me, as if I was joking.

"I took a whole pill by accident," I explained, willing my brain to think, but to no avail. "Isn't it Sunday?"

He sighed, heaved himself from the floor, and sat on the bed.

"It's Saturday, Honey. It's still very early. Are you sure you took one at all? Maybe it was a Tic-Tac." His lips pulled into a wry smile. Impossible. I sat up and looked for the container on the table. It wasn't there. I was sure I took one. I remembered almost spilling it.

"Where is it?" Panic was raw in my voice. I put my hands on the floor, looked under the bed and, relieved, I picked it up.

"See? I did take it. I panicked after realising I'd taken a whole one." He took the container and read the label; his eyebrows raised.

"Looks like you've declared sleep your mortal enemy since you're fighting it with everything you've got. I'm sad to say you're winning the fight." He sighed. I was disturbed by the fact that I'd woken up so soon after that dosage. Maybe it had something to do with my brain chemistry. Tji-Tji meowed again, and my dad petted her. I wondered when she had arrived since she wasn't with me the night before.

"Maybe we should go old-school and try some honey and warm milk?" He quipped after a while, excited at the thought.

"It's worth a try," I agreed, and he rose.

"Well, I think you should try sleeping some more. I was just checking to see if you're okay. You forgot to barricade yourself…" He was right, of course.

"If I see your face before ten, I'm dragging you back to your tower." He closed the trapdoor to a sliver, glowering at me through the crack, and I laughed. So villainous. I turned and held Tji-Tji against my chest, warmed by her comforting presence.

The light was dim, and I turned on the bed, onto my knees, and looked out the window. My right knee was sore, so I shifted my weight off it. The lake was the same solemn grey as the day before, and mist bulged and crept over the water. It looked eerie; the forest green was lucid against the sombre greys. The disturbing beauty stirred something deep within me.

I slid off the bed to retrieve my camera from the desk. It would do the scene better justice than my phone camera. My mom had last used it to photograph the butterfly, which felt like a lifetime ago. As I walked past the chaise, I stopped. My bare feet felt sand strewn beneath them, almost imperceptible. I crouched to investigate. It trailed from the chaise to the edge of the mirror. My heart rate climbed at the faintest whisper of a dream about a forest, but try as I might, I failed to grasp the memory. My head hurt, and I relinquished. The sand probably came from Dad's shoes.

I fetched the camera. The rays from the rising sun peeked through and scattered in the mist. It looked spectacular, and I took a few photos, Tji-Tji happily looking out the window with me. But exhaustion soon enrobed me, and I climbed back into bed, snuggling with Tji-Tji.

Sleep won this round.

I woke again after nine and checked my phone, finding messages from Laura. One was from the day before, but I had missed the notification. I messaged her back and slipped out of bed. Funny how a few extra hours of sleep had me feeling much better than the whole of the previous couple of nights combined.

A coolness occupied the house as I descended. I found my dad sitting on the porch under a blanket, reading and writing in his notebook. Mom was in town for business, and where Andrew was, we could guess. I crossed my arms against the bite in the air. Dad jumped up and draped a blanket over my shoulders. He ushered me back into the house where we brewed coffee and got me breakfast before returning to the porch. It was a delightful morning, and the forest looked magical, so green it hurt my eyes. When he asked about my plans for the day, I confessed I had none. What I didn't say was that I hoped Adrian would come. He headed into town to meet someone about his research after I'd finished my oatmeal.

My day passed in a slow, painstaking drip. I found myself looking out the window often, hoping to see Adrian, but he never came. The more I thought about how he had just left the night before, the angrier I became. But he owed me nothing, I realised, just as I thought I'd yell at him when I saw him again. I don't think I ever could. Feeling a fair bit disappointed, I went to bed early and took half a pill. It felt redundant, but I figured the worst that could happen was I'd have more of the same. Best case, I would sleep well for more than three hours. As an extra precaution, I drank warm milk with honey and fell instantly into a dreamless sleep.

Chirping birds roused me to consciousness, pulling me back to the realm of the unsleeping, as blinding light cut through my room. A gentle, sweet, and unfamiliar scent hung in the air. I didn't have to wonder about its origin for long. On the pillow beside me lay a stem with three purple and blue orchids. I gasped and sat up. The colours made me wonder if I had shifted, and I looked around. The room looked normal enough, except for a faint red twinge that might have been my imagination. I picked up the stem, filled with awe at the colours. Their scent was subtle and pleasant. Maybe Dad had left it. I slipped out of bed and placed it in my glass of water.

It was a beautiful, sunny day, and the lake glistened like it hadn't in a while. I wondered if the water was safe for swimming. As I stared at the water, I felt something… *off*. I opened a window, poking my head outside. It was quiet. I would falter in explaining what exactly disturbed me, but I sensed a peculiar undercurrent in the atmosphere. I pulled back from the window and went downstairs. Silence permeated the house until midway down the foyer stairs when laughter echoed through the closed ballroom doors. Those doors were never closed. I couldn't recall my parents mentioning guests coming over. I lingered, waiting to hear something, but continued down, stopping in front of the double doors, listening. Something was off. I felt it in my bones. All I heard were mumbling voices, and I couldn't tell by how many people. I opened a door slowly and peeked in, trying to be as noiseless as possible.

Soft light streamed through the windows, giving the room a disturbing, ethereal, dream-like quality. At the centre of the massive room were my mom, dad, Andrew, and Adrian, seated around a table. In unison, their heads turned to look at me, but no one spoke as I approached. They all gave me identical smiles as I met each of their gazes and felt myself clam up. I stared at the scene, half expecting to wake up. An eerie silence lingered. My stomach twisted, as it did with puppet shows. Dad sat at the head, Mom to his right and Andrew beside her, all their postures rigid. Adrian sat opposite them.

I reached the table, set for an elaborate meal, with a single open seat beside Adrian. His soft smile ignited my heart, even though I was too shocked to return it. His eyes drifted over me slowly, gleaning me, and I realised I was in my pyjamas—my cheeks flushed.

"Perfect timing. I was just about to call to you." Adrian finally broke the silence, his rich voice resonating through the room. His address seemed oddly intimate, making me feel uncomfortable and guilty, as if it were a sin to talk to him in my family's presence. I swallowed but couldn't speak. My family's stilted expressions creeped me out, and I looked away. The artificial congeniality of their faces twisted my stomach. I had to do *something*. Adrian stood and pulled out the chair, and I awkwardly sat. As he pushed it back, he surreptitiously stroked my arm and flames erupted over my skin. Nervous about the act, I stole a glance at my family, whose disturbing gaze continued as the silence hovered over the table like a bird of prey.

I pushed open the ballroom doors.

"Ah, Honey! It's as if you were summoned." My dad exclaimed when he saw me. He and Andrew were setting the table, both in a cheery mood. I stood frozen for a moment. Did I just sleepwalk into the room? My shoulder burned. I frowned at him, and he stopped, his expression turning concerned.

"Are you okay?" I wondered if I was awake and I looked at my hands. They were fine.

"Deja vu, I guess." Mom entered from the hall entrance on the other side, carrying a tray.

"Oh, Josilyn, perfect timing! We were just about to check if you were awake."

"Something like that, yeah." Head still spinning from the dream I'd just had, I was closing in when Adrian entered, carrying a tray with coffees and a roguish grin. I stopped in my tracks. His eyes glinted.

"Good morning, Sleepyhead."

"Adrian?" My shock must have been obvious, and my parents laughed.

"He was the one who suggested a large breakfast, and he helped with the cooking." Mom lifted her eyebrows at this last bit of information, visibly pleased. My lungs swelled and burned inside my chest.

"Did he?" I hadn't intended to say it aloud.

"Don't be so surprised," he responded.

"I am surprised, though."

He looked me up and down as he put the tray down and I crossed my arms.

"Is that all of it, Adrian?" Mom asked.

"Yes."

Adrian placed a coffee beside each plate.
I looked at my hands again.

My dad sat at the head, my mom on his right, and Andrew beside her. Adrian pulled the chair out, and I stared at it.

"Sit," he said after a second, and I did. He pushed the chair in, and I looked at my left shoulder, anticipating his touch, just as his index finger slid over the spot. It burned again.

"How'd you sleep, Hon?" Dad asked as Adrian found his seat but continued to stare at me, interested and focussed. My cheeks flushed, and I forced myself to focus on my dad.

"Great, actually. I slept so long—almost can't believe it. Maybe the honey and milk did the trick." I refrained from mentioning the episode from earlier. No need to taint the good news.

We dished up from the impressive selection. Mushrooms, bacon and cheese omelette rolls, fried banana, eggnog French toast, fruit salad and yoghurt. My mouth watered and my stomach growled. We ate like royalty. Even the coffee seemed infused with more flavour than I'd ever tasted. The heaviness of Adrian's gaze weighed on me often. My heart raced at such boldness in present company. Mom mentioned he'd made the omelette rolls himself. He had won her over. Andrew seemed unconvinced and eyeballed him warily whenever he spoke.

"Oh, Adrian, you were telling us about picking up a slug?" My dad asked halfway through the meal, and my fork clattered on my plate. Everyone stared at me except Adrian because he knew why I dropped it. His hand was on my knee beneath the table, burning. I wished I could glower at him.

"Sorry," I looked at my plate and picked up the fork. My heart raced. My parents laughed.

"That was our reaction, too," Mom giggled. I doubted. Adrian spoke, and everything else stilled. I didn't even want to chew.

"Well, I was wearing gloves, so it wasn't until I was about to hit the nail that I noticed I'd mistakenly picked up a big slug instead of a hammer." My parents broke out into laughter, my mom cringing at the disgusting thought. I would've laughed if my mind was unclouded. The heat spread to my head like wildfire through dry brush. The conversation carried on, but it was gibberish to my ears. While still engaging like an attentive participant, Adrian moved his hand up my leg, sending a jolt through me. I yanked my free hand under the table to push his away. He simply enfolded my hand with his and settled back on my knee. Sneaky. I stole a glance at him, noticing the corner of his mouth lift ever so slightly as he continued to speak. My pulse raced, and the heat became almost unbearable when he gently stroked the back of my hand with his thumb. I tried pulling away, but he tightened his grip. I was self-conscious but couldn't struggle while my parents' eyes were on us. Maybe they already noticed. I glanced at them, but they seemed oblivious. Adrian continued with the conversation and carried on as if everything was normal. He knew the effect he had on me and enjoyed torturing me—I'd bet.

With my heart lodged in my throat, I managed to finish my food, though it took considerable effort. Before I could fully push my chair back, Adrian was already on his feet, finishing the task and leaving me dazed.

"I'll help clean up while you get dressed," he picked up my plate before I could.

"But you cooked," my mom and I protested in unison, but he had already gathered all the plates.

"I don't mind."

Andrew seized the opportunity to excuse himself. My mom had a big smile on her face, and she glanced behind her and whispered.

"He's been here since nine. I thought it would be an ideal opportunity to break ground with him," She leaned closer. "He's great, Honey. Such a gentleman. And an excellent cook. I'm happy for you." She winked at me. I blushed, praying he didn't hear that—I burned like a cinder. She was about to say something else, but he emerged, eyes dancing and a smile that melted me. She refrained.

My dad smiled at me with amusement.

"That's weird; your clothes look exactly like your pyjamas." Adrian poked fun at me as he collected more items from the table. My dad snorted. I took the hint and withdrew to my room to dress.

The orchids were so vibrant in the bright light they looked fake, and I touched the delicate, smooth petals. I opted for jeans, black sneakers, and a soft, light green long-sleeve t-shirt. Uncertain about the plans, I grabbed a black crocheted sweater.

Adrian stood at the foyer, waiting at the bottom of the stairs, and looked up as I descended. His gaze made me clumsy. My parents talked in the parlour. I reached the last step, and he held out his hand. Awkward, I took it, my eyes flickering to the parlour. Adrian noticed, and turning, put himself between me and the doorway.

"Only slightly more decent," he whispered. My parents greeted us as we walked past, our hands hidden from them. He opened the front door and let me walk ahead, my arm burning.

"Where are we going?"

"I thought some fresh air would be beneficial to you. Your father had me swear not to let you do anything strenuous, so I'll do my part, but you'd better behave." Still holding my right hand, he stepped forward and faced me, and walking backwards, took my left hand and winked. We walked towards the obscured path leading to the pier. I hadn't been back there again. My heart swelled at the thought of being alone with him, perhaps longer than usual? He was always in a hurry to leave. I wondered if we'd sail on the boat again. We entered the forest, the trees canopied above, and bird songs echoed through the dense space. My senses drifted. He stopped and gave me a questioning look. Had he felt the jolt going through me? He kept staring, and I couldn't break his gaze, but was unsure how to explain. After a few seconds, his expression changed to one of understanding.

"That happens often, doesn't it? I've felt it before but was unsure what it was." Tenderness suffused his voice. I never considered that another person could feel my shifts. And he was accountable for several of them.

"I do get them often, yes. I can't always predict them, but it's usually when there's a sensory overwhelm. Like, when I'm surprised, or something unexpected happens."

"Like this?" his arm circled my waist and swung my weight to his other side, dipping me. My senses crumbled, and the *Pulse* shot through me. I squeezed my eyes shut, and my body stiffened. I was inches away from the ground, supported only by his arm. His warmth spilt over me. I opened my eyes to green flames that melted me.

"Yes," I breathed. His lips curved into an amused grin and his eyes explored my face—heat tinging my cheeks. Involuntarily, my lips prickled, and I broke my gaze, embarrassed.

"Hmmm, I see." a smile wove through his voice. He swung me upright like I was weightless. My head felt light as he took my hand and continued walking. My feet were numb, and after the third stumble, he snorted and stopped.

"Well, this is not going to work." He hunched, wrapped his arms around my thighs, and lifted me over his shoulder. I gasped.

"Adrian!"

"I have promises to keep. If I brought you back with a broken ankle, your father might disallow me from seeing you again." The heat crawled into my marrow. I was mortified, my legs dangling as I tried to find a grip on his shoulders. His muscles shifted beneath my hands, and I swallowed. The heat of his hand on my outer thigh spread and seared. I was so high above the ground that I felt a rush of vertigo. I took a deep breath, calming myself, and gazed into the forest, catching a quick, bright blue flash.

"Did you put the orchids on my pillow?" My stomach fluttered.

"I did—snuck in while your parents were in the kitchen. I thought it would be pleasant to wake up to. Do you like them?" He had been in my room while I slept.

"Yes, they're beautiful, thank you." An edge peeked through my tone.

"Galaxy orchids. Indigenous to Ostia. They reminded me of you. I picked them in the forest this morning." I smiled, my lungs feeling hot inside my chest. *How thoughtful.*

"I love them, thank you." My voice betrayed the profound effect the gesture had on me. He squeezed my thigh in acknowledgement. At the water's edge, he placed his other hand on my back, sliding me off against him until my feet were on the moss-covered bank. I cleared my throat and took a subtle step back, glowing from the prolonged exposure to his body heat. My gaze escaped to the lake of the secluded cove and the bright blue water stung my eyes. It was peaceful.

"How do you know about this place?"

He looked over the water, a smile dancing in his eyes and curving his lips.

"I know this area like the back of my hand. You would, too, had you lived here as long as I." A thought pulled his eyes into a smile, and he looked down, stepping towards the water. The sudden absence of his heat sent a shiver through my body. He scouted pebbles from the lake's edge and skipped them over the water. I approached the pier, resting my hands on the post. The stones skipped so far that I couldn't see where they landed.

"Wow, that's impressive." A breeze slurred over me and through my hair, and I closed my eyes, drinking in the wind through the trees, the soft sloshing water, the birds chirping, and the delicate slashes of the skiing pebbles. The rich forest scent permeated my nose. My senses drifted apart, and the lake turned into a black hole, the dark waves lapping at my feet. I stepped back, sobering up. The spot where Adrian had stood moments ago was empty, and I turned to see him sitting on the bank, arms on his knees, gazing at me with dancing eyes.

"Come here." Something irresistible stained his voice. I obeyed. He offered me his hand when I reached him. I never acclimatised to how hot they were. My cheeks glowed as I sat. He pulled me closer than I intended. I could sense him staring at me, but it was too much to handle, and I gazed over the water. Butterflies fluttered in my stomach and in my veins. He touched my cheek, wiping away a loose strand, and I looked down. My heart raced. I was aware again that my hand was sweating, but when I attempted pulling away, he tightened his grip. I pursed my lips and looked away, raking my brain for something to say.

"Why didn't you come yesterday?" My voice sounded raw.

"I wasn't aware that I should have." My stomach churned. He was right, of course. He owed me nothing. I felt silly. He chuckled, nudging me with his shoulder. "I'm joking. I thought I'd let you get some rest. Did you miss me?"

I looked away as my heart burned. It felt as if my head was going to explode from all the blood. "I missed you," he whispered, squeezing my hand. I dared a glance at him, and he was smiling, his eyes endless chasms.

"You abhor being vulnerable, don't you?" he asked after a moment.

"That's a paradoxical question."

He chuckled.

"Alright." He sighed and looked up, his eyes changing as they skimmed over the lake. I couldn't imagine where his thoughts were, distant as his eyes seemed. I followed his gaze, and we watched the water in silence while he absentmindedly stroked the back of my hand with his thumb.

"How will I bypass the water?" I heard myself say, unsure where it came from. Adrian's thumb stilled, and he looked at me with a frown.

"What?" His voice was low.

I frowned back at him. "I—I don't know."

He looked back at the water, his thumb moving again.

"You said you slept well last night?" he asked after a while.

"Like a rock. It was the first night in recent memory without strange dreams."

He looked at me with curious eyes.

"You have yet to tell me the full extent of things. I am quite interested in these dreams of yours. What are they about?" A chill ran down my back at the thought of them, as if they were monsters hiding in the shadows, shying away from the light searching for them.

"Well, that's the odd thing, I can't recall—" I began, but stopped as my senses flashed for a second, bright and violent. Faint fragments of a dream seeped into my mind. My throat tightened, and I caught my breath. Something had stalked me in the woods. Concern framed Adrian's eyes when I met them.

"Did it happen again?"

"Yes," a bare whisper.

"Why?" His eyebrows furrowing.

"I don't know, but I just caught glimpses of my dream."

Intrigued, he leaned closer.

"How peculiar. Tell me?" His voice dripped with deadly allure, and I struggled to focus.

"I'm still not sure. I… woke up within my dream, and the mirror was vibrating again—"

"Again?" he interrupted, exhilaration glistening in his eyes. I found it surprising I hadn't mentioned the mirror before. Had I just remembered now?

"Didn't I tell you? It happened once before, but this time I think I walked through it. And there was a forest, but I can't recall much else. It ended with overwhelming fear."

Elated, his eyes buzzed with life as they met mine, as if he could see what I saw. He inhaled a slow, deep breath and cut his gaze to the lake. It felt like the sudden release of pressure.

"How often do you have these dreams?" His distant tone caused some concern within me.

"Um, if I'm honest, strange things have been happening since we moved here. But the past week has been quite bad. This dream was the longest and most detailed. It felt so real, slower than dreams usually are." He nodded, inhaling deeply again.

"Dreams illuminate the subconscious mind, a lens into your soul's yearnings and troubles. Perhaps you're trying to escape something."

Ironically, all I was trying to escape were my dreams.

"I don't want to escape anything."

He didn't respond and continued looking over the water. I wished he would look at me.

"Perhaps your conscious mind is still unaware of the things beneath the surface."

"Well, then, I wouldn't know," I replied.
He nodded.

"Your dreams are speaking, Josilyn. Maybe they linger because you're not listening."

I shrugged. "I can't listen if I can't remember."

He snorted and nodded. Leaning closer, he kissed my cheek, and I felt the heat spread, shadowing my blush.

As he pulled back, he frowned at me.

"There's a shadow in your eyes that wasn't there before." He studied my face, coming closer again. I couldn't linger on his peculiar comment for long. The proximity was intoxicating, and I felt a little dizzy. I rummaged through my mind for a distraction.

"I think I dreamt you play the viola, and we played together." He smiled and pulled back a little. I continued, "It made me realise we have classes together, but I don't know what instrument you're majoring in."

"I'm not majoring in anything. Yes, I have some music subjects, but I'm also taking a few maths and physics courses. I have a hungry mind. The moment I understand something, I get bored."

It seemed fitting, but as I absorbed this, I wondered: Would he get bored with me, too?

"How do you manage that? To take different courses, I mean."
He smiled.

"Oh, I have my ways. And I tend to get what I want." Subliminal meaning shone from his eyes as he looked at me, then looked at the sky—his expression losing amusement.

"I'd prefer you didn't change the subject, though."

Blinking, I tried to recall which subject I had changed, but couldn't. He ignored my confusion.

"You are more cautious than most."
I was lost.

"Cautious with?"

"Yourself."

I blushed, realising we veered into uncomfortable territory again. I did indeed change the subject when it nudged closer. My heart knocked against my chest.

"I'm more observant than most."

He chuckled. "And more guarded. But you can't hide from me, though your attempt is valiant." He was on a mission to expose me.

My face burned like a lantern, and I looked away. How would I even respond? I wanted to pull my hand from his but forced myself not to. As if he sensed the impulse, he squeezed and tugged it.

"I'm falling for you, Josilyn." My name on his tongue was an incantation, and I looked at him. His eyes shone like the sun, and I was a celestial moth; the naked flame inside him terrified me, but I couldn't break my gaze as it inhaled me like oxygen. He continued, "With every thought of you that crosses my mind, which is every second, I fall further. You have entrapped me. Not all things in life are logical," he paused and shook his head. "It took everything inside me not to come yesterday. My anima has latched to you; this pull between us is an unbreakable tether. I *want* you—I would inhale you if I could, so you'd be inside my chest, like the oxygen I need to survive. I don't quite understand it, but I am transfixed."

The *Pulse* bristled inside my bones, itching as he spoke, and my heart screamed. I edged closer to exploding and shifting into another dimension altogether. His words didn't ease but ignited, and I felt even more exposed, utterly bare. My thoughts were a mess, and I wanted to run away, but I doubted I could outrun him. And he would follow. I knew at that moment that he always would. Panic rose and filled my throat. I sucked a deep breath and, with violent effort, broke my gaze away from him to the lake. I lacked the courage to say what tumbled inside me. He had taken the first leap, though, and like ought to meet like.

"That is a lot to take in," was all I could manage to whisper.

"It is a lot to feel, also," he whispered back.

My senses disintegrated, and I tasted flames; my eyes burned. I was squeezing his hand hard. My heart was hot inside its cavity, and I took a deep breath, imagining it would help cool it.

"I feel it too. I'm detached from my body when I'm with you. You've clouded my mind since the first time we met. I don't understand, either. This is a first for me, but if what I feel is not me falling too, I don't know what it possibly should feel like to fall." The words flowed out, unstoppable. My head was too heavy for my shoulders, and my eyes pounded. I didn't dare look at him. I loosened my grip on his hand, and he wove his fingers through mine.

"You are mine." His voice was deep and sticky. My heart swelled, and I looked at him. From somewhere at the back of my brain, the thought forced itself from my mouth:

"We should go slow. Take time to get to know each other."

He made a face.

"Time is a cliché. The world would perish before us if we always waited. Is it possible to ever know someone fully? Is that not the reason people can love each other for decades? Just when you think you know someone, they surprise you. We are infinite." He turned towards me fully and cupped my face and neck with his burning hand. His eyes were desperate as they searched mine. No matter how much I tried, I couldn't turn or even look away. It would offer little escape anyway. "Josilyn, why waste a second of *this*?" His scent washed over me, and my senses boiled beneath the surface. He touched his nose to mine briefly before pulling back. I inched towards spontaneous combustion.

"I have to try and maintain my sanity," I whispered, raw with the intensity of the moment, as tears burned in my eyes—mortified when he gently wiped away the escaping traitors. His voice was hoarse when he spoke.

"If this is insanity, I would gladly pledge it."

I could not escape him. He would counter any argument I could bring to resist the pull. His eyes bore into mine; the fire burning there terrified me. I loved everything he said—it all sounded so good, and it was killing me. Perhaps my own true enemy was me.

"Taking things slow doesn't diminish anything." My eyes pleaded. I was unsure what *not* going slow would even mean. He smiled and stroked my cheek with his thumb.

"You're right. Nothing could snuff this out." Relief washed through me, and I felt like I'd accomplished something. I might have been mistaken. My blood reacted fiercely to his hand on my cheek. His smile was soft as he leaned closer and pressed a sweet kiss on my lips, setting them ablaze. It was difficult to breathe, as if my lungs were no longer compatible with the atmosphere. The allure of his scent overwhelmed me, a divine fragrance that lingered and burned. His eyes danced with amusement as he pulled away and leapt up, walking past the pier. The absence of his heat sent a cold shiver through me. It was all so bizarre, and feeling lightheaded, I lay back on my elbows. He walked along the water's edge, looking at the ground. The branches above canopied over me with tiny purple flowers hanging like grapes. I felt spent after the intense conversation. The sun seemed lower than it ought to be in the late morning.

Something hovering above the water interrupted my thoughts, and I sat up. As it approached, I realised it was a black and orange butterfly. The sun bouncing off its wings made it look like a small, brilliant flame. It swirled around before settling on my knee. Strange, how this kept happening. My senses shuffled, and instead of the usual blues and purples, the butterfly had a flame-like mist around it.

Another piece of a dream dropped into my consciousness. An annoying butterfly preventing me from touching... touching... something. It looked at me like the others had. With care, I moved my hand closer, and it seemed aware of it. It climbed on my finger, tickling me.

"What secrets is he divulging to you?" I was startled to find Adrian standing over me, but the butterfly hadn't moved. It seemed rather aware of Adrian's voice, as I was, and looked like it was listening to us.

"It was telling me how beautiful it is."

He laughed and sat down beside me, leaning back on his hand, half lying. The butterfly followed his movement.

"I think you heard wrong." A smile laced his tone. Captivated, I stared at the shimmering wings in awe. They looked so soft, and I wanted to touch them, though I knew not to. A strange, majestic moment.

In a blur, Adrian's hand swooped in and took it captive. A frenzied fluttering erupted inside the cage of his fingers. It sent a shock through me, and my eyes darted to Adrian, who lifted his hand to his face and inspected it while murmuring something inaudible.

He caught me frowning at him.

"Did I hear wrong?"

I jested at his earlier comment. He smiled.

"Butterflies are messengers."

"From whom?"

His smile broadened.

"Anything that has something to say."

"So, what does this one say?"

His eyes were soft, and a smile curved his lips as he opened his hand. The butterfly had settled on his palm and seemed to look up at him. *Eerie.*

"That I must go, unfortunately." Unexpected. Disappointment sagged into my stomach. The butterfly lifted off and fluttered into the forest. "Take this as a token of my apology." From behind his back, he lifted a white lotus flower.

"Wow, it's beautiful." It was still a little wet. He must've fished it from the lake. I took a whiff of its fresh fragrance.

"Just like you."

I blushed. It was the first time I'd been called beautiful.

"Let's get you home." He was standing and offered his hand. I must have glitched because I hadn't seen him rise. Distracted, I placed my hand inside his and the next thing I knew, I was flying through the air as he tossed me above him. I gasped, and the flower dropped from my hand. My senses scattered, and it felt like everything happened in slow motion. His arms caught me around the waist as he turned, smiling. My heart hammered. Perhaps telling him about the jolts was a bad idea.

"You dropped something." He handed me the flower. When I could breathe again, I asked him:

"What does it feel like to you when I… when it happens?" His arm around my waist was scorching.

He inhaled and looked off into the distance.

"Hmmm… It feels like an electric current running through your skin. Not unpleasant. Does it hurt?"

No one had ever touched me while it happened. Except maybe my mom or dad, but they'd never mentioned feeling it.

"No, it doesn't—not exactly. It's a little uncomfortable, though… Like putting a glove on your foot instead of your hand. Not quite a fit."

"That's interesting…I'm glad it is painless; I would have felt helpless knowing something was hurting you and not being able to prevent it. And I would need to supply profuse apologies too." He smiled down at me softly, rocking us from side to side. Sighing, he kissed my hair and unwrapped himself from me. He took my hand, and we walked up the slope as he held me steady.

"What are you doing on Tuesday?" He asked after we'd walked a while.

"Um, I'll be at class the whole day. Why?"
He chuckled.

"Well, you'll be the only one." He saw I was confused. "It's a public holiday."

"I didn't know." A bonus resting day.

"I can come by if you want me to." My heart bloomed.

"I do." He smiled and released my hand when we reached the trail's end.

"How do you get home?" I asked, realising as we neared the porch that there were no vehicles around.

"I prefer walking. It keeps the blood warm." His blood needed no heating.

"I think you're warm enough as is."
He pulled me closer.

"Are you saying I'm hot?" I attempted pulling away, afraid my parents would see, but it was futile, like pushing against a mountain. "They can't see us," he whispered in my ear, and my face burned. My senses were close to the edge and my heart contracted. We were at the front door. A soft laugh reverberated through his chest.

"It's amazing. I can feel it prickling beneath the surface." A chill ran down my spine. He felt it when I shifted, but I hadn't realised he could feel it build too. He enveloped me in a warm hug.

"Now, please rest well. Don't tire yourself running after butterflies."

He released me. "I'll see you tomorrow." The promise gladdened my heart, but I still wanted him to stay.

"You're the one running after a butterfly," I joked.

"I suppose so," he winked and walked down the steps, towards the stone arch. I watched him walk all the way and wave over his shoulder without looking back right before disappearing. A coldness enveloped me in more ways than one and I reluctantly went inside.

I stopped when I saw my dad in the parlour, reading. He regarded me over his spectacles—I hoped he didn't hear or see anything.

"Hey, Hon. Where's Adrian?"

"He had to leave. Seemed in a hurry." I fell on the couch. He nodded, looking back at the book.

"You were gone a while. Are you hungry?" I looked at the clock and started. It was after three already. "What?" he asked.

"I… I didn't realise what time it was. It felt shorter."

"Hmmm." I preferred not to delve into the subtext of his tone.

Eager to change the subject, I asked how his book was coming along. Sighing, he put the book down, removed his glasses, and rubbed his eyes. He had hit several dead ends with the native and locals' stories. As he talked, I realised how worn out he looked. I was aware of my unwanted influence there, and my face burned with guilt. When I asked how he was sleeping, he joked he should take one of my 'Tic-Tacs'. I went to the kitchen to brew coffee and heat some leftovers from lunch. When I returned with the coffee, we talked about his project. He was writing a historically accurate romance novel about Ostia's origin story and wanted to stay as true to the facts as possible.

Movement at the stairs caught my eye. Tji-Tji peeked around the corner. When our eyes met, she ran over and jumped on the couch. She stared at me, meowing.

"Hey, Girl. Where have you been?"

"She's been in your room all day, refusing to come out."

That was unlike her. Something strange dawned on me: the previous night was the first time I didn't have a bizarre dream and the first night she spent in my room. She had been sleeping in my parents' room for the past week for some reason. The way she looked at me now was discomforting. I squirmed at the path my mind roved towards. Cats had uncanny senses. As I stroked her, ice prickled down my spine with a thought.

"Dad, do you think this house could be haunted?" My voice sounded hollow as the words escaped uncensored. I shivered. He stared at me, taken aback.

"Um… I don't know. I've heard rumours and tales of supernatural things, but not ghosts and hauntings."

"What supernatural things?" The *Pulse* simmered beneath my skin.

"Well, that's part of where I'm stuck in my research. Some stories don't tie together. One dispute is over the name Ostia. It means the veil or the doors. Doors to what? No one knows. And, of course, as amazing as it is, it is an anomaly that this house has remained intact for half a millennium. The natives believe there's an underground cave system where creatures dwell, exuding magic that preserves the town. Others believe the mysticism in the name might refer to the two brothers who discovered the secret of their birth against all odds, like a veil which was drawn back."

My senses swayed as I remembered my dream and the big, stalking creature in the forest. But I'd never heard of it before; how could I dream about it?

"Are you getting your info from the natives themselves?"

"In a way, yes. They live right behind this mountain, in the reserve. But they are quite primitive. I've found a native contact, Komelsha, who lives in town and has learned English. This caused huge issues with his tribe. Their traditions and legends have been exceptionally well preserved. I met him in town yesterday."

I was a little disgusted with myself for not even knowing about this. It was something Dad would have been very excited about.

"Well, it's great that you have such a raw source. What's the tribe's name?"

"Mjesecai. The creatures are called Nakshati, or some variation of that."

"I like the sound of it. Does it mean anything specific?"

"There's speculation that the name comes from Nakshatra, which involves the zodiacs, but I don't see how that would be possible. They've been here, maybe even longer than this town has."

I was referring to Mjesecai, but he was clearly more interested in the creatures.

"So, the Nakshati have nothing to do with the zodiac, then?"
He shook his head.

"Not exactly. The Mjesecai think they have something to do with the moon."

"Like, werewolves?" I snorted.

"Well, no… but they believe silver keeps you safe from them. Some old townhouses have silver hidden inside the threshold, preventing access. But apart from the moon and silver, there are no other similarities. There used to be many disappearances in this area, but they stopped, for the most part, twenty-five years ago. Many were blamed on the Nakshati."

"What changed twenty-five years ago?"
He shrugged.

"They don't know."

"What do they look like?"

"No one knows. The theory is that they are invisible. Their presence can be felt, but there's never been a sighting."

Goosebumps rose on my skin.

"That's not creepy at all."
My dad snorted.

"Nope." He stayed quiet for a moment, then frowned. "Hey, what are you doing on Tuesday?"

I thought about Adrian.

"Nothing specific. Why?" It wasn't a lie.

"Just wondering." He was planning something, but I'd have to wait to find out what. After a while, he asked if I'd play the cello for him—something he usually did when he was stressed. When I returned from my room, he had settled on the Chesterfield, prepared to relax and doze off. I kicked off with an adagio and merged it into an interpretation of Sarasate's Zigeunerweisen. I played without pause for a long time, pouring everything into the electric, familiar ultraviolet world. Mom and Andrew joined at some point, which I only knew because Andrew bumped into the coffee table, and it jangled through the composition I was immersed in. When my fingers couldn't take it anymore, I stopped. My energy sapped away like cotton candy in water, but I kept up appearances until after dinner. I excused myself early and went to my room. When I saw the orchids, I realised I'd never brought the lotus flower into the house. I must have dropped it somewhere on the walk. The thought made me sad. I was sure Adrian gave it back after throwing me in the air.

~

I arrived on campus after an uneventful night, and Laura jumped on me for a tight hug as soon as I climbed out of the car.

"She's alive!"

"Corpse bride no more," I joked.

"I'm glad you're back. I was planning a manhunt."

"For whom?"

"I mean, I wasn't sure you were the one texting… It could've been anyone."

"Who would be your first suspect?"

She looked at me, eyebrow cocked. "I mean…"
I knew she was implying Adrian.

"He's not that bad."

"I'm not saying he's bad, but he'd be my first suspect. That's how these things go. I don't make the rules."

"Which rules would those be?"

"The rules of love and murder. A thin line, I am told." I laughed, shaking my head.

Adrian was sitting in Dagworth's class when we arrived. For some reason, I wasn't expecting him. He was looking at the door when I entered, as if in anticipation. I stopped at the door, and Laura walked right into me.

"Oof," she gasped, "Why'd you do that?" She soon saw Adrian. "Oh, fair enough." I shook my head at her.

He was smiling as we approached him, and my cheeks burned as yesterday flashed through my mind.

He smiled when I reached him. "Why are you so surprised to see me? I told you I'd see you today." I didn't understand why I felt naked when he talked to me in front of others. The black button-up shirt against his tanned skin did something to me.

"I don't know. I haven't seen you in class for a while." Feeling clumsy, I sat down beside him. Laura, quite unusually, remained silent, only waving to him in acknowledgement as she sat next to me.

"I forgot to give you your actual notes." He handed me a sheaf of papers.

"Great, thanks." He laughed at my unintentional sarcasm.

He took my hand beneath the desk, and I leaned forward so Laura wouldn't notice and ask questions. I didn't listen to a word Dagworth said. Adrian didn't attend the other classes, but said he'd see me the following day. Laura and I caught up between periods, but I didn't tell her much about Adrian because it felt too private—too new. She wanted to go hiking the next day, but I told her my dad had something planned. I said nothing about Adrian coming by.

When I arrived home, I walked to the trail to search for the lotus and found it lying a little way into the tree line. I retired early and took a whole pill, which knocked me out within minutes. My dreams were heavy and exhausting as I fell deeper and deeper into my insentient state. Even in my dreams, I sensed it was a mistake to have taken the whole one. Further… further I plunged.

If I could have had emotions then, I would have been beside myself with fear because it felt like I was dying.

Vigorously, something yanked me back.

Chapter 10

I had fallen so deep, so far, the pull felt like being torn from my body. But I was stuck inside a tar ocean, and the force summoning me to the surface did not have it easy, even as my awareness prowled back. My soul burned with heat, and my body felt numb, as though my senses had been shut off. Heart beating faster, they returned slowly, starting with touch. A pressure lingered on my back. Oxygen filled my lungs as I inhaled. Orientation came next, but slowly. I was on my stomach—heat spreading across my back. Was Tji-Tji lying on me? My auditory senses woke, but there was no sound. I opened my heavy lids to a slit. Limp, I tried wiggling my fingers. My body overheated and my heart rate climbed. I groaned into the pillow. I yearned to sleep more but stretched, and life flowed through my nerves, waking me. My bones crackled, but the heated pressure on my back remained unmoved. Still reluctant to surrender my sleep, I tried turning onto my back but couldn't. A sliver of panic coiled around my heart. I tried again. Breathing heavier, I wondered if I was about to have another night terror. The thought alerted me. My neck was stiff from lying in that position for who knows how long.

The bright light stung my eyes.

"Get off" came out as an irritated mumble. I tried swatting her off, but could not lift my arm. I wiggled my body.

Soft laughter reverberated through the air, and my eyes shot open.

"Good morning." His voice, hued with a smile, oozed into my brain. Familiar yet delicate, he squeezed my back, and I realised it had been his hand pressing on me. Just like that, I was wide awake. Adrenaline burnt a path through my veins, and my throat tightened, itching to scream. I jolted upright. His hand moved to the bed beside me, positioning his face inches from mine as he leaned over me. I swallowed. His green jewelled eyes sparkled—both of us were taken aback—and I saw a shadow flicker across them. His gaze dipped to my lips, and I realised I had morning breath. I leaned back to create distance, but his other hand burned on the back of my neck. It startled me—it hadn't been there a moment ago. He caressed the back of my ear with his thumb, and it prickled from the heat. His chest heaved fast as he looked over my face as if searching for something. Sobriety returned, and I realised anew that he was in my room, and someone could come in at any moment.

"What are you doing here?" My voice was a raw whisper. He smiled while frowning, and my heart hammered.

"I told you I'd see you today, did I not?"

"No, no, I mean, what are you doing *here* in my room? What if my dad comes in?" The edge in my voice rose as I spoke. The scene played out inside my head and distilled the hysteria. His expression shifted to one of mischievous expectation.

"Oh, I have uncanny reflexes. You don't have to worry." Eyes alight—lips curved wickedly.

"How'd you get in here again? Is there a secret entrance we don't know about?"

He shook his head, laughing.

"No, I'm just very sneaky." Sneakier than I'd realised, it seemed. He looked at my bedside table, smiling. I followed his gaze—the orchids and the lotus. I turned back to him, startled when his eyes lingered on my face in a way that made my lips tingle. His scent spilt over me as he inched closer.

Panic jolted me as the trapdoor creaked open slowly. My senses scattered, and I stifled a horrified gasp. My head was about to explode with the thought of my dad's face if he saw Adrian on my bed. I was about to tell him to hide, but he was gone. The spot where he'd been just a second ago was empty. My head spun with violent confusion, my heart raced, and I tasted iron on my tongue. I scoured the room but saw him nowhere. Did I dream again?

All this processed as the door rose.

I fell back, pretending I'd just woken up and hoping my eyes did not shine with adrenalised shock. Dad's head peeked into the room.

"Morning, Dad!" My greeting came too quickly and my voice betrayed anxiety. It was the worst possible day for breakfast in bed. He frowned and opened the door completely, holding a tray.

"Well, aren't you a bottle of sunshine…"

"I just woke up, and you startled me." I fought the instinct to look around the room. Where was he? He was too big to hide behind my wardrobe or desk. I didn't even hear him move. The only place I could think of was under my bed, but my dad was looking directly at it. Maybe he was invisible. Wouldn't surprise me much. The suspense was killing me. Dad's eyes focused on the space underneath my bed, and he frowned. My heart skipped a beat and then raced. *Oh no.* I breathed faster, wondering how I'd explain a full-grown man under my bed. He blinked and shook his head.

"Sorry, Honey," he said, wobbling up the steps. "Didn't mean to give you a fright."

'*Fright*' was the fiercest understatement imaginable. Near-death was closer. I wondered again if I'd been dreaming, but my prickling skin was evidence to the contrary.

"It's okay."

He hovered before placing the tray on my bed and sitting down.

"How'd you sleep?"

"Like the dead."

"Well, welcome back then. Any good news from the other side?"

"Don't do drugs."

He snorted and smiled, nodding, and looked at my bedside table. His eyes flickered.

"Ah, wow. Those are beautiful." I had forgotten about the flowers. My cheeks burned.

"Uh, yeah." Silence lingered for a moment.

"Adrian?"

"M-hmm," It sounded shrill. A terrifying thought crossed my mind. If he talked about Adrian now, he might as well set up funeral arrangements because I would die.

"Honey," *oh no*, "I was wondering," *please, no*, "do you remember the conversation we had the other day," my head spun, "about the Mjesecai tribe?" *Relief.* I breathed out.

"Yes, of course. Why?" my voice was rough.

"Well, I've be—" he stopped, frowning, and looked at his feet. My heart dropped. He bent forward and looked under the bed. I could just imagine Adrian using the opportunity to mess around, and my heart hammered against my chest. I felt cold air on my eyes as they widened.

"Hmm," was all he said, straightening up. "Weird, I thought I felt something. Anyway, where was I? Oh yes. Well, I've been arranging a meeting with the tribal chief, and Komelsha let me know late last night we have the green light. The thing is, they're matriarchal and would prefer that a woman accompany us, as a sign of goodwill and diplomacy. They know it's our culture to protect women as the physically weaker gender, so to bring one with us creates trust and shows our visit is peaceful. I asked your mom, but she has a lot to do today, and I was wondering if you might want to go? It could be a wonderful experience." It did sound incredible but also scary. I didn't know much about matriarchal tribes, apart from the Amazons. This was why he'd asked about my plans. I was torn, even though Adrian and I didn't technically have plans.

"Um, it's a little unexpected, but yeah, okay. When are we going? And when will we be back?" Disappointed to miss a day with Adrian.

"It'll be about an hour's travel to the village, so he said he'll try to be here by nine-thirty. I doubt we'll be there longer than two hours if that. So, four hours total."

I looked at the clock. Eight. We'd be back by three at the latest.

"I wanted to give you enough time to prepare or give myself enough time to find someone else." He smiled. I slipped from the bed and approached my wardrobe.

"Thanks. I'm not sure if I have the right shoes." When I reached the wardrobe, I did a sly check behind it, but he wasn't there. I took out two pairs and asked my dad which would work better, sneaking a look under the bed. Nothing.

"I think the brown ones with the ankle support would be best." I returned to the bed, feeling nervous. He stood up and left to pack snacks for the trip. The hatch closed, and I turned to scour for Adrian, but there was no need. I stumbled back in shock when I found him standing right before me, grinning, his eyes burning with amusement. My senses rushed, and I clasped my chest as if that would stop my heart from thrashing.

"You see, I told you, I'm fast." His voice raced with exhilaration.

"Freakishly so, yes! Where were you?" Breathlessness weakened the demand.

"Under the bed. I itched to grasp your ankle when you stood, but you would've screamed."

Horror surged through me at the thought.

"Of course I would have! Did you touch my dad?"
He laughed, and his eyes confirmed it. I took a deep breath.

"Are you crazy? Why would you risk that?" My brain struggled to access oxygen.

"It's okay, Josilyn; nothing happened." All amusement.

"But how'd you do that? He looked under the bed and saw nothing. I saw nothing. Are you invisible?" He smirked, laughing again.

"I told you, I'm good at hiding."

"In plain sight?" My voice was shrill, and the anxiety thickened. His eyes shifted a measure, and a small crease formed between his brows.

"Sometimes." His voice softened, and he slid toward me. I tried backing away, but he moved faster and pulled me into his arms. For a moment, I wanted to push away, but instead, I clung to him. It was unsettling, and I was unsure why my reaction was so severe. Swaying, he pressed his cheek to my head, and the warmth enveloped me. His scent registered, and I could feel the dopamine rush through me.

"I'm sorry—I didn't mean to unnerve you. I thought it was exciting." I didn't respond but closed my eyes, listening to his heart—certain it beat slightly slower than in the past. When I'd calmed down, he pulled back and slid one hand to the nape of my neck, melting me with a penetrating gaze.

"I *am* sorry, truly," he said tenderly. "It is a good thing I snuck in; otherwise, it seems I wouldn't have seen you today." His tone betrayed disappointment, shaded with low hues. My stomach twisted, and I felt terrible.

"I'm sorry about that—didn't see it coming. And I would've felt bad to say no."

"I know," he replied.

"You didn't have something specific planned, did you?" My guilt smothered me.

He chuckled, easing my anxiety somewhat.

"Well, not more than usual, just to lure you away."

"Would you stay a little longer?" The words came out unbidden, and I blushed at their boldness.

"I'll stay as long as you want me to."

My heart swelled as he squeezed me, the heat seeping into my bones again. He released me. I took the tray and sat on the windowsill, and he lay down on my bed, propping himself on one elbow, and gazed at me. He was too big for the bed, his feet hanging off the edge. He painted quite an image, draped across my bed; his thick burgundy hair, short-sleeved navy button-up shirt, dark jeans, and leather boots contrasted starkly against the soft grey voile swaying in the gentle draught.

"So, your father is meeting with the Mjesecai."

"Yeah, he's writing a historical novel and wants his information to be accurate."

He smiled, nodding.

"If facts are what he's searching for, asking a superstitious primitive tribe might not be the best route."

I shrugged.

"Well, it's not a history book. Stuff like this is interesting to him. He might get nothing from them, or even use whatever he learns. His interest lies more in the town's origin, and they've been here since the beginning. So, it makes sense he'd want to hear what they have to tell."

"Nonetheless, don't take everything they say too seriously."
I nodded and continued eating.

A little after nine, I realised I'd better dress and head downstairs before my dad came looking for me again, but when Adrian stood, my heart sank.

"What will you be up to later today?" I kept blurting these things out which had no permission to do so.

He smiled, eyes dancing as he stepped closer and wove his fingers through my hair.

"Sounds like I'll be here." My heart fluttered. He bent lower and pressed a delicate kiss on my lips before pulling away. I nearly stumbled forward, following his sudden retreat. "Take care of yourself out there." He stepped back and opened the trapdoor. I was about to protest, but after the magic trick he'd pulled in plain sight earlier, I believed he'd walk right past my parents unnoticed.

"I'll do my best."

He descended, but right before closing the trapdoor, he stopped and looked up at me, curling his index finger, summoning me closer. A little confused, I crouched down. He shot forward and kissed me on the cheek before drawing back into the hollow and closing the door. Taken aback and blushing, I smiled.

I dressed in a rush, grabbed my backpack, and ran downstairs. While waiting on the porch, we heard Komelsha long before we saw him. Wide-eyed, we looked at each other as the ruckus approached. The colossal custom truck crawling from the forest was unlike anything I had ever seen before. Under a layer of mud, the monstrosity appeared to be beige. The bumper looked like something out of a dungeon; huge, jagged spikes pointed in all directions, with branches stuck between them. The wheels were gigantic, and their diametre seemed scarcely a few inches shorter than I was. It sounded like a pained whale as it approached. I questioned my decision.

"It's huge," I spoke as it circled around.

"Right? He built her up himself. Rkelta, the monster in Nomratj."

Rkelta stopped and the sudden silence rang in my ears, my senses dipping. The massive door cracked open, and I gasped under my breath at the striking man who appeared. He was as dark as strong coffee, but his smile was a bright, shining sun.

"Morning, Sir Joseph," he spoke with a heavy accent, and jumped down, a graceful shadow landing on the ground. He was lean and tall, with sleek black hair tied into a long braid.

"Good morning, Komelsha. This is my daughter, Josilyn."

He looked at me and bowed his head. His eyes were dark, but vibrant and sharp. I guessed he was in his late twenties.

"Josilyn," he placed his open hand on his chest, "Beautiful hair. Every woman's crown. For us, it shows authority and power, like a fur coat on a leopard. Let me get the ladder." He turned and, with a little run-up, jumped on the rear wheel and swung himself over, disappearing into the back. Surprised, I looked at my dad.

"That's impressive."

"I think my knee popped out just looking at that." He wiggled his leg, and I laughed. Komelsha reappeared holding a wooden ladder and jumped to the ground. I gasped, but he landed on his feet as easily as if it'd been only a few inches. If it were me, I would be writhing in agony on the ground. He walked around back, and Dad and I stood there awkwardly, awaiting instructions.

"Miss Josilyn, please?" We followed him around to find the ladder propped against the truck into the cabin. He held it as I wobbled up. The passenger seat was a wide two-seater upholstered with stained yellow leather. The air was heavy with the smell of oil and mud, making my nose itch. Dad clambered in, and Komelsha closed the door with a loud creak and a bang. We heard him climb on the back and put the ladder down, and my heart dipped when he swung himself into the driver's side from the back. He would be an extraordinary stuntman. The monster roared to life, and I struggled to hear myself think. My stomach churned, and I clutched the backpack against my chest.

"You'll get used to it," Komelsha yelled, his full mouth curved in a smile. Not convinced, I smiled back. We moved forward, the high vantage point strangely disorienting. Nausea built up in my stomach, and I pulled the backpack closer. Komelsha drove fast, and we flew down the stone path, the trees blurring past. It felt like I was travelling down a portal. A bumpy, uncomfortable portal. He turned into the road we had used the first day we arrived, and after what felt like a thousand kilometres, he slowed and turned right, back towards the mountain. A concealed entrance and a sharp turn took us onto an unmaintained gravel road, the forest encroaching on it like an ancient, hungry creature. As we were immersed in the shadow of the forest, the atmosphere shifted, and I shivered. My dad and I looked at each other as if we both felt it.

Komelsha laughed.

"Don't concern. Is normal." We could only stare at him.

Maybe he was waiting to see if we noticed. I'd give Rkelta that: there was little difference between driving the tar road and the gravel road. We climbed first and then descended, only to rise again. The deeper we moved into the ancient forest, the more it swallowed the road. The massive, spiked bumper made sense now.

"Isn't this a maintenance road?" My dad asked when we hit the third blockage of branches on the road. Komelsha smiled.

"Maintenance for what?" He looked at the road ahead.

"Don't you come here often?" My dad pushed, and Komelsha went quiet for a moment.

"No, Sir Joseph. I leave, remember?" A shadow of sadness tinged his voice.

"How did you confirm we can come today?" Dad's voice had an edge. I elbowed him, and he flinched, scowling at me.

"It's take long time, but I got accepted a walkie-talkie in village. I stop at tar road and call. Is young warrior." It took some concentration to follow.

I tried lightening the mood. "Is it battery-powered?"

"Sun." Sensible. We approached an overgrown dead end, and Rkelta slowed, then quieted when Komelsha cut the engine and cracked open his door.

"I come now." He swung himself into the back again. With much effort, my dad opened the door on his side and looked at the ground far below.

"Boy, I didn't quite plan on breaking my legs today, but I supose I must make some sacrifices for an exciting story."

"Yes." I placed my hands on his back and pretended to push, a jolt shot through him.

"Hey!"

I laughed.

Komelsha materialised below us, holding the scariest blade I'd ever seen, huge and rusted but far from blunt. My dad and I froze.

"Did you bring us all the way to murder us?" Dad asked. Komelsha looked confused at first, but then his white smile beamed as he pegged the blade into the thick undergrowth.

"Panga, for the forest." He held his arms up. "You jump? Don't worry, Sir Joseph. I catch you good, don't mind." I wondered what Nomratj sounded like.

"Uh, no thanks, Komelsha." My dad turned in his seat, found his footing, and grabbed hold of the bar beside him as he lowered himself. He had a determined look on his face. I could see Komelsha below, lips pursed, and arms outstretched, as my dad dangled from the cabin, searching for, and not finding a foothold. My dad grunted, and I suppressed my laughter. Finally, it looked as if Komelsha couldn't take it anymore and he stepped closer. I don't know what happened, but my dad's eyes widened.

"No, no," he protested but swiftly found himself on the ground, where he commenced clearing his throat and straightening his clothes. Komelsha smiled and looked up at me, arms outstretched.

"You jump butt first. I catch."

I inched closer to the opening and found my footing. It was a near two-metre jump.

"You gon need to trust me." Telling myself not to think about it, I jumped. I felt surprised to feel almost nothing as he gently caught me, like a shock absorber, and placed me on the ground. Disorienting— having expected a larger impact, or pain even. A sudden unease fell on me as I stood there. A sense of not belonging. As if a thousand sets of eyes—and one—were gazing at us, inspecting. The thick air pressed against me, and the birdsong stirred up a sense of entrapment. Nowhere to run. Nowhere to turn. Stuck between walls and walls of green. Right behind Rkelta, the volcano loomed, tall and sharp. My stomach twisted, looking at it.

"Welcome to the forest. Is different to be inside." Komelsha announced with arms spread wide.

My dad nodded. "You're quite right there. How far is the village from here?"

"Few kilometres." He turned, and we followed him around the truck where there was a break in the treeline. He entered and Dad followed, but I lingered a short distance from the border, my heart pounding. My senses drifted, and my knees buckled. The ultraviolet world writhed with life and energy, but it was overwhelming, and my throat tightened.

"Josilyn?" The forest called with a muffled voice. I took deep breaths and closed my eyes, forcing my senses back into order.

"Coming! Give me a moment." My voice trembled, straining under the weight of my emotions. Senses slurring back into place, I stepped forward. A rough path stretched before me, bending, curving, and dipping. Moss-covered roots stretched over it like tentacles. A memory itched for remembrance but evaded me as I reached for it. Komelsha stood at the furthest bend, waiting.

"Keep close, please."

I moved faster. The path was spongy beneath my feet, cushioned by layers of leaves and moss. It was an ancient, forbidden wilderness. The birdsong echoed in surround sound around us. I took controlled breaths, focusing on each step and trying to suppress the simmering *Pulse*. Chills periodically ran along my spine as I walked on, gazing through the endless row of knotted tree trunks.

"These look like the ones in your room," my dad pointed at a galaxy cluster of orchids a little way off the path.

Komelsha looked.

"Latrjimea, tears of the moon. We use tea for sleep and clothes dye."

"Huh. Maybe you should try that, Hon."

I couldn't see myself making tea from the flowers Adrian gave me. The path breathed—narrowing and widening in turn until we reached a section that was completely overgrown. Komelsha hacked away, opening a path.

"Every day, there is village watcher. They will find us and bring to village. Only one is bad news, but I make certain it's not them today. For the warriors, don't make long eye contact. It is rude." Strange. At least he gave us a warning.

Progress slowed as we walked further, and I was unsure whether it was my lack of fitness or the pressure that increased, but it became more and more difficult to breathe.

We stopped a few times for water and to rest. The entire expedition lasted about an hour but felt like an eternity. My dad had fallen back, but in his defence, he was also taking photos, when Komelsha stopped short, and I bumped into him.

"Sorr—" He interrupted my apology by turning around and putting a finger to his lips. Ice dripped down my spine. His breaths came fast and wide, alert eyes looked up—scanning the trees. I followed his gaze, searching, when my eyes were drawn to a specific area. Komelsha looked there too, and I thought I caught a movement a second later. My senses dipped, the world lit up, and I looked down. Komelsha's body was rigid. I was aware of Dad being further back, frozen in place. The distance between us felt like an entire world. Komelsha cursed—in English—under his breath.

"El kajiti, par quell tah!" His voice was raw with nerves. The language was strange in my ear. Everything became ominously quiet; seconds dragged by, and my pulse raced. I held my breath.

"Ajenter gorev chel," a deceptively casual and deep female voice slithered through the trees. It stunned me, though it shouldn't have. It was a matriarchal tribe, after all. Komelsha's face distorted with apparent shock, which was discomforting. I ached to know what was said.

"Quell tah, paros," he hesitated, "Orchendas."

Whoever was in the trees remained quiet for a long time. Tension strung the air, and I looked for my dad; wondering if we were in actual danger.

"Bürg ajeldon, Orchendas." Her voice sounded hostile. It felt like she was gone as her words died. Komelsha blew out a breath, which he was holding, and faced me. He signalled for my dad to come closer before whispering.

"Luck was not ours. I don't understand. She must've caught word after I asked. That was Xorvelca, a most fierce warrior. Not friendly. I say you visitors for Great Mother. She's gone ask permission. I'm sorry. Another would let us just go along. We will wait here."

A most fierce warrior. That was not reassuring. I wondered whether 'Orchendas' was The Great Mother. He had spoken the word with reverence, and she had repeated it.

"Are we safe, though?" My father voiced my concern. Komelsha looked away.

"For most part, yes."

"I need more than that, Komelsha. I brought my daughter out here thinking it's safe."

"Xorvelca is different from the others. You will be okay." Dad gave me a look.

"Wait here," Komelsha instructed and walked off.

"I'm sorry about this, Josilyn. Not quite what I thought it would be like."

"How could you have known? Besides, he said it would've been different if it was another one." I didn't want to talk because it felt like everything was listening. My heart pounded faster. Komelsha returned and told us to follow him. A little way further, there was a small clearing where we stood waiting, and Komelsha started pacing around. My dad asked what would happen if permission was denied. Avoiding eye contact, he said it was unlikely, but something about the way his voice sounded was unconvincing. Perhaps I was naïve, but I couldn't imagine what the horrible repercussions would be. Surely, she wouldn't just kill us. The tribe wouldn't be so easily accessible to the public if they were an actual threat. My dad looked at me and sighed.

"At least it would make a cool story for our tombstones."

"Maybe someone will write a book about it." He grimaced.

"Orchendas tarov paros cal." The voice came from nowhere, startling us all. Komelsha expelled a breath. Somehow, I had the feeling that she'd been watching from the shadows a while before saying something. I guess we won't get slaughtered just yet.

"Kell jon," relief flooded his voice. He faced us.

"The Great Mother consents. Xorvelca will escort us from the trees."

We proceeded at a slow pace, Dad and I speaking in subdued tones. The path faded, forcing us to climb over roots and scout for the way. *She* remained hidden above us, covered by the thick leaves. Komelsha reminded us not to keep prolonged eye contact, especially *'with the one above'*, no matter how difficult it may be. He avoided using her name. She may have had a sixth sense, though, because she spoke to him right after. I wondered why it would be difficult but refrained from asking. Perhaps she was deformed somehow. My mind kept trying to conjure an image of her. It curdled my blood. My dad asked what she'd said, and I gave him a look. Apparently, she wanted to know if we were alone. The question sent a shiver down my spine.

The trees thinned ahead, leading us into a small clearing where water flowed over moss-covered rock formations and the ribbiting of frogs filled the air. My eyes absorbed the details, and it all overwhelmed my heart. Then, a statue amongst the shadows seized my attention, incongruent with the trees.

Except it wasn't a statue.

Hunched on the ground, hands touching the earth like she'd just landed or was about to pounce. She looked like a panther—the wildest, most beautiful thing I'd ever seen. The breath caught in my throat at the sight of her.

"Xorvelca," Komelsha breathed. Slowly, she straightened to her enormous height, making her appear even more frightening. She was a feral goddess cut from obsidian. Her pitch-black braids jostled at her hips. I absorbed all I could while trying not to look into her eyes. I was too frightened, but knew I had to. My senses brimmed, shifty, and goosebumps rolled over me. I looked up and caught an audible breath. She was staring at me with piercing, ice-blue eyes; what lay behind them, I couldn't fathom. I looked down, unnerved that she was staring at me. My pulse surged, and I felt lightheaded. My senses drifted, and I focussed on locking it out.

Fascinating, how adrenaline causes hyper-observance. After only a glimpse of her, my mind had a detailed picture. She was a stunning beauty by any standard with her full lips and satin smooth skin. A section of her hair was braided against the top of her head into two Dutch braids, but the rest hung loose like a curtain. Peacock feathers dangled at the ends. It showed how deceptive beauty could be—If I'd seen a photo of her, I would have thought her harmless. But she was dangerous. One look into her eyes confirmed she knew no fear. She would run into hell without flinching.

She shielded her eyes with one hand before extending it to him. He did the same.

"Komelsha," she finally said after a sticky silence. Her voice was almost sultry. I couldn't help but stare now. She was mythic. Garbed in what looked like a layered miniskirt of dark midnight blue leather, it blended into her skin. The top was the same blue but with patches of fur. Strange furrows dug into the skin of her stomach, which, at first, I took for scarring, but then realised were leather straps. They looked uncomfortable. I wondered about their purpose.

"Galitavi dol matjes." She barked, startling me. I stopped myself from looking up—a difficult rule to abide by.

"Um, Josilyn, she don't like you stare at her." Komelsha sounded nervous. My heart skipped a beat, and my senses boiled. She had to have been looking at me.

"Teca." She turned and walked into the forest. Komelsha followed, and so did we. Dad looked at me with saucer-sized eyes, communicating what we were both feeling. He squeezed my shoulder and let me walk first.

Progress was slow through the forest. In the distance, I could hear rushing water from a river or a spring. Several times I looked around me, thinking I'd heard a whisper in the wind. I wondered again about Xorvelca asking if we were alone. Who would have followed us? The light up ahead brightened, and the pressure seemed to lift—breathing became easier. My senses bristled with relief and excitement, and I itched to walk faster.

Komelsha turned.

"Would you loose your hair? See as peacock opening his tail." His smile had dimmed compared to earlier. I unwound my braids. Usually, my hair felt like a shield, but I felt exposed as I spread it around me.

We stepped out from amongst the trees into a fantasy. A tranquil green meadow glowed in the new light. I squinted against the new brightness. A river meandered around it to our right, white moss-stained boulders lining the edge and scattered across the width. The water was bluer than the lake, which was saying something. Trees bordered the other half of the circle. The meadow—which held the village—was partially under the volcano's shadow, and something about the sight was alarming. We were near its base, colossal from our current vantage. My senses lilted, and I staggered.

Right at the centre of the meadow stood a massive grey tree, which looked like a baobab, the trunk as thick as a car. The solid branches reached towards the sky like begging arms, but at the top, they cradled a hut fashioned from grey branches or grass. Strange lights on the branches refracted and glistened in the filtered light. An overcast sky painted a melancholic coat over the entire scene. I looked at my hands, feeling weird for some reason. The clearing was scattered with a few smaller trees of a similar kind. They, too, had huts atop them, but most of the zome-shaped huts were on the ground—all composed of the same grey twig. Domed frames hosted grass pods that hung inside them from the apex and looked like teardrops in a cage. I was uncertain what they were.

Some natives were busy at the river, both men and women wearing vibrant blue smocks adorned with leather, feathers, and what looked like crystals. This was so surreal. The *Pulse* simmered inside my bones, itching to explode. A few kids peeked around the huts but quickly disappeared. It felt like we were intruding.

Xorvelca emitted a sound so frighteningly like a jaguar that my senses spat, my eyeballs vibrating from the spiky sound. The villagers at the water looked at us and stared. My cheeks burned.

"Teca," she said again and stalked towards the large tree. Komelsha followed, and so did we. As we passed the huts, the scent of smoke and tea permeated the air. A few villagers were sitting at the entrances of their huts, poking their fires. They all stared as we passed, and I avoided prolonged eye contact. Some greeted Komelsha, or Xorvelca, with the same gesture I'd seen them use earlier. A circle of white rocks lay arranged in front of the tree—firepit in the middle. It looked like a communal gathering place.

Against the tree trunk was what I would describe as a primitive throne out of the same white stone. Grey branches fanned out behind it, woven through with bright blue webbed strings encrusted with a rainbow of crystals. On either side stood a tall man—dressed differently from the villagers, and I assumed they were warriors because they both held short spears at their sides. A drop of sweat trickled down my neck. I looked at my dad, and he leaned closer.

"It's a lot to take in, isn't it?" I nodded, afraid to speak. Komelsha sat a few rocks away from the throne and urged us to do the same. He seemed nervous, which made me nervous too. In answer to Dad's whispered question, he said the village had around a hundred and thirteen people living there.

"Only look when she's sit," he whispered when we heard movement up in the large tree. Some villagers sat down on the rocks furthest from us. In my peripheral vision, someone trudged to the throne with the slow and rigid movement of an old person. My heart raced. It felt like I was trespassing, more out of place than I ever had, which was saying something.

I bore a shock, my senses shuffling when Komelsha nudged me with his knee. I frowned at him, and he indicated I had to look at her. Unprepared, I took a deep breath and looked up. Her solemn gaze was directed at me, waiting. The black, misty eyes seemed wary; their depths unfathomable. My heartbeat slowed as if the world had been thrown into slow motion. Her hair was whiter than snow, the length indistinguishable because it blended with the light grey fur cloak she wore. I wondered where they had sourced the fur from.

"Belvre, Orchendas," Komelsha spoke, and I looked at him.

"Belvre, Komelsha," her voice dripped wisdom. It sounded much different hearing his name from her.

"Quell tah paros cal, Orchendas." He said after a moment.

"Betica."

I wished I knew what they were saying.

"Sel Keptah, dwano kin partonu, verto, sel empa." His words were gentle.

"Betica."

He breathed relief at her answer.

"Great Mother approves the translation. What do you want to ask Sir Joseph?"

"Let me just get—" my dad dug in his pocket, producing a small notebook and pen. Pandemonium broke out as Xorvelca thrust her dagger toward him. My senses cracked like an egg. I closed my eyes, trying to settle them, as red heartbeats pulsated the air.

"Telma dar! Telma dar! Wison kolen!" Komelsha jumped up, yelling and pleading, his arms outstretched. My dad froze, pen still in hand. Xorvelca stopped and looked at the Great Mother. We all did. She seemed as calm as a breeze, a stark contrast to my pulse, which was flying through my head.

"Wison kolen, epta," Komelsha said, breathless. The Mother nodded, the energy dissipated, and he sat again. Why was Xorvelca so hostile?

"Your pen; she thought it's weapon. You tell me everything before, please. This one's in a mood." I tasted the blood on my tongue. My poor dad was as pale as a corpse, and I reckoned I was, too.

"I—I'm sorry, Komelsha. I—the thought didn't even cross my mind." His voice was hoarse with fear. A peculiar feeling coiled around my stomach and over my skin, like a magnet pulling me to the point of nausea. I yielded and looked up to find Xorvelca staring at me, an odd expression on her face that I couldn't name. Did my staring at her earlier warrant such hostility?

Komelsha and my dad discussed what he wanted to ask, and once translated, she thought for a while before speaking.

"Mjesecai settled in region and was first to live in open. Others were here before us, yes, and they remain still, but are unseen. They are devils, but they don't disrupt our village often, only on occasion. It used to be worse, in the beginning," Komelsha paused because she had. "The Ivories came many generations after. First was road, then the stop, then the house. Later came the mining and the rest. They popped up like mushrooms but didn't bother us, and we not them. The wild animals don't cross the mountain, so we were unaffected."

I endured violent chills at her speaking so openly about supernatural things. I wanted to ask, but I was shell-shocked and too afraid.

"Ivories?"

"White folk."

My dad nodded and wrote. I knew he was interested in hearing more about *'the devils'*.

"And who made first contact?"

"We. The road brought many travellers to the stop, and warriors kept an eye but was not a threat. They didn't come this side. The mountain repels them. Clogs the mind."

I frowned. Why would the mountain clog minds?

"The stop, is that the original inn?" Directed at Komelsha, and he nodded. My dad stuck to the basics—it gnawed at my brain.

"She said it was the road, the inn and then the house. Which house?"

"The one on the mountain's other side—your house, sir Joseph. They made big noise that could be heard here, and it frightened the people. We sent warriors. They made big fire and smoke. They wanted into the mountain, but they don't know they'll never get in."

Our house. Goosebumps rippled over my skin, and I rubbed my arms. Xorvelca's gaze weighed on me still, I knew.

"Hmm, I'm not sure they were trying to get inside. They tried building the house into the volcano. Why did she say they will never get inside?"

"The Dwellers. They made a shield. You will never get in."

There it was. The *Pulse* smouldered inside me.

"Dwellers?"

"Mountain creatures. They live inside the mountain and hunt in dreams. They come out by the waters."

My senses tumbled, and for a moment I saw fog and forest and fear.

"What did she call them?"

"Dwellers."

"No, in Nomratj."

"Oh, Namlakshati."

"Why do they come out by the waters?"

"All waters connected by underground caves. They use to travel. The caves lead into mountain."

My nails pressed into my palms, and I focussed on releasing them.

"What does she mean they hunt in dreams?"

The Great Mother stayed quiet, and my nerves tightened.

"You are awake in your mind. They play games."

My heart raced, and it took violent effort to suppress the *Pulse*.

"What do they look like?"

"You never see them. They too fast. But we think they look like panthers. Unfamiliar footprints have been found around our compound and at the water's edge. Can't tell if they are feline or canine. But the prints were bigger than hand." She held up her hand and spread her fragile fingers wide open. Excited, my dad wanted to know if there were any fresh prints nearby, but there weren't. I looked up on impulse. Xorvelca was gone. I didn't notice her leave, and I looked around.

"So, they're animals?"

"Perhaps. Or more. They are too smart for normal animal. There's not much knowledge other than their existence. We know they are more active on full moons."

I remembered going into the mountain. Something was there. My heart thrummed, and I looked at the ground, trying to restrain the *Pulse*. She continued.

"You can't hide anything from them. They see. They always do. Our ancestors warned us. They lurk in the shadows and listen to our heads, spying on our dreams. That is all."

Indicating the subject was closed. Pins and needles pricked my skin. My senses lagged.

"Okay. Why don't the animals cross the mountain?"

"They're too afraid."

"Alright." My dad scribbled on his notepad for a while, and I took a deep breath. For some reason, I struggled to breathe again.

"Why are you so certain about these Dwellers? Maybe they're just normal animals." I heard myself speak for the first time, and it caused a stir. Komelsha seemed to have forgotten about me. He translated, but she remained silent. Xorvelca appeared from behind the trunk and approached her, whispering something in her ear, which made her look at me. My heart dipped. Xorvelca straightened and stepped away, while I looked into her icy eyes again. I had instigated eye contact multiple times, but she still hadn't attempted to take my life. The Great Mother spoke, and Komelsha frowned, repeating the phrase. They exchanged more words, and I thought I heard a distorted version of my name.

"Um, Josilyn, she wants you to come closer." I felt lightheaded.

"What?" My voice sounded as bewildered as my dad looked. I should've stayed quiet.

"I don't know, but it's best you do."
My dad and I exchanged looks, and he squeezed my knee.

"I'm sure it'll be okay," he whispered. I gulped and stood, though I felt tied to the boulder. Komelsha rose, too. I approached the throne on unsteady legs as if I'd forgotten how to walk.

"Kneel before her," Komelsha instructed when we were close.

Aghast, I looked at him.

"Excuse me?" I was unaccustomed to kneeling before anything or anybody.

His lips pulled into a grimace.

"It doesn't mean what it do to you. She is Great Mother, not a god. Kneeling is giving trust." But I didn't trust any of it. The *Pulse* boiled inside my veins, fire in my bones. I sucked a deep breath, subduing the peculiar rage I felt out of the blue.

I kneeled, my throat tightening, and looked at her bare feet. They were clean and well cared for. She leaned forward and said something to Komelsha.

"She wants you to look at her, in eyes." He sat to her left on a boulder, and I frowned at him. Wasn't that what I wasn't supposed to do?

"I thought eye contact was a no-go?" My defiance surprised even me.

"Eyes are doors to spirit. You don't walk naked before strangers. It is honour to be granted the eyes." That deepened the meaning of how they greeted each other. It would've helped if he'd mentioned it earlier. The *Pulse* bristled in my neck; I looked up and locked eyes with her. Her face was close to mine, and the energy vibrated beneath my skin. Unnerving—staring into the wise black pools. Her irises were dark and indistinguishable from the pupils. She stared into me like she could read my insides like a book. My soul rose inside me, and my breathing increased. I felt naked indeed before this stranger and fought the urge to look away.

"Lacrita cletsova!" Xorvelca spat. Mother didn't move, but a jolt went through me, and my senses tilted. As soon as I closed my eyes and pulled back, Mother clasped my face between icy hands. I couldn't suppress the shudder as she looked deep into my eyes again. I felt the compulsion to pull away. She whispered something to Komelsha, but he didn't translate. He hesitated before kneeling beside me and leant closer. I tried to look at him, but my face was still held hostage.

"What's going on?" Anger simmered at the seams.

"She wants only you to hear," he whispered. She released my face but stayed close, eyes on mine. My heartbeat slowed as the madness waned. When I had calmed, she spoke.

"Your eyes have seen things no human is supposed to see, Child. I see the scars."

I frowned, but her expression remained blank. She was right—I did see things others didn't. Before I could ask for clarification, she continued.

"Like splitting branch, your life has come to a fork. You decide which branch you're going to walk on."

Ambiguous.

Xorvelca knelt and grabbed Mother's arm; her eyes pleading. The meekness and vulnerability on her face caught me off guard. I wondered if this was *her* mother.

"Lacrita cletsova," she repeated feebly.

"What is she saying?" I thought out loud, flinching when I realised I had spoken. They took no notice of me, which was a relief.

Komelsha took a moment to respond. "I smell it on her."

A chill ran down my spine. What did she smell on me?

"What?" I barely managed.

"I don't know. They aren't speaking."

But the question was intended for him. Didn't he know what they meant? I was relieved when she turned to me and spoke again, but it was short-lived. Her words were disturbing.

"Seems they have a taste for strange beauty. The battle could already be lost."

My brain had no idea what to make of that. Adrian's words came to me, *'Don't take everything they say too seriously'*. I decided not to let cryptic native ramblings upset me.

"I've seen what I wanted." She drew back and straightened. When she removed her eyes from mine, I felt naked again. I stood and joined my dad, who looked distressed, searching my face. I scrunched my eyes briefly, trying to convey that I was okay.

"Anything else, Sir Joseph?"

Dad took a second to resurface from his thoughts and asked. I didn't listen. My mind raced, and I just wanted to get home. I hoped Adrian would still come.

"…—I think what you want to know is about the girl," drew my attention back.

"Uh, yes, please." Dad sounded excited.

"She was the daughter of the sun, her skin white as snow, her hair flax. Our ancients thought she was a goddess or an enchantress. But she just child then. She returned later when she was older. She wasn't the enchantress, but one was with her. That's all we know."

I could just imagine their reaction to seeing a fair-skinned blonde for the first time. Dad asked about their name for the town. They called it Del-Crovar, not Ostia. It meant the Dream Veil. In light of what they'd said about the Dwellers, Dad asked a few more questions. I checked out, eager to leave. Finally, they stood, and after the greetings, we headed back. It seemed we would be without an escort, and I was thankful, ready to get away from there. I had the weird sense that my presence had made them uneasy.

As we moved through the forest, I wondered, in the back of my mind, if a warrior followed us because I had the same sense as earlier—of being watched. But I'd felt that since we entered the forest and I didn't think about it too much. My dad engaged Komelsha on the walk back, and I caught bits and pieces of the conversation. When Komelsha was young, he and his mother became sick to the point of near death, and none of their traditional medicine helped. His father, afraid of losing them both, decided to trek to Ostia for help. His mother didn't survive the journey, but Komelsha spent two weeks in the hospital and received physical therapy for a month. That's how he learned English. A non-profit organisation covered all the medical costs. When his father died six years ago, he moved to town permanently. It was sad to think that his mother might've still been alive if the villagers had been willing to accept help from outside. The conversation sped the time, and before we knew it, we saw the truck ahead. I was happier seeing it this time around, and sitting on the soft seat was a sweet relief. Komelsha executed a fifty-point turn in the opening, but the drive back felt smoother.

I asked him why only Xorvelca's eyes were blue, and although he seemed hesitant, he told the story: Her eyes had been as dark as theirs when she was born, but one night a Dweller snatched her mother right in front of her. After that, her eyes turned blue. The rumour was she'd laid eyes on the creature, but she never spoke about that night. I felt a swell of empathy for her. It must've been uncomfortable—listening to us talk about them. And me asking if they were even real. No wonder she wanted to gut me. Dad was perusing his notes, so I took the opportunity to ask Komelsha again what she'd meant by smelling it on me. He shrugged, saying he had no clue and not to worry about it too much. She was, after all, a bit offbeat. I wondered what he meant with that because the same could be said about me.

We arrived home around three o'clock to find Andrew and Mom sitting on the porch. Komelsha had mercy on us and retrieved the ladder so we could climb down. I wondered why that hadn't been an option earlier. Andrew seemed fascinated with Rkelta and Komelsha indulged him, even letting him climb on the back. Mom asked for a rundown, and I relayed our experience, leaving out the creepy, scary bits. The peace of being home and not under threat soon sapped all my energy. I was drowsy but unwilling to climb stairs, so I lay outside in the hammock. Soon, I drifted into sleep, the swaying hammock morphing into a boat, and I drifted down a river. The volcano towered to my right, and bird songs echoed around me.

"Josilyn," my name—whispered across the waters. I stayed still, listening, and the boat glided into the mist. The whisper came again, surrounding me—I couldn't tell from where. I attempted to sit, rocking the boat.

I was sitting in the hammock, awake.

"Josilyn, you have a visitor." *Mom.* Excitement trilled in her voice. The meaning of her words didn't register as I was disoriented, shifting from one environment into another in a blink. I looked at my hands, but they were fine.

"What?" I found my voice, though rusty. I looked up to see Adrian standing on the porch beside my mom. My heart galloped at his lopsided smile.

Mom's eyes were sparkling, even from the distance, and she offered him something to eat or drink. He graciously declined and came closer.

She winked at me and quickly walked into the house. *Subtle.* My cheeks burned as Adrian approached.

"Hey," I managed as I struggled to escape the hammock. Adrian bent, took my ankles, and pivoted my legs to dangle off the side. He sat down beside me, and I shrieked as I rolled over, ending up squished against him. He laughed and lay back, relaxed, his long arm stretched to the side and his feet still on the ground. His heat spilt over me. Feeling awkward, I tried pushing myself into a stable position, but the only thing I could push against was him. My pulse raced, and my face burned.

"A warning would've been nice."

"You've had enough warning," he chuckled. I found an almost comfortable position. "How was your tribal experience?"

I told him everything except about the Great Mother calling me closer and what came after.

"They said there are Dwellers living inside the mountain, and they're like panthers."

"Panthers?" He repeated, "Interesting." He placed his fingertips on my head, half massaging, half caressing, while we spoke. When my dad appeared, my face lit up like a glow stick at our compromising position. Unfazed, Adrian stood up and shook his hand. He enquired about the book and the trip and, from Dad's reaction, I could see his interest meant a lot. Adrian left around five o'clock with the promise of seeing me the next day.

I had loads of work to catch up on, so I went to my room after dinner. I snubbed the pill, fearing I wouldn't wake up in time for my eight o'clock class. As I struggled to fall asleep, I had the perturbing feeling someone was watching me.

Chapter 11

I dreamt of the forest, the Mjesecai, Xorvelca's icy gaze, and Mother's strange words. But they were normal, to the extent that dreams could be. I was delighted to be woken by my alarm, feeling rested despite my legs feeling heavy from the exertion of the day before. Tji-Tji was curled up between my pillows, meowing for attention. Ominous dark clouds loomed outside. My skin felt sensitive under the shower's warm water, and I adjusted the temperature to colder than usual.

As usual, I was alone on the stone road. Mist seeped through the trees and onto the road all around me. In the rear-view mirror, the volcano looked dark and portentous, shrouded in a thick, heavy mist that spilled over and lingered between the glens. The sun rallied as I drove, breaking through the clouds here and there, sunlight shimmering on the mist like a creeping flame. Mist tentacles on the lake fought against the sun's heat, swirling, begging, and it stirred something within me. My pulse climbed. Somewhere in my mind, a door shivered and quaked to be opened, but I refused, turning my gaze away from the volcano and the waters. A thought slipped through. I dreamt about something I had been unaware existed, and Mother said they were like panthers. Predators. The hidden creature from my dream had four legs. I pushed the thought away.

As I turned the corner, I slammed on the brakes, my senses dipping. The lawn was flooded with people, which was strange given the weather and the time, close to eight o'clock. I found a far-off parking and curiosity burned as I hurried closer—energy simmering. Nothing in the snatches of conversations I heard in passing clarified what was going on. The crowd thickened near the main building, and I couldn't see Laura. I searched, searched, still catching conversational bits and pieces, but nothing solid. I lifted to my tiptoes to look up at the building, eyes stinging in the filtered light.

"Yeah, no, I don't know either," Laura's voice drifted towards me. She was standing to the left—thick padded clothes against the weather, her hood pulled up, speaking on the phone. Someone standing about two metres away from her caught my eye. He was exceedingly tall and muscular, with his back towards her and his right side facing at an angle towards me. His height reminded me of Adrian, prompting a double take as I inspected him. Apart from the height and olive skin, there wasn't much of a resemblance. Almost none at all, actually—strange that I even thought it. He had short, medium-brown hair and wore a khaki T-shirt, dark jeans, and walking boots. The loose T-shirt accentuated his back muscles, which were bulky and tensed, a thick vein network curling over his thick arms. He seemed unbothered by the cold. I found it impossible to break my gaze, and the *Pulse* simmered through my body, prickling like goosebumps. I felt certain he was not a student. He had a rugged, primal yet military look about him, like a prowling lion, head dipped low as it stalked its prey. *Why would someone like him be here?* He stood motionless apart from shifting his head a little, as if listening. I could see more of his face, poised in a frown, his prominent jaw clenched enough to show striations.

"There you are!" A jolt shot through me, my senses shuffling, when Laura yelled. When they settled, I looked at him. He remained a motionless and focussed statue.

"What's going on?" My voice sounded strange, and I cleared my throat.

"No idea. Someone said there's something inside which must be removed, but I don't know what. No one's allowed inside."

"What do you mean they have to remove something?" She shrugged.

"I don't know. I saw a few people enter with cages and nets. Maybe it's a rat infestation or something."

"Ew. That might take longer than a few hours." She wrinkled her nose as we looked up at the building, searching for telltale signs.

"It's so cold, though. Maybe we can wait in your car…" her voice trailed off as her eyes widened. She stared at my left shoulder. "I think I know what it is."

"What?" I looked down and saw a blue so radiant, it hurt my eyes. It took a second before recognition dropped. *Peleides Morpho*, large and alive, sitting on my shoulder. An icy breeze rose and levitated my loose hair around me like a dark halo. My senses thumped, and Laura caught her breath.

"Stay still. I'll call someone," she left while speaking, and my senses roiled like waves. The world spun and exploded into ultraviolet colours. My heart raced as a hurricane of light and mist engulfed me. Heat radiated against my left shoulder, pulling me back to reality. As my senses settled, a pair of hostile brown eyes confronted me, unyielding as an earthquake. I stumbled backwards, my senses drifting again. A black mist corona where he stood—I turned my face away. The butterfly rose but then resettled on my shoulder. I turned back. It was *him*. Was I hallucinating? My pulse hammered against my throat, my lungs burning as we looked at each other—or as I looked at him. For his part, it seemed he was glaring in a way that went beyond mere eye contact. His piercing, virulent stare burned with a fury I had never seen before. Inwardly I squirmed, recoiling from his glare, but no matter how much I itched to run away, I couldn't move. My mind was empty—pure emotion distilled into fear. His mouth constricted into a stiff line as he towered over me—a statue of a disdained god. Nothing moved, not even his eyelids. From somewhere, a thought slithered through as I looked at him. Something about his eyes looked familiar, but I couldn't place it. My soul was bared before him; his radiant heat lashed at my skin. My breathing was shallow. I tried speaking, but opening my mouth was impossible.

Nervous chatter approached in the background of my consciousness; the words indistinguishable. My throat burned and pounded with the urge to scream. His expression of unbridled loathing had somehow intensified. The next moment, he turned around and darted through the crowd at an eerie speed, like a fleeing ghost. I kept staring until he disappeared. My nerves twisted, my senses spluttering again. Tears burned behind my eyes. What had I done to provoke such vehement hate? Flustered, I turned around, intending to go straight home.

"Wait!" A man wearing a white overall stood facing me, his palms out. For a split second, I thought of an asylum orderly coming to take me away, but the bright blue in my peripheral reminded me of the *Morpho* on my shoulder. I was trembling, stunned by the hate from someone I had never met. My inner turmoil stilled when Laura touched me. I shook my head, clearing the clutter.

"Hey, are you all right?" She was frowning, visibly concerned. The man and the butterfly were gone.

"Oh, sorry," my voice was hoarse, and I tasted blood.

"What's going on?"

I pulled my arm away.

"I'm freaked out. Did you see that guy standing here?" She looked at the ground.

"Uh, no… I don't think I saw anyone. Why? What happened?" I was taken aback. How did she not see him?

"You didn't see him? He was standing right here!" I asked, incredulous. Huge and imposing.

She shook her head.

"No, sorry."

"Well, anyway. I noticed him earlier, but as soon as you left, he accosted me, staring me down like he hated me enough to kill me.

I couldn't move. It frightened me half to death. I've never even seen the guy before."

Distress alchemised into anger, and she mirrored it.

"What the heck? Are you serious?" She looked around. "Where is he? What does he look like?" I had no doubt that if she hunted him down, he'd be sorry.

"He left. I don't know where he went. But honestly, I can't imagine how you missed him. He's as tall as Adrian, brown hair. Wearing a short-sleeved khaki T-shirt."

"A short sle—Well, that explains it. He's clearly crazy."

"What's *crazy*, is you not seeing him." A spike of fear licked my neck. What if he wasn't actually there?

She brushed that aside.

"No, no. He might be tall, but he's obviously a small man to act like that, and I don't notice small men. But I *do* notice bright blue butterflies about to fly away. That's the hold-up, by the way. Somehow, a *Morpho* swarm invaded the faculty yesterday, and they're trying to catch them. Main building classes will move to the satellites, but they're figuring it out. So, we wait." She walked off, and I followed, unsure where to.

"Even the insects are going crazy. This town keeps getting weirder." I thought out loud.

"Only since you've arrived. Before that, we had reasonable measures of odd; now it's just overflowing," Laura smiled—a joke, but was it, though? Life had tipped over into the eerie since we'd arrived. She negotiated her way through the crowd towards the fountain across the road and sat on the edge. I joined her, shivering on the icy surface. The last time I was here, I had that weird experience.

"Where is your boyfriend?" I was taken aback, confused at first by the word. It seemed ill-fitting. He wasn't, though. Was he?

"He's not my boyfriend." I said quickly, "But I don't know. He might be around." As I cast about for wine-red hair. I realised I hadn't thought much about him at all until then. Odd.

"But he's not *not* your boyfriend either, right?"

"He didn't ask to be my boyfriend." He did, however, tell me I was his, which might be a shade more serious. "I don't really like that word."

"Would you go on a romantic date with another guy?"

"No." the idea discomforted me.

"Not even the blonde guy from the ball, if he materialised?"

I frowned.

"What blonde guy?"

Her turn to frown, she looked away as she pondered.

"The blonde guy you danced with at the ball…?"

"I don't remember a blonde guy. I only danced with Adrian and the dancing aides. No blonde one."

Where had she seen a blonde guy? As we contemplated, I felt the prickle of someone staring at me and looked up into Brinelle's pensive frown. He was leaning against a tree across the road. My heart skipped a beat, and I only half-listened to Laura commenting about Adrian's weird vibe she couldn't put her finger on. I looked away—hoping it was coincidental eye contact—and noticed the crowd moving away from the main building.

"Something's happening." I rose. "I forgot my bag in the car. Message me where our class is; my phone is in the bag." She crossed the road as I rushed towards my car, which I realised was parked quite far away. At least I'd had the presence of mind to lock it. I was power walking back, anticipating Laura's message and texting my dad about the *Morpho* infestation, when someone stepped into my path. We almost collided, and I nearly tripped over my feet trying to sidestep him. I met Brinelle's confused gaze. My heart sank. Neither of us spoke as we stared at each other. His eyes were cloudy and dazed, forehead creased in a frown. He opened his mouth but only spoke after an awkward pause.

"Do…" he paused, "do I know you from somewhere?" He seemed sincere enough, like he genuinely didn't remember me. *Was he being clever?*

"We've… exchanged words," I replied, as vague and curt as possible. His frown deepened.

"Ha… your face looks faintly familiar, but… I can't recall… What did we talk about?" His eyes were dim and foggy. Did he honestly not remember? I scrutinised his face for any false twitch but found none.

"Um… we… talked about music." An understatement, sure, but I assessed his amnesia. His confusion didn't dissipate.

"We did? I can't…" he looked as puzzled as I felt. I preferred not to linger until he remembered the actual conversation.

"I must get to class, so please excuse me…" I started past him, half expecting him to block me like before, but he stepped aside.

"Of course…" he seemed lost in thought. Perplexing that he'd forgotten our encounter. He'd have a hard time as a musician if he had actual amnesia or memory problems.

Laura was nowhere to be seen, but a message had come through. The class was in an unfamiliar satellite building. She'd sent landmark photos en route. Confused students filled the narrow alleys between the satellites. I folded, looking around for Adrian. He wouldn't know where the class was if he came. I wondered where he was. He said he'd see me today.

I found the class and squeezed into my seat. The classroom was small, and I scanned the room for his red hair, but the search was moot. I finished the text to Dad about the *Morphos*. We barely had a first period, and the rest of the day was chaotic with the changes. After each class, I searched for the wine-red hair, my heart speeding up with anticipation. The disappointment became more pronounced each time I came up short. I hoped nothing had happened. His absence stirred up my anxiety, and I struggled to concentrate as the day wore on. Dad invited me to lunch at a nearby café, and just as I headed there, the rain started pelting down. Dad laughed when I arrived soaking through and cold. At least they had a fireplace, which I was tempted to climb wholly into. The staff were nice enough to offer me blankets. Time passed, but I was anxious to return to campus, in case I missed Adrian. Dad drove me back and handed me an extra jacket he had in the car—grey with brown sheepskin inside, warm but quite large on me, the sleeves pooling at my wrists. I failed to suppress the anticipation of seeing Adrian at the afternoon classes and looked around, seeking my vermillion as I walked to the satellite building. Laura stood under the cover of a doorway.

"Looking for something?" A little smirk on her lips.

"Yes, you." A lie—but an easy one. We reached the building just in time to miss a fresh downpour. He didn't attend the afternoon either. Had he mentioned skipping classes today? Maybe he meant to stop by the house later. It upset me more than it should have.

Rain pelted down as I drove home, the volcano and lake hidden by the haze. My car felt particularly small as I drove up the stone pathway with the massive, drenched trees hunched over the road. I turned on the radio and, through the static, heard the announcement that a storm had rolled in. The canal was closed to boats due to dangerous waves. My pulse climbed. What if something had happened to Adrian?

"Where are you?" I said aloud, feeling weird for doing so. I cleared my throat and turned the radio down. The rainfall hit harder when I drove into the clearing, not broken by the trees anymore. I parked by the porch steps to avoid getting soaked while trying to unlock the kitchen door. I almost slipped running up the steps but caught myself on the balustrade just in time. A flash of lightning lit the surroundings, thunder grumbling above. My senses rolled. Weatonburg had thunderstorms, but nothing like this. I brewed coffee and took warm blankets outside, where I sat on the porch and watched the rain pour in torrents. I could not see beyond the tree line leading to the lake. Though illogical, I found myself anticipating Adrian's appearance, as if he might materialise from the rain. Maybe it was the eerie sense of someone watching me again. He possessed my mind more and more, to the point where I struggled to think about anything else. It drove me crazy, so I went inside to review my work as a distraction. Sitting on my windowsill, I watched the rain flow down the glass. The task proved more difficult than expected— futile, even.

I kept looking outside, rehashing everything he'd said the day before. Suddenly, it hit me I hadn't done anything about Giovaniello's composition assignment for Friday. My mind was too cluttered and clogged while playing, leaving me unable to connect with myself. The *Pulse* felt like a light with a flat battery—flickering occasionally but never reaching consistent, full brightness. I struggled to identify the subliminal angst that tensed me like a trip wire. When my dad's car pulled in, I ran downstairs, hoping his company would ease my knotted stomach. But it didn't. I helped with dinner, and Dad noticed I was on edge—leg bouncing when we sat to eat—and asked if I was okay. I was honest, confessing that I felt anxious but was uncertain about what. He suggested it might be the storm. After dinner, I excused myself and tried to relax with a bath, letting the music wash over me. But I couldn't relax; I didn't even shift once. All I wanted was to see him and know he was all right.

All out of ideas, I climbed into bed, holding Tji-Tji close. I tried to control my breathing and force all thoughts from my mind. I squeezed my eyes shut and focussed on counting each deep breath, losing count after hundred-and-sixty-two.

I dreamed, and I knew for certain it was a dream. I was wandering around an unfamiliar cobbled square in town. Sombre throngs of aimless people drifted around. Their clothes ranged from light grey to black, and I realised the dream's colour was missing, like an old movie. Their faces were rigid and emotionless. Some sat at coffee-shop tables motionless like statues set in stone, while others walked around like militia. What struck me was how tall they all were; and I was as unnoticed as a ghost. I ambled forward slowly, looking down when something brushed my ankle. I was wearing an archaic sleeping gown, white and ruffled, my feet bare. A scurrying movement caught my attention in my peripheral. It was an old, hunched man wearing dirty white rags. He moved with determination but seemed wracked with immense pain. His eyes were on the ground, but he seemed to know where he was heading. It took me a moment to notice the jagged stick clenched in both hands, knuckles bone white from the grip.

A wave of empathy washed over me as I watched him struggle. I walked towards him, but he was faster than I thought and disappeared around a corner. I ran to catch up, and when I turned the corner, he was already some distance down the narrow passageway. "Wait!" My cry sounded like a ball landing on a soft cushion. I continued towards him. He stopped, his back straightening as he slowly turned to face me. As in dreams, I suddenly stood before him.

Only now, he was young and attractive—someone I both knew and didn't. I stared up as he towered over me, even taller than the rest. Despite the sudden proximity, I was at ease. His tender gaze weighed on me, inching his head closer, lips curved in a soft smile. He seemed to know me well, though I couldn't place him.

Another stranger approached and spoke to him, and I was dwarfed between them. I couldn't comprehend their conversation, but the young man seemed absent-minded as he gazed at me with a bemused look. To me, his responses were akin to the forced, expected conversation of a well-known person. The second man disappeared, and suddenly we were standing in a forest. He reached out to touch my face, but everything melted into fog as I began to wake up. I resisted, but his face faded even as his gentle eyes lingered on me. I couldn't recall their colour. Tji-Tji lay beside me, curled in a ball. It was a little before my alarm, which was a delightful surprise.

Andrew drove in with me, and I dropped him off at school in the newer area near the university. He surprised me with a hurried kiss on the cheek before running off. The thought of seeing Adrian again made me speed up, even as the same anxiety from the day before twisted inside me, lingering. I kept looking around, hoping to see his dark auburn hair, but never did. Laura noticed, I knew, but was gracious enough not to say anything. It was a helpless feeling, having no way of finding out what had happened to him. The storm weighed on my thoughts. What if he'd gone out on the boat? What if he was in the forest, slipped, and hit his head? What if lightning struck him? My mind raced, and the anxiety thickened.

That evening, I forced myself to play something for the next day's composition practical. It sounded mundane—my senses remained fixed throughout—which vexed me. I was ashamed to admit that while I could play something, improvising a composition without my gift would be difficult. I gave it my best shot but forfeited after a while and crawled into bed. The memory of the man who had stared me down with such hatred the day before, combined with Adrian's continued absence, made my emotions well up inside me. I fell asleep with tears prickling at the surface. Dreamless, I slumbered until a noise awoke me in the dark morning hours. It was a thudding or a grating—indistinguishable from one another as I made my way back to consciousness. Slowly, my mind cleared, processing. Something scratched on a surface.

"Tji-Tji?" I mumbled, my voice hollow and weak. Moments dragged by. As I woke up, I realised it could not be her—the sound too ferocious. My eyelids fluttered, weak when I tried to open them. Limp, I squinted into the room's darkness but saw her white fur nowhere. The sound was irritating and troubled my sleepy mind. I clawed my way out of bed, feeling drunk as I tried to locate the source. It dragged into place after a second. The mirror. My heart sunk into the earth. Appalled, I focused on the back wall but saw nothing. Reluctant, I stepped closer, my pulse racing. The robust tearing persisted, louder than I had first registered. Had it just started? It was unimaginable that could have slept through it. It was so loud I half-expected my dad to come running into the room. I wondered if it could be an earthquake or the volcano erupting, but nothing else was shaking. Only the mirror. It vibrated as if the wall trembled, not the eerie way it did when I dreamed. Fear coiled around my spine, tightening its grip. The wall shuddered as if something huge was pounding against it. Adrenaline raged through my veins, but my senses remained locked. I looked at my hands, but they were normal.

Did that even work? Along with the thudding, I discerned a scratching sound. Something was trying to come inside. Or get out. Ice ran down my back. I tried pushing the thought away, but it forced itself in: Dwellers. Unwilling to wait for confirmation, I scrambled to the bed and grabbed my duvet and pillow. In my rush through the dark, I nearly tripped over the duvet on my way down. Itching to be as far away from my room as possible, I ran to the downstairs parlour. With my heart thrashing inside my chest like a wild thing, I threw the bedding on the Chesterfield and then lay down, trying to calm myself. I swore I could still hear faint scratching and thudding. As I lay there, an eerie feeling crept over me. A disturbing awareness that someone was staring at me. I bolted upright and switched on the lamp—which magnified the feeling—and quickly scanned the room before switching it off again. I gulped and stood. My senses didn't shift, the weak *Pulse* rose lazily beneath my feet. I approached the window, trying to sense where it originated from. As I stared into the forest, it became stronger. Only the trees were visible through the dark, nothing else. I yanked the curtains shut and ran back to the couch, cocooning myself in the duvet like a shield. Perhaps it was just in my head, but I still heard the thudding. I started counting breaths again, pushing all the other stimuli from my mind.

My dad found me like that a few hours later when the light broke through.

"Uh, morning, Hon," worry stained his voice, despite his attempt to lighten it, "I don't believe metamorphosis works for humans."

My mouth was dry, and sitting up felt difficult.

"Morning," I croaked, thawing my tongue with a wiggle. I was so tired.

"What happened? Are you okay?"

"Yeah," my voice was husky, and I cleared my throat. "Yeah, there were strange noises in my room. It could've been Tji-Tji." On steroids. "But I couldn't find her." I refrained from telling him I'd hallucinated Dwellers attempting a break-in. Or out. He nodded, looking like he wanted to say something, but thought better of it. Instead, he offered me coffee. I stumbled to my room, the bedding heavier than it ought to be. I would have forgotten to take my cello if not for the sheet music strewn about the floor in my attempt to write something. Before eating breakfast, I deposited my cello in the car, which was still parked by the porch. I contemplated telling Dad the truth about the noises and the feeling of being watched but had no clue how to do it without sounding crazy.

The weather was less miserable as I drove in, but I felt worse. My heart ached with conflicting emotions. I yearned to see Adrian while also trying to manage my expectations to prevent further disappointment. When I arrived, I forced myself not to look around for him. My thoughts wandered during class, and the same feeling that someone was watching me returned. At times so potent that I failed to resist the instinct to look around, but I never saw anyone looking. It was an unexplainable phenomenon. It was inexplicable how I knew, but I just did.

Giovaniello's class came, and my thoughts were snuffed as I listened to the others play. My senses remained steady, and I didn't know what to make of it. I couldn't recall ever going so long without them shifting. A form of fear unfurled inside me as I considered the possibility of being unable to play and making a fool of myself. On cue, Professor Giovaniello called me forward, and I stared at her like a deer in the headlights. A crease formed between her brows. I swallowed. My nerve endings felt sedated as I stood and walked forward. My heart battered inside my throat, and I felt lightheaded. I positioned myself and couldn't feel my arms. Giovaniello lingered close by. I inhaled a deep, burning breath.

"Professor, if necessary, please stop me." She seemed perplexed by this, but I had no idea what would happen. I might need to be pulled back. She smiled and touched my shoulder. Her hand was blisteringly warm, and she snatched it back as if she'd touched a hot plate, then turned and walked to her desk. The peculiar response caught me off guard, but I didn't have the luxury of dwelling on it. I cleared my mind and took another deep, focused breath, hoping I wouldn't embarrass myself. I thought about my life in Weatonburg and the move to Ostia, and how everything had changed. How I had changed. And Adrian, most of all.

Sluggish and afraid of what was coming, or not coming, I dragged the bow over the strings. I almost cried out with exhilaration when the *Pulse* returned and swallowed me whole, taking command of all my faculties, every thought, and every movement. Excitement and joy bristled beneath my skin and mixed with the *Pulse* as the waves rolled through me. The melody was unexpected and eerie, with shades of melancholia and rock. I tapped my heel on the wooden platform, which merged to perfection. When the creeping energy reached my neck, an external heat source interfered. My cue. I pushed against the energy, gradual but urgent. It proved difficult.

My senses lumbered back into order, and the normal classroom sounds registered. I lingered a while.

"Thanks," I was out of breath. Her hand burned on my shoulder, and she removed it.

"Thank you, Josilyn. That was astounding." The class erupted into applause and cheers, drowning out whatever she might've wanted to add. My cheeks burned as I walked back to my seat. Giovaniello quieted the class and talked about the style and progression, but I couldn't listen. The praise didn't feel like mine. I looked at Laura, and she wasn't listening either. Her mind seemed to be elsewhere as she stared ahead, her eyes large even viewed from the side.

"I'm speechless," she said after a long moment without looking at me.

"Hopefully, in a good way?" I felt suddenly insecure that it didn't sound the way I thought it did. Blood stained my cheeks. She lifted her eyebrows, still not looking at me.

"That was beyond amazing, Josilyn. It took me somewhere," she finally turned to me, frowning, "somewhere I'm not sure I wanted to be. Scary. Eerie. But breathtaking. I would've cried if I wasn't so carried away."

Such praise from my friend caught me off guard, and my eyes burned. I bit my lip. The next student stepped onto the stage.

At lunch, Laura and I lay on the grass watching the odd arrangement of clouds. The fluff looked like white, cracked clay with sunlight creeping through. She seemed reserved, but I didn't want to pry, fearing she'd ask questions I'd fumble to answer. I took deep breaths and forced myself not to look around for Adrian. As if she'd read my thoughts, she asked me where he was. When I said I'd no idea, she let it go. The day dragged on sluggishly, and I was glad to arrive home. I passed out in the hammock, imagining Adrian coming up the road.

On Saturday morning, Mom and I went shopping, and I met Laura at a café in the afternoon. I was on edge whenever I was away from the house, fearing Adrian would show up while I was not there. My emotions were a mixture of sadness and anger. If others didn't ask about him, I'd have thought him a hallucination. The anticipation of his presence nearly drove me to lunacy, and the days were bleak.

By Tuesday, I convinced myself that he had moved away and forgotten about me. The thought hurt me in more ways than I could understand or describe. I replayed our encounters, searching for clues, things I might've said to upset him. When I remembered him saying he became bored with things he understood, tears burned. Maybe he'd figured me out, and I left much to be desired. I tried hiding the lurking misery from my dad, but it was apparent he had picked up on it. On Wednesday evening, while hiding in my room, staring out the window, waiting, he called me to the first-floor parlour.

"How have you been, Hon? I haven't noticed any strange nighttime activity from you recently."

"Sleep has been fine. I haven't had an incident in a while." Ever since we went to the Mjesecai, to be exact. Ignoring the night I heard the scratching. "And you? Making progress since the tribe visit?"

"I'm good. Yeah, I'd say so." He wasn't planning on talking about himself. "I haven't seen Adrian around for, what... two weeks?" It hurt hearing it out loud and my heart cringed at Adrian's name.

"Me neither." My voice cupped disappointment like a basin. He nodded, pursing his lips. "I'm sorry to hear that. Did he say anything?"

I shook my head, looking away.

"I see. Well, I'm sure there's a good reason, Hon. He didn't seem like the type to just disappear."

"None of us know him that well if we're being honest." It was true. He'd only been in our lives for about two months. Dad's face pulled into an expression of acknowledgment, and he nodded sombrely—the conversation drifted into safer waters. Time ticked by, and when everyone retired for the evening, I remained. I was reluctant to return to my room, though I wasn't sure why. The *aloneness* crept into the room and wrapped around me like a shroud. The feeling was back, that someone was staring at me through the open curtains. My pulse climbed as I looked there, but of course, I saw little in the dark. I needed to escape those eyes, whose or whatever it was. I jumped up to close the curtains and switch off the light, adrenaline coursing through me. But I was drawn back to the window and peeped outside. The moon cast a glow on the surroundings, but too faint to see much. I waited, but nothing moved. Unsure if I was relieved or disappointed, I stepped away and headed for the stairs.

A sound on the porch stopped me dead in my tracks. My senses drifted, and I felt a mix of happiness and fear. Electricity bristled over my skin. It sounded like something was being dragged across the floor. A chair? Ice stabbed my neck at the thought. Frozen, I stood at the foot of the stairs, senses sharpened, two instincts warring inside me—to run or to know. The noise stopped, and the silence rang, thick and sharp. I waited for something to happen. Nothing did. A shiver ran through me when I turned around, which I wasn't sure I decided to do. The lights were off, giving me a semblance of peace, knowing I was not illuminated. Careful, I tiptoed to the large window by the front door and peered outside. Nothing moved out there, but one chair stood by itself near the door, facing me. I gulped, my throat dry and my pulse racing. Was someone playing a game? I leaned closer to the glass and jerked back when my nose touched the cold glass.

A trembling finger flicked the switch for the porch light. My heart pounded with anticipation. The sudden brightness revealed nothing the darkness had been shielding. Maybe it was my frustration with Adrian's disappearance, or anger at being watched from the shadows for weeks, or the *Pulse* abandoning me. Or perhaps it was all the above. But I was determined to know what was going on. Adrenaline pulsed through me when I turned the cold doorknob. A small part of my mind screamed profanities at me to stop. But felt something was taking control, and I had no power anymore. Inch by inch, I pulled the doors towards me, heart hammering. I scanned the porch. Panic urged me back into the house, but something stronger pulled me outside. I stepped forward, blood pounding against my neck. I felt like an observer within my own body. My eyes absorbed everything visible. The only thing amiss was the chair, taunting me. My senses shifted, leaving a trail of relief and confusion on my nerves. Against my conscious will, I approached the steps. My heart raged, spewing fear like a war drum. Chasing breath, I peeked around the corner. Relief washed over me. There was nothing nor anyone. But I wasn't eased; why had the chair moved? Perhaps a gust of wind had caught it at the perfect angle. I grew uneasy, realising the porch light illuminated me and turned to head back inside. But my movement was halted before I could complete the step. A hand from behind covered my mouth just as I was about to scream. Even as pandemonium erupted inside my head, my body froze. A scream congealed in my throat. Why had I been so stupid to come outside? An arm girdled my waist and crushed me against a strong, massive body. Every ounce of breath expelled from my lungs, and my senses scuttled around like I wished my body would. As my consciousness slipped away, I thought of the hostile stranger on campus. He'd come to kill me. My body remained unresponsive, no matter how many signals my brain sent. Tears pooled behind my eyes, and I went numb.

"That was too easy." That voice. My brain lit up like a bomb. The foreign, hostile touch shifted suddenly into something else entirely. He whirled me around to face him, encircling me in an embrace. My heart swelled. No library could contain the thoughts rushing through my mind, but I was mute, limp with shock. His scent washed over me, the familiar heat thawing me out as I returned to my body. I threw my arms around him, the days of longing spilling over like hunger. His embrace was like an iron cage, and I struggled to breathe. He relaxed his hold slightly just as I realised it, and I inhaled a deep, stinging breath. Sobriety seeped back into my mind, and anger brewed into a thick paste.

"What were you thinking?" My voice was strained raw. I unwound myself from him and tried to pull away, but he locked his arms. "Why did you do that?" I looked into his eyes, and their softness disarmed me. He seemed caught off guard, oblivious to how messed up his game had been.

The concern soon shifted into a playful glint, that mischievous smile pulling over his lips.

"It was a test. You failed, I'm afraid."

I melted further at the sound of his velvety voice and found myself smiling.

"A test?"

"Yes, to see how much of a safety risk you are to yourself." He was joking, but an undertone simmered beneath.

"Well, I'm not accustomed to being lured out and pounced upon." His eyes danced, and his skew smile spoke subtleties.

"Oh, well, you'll have to get used to that." He brushed his knuckles over my cheek, setting my veins on fire. His eyes changed, and I swallowed hard as he slowly drew nearer. He touched his lips against mine for a delicate moment. My heart ached with weeks' worth of longing. I inhaled him into my aching lungs.

"I missed you." His words trickled with honey. He furrowed his brows, and the anxiety I'd felt while he was gone flared.

"Where have you been? Do you have any idea what you put me through? I thought you'd moved away, or something had happened in the storm. You could've called or let me know you were okay." My voice rose with unleashed emotions. He put his hand on the back of my neck, caressing my cheek with his thumb.

"I know, believe me. It was maddening, but I just couldn't reach you, no matter how much I wanted to. It tore me apart. Please forgive me?" My heart thawed at his pleading expression, his eyes searching my face. His pupils were so dilated that his eyes seemed black, hypnotic. At least it sounded like he'd been tormented too, which made me feel a little better. I couldn't refuse him, even if I wanted to.

"If you promise not to do that again." He smiled and pulled me closer, kissing my head. His scent enveloped me, and I inhaled so deeply that the fragrance burned in my lungs.

"If I had my way, I'd never have you from my sight again." His voice was so intense, my heart omitted a beat.

"But where were you?"

He stayed quiet for so long that it unnerved me, and I pulled away to look at him.

"I… had a situation at home, and I simply could not break free, no matter how much I tried. I had no opportunity to leave."

It sounded serious, but I didn't want to pry.

"Oh, okay. Has the… situation been resolved for you to be here now?" I itched to know more but wouldn't push it if he didn't share on his own. He looked at me for a while and sighed.

"It's complicated. But I'm here now."

He glanced behind me for a split second, so fast I thought I'd imagined it. Before I could turn to see what he'd seen, he spoke.

"May I come in?" He paused, a tentative smile staining his voice. "Or would you prefer me to leave?"

"No, you can't leave," I exclaimed, aghast that he'd even suggest it. A low laugh vibrated through his chest.

"Just checking." He placed his arm around my shoulders, and the heat seared my skin. As we stepped through the door, I realised I hadn't thought it through. What if someone came downstairs?

"I don't think it would be such a big problem if someone came down. But if you need me to hide, you know I can do it well." He chuckled.

I froze and stared at him.

"How did you know I was thinking that?"

He rolled his eyes and sat us down on the Chesterfield.

"Oh, please. You stiffened like a pole the moment we walked in. It took little effort to deduce what you were thinking. Besides, am I not allowed to visit you?" This last bit in a sweet voice. Devilish. I was not as stiff as a pole. I purposefully relaxed my muscles as proof.

"You are, but I'm not sure about the curfew. You haven't been here often enough for my dad to put one in place." That didn't come out quite how I meant it. He sighed and slid onto his knees before me. My stomach came alive with butterflies.

'*That's not what I meant,*' I wanted to say, but my cheeks burned instead, as did my hands in his. His eyes shone bright, burning, and my heart was engorged with blood.

"Josilyn," he paused, my name a spell on his tongue, and the butterflies ran amok. "I apologise for not visiting often enough to affect domestic time barriers for you. How may I atone? I would do anything." His lips curved into that wicked smile. Warm, saccharine breath washed over my face. My head spun. It stirred something peculiar inside me to have such a large man on his knees before me.

"I didn't mean it like that. I've never had visitors at night, so we've never had to talk about it." Instinctively, I leaned closer. His face went blank, but his eyes didn't, drifting to my mouth.

"Good to know," he whispered. My heart was going crazy. He held my jaw delicately with his thumb and index finger. It burned, but I leaned into his hand, and he cupped my face. I closed my eyes, feeling the heat seep into my brain. Breathing fast, he pressed his forehead against mine. After several intense moments, he took a deep breath, pulled away, and sat beside me. My head cooled at the loss of his touch, and I sat back. He was lounging in the corner, his arms resting on the back of the sofa. Discomfited by the sudden distance, I folded my arms and leaned further back.

"How was the rest of your week, regardless?"

I was ashamed to realise how much his absence had affected everything else, and I wasn't about to let him know.

"It was okay. We started our practical compositions on Friday. Mine didn't end up as bad as expected. Oh, and there was a butterfly invasion last Wednesday, which disrupted class."

His eyes shifted slightly.

"Interesting." He seemed guarded. "Why did you expect your practical to go badly?"

My face flushed, unwilling to admit the impact of his absence. I was ashamed and didn't understand it myself.

I shrugged.

"Sometimes you're Batman; other times, you're just Robin."

He frowned, and I wondered if he understood the reference, but then he smiled and nodded.

"Off day."

"One could say so, yes." More like an off week, but no need for details. I thought of the man who had stared me down, and was about to tell him about it, but my mind recoiled from the thought. Like a sneeze that never happened, a veil obstructed the memory. I frowned.

"And now?"

"I was about to tell you something but can't remember what." He seemed serious, waiting for me to try and recall. No matter how hard I tried, I couldn't. Like a familiar word on the tip of my tongue, but just out of reach.

"I think I know what it is." Taken aback, I looked at him. He leaned forward and pulled me closer. Before I could register what was happening, my head was on his chest. I was caught off guard, but even if my instinct was to pull away, I was trapped by the burning columns of his arms wrapped around me. His cheek rested on my head, and soon the rhythm of his heart had me spellbound. It was beating fast again.

Maybe I imagined it slowing the previous times. Or he was nervous. He stroked my hair, and my body burned. He had the heady scent of earth after rain.

"Why are you so warm?" I blurted. His chest vibrated under my cheek.

"I have fire in my blood." He whispered against my hair, sending a thrill down my spine.

"You know, this town is so weird; I might just believe that." I wasn't joking.

"It depends on the eyes observing, as in all things. Not everyone sees things as they are. Still, others choose not to see, though they have the sight."

"Do I?" My heart skipped a beat as if I'd asked something forbidden. He stayed quiet for a second.

"You see more than you even realise."

My breath quickened. I thought of all the things I had seen because of my gift.

"You're not wrong."

Silence lingered—then he shifted his body so fast I thought I'd blacked out for a moment. We were lying down, his back to the edge of the sofa, leaning on his elbow and gazing down at me. My senses drifted, and I closed my eyes. He breathed out and ran his fingertips down my arm.

"Hmmm, there it is." My cheeks flared up, and goosebumps rolled over my skin. Feeling wickedly exposed, I turned my face away, into the sofa seat. His warm breath caressed my skin as he drew closer. My heart pounded. He pressed his nose against the base of my neck and trailed it towards my jawline. Chills ran through me. The feverish temperature of his skin radiated like the sun.

"Your scent is maddening." My head spun as he traced my neckline and jaw, inhaling deeply. Tingles prickled down my neck, and a shiver ran through me. He pulled back and laughed darkly—face too amused for the circumstances. His thin silver chain had slipped from his collar—a small, warped coin hanging from it.

"Are you cold?" His eyes glinted.

"No, it tickles." My voice feeble. Wicked light dawned in his eyes, and I lost my breath.

"Oh, you shouldn't have said that." His voice was thick and low—I stiffened. He clasped both my wrists in one hand, and my veins ignited. His other hand was underneath my head, his fingers gathering my hair. I stared, wide-eyed, at him as he came closer. That wicked smile on his lips. He dipped lower and pressed them to my neck. My senses rolled, and I closed my eyes, gasping as the energy ran over my skin. I squirmed but he held me in place, kissing the delicate skin of my neck with burning lips. It was so ticklish I was breathless. Goosebumps erupted over me along with hysterical giggling. I writhed to loosen myself from him, but it proved useless. He tightened his grip. I felt him laugh against my neck but froze when his teeth pressed against my skin. My eyes shot open. He seemed unfazed by my reaction and gently nipped me. Chills ran through me in waves, and my stomach twisted as I gasped and shot up. He released me but remained in his lounging position. My veins glowed inside my body, and my pulse raced. It didn't hurt, but a strange, powerful feeling pulled at my insides. The moment was too intense, so I sat with my back to him, trying to regulate my breathing. The *Pulse* simmered inside my bones. I could feel his eyes bore into me, followed by his fingertips caressing my arm. Electricity ran through me, and I breathed deeper. My blood rushed. He ran his fingers through my hair and down my back before sitting, pressing his nose to my hair.

"For the sake of decency, I must leave," he whispered in a dark voice. My first thought was to protest, but another, stronger one overruled it. His bite still pulsed hot on my neck.

"If you must." I was taken aback by how rough my voice sounded. He exhaled loudly and stood up. The heat syphoned away from me, and I shivered. I swung my feet to the ground and rose as he stood waiting. His eyes burned, and he seemed to fight whatever impulse simmered behind them as he took my hand, walking to the door. The heat travelled up my arm. At the door, he faced me and cupped my face with his fingertips. Between the Chesterfield and the door, his eyes had changed. He bent down and gave me a quick kiss that left me wanting.

"You have marred me, Miss Grey." His face was solemn. I wasn't sure what he meant, but ignoring my frown, he opened the door and stepped outside. I waited for him to turn back, but he didn't. He just disappeared into the darkness like a ghost. Perplexed by his comment, I closed the door. The warmth of his touch on my skin was fading. Still, the ache in my stomach grew. Maybe I was hungry.

The moment my foot touched the landing in my room, the awareness of being watched returned. Frustrated, I peered outside. As expected, I only saw the trees in the shadow-painted landscape. My heart oddly sped up as I squinted around and I shut the curtains.

I was in bed when Tji-Tji jumped on out of the blue, and my senses scurried.

"You scared me! I didn't know you were here." I pulled her close, but she whined and wiggled. "What is it, Girl?" something about her urgency disturbed me. I tried calming her but to no avail. She shrieked and jumped off the bed as if hurt. My heart thumped, and the adrenaline spurted. She scratched at the trapdoor like a maniac.

"No! Stop that!" I scolded, but the frenzied scratching continued. I got up and to let her out and the door was barely open, when she slipped from sight. My pulse was erratic, and I felt a numbing sensation that often followed the release of adrenaline. Another unidentifiable feeling was also present, though diluted. Eerie but unplaceable. Exhausted, I turned back to bed, ready for sleep.

The mirror summoned my attention, and I looked at my reflection. Except it wasn't mine. She looked younger. Her skin was as pale as mine, golden white curls dangled at her hips. I caught my breath. Her beauty pacified the fact that what I saw was bizarre—still frightening, with her expressionless stare. The room's reflection was normal; I was the singular item which had been replaced. The house was haunted, after all. As the thought rose, one corner of her mouth lifted into a menacing smile, and her chin lowered. Creepy. My pulse raced and my breathing became shallow and fast. Maybe I was having another hypnagogic episode. I stepped towards my bed, and her head lowered as she seemed to focus on the movement. I froze.

The reflection was altered. No longer was she in my room, but was standing on burnt grass, surrounded by burned trees. A swarm of butterflies, blacker than oil, appeared out of thin air and swirled around her like a cloud. She opened her arms and twirled around, smiling. The butterflies changed into fog, and she turned back to face me, expressionless again. After a while, she turned around and walked into the mist. She was gone. The fog crept closer and thickened until the mirror looked like a holding glass containing a storm. Like a switch, the reflection went back to normal. Stunned, I looked at my hands; they were normal.

A sort of rage awoke inside me. I was fed up. With the room. The mirror. All the weirdness it caused. I marched forward, dragging the chair along. Though I didn't want to destroy it, it was coming off or getting covered by a blanket. I clawed at the frame from the floor upwards, looking for purchase, wanting to remove it. Or maybe to open it. Anything. I stepped onto the chair and stood on my toes. At the top the fusion between the wall and frame was flush. Frustrated, I yanked at the edge, grunting. Thick dust collected under my nails. The *Pulse* rolled through my feet, and my senses drifted. I toppled back, nearly falling, but grasped the frame. My heart raced as my breath fogged the mirror. I gathered myself, relaxing my fingers and stroking over a protrusion. And froze.

Chapter 12

I flinched, thinking I'd nicked my finger on something, but no pain followed. After a deep breath, I returned my hand to where I'd felt the ridge. I fiddled around delicately, trying to decipher if there was a mechanism of some kind. My breath fogged the mirror, and my arm grew tired; the *Pulse* prickling beneath my soles. I didn't know what to expect at all. Would the mirror open? Pushing it back and forth was fruitless, and I tried sliding it left and right instead. I yanked my hand away when it yielded. Chills ran over my body, and my senses dipped.

"Josilyn," a whisper wrapped around me, and I almost toppled off the chair again, grabbing the frame just in time. The *Pulse* coiled around my ankles, and I wiggled my toes. The mirror remained closed. I pulled at the frame, testing, but it remained as solid as ever. My head spun as I slid my hand back, detecting an opening beneath my fingers. I explored the edge of the cavity, unnerved by the lack of visual input. Heart racing, I lowered my hand into the hollow. The descent was short, as I soon felt a texture beneath my fingertips. My heart dipped, and I reached both hands in. Although covered in dust, it felt like a leather something. I wiggled it around, gauging if it was loose, then took hold of it as best as I could. It weighed heavier than expected and slipped from my fingers, causing a dull thud. Grabbing hold once more, I pulled it out with great care. I gaped at the dusty leather rectangle in my trembling hands. In a trance, I stepped off the chair and moved it back to the desk where I sat down. Placing the precious discovery on the desk before me, I sat there a long time, simply staring at it. I didn't know what to do. I considered waking my dad; this should probably be handed over to a museum or the library. But I didn't know with certainty what its significance was, if any. Who knew? Maybe it was Aunt Catherine's secret stash of photos she didn't want anyone to see. I smiled, imagining handing it over to officials and causing embarrassment for all.

The leather was merely a wrap, crisscrossed with leather straps which held it fast. When I blew over the layer of dust, a cloud rose around me that had me coughing, and nose itching. I wiped at it with my sleeve, but it needed oil. I wondered if the straps were brittle and if they'd break if I unwound them. Careful, I picked it up again, turning it around and saw the simple knot at the back. To my surprise, the knot was slack and loosened when I tugged at it. My pulse raced as I continued to unwind the long string, with a vague sense that I should stop. I didn't. With great care, I unwrapped the securely folded leather cover.

Underneath was a second layer of leather, and beneath that, a coarse cloth. Someone had been determined to not let whatever was inside decay. Under all the covers was a wooden box. No wonder it was so heavy. The *Pulse* licked at my ankles, my senses edging. The top of the wooden box had a lotus carved into it, in the same style as the front door. An inscription below read: "Cordis Arca". A current ran through me, raising the hairs over my body.

Not Aunt Catherine's.

I cast a wary glance over my shoulder. The curtains were closed. My heart rammed against my chest as I lifted the lid to reveal a delicate white handkerchief. Or one that had once been white. Underneath was a stack of browned papers with writing on them and a coiled-up lock of long, light gold hair. It was hers; I knew. It shone and looked as if it had just been cut. I left it untouched. Trembling, I picked up the top sheet—much thicker than expected. The ink was faded but still legible. My eyes blurred looking at the strange script; it took a moment for my brain to recognise the words. I guess I expected another language other than English, though I was uncertain why. I scrolled over the page, and my eyes burned when I realised it was a diary.

I looked up, my pulse racing violently as my chest heaved. Torn between curiosity and uneasiness about violating someone's privacy, I skimmed through the pages. They were arranged from the earliest, dated December 17th, 1756, to the latest, October 3rd, 1757. My throat burned. I stood, leaving the papers on the desk, and paced around the room, wringing my hands that burned with the need to read them. The discovery was momentous—not just for my dad, but for the town. As close to a sacred text as one could come. I couldn't believe that no one had discovered it before. Perhaps it had, but for whatever reason, had remained unrevealed. Maybe it contained secrets people preferred to keep.

I found myself seated at the desk again, feeling lightheaded. Afraid my clammy hands would ruin the papers, I kept them inside the box while I conducted my questionable act. I read the first entry with a feral heart.

December 17th, 1756

Oh, how wretched a thing. Oh, how wicked a thing a heart can be! I am afflicted with the most terrible and most glorious of torments. My heart has been captured and shackled by the most handsome of all men, and I languish! How careless and thoughtless have his actions been, enrapturing me? He called on me by the gardens again today. I confess, my sins are plentiful. The first was tricking dearest Helda into leaving me unattended by feigning a sudden malady. I gave her a litany of detailed yet deliberately vague and confusing instructions, then rushed her away. Oh, what a wicked girl I am!

I blush at my trickery. Mother would be absolutely horrified if she knew. My soul triumphed in such a salacious way at his embrace. His eyes are bluer than the ocean on a bright summer's day, and his smile, oh, his smile sets my soul on fire. I am unable to refuse him anything. I am his servant in love and desire. The remainder of my sins cannot be named. As my love for him grows and groans, so does the guilt. I long to be with him, and his, always. Whatever shall I do? What would my parents say if they discover my affection for a suitor who is not my betrothed whom they have chosen? Oh, how horrendous the thought. I am sickened by the thought of another's touch! I cannot bear it. I long only for his arms and dread the thought of what is to come. But I cannot deny this aching inside of me.

Aurelia

Aurelia. I sat back, taking a moment to let it sink in. I could hardly believe it. This was *the* noblewoman from the stories my dad had told me. The blonde girl the Mjesecai mentioned. It must be. I was struck by the magnitude of what lay before me. This was my ancestor. The *Pulse* prickled on my skin, and my senses shuffled. In a way, her blood flowed through me, and I realised she'd been in this same room, maybe even sitting on the same chair as she wrote. Chills ran through me. I set the page on the desk and continued reading. The first few pages retold their forbidden love and their trysts, including a couple of comical attempts to elude her chaperone, Helda, which had me giggling. But an undertone grew as one page followed the other, and by mid-January, the man, whom she never named, chose to leave for 'honour's' sake, as they were both betrothed. I was not sure how much *honour* remained. I wondered if they couldn't have found some way to be together. The sudden separation debilitated her. She became what we'd call depressed, and her parents sent her and Helda here with servants to recuperate. The journey by ship and carriage took a month. It had been years since she'd visited Ostia, and she enthused much over the place's ethereal beauty. The inn was already established.

The entry dated March 4th sent a shiver through me. She wrote an offhand comment about strange things happening while she slept and wondered if her mind had broken along with her heart. She saw things she shouldn't, uncertain if she was awake or asleep. I swallowed and stopped reading. Energy gathered within me, my heart racing. I read on, ploughing through the letters. The archaic language made just skimming them impossible.

A later entry described the room filling with mist as if she were outside on a gloomy day. *So, she experienced the mist just like I did.* I sat back, chills assaulting me until I trembled. The *Pulse* shot through me, my senses spinning out of control. In equal parts, I longed for more, but also to stop.

She spoke about butterflies coming into her room and saying peculiar things, on which she didn't elaborate. They also came while she read by the lake. She called them her winged companions, speculating whether they were disguised fairies. A drop of ice ran down my spine when I remembered Adrian telling me that butterflies were messengers. She contemplated and seemed unbothered by the idea of losing her sanity. In fact, it seemed a welcome distraction from the pain. Her writing had subtext as the entries progressed, and I was engrossed, as if spellbound. She dreamt her departed lover called on her, as scandalous as it was, in her chambers. My room. She noted he appeared much taller than she remembered him. And his eyes were as bright as jewels. She withheld the details, but the insinuation had my face burning. My brain took notice of certain details. Tall. Bright eyes. Dreams. My mouth was dry. Her dreams became more frequent, more intense, with an incident when she was on a walk by the lake and thought she saw him there. The page trembled in my hand. She described her amazement at how warm his skin was in her dreams. I froze. My senses dipped, and nausea rose in my throat. It felt like searching for a familiar light switch in the dark; I should have found it quickly, but it evaded me. Something important waited for the light to cast upon it. Sick to my stomach, I continued reading. She confided in Helda about her night-time experiences, feeling soothed by the visits yet found them outlandish. The account disturbed Helda, who told her it might be an incubus visiting her at night. Aurelia didn't take that seriously, but humoured Helda when she gave her a garnet ring for protection, swearing she'd never take it off, even at night. Her dreams stopped, but Helda grew suspicious when she saw a tall man wandering around the lake one night, so she cast protection on the house. It seemed Helda practised magic, which reminded me of the Great Mother's mention of an enchantress accompanying the noblewoman. She forbade Aurelia to leave the house by herself, to her displeasure. Months passed without more nightly visits, but Aurelia noticed changes in her body. She was convinced she carried a love child from the ill-fated romance between her and the betrothed *'gentleman'*. The *Pulse* simmered in my bones, and goosebumps spread everywhere. Nowhere did she mention going into the mountain. My heart sank when I reached the last page.

October 3rd, 1757

My winged companions visited today while Helda and I walked down to the lake. It has been such a long time, my heart nearly exploded. I thought I'd imagined them, like so many other things. They remained with us longer than before and played with me, tickling my cheeks with their gentle touch, sitting on my swollen belly. Helda seemed perplexed at the display and remained silent, even after I told her they spoke to me. Harbingers of a dark message that I was unsure I wanted to receive. They left with a bittersweet departure. The omen: in fourteen days I shall birth two perfect, healthy boys. I was overjoyed by this, as I'd suspected that I had been blessed with more than one. They were hesitant to say more, but after I encouraged them, they revealed it, and their sadness was named. I could scarcely place my turmoil. Frightened. Scared. Sad. All of these, but mostly, I am fearful for my two sons. It will be difficult not knowing their mother, father, or family. The thought pains me more than anything else. I told Helda what would happen. She wishes to dismiss it but she cannot hide from me that she is stricken with grief, perhaps even more than I am. Then again, she will bear my loss in a way I will not. She must keep the cause of my death a secret to spare my family the shame. Here I will die, and here I will be buried. She will give my sons to a respectable family in this foreign country. I've made her swear on my life.

This will be my last entry. I shall place these pages somewhere safe, in the hope that one day they will return, as I call them, and they will find them. They will then know a small fraction of my life which was my happiest, and most tragic.

Dorian, & Myron, I love you more than my life, and though I am terrified, I hope to hold you both at least once. You are my crown.

Farewell, and all the love in my being.

Your mother

Tears streamed down my face, my skin cold and tight from the wake of earlier spells. I wished there was more. How horrible, knowing the day you are going to die and being unable to do anything about it. Waiting and knowing as the day came closer. But the implications held such blatant sinister hues. What I said earlier about her blood flowing through my veins took on a different meaning now. I pushed that train of thought away. Overwhelmed, I stared at the pages for a long time before placing them back, arranging everything in the box the way it had been, and re-wrapped it. Just as she had done centuries ago. I wondered if her sons had ever discovered it. It seemed not, which would be dreadful. And yet, it might not have provided the solace she'd hoped. Frankly, I doubted I should give it to anyone.

I left it on my desk and climbed into bed. Although exhausted, my mind was reeling, and it took a long time to fall asleep. The diary swallowed me into its story, an observer of a foreign life. I saw Aurelia, as she had been in my mirror earlier, sitting on the windowsill when the trapdoor opened, and a man entered. As tall as Adrian, with bright blue eyes. His hair dark brown, medium length and wavy. The dream jumped from scene to scene, depicting everything I had read, until I was lying on my bed covered with butterflies, foreboding and pitch black. I sat, and they spilt away like water. Their tiny legs tickled my skin and caused goosebumps.

"*He cannot be trusted.*" A whispering choir.

Gasping, my eyes flew open and, stuck between two states, I *saw* into my dream. I was immobile—my room was covered with black butterflies, like harbingering shadows. My breath came fast, burning in my throat. With their synchronised flapping wings rose a faint mist. The *Pulse* prickled over my body. With a sudden burst, they flew up and whirled around the room like an eerie black storm. In an instant, they vanished into thin air as if they were never there. The weight on me lifted, and I shot up, frantically scanning the room. Another jolt hit me— my alarm piercing through the thin air. I slammed it so fast I might've broken it. My heart pumped wildly. What a way to wake up. I took a few breaths, trying to calm myself. The skin on my neck prickled, warm, and I placed my hand there, realising it was where Adrian had bitten me the night before. I shivered, cotton in my mouth. My eyes found the diary on my desk. Undecided about what to do with it, I slipped from bed to prepare for the day, first checking my neck in the mirror. I was relieved to see no mark or anything else sinister. A phantom sensation, as it were. Feeling a sudden self-consciousness, I dressed out of view from the mirror; considering whether I should move rooms for a while. Before heading down, I pushed the chair against the mirror and placed the wrapped box on it. I opened the curtains and went downstairs. My dad was in the kitchen, eating a sandwich. A hand squeezed my heart, but I tried to act normal.

"Ah, good morning, Hon. I made you coffee and an egg sandwich."

"Thanks." I swallowed, telling myself to focus. When he asked how I'd slept, I told him not bad but refrained from details as I mentioned having some strange dreams. He remarked that I seemed in better spirits than I'd been for a while. Ironic. I thought of mentioning Adrian had stopped by but decided against it. I managed to keep my cool with our exchange and left with Andrew. The sun shone bright, the shimmering light reflected off the lake, blinding me. I was delighted at the sight of friends waiting when I dropped him off—glad he'd settled in here.

I arrived earlier than usual to a barely filled parking lot. Laura wasn't there yet, and somewhat aimlessly, I wandered around. I found a bench near the main building and sat down. I fished out my phone and typed a message to my dad. "When you have a moment today, go to my room." With a hammering heart, I hit *Send* and put the phone away. The whole situation unsettled me and I thought that perhaps sharing the burden with my dad would ease me. I drew a deep breath until my lungs burned and closed my eyes, lifting my face towards the sun. It was a lot to process, and I wondered what my dad would gather from it all, not knowing the details of my dreams. Thank goodness I had not experienced everything she had. What would have become of her if she'd survived?

Would she have confessed it all and raised her sons in shame? Would she have outed the nobleman? Who was the man Aurelia and Helda saw at the lake, and why did he look like the nobleman? Whose babies had she conceived? Troubling thoughts. I wished she'd mentioned his name. The story did go that Helda found the twins when they were grown men. I guessed she would've told them the truth. Well, maybe not the *whole* truth. So many complications. To think the entire tragedy was caused by two people's forbidden love.

"Your thoughts trouble you." Adrian's abyssal voice carried statement and question, and I jumped as my eyes flew open, my senses buckling. I grasped at my chest.

"You!" I was uncertain what I intended to add, and he chuckled, his green eyes sparkling. My stomach twisted, recalling the diary, and I looked away. His eyes were jewels too.

"How long have you been sitting here?" I was breathless.

"I don't see how that is relevant. This is a public bench; anyone may sit here." His eyes bore into me, that crooked smile on his lips. When his eyes drifted over me, my thoughts faltered, my heart melted, and my cheeks burned. His heat reached me across the space between us, and I longed to move closer.

I swallowed. "It's rude to stare." Blood flushed my skin.

"Then I'm a primal man." My pulse raced, and I looked away once more. He seemed even more brazen than usual, which was quite a lot already. I recalled him telling me I had marred him. And the bite. Just the thought had my neck prickling. The *Pulse* swirled beneath my feet. He spoke again when I didn't.

"What was upsetting you?"

"Well, would you look at that? I thought you'd been abducted!" Laura's voice approached and her presence dissolved the thick air. I took a deep breath.

"Only in body." He smiled, his eyes glinting. "I wouldn't want to miss any more of the… *weird vibes* which have been going on." The way he said 'weird vibes' seemed pointed. Laura frowned at him.

"I mean, I'm pretty sure you'd never run out of weird vibes, no matter where you go." She said this, smiling sweetly, cocking her head to the side. I couldn't identify her tone—whether playful or serious, but her eyes held traces of fire. It was comical seeing someone trying to be threatening with a man thrice her size. Her subtle hostility took me aback. He rose—smile and glint intact—and her eyes widened as he reached his full height. Indeed, he seemed more immense than usual. Her valour dipped, and I couldn't fault her for it.

"Quite right."

I realised I was standing too, though I couldn't remember rising. My heart raced and my senses wobbled. The air held a red tinge, and I rubbed my eyes. Adrian's gaze scoped the lawn and then settled on me.

"I'll see you next period," With smiling eyes. He looked at her. "Laura." He turned and walked down an alley, Laura and I staring after him.

"Dude's intense," Laura commented as we headed to class. My nerves burned inside me, and the *Pulse* simmered. I felt queasy and looked around, though uncertain what for. My senses dipped and my knees buckled. The air was red-hued as we approached the main building.

"Are you okay?"

"I feel weird."

"Me too." She frowned and cleared her throat. "Did something happen?" The question caught me off guard, and I refocused.

"What do you mean?"

"Before I came. You seemed upset."

A knot tightened in my stomach.

"Oh, don't worry about it." I tried to brush it off and smiled.

"I do." She looked at me, her green, no, her yellow eyes penetrating so deep into me I looked away.

"It wasn't him if that's what you're getting at." Well, not directly.

"You can tell me." I thought her voice was lower than usual.

"I found something last night." The words weighed too heavy and ripped through my restraint. My pulse raced as that weird feeling came over me again. She looked at me, expectant. We were near Giovaniello's classroom.

"I… uh, found a… diary of some sort behind my mirror." It felt like a weight lifted from me, but I looked around because it felt like a third person was part of our conversation.

"A diary?" Giovaniello wasn't there yet, and we found our seats. Scooting in, I brushed against her and frowned.

"Do you have a fever or something? You're burning up."

She slowly dipped her head to look down at her hands, as if moving exacted great effort.

"No. Did you read it?"

My freedom redacted, and I felt suddenly guarded. Her reaction was not what I'd expected.

"I skimmed it. It's old English. The dates are from the 1700s. Written by a woman called Aurelia."

"Aurelia." She repeated. My heart pounded like crazy, and my senses gnawed at the surface. "Where was it?"

"Behind my mirror, inside a hidden compartment."

Her gaze shot up to meet mine.

"Behind?"

I frowned.

"Yes, behind the frame." Where else did she think I meant? I looked around, seeking the eyes I felt.

"Where is it now?"

Giovaniello entered the room.

"It's with my dad." I took my phone out to check if he'd said anything, but the action was cut short with her response.

"Hmm?"

"It's with my dad," I repeated.

"What is?"

Confused, I looked at her. A deep frown etched into her forehead.

"Are you okay?"

She rubbed her forehead.

"Yeah, sorry. I think I'm getting a migraine."

Giovaniello began the lecture, informing us the practical would continue in the second half. I noted inquisitive glances in my direction throughout the lecture, and it made me nervous, but she didn't call me afterwards. As Laura and I headed to the next class, I asked how she felt. She said the headache was gone and—more in line with my expectations—asked if she could see the diary sometime.

"What diary?" Adrian spoke from behind us. We started—gasping. My senses drifted, my knees buckled, and I felt heat cup my elbow.

I heard Laura snap at him, calling him a sociopath.

"Are you all right?" His voice drowned out all other sounds. I waited until my senses slurred back and nodded.

"How do you manage to be massive and sneaky at the same time?" Laura asked him, her eyes still a little wild. He tore his gaze from me and looked at her.

"You weren't paying attention."

"Oh, I pay attention."

"What diary?" he asked me, eyes alive and bright. I swallowed hard, thinking about the man described on those pages. The things he did. If I were secretive now, it would be too obvious.

"I think I found the diary of our house's original owner last night." I studied his face for his reaction. A small crease formed between his brows.

"Original?"

"Yes. The noblewoman from the town's origin stories." Aloud, it made the gravity of the discovery sink in, said like that. His eyebrows lifted, and he slowly nodded.

Laura interjected and hurried us to class. On the way, she repeated that she'd love to see it sometime, and an idea struck me.

Seated in class, wedged between them, I finally checked my phone. My dad had phoned several times, and I had thirty-one unread messages. I messaged my mom first, asking if Laura could sleep over. My dad's messages started out with curiosity over being sent into my room, but grew progressively more intense as he found the box and eventually discovered the hidden compartment. Writers could captivate, and I was engrossed in reading the updates, losing track of my surroundings for a second. But something licked at my brain, and I looked up and caught Adrian's eyes shifting up to meet mine. He'd been reading my messages, I was sure. My phone vibrated with my mom's enthusiastic reply. It would be my first sleepover. She was concentrating on the lecture, and I sent her a message. Her phone lit up beside her and she read the text, looking at me with a wide smile, eyes bright.

"That would be epic!" She mouthed, barely a whisper. "I'll get my things after class. I must do something for my dad, but I'll drive through straight after." My enthusiasm matched hers, my heart warm from the excitement of this novelty yet to be experienced. I settled in to focus on the lecture. After a few minutes, I felt Adrian's eyes on the back of my head and, like a compulsion, turned around. He was leaning back in his seat and looked at me, smiling with swarming eyes. My heart squeezed. I smiled at him and turned forward, thankful that my hair formed a curtain over my shoulder, giving me some privacy to burn in private as my cheeks stained red. The thought barely registered before his burning fingers brushed my hair away, exposing my neck and sending a shiver through me. He chuckled under his breath, and the wake of his touch prickled my skin. Heat radiated over my back, and I knew his arm was draped over the back of my chair.

I struggled to concentrate; his scent saturated the air. He seemed utterly disinterested in the lecture, and all the ones that followed. My face burned at his fixed attention as if all was mundane apart from myself. Embarrassed by being the sole focus of such intense scrutiny, I tried to catch him out by asking what the one lecturer had said. That backfired. He repeated, verbatim, what had been said, even adding information, eyes glinting. I just shook my head. Laura wanted to speak to the lecturer as the class before lunch ended, and Adrian and I went outside.

"I must go." He moved a few steps down and turned towards me. "I will come to you when I can." I nodded, experiencing a peculiar cocktail of emotions. He encircled my waist with one arm and pulled me closer, planting a kiss on my hair. I blushed at the public display. He pulled away, and I unconsciously followed, losing my balance and almost stumbling down the steps. He steadied me just in time. *Embarrassing.* He smiled and tapped my nose with his finger.

"Try not to fall while I'm away." He walked backwards and disappeared into an alley.

After classes, Laura left to do her chore and pack her things. As I drove home, a knot twisted my gut. I'd never read all of Dad's messages, and an uneasiness settled over me, my heart rate climbing while I drove up the winding stone path. His car was home. I parked beside it by the kitchen door.

The house was quiet. Dad wasn't on the first floor. The light through the skylight scattered down the main staircase—the marble swirling as I climbed. Maybe I should've read them all first. As I walked towards his study, Tji-Tji came running toward me from the hallway.

"Hey, Girl," I kneeled and stroked her.

"Josilyn?" His voice came from the study. My mouth went dry at the thought of the impending interaction.

"Yes?"

His chair creaked and my heart dipped. I picked her up and held her close as I rose.

"You didn't reply to my messages." His hands in his pockets, he stood at the entrance of the hall.

"Sorry. I didn't get through them all. Did you read it?" My heart hammered as he nodded slowly, his eyebrows lifting.

"I did… I read it all. Twice. Reading it a third time now." He paused as I nodded, impressed but not surprised. "It's quite a discovery, Hon."

"I realised that."

"Did you read all of it?"

I tried to swallow—difficult with a parched mouth—and took a deep, obvious breath.

"I did."

He nodded and turned towards the hall.

"Let's sit."

I followed him into the parlour, where we sat down, the sun casting a heavenly halo on the high-ceilinged room.

He looked at me for a long time before speaking.

"Quite a tantalising read, isn't it?"

"It's definitely something."

"Did you tell anyone about it?"

I wasn't expecting a question like that.

"Um, yes. I told Laura and Adrian. Not much though, just her name and the dates."

He pursed his lips and nodded.

"Well, one could hardly have expected you to say nothing, I suppose. But that's why I kept calling and sent you all those messages."

My pulse spiked, and I frowned at him.

"Am I in trouble?"

He shook his head and sighed.

"No, not exactly. Look, Honey, what you've discovered is massive. After reading it, I called Hector. You remember him?" The mayor from the library. I nodded. "Well, I told him what you found and where. It's a historical find, of course, but they need to authenticate it. Should it be genuine, ownership becomes a question. It's our house, but the diary might belong to the town." He made a dismissive wave with his hand. "Whatever they decide on that front, I have a non-disclosure agreement on my desk waiting to be signed." He grimaced. "The fact that I'm a writer researching this specific topic has raised some questions."

I couldn't believe it.

"They think you fabricated it?" My voice was hoarse.

"They wouldn't be so direct. The lock of hair does add a layer of authenticity, though. That's why they need time to do some tests. I think that's fair. But in the meantime, neither of us can talk about the content of those pages to anyone else."

My heart sank.

"Laura is coming over to look at it… she's sleeping over."
He shrugged.

"Well, you'll have a good excuse. You can blame it on me. It's not here anymore."

"What do you mean? Where is it? I thought you said you were reading it?"

"Pretend you don't know that. Hector sent someone to collect it and take photos of the compartment. He took some samples too." He frowned. "Tall guy."

The *Pulse* bristled beneath my skin.

"Maybe it was the tall man from the diary coming to collect his dirty memoir."

My dad gave me a pointed look.

"He didn't have blue eyes."

My phone vibrated. Laura. I answered the call, and my dad, with feigned drama, commented on how I answered *others'* calls before he stood and left. She was at the turnoff we took to the tribe and needed directions. I told her to keep straight and park to the right of the house when she entered the clearing. The car was a grey Honda I don't think I'd seen before. As I hung up, Dad returned and placed the paper and pen on the table before me.

"Sign it. For my sake."

This was an unfair card to play. Seeing my hesitation, he said the authentication should take less than a few weeks. I heard Laura's car go silent outside and put my signature next to his.

"This relates specifically to the content, right?"

He nodded. A good thing—it would've been real awkward to suddenly not be able to talk about it at all. I left saying nothing else. Laura was standing in front of the house, gaping in awe and looking like a pack animal.

"I've never seen the place in the daylight before…" she said dreamily as I went down and relieved her.

Tji-Tji came bounding down the steps when we entered the foyer and Laura dropped everything to pick her up. She mentioned that having a cat was one of her greatest desires, but her dad was allergic, while gushing about how soft her fur was. I showed her to her bedroom on the second floor, next to Andrew's room.

"But if you want, we could camp out on my floor."

She put her things down, Tji-Tji still under one arm. "Give me the full house tour."

I showed her the sunroom first, which was on a level between my tower and the second floor, removed from the rest of the house. My mom used it as her study, but it was neat as a pin. My dad met us at the second-floor parlour on our way to my room. He asked about her family and whether she'd known our Aunt Catherine when she lived there, which she didn't. He promised to ask more questions later, and we continued with the tour, Laura holding Tji-Tji the whole time.

We entered the stair hollow, and the trapdoor was open, light streaming down the steps. I let her walk first.

"This is so epic."

I smiled, remembering my first time experiencing it, too. She reached the landing and gasped.

"What! Oh, my soul, this is a dream!" Her eyes were wide and dazzled as she looked around. She climbed onto her knees on the window seat and stared out. Tji-Tji wiggled from her arms and jumped onto the bed.

"Wow. I could sit here for hours, just staring. Look how beautiful the town is from here."

I stood beside her, absorbing the view. It looked fantastical.

"You are so lucky. It's unreal."

I thought about it. Yes, it was spectacular, but it came at a cost I didn't yet understand.

"It is indeed beautiful."

She scooted off the sill and turned back towards the room.

"That is quite a mirror." She approached it, slowly. "Where did you find the hidden compartment?"

I dragged the chair against the mirror.

"Up there," I pointed and stepped back. "It might be closed now, but you'll feel a bump. Slide it left." She stepped up and her fingers searched.

"I feel something." I heard her slide the compartment open and saw her smile in the mirror. My senses prickled, and I looked away, closing my eyes.

"Josilyn?" I opened my eyes, and she stood in front of me—the chair back at the desk. I frowned—must've phased out.

"Sorry."

A small crease was pressed between her brows, but she smiled.

"I asked where the diary is?"

"I'm sorry, but it's not here anymore. My dad let the mayor know and they collected it to test its authenticity."

"Oh wow, that serious, huh? Well, it makes sense, I guess. Seems like I'll have to wait a while to see it." She smiled, seeming unbothered by the fact that the item which motivated the visit was no longer here.

"Yeah, sorry about that. My dad only told me when I got back."

She brushed off the apology, and we went downstairs, brewed coffee, and drank it on the porch. Tji-Tji stayed close, winding around Laura's legs to her great delight. My dad came to check what we wanted for dinner. After he left, she was quiet for a while before asking me if my dad and I were close. When I confirmed we were, she said hers owned a business that often took him away from home. Mom and Andrew arrived after a while, and he disappeared into the forest soon after. Laura wanted to follow him and see what he was up to, and though I was tempted, I dissuaded her. Mom was excited to meet Laura and sat and chatted with us before heading in.

The more time we spent together, the more I realised how easy it was to be her friend. The thought crossed my mind to share about my gift, my heart skipping a beat as it did. I tested the waters with some quantum physics theories, and she seemed pretty interested. We helped with dinner and somewhere during the meal, I reached a turning point and decided I would tell her my secret. In response, the *Pulse* simmered and shot through my body, my senses dipping. My fork clattered on the plate and startled everyone. My family pretended nothing happened and Laura followed suit. After dinner, we went to my room, planning on watching a movie.

She cast me a probing glance. "So, I must be honest. I didn't want to say anything earlier, but your room is a bit… eerie. Like, right now, it feels like someone is watching me." She turned around as if searching for invisible eyes. I was taken aback, not just because she said it aloud, but because she felt it too. It cemented my decision to share my secret with her. She sat on the bed and Tji-Tji settled on her lap.

"I love this cat! I would steal you if I could."

"Would you prefer to go to another room? If this one makes you uncomfortable."

"No, I'm good."

It would be too easy to tell her—but I didn't know how. She took out her laptop, and I joined her on the bed, my heart racing and my jaw open, just waiting for me to say the words. With her eyes on the screen, she spoke.

"Can I ask you something?"

My pulse raced, unsure what to expect.

"Sure."

"What happened at dinner? When you dropped your fork, everyone pretended nothing happened. I don't mean to pry, but I've noticed you check out of the moment sometimes. More than most people do."

Bless her for creating an opening.

"Funny that you're asking, because I was planning on talking to you about that." My heart raced, and as she looked at me with curious eyes, my mind drew blank. "Um, I don't know how to start." It had been different with Adrian. When I'd told him, I hadn't planned on saying anything. It just flowed out like a tap had been opened. "So, you saw me perform at the ball, and in class—"

"Which was damn near supernatural, by the way. I've wondered why you're even bothering with a degree." She interrupted, and I smiled.

"Well, you're not too far out off the mark, actually." I paused, expelling a nervous giggle, and she smiled. "I... have a way with music. Well, with sound, to be more specific." She frowned, but waited for me to continue. "How can I put this? Um—the cello isn't the only instrument I can play. It has to do, um, I think, with the frequency of matter." My mouth was dry. "That sounds stupid, I'm sorry." She shook her head.

"No, no. It doesn't sound stupid. Look, I've heard you play, and I've seen you react in certain ways. You can be honest." My heart warmed at this reassurance. Her eyes burned with fixed attention and questions.

"Okay, well... I can master any instrument by touching it. I have a synaesthesia-esque condition where I can see the radiance of matter. Sometimes the signals from my senses get mixed up, and I hear colours or taste sounds. So, when I touch an instrument, it's like I connect with its frequency, its energy fibre, or its essence, in a way. And then I just know what to do, how to play it. I don't know exactly what happens, but it's like there's this entity inside, separate from me in some way, and it takes over. Sometimes it lashes out whenever it wants. I call it a *Pulse* because it feels like electricity running through my body. I was born with it, as far as we can tell." Wide-eyed, she absorbed the information like a sponge. It felt like I had opened my ribcage for inspection, and it made me queasy. Thoughts raced behind her eyes, but there were no shadows telling me I'd made a mistake in sharing.

"Wow, that's a lot to take in." She looked into the distance. "But I've noticed when you play you become this whole other person. Like you're not there. I thought you were just engrossed in the music. I guess in a way you are."

"Yeah, it's like a compulsion, like being pulled into the ocean by a current… I can't swim against it."

She nodded.

"Is that why someone needs to stop you? I noticed at the masquerade and practical."

"Compositions are a little different. The music is never truly done, I could go on and on. It's difficult to stop."

"Wow, so you're like a musical superhero or something."

A frown replaced the smile. "Does it hurt? It seems so. Especially at the ball."

It hit me then that I had underestimated her. She was much more vigilant than I'd thought.

"That one had an extra layer to it. It was what I call a heart song, where I see people's memories and their most run-through emotions. When people sing or hum, I pick up the frequency of their thoughts and feelings, like with an instrument. And then I play them like one."

Her eyes were as large as saucers now. She jumped up.

"What?!" She paced around, hands cupping her face. "My mind is blown." She said nothing for a while. "So, if you compose a song for someone, like at the ball or the practical, that's what that person would sound like if they were an instrument?"

I thought about it and nodded, impressed with the deduction.

"Yes, but for a limited period… people change a lot over time. It will never stay the same."

She sat down on the sill and stared at me as apparent fascination emanated from her face.

"Wow."

Goosebumps rose over my skin, and the *Pulse* itched inside my bones. My face flushed red at her unveiled awe, and I heard myself speak, swept away by the overwhelming feelings.

"Would you like me to show you?" My voice was thick with the same emotions that stung my eyes. I was certain seeing her song would be a treat—curious and colourful.

"Are you serious?" She looked shocked. I nodded, rose from the bed, and dragged the chair into position. She moved to the chaise, bouncing and smiling. I retrieved the cello and sat, hands shaking. Not with fear or anxiety, but with excitement and joy about sharing this part of me with her.

"I'm so nervous! It's like looking into a weird mirror." She laughed. "What do I do, just sing some random notes? Do I think about it or just go for it?" I met her joviality with my own laugher.

"Do whatever you feel is right."

"Okay, all right." She closed her eyes and took a deep, exaggerated breath. Then she cleared her throat, her hands fluttering in the air before her. Quieting for a moment, she hummed half a dozen jittery notes, which shaped a melody. I closed my eyes and repeated them inside my head, my senses building, the *Pulse* glowing in my feet. It broke and burst through me in small explosions. I felt nothing but immense happiness and excitement, and my hands bounced over the strings. A sweet, high-paced sound that would make anyone smile. Her memories showed her playing the piano with a cup of tea steaming beside her. Her reading a romance book, cuddled up in bed. Seeing me at the faculty. The only dark note slipped in when she saw Adrian looking at me. Her seeing our house; enjoying and laughing with my family. Listening with admiration as I told her my dark secret, which to her seemed like a bright sun. Tears ran down my cheeks. I was disgruntled when I felt a hand on my knee. I did not want to stop. It was the most serene and peaceful composition I'd ever played or heard. It felt like comfort and acceptance. The touch became more insistent until I relinquished and stopped. I waited until my senses dragged into place before opening my eyes to meet Laura's beaming face as she was kneeling in front of me. She was the purest soul.

She squealed and jumped up.

"Oh my word, oh my word! Josilyn! That was *insane*. Like hearing the most perfect song for the first time, yet also feeling you've heard it before, but you can't place it! Wow, that was so weird." I was as overwhelmed as she was, but perhaps for different reasons. I put the cello down—a bit too roughly—and before I knew it, I was hugging her. She was a bit taken aback but hugged me back without reservation.

"Thank you," was all I managed in a whisper as I released her.

"No! Thank you!" She twirled and danced and hummed the song I'd played. My senses buckled, and I turned my face away, out of habit. But then I had a thought.

"Laura, may I ask something a little odd?"

"Yes!" she answered before my words were cold.

"I want to see what you look like when my senses shift and the lights are off."

She indulged me and switched off the light. My senses drifted a second later, and I forced myself not to look away. It was so unexpected that I caught my breath. She was a radiating glow of energy, a white flame in an ambiguous humanoid shape. I saw her heartbeat pulsing the air, sending vibration waves everywhere. Goosebumps rolled over me. I couldn't believe that I'd never seen it before and wondered if it differed from person to person. I recalled the vague memory of Adrian on the boat. When I'd shifted, he looked like a thin black mist, the exact opposite of Laura. I was transfixed by her glowing form when a faint glow behind her caught my eye. At first, I thought it was her reflection in the window, but in the next moment, it vanished. My heart jumped. It had been outside. I couldn't identify a shape, but I guess it could've been an animal. Laura's glowing form drew my attention again.

"I wish you could see what I do. It's incredible." The ball of energy skipped towards the bed and plunged onto it, emitting a swirl of light in the glowing room. She was still humming. The *Pulse* sizzled in the air. Another glow came from underneath the bed. Tji-Tji. Hers looked different, so I stooped and looked at her. A dark blue mist curled from her, like heat evaporating from a warm body in the cold. She looked like herself but with a navy mist halo.

Laura stopped humming. "Describe it to me then." Her voice was thick. My senses slurred back into order, but I still had goosebumps over my body. The sight seared into my mind.

"Um. Light. You're made of white light. I could see your heart beating in the air." It was legions to absorb, and I sat on the windowsill.

"Wow, Josilyn… That sounds so cool. I wish I could see the things you do. It must give you an amazing way of looking at the world."

I kept quiet, feeling guilt over my mostly negative feelings towards my condition. I realised I'd allowed myself to feel resentful towards people instead of *looking* at them. She was right. Seeing the things I did should cause a profound appreciation for the world and the multiple dimensions it possessed.

"It should," I answered after a while.

"You know, sometimes we're given shoes too big for us that we need to grow into. Maybe we're not supposed to understand why we go through the frustration and the bad stuff before the shoe fits."

Her words sunk in deep, like a stone plunged into dark waters, disturbing the debris that had lain untouched in stagnation for years. It shifted something, no doubt, and the *Pulse* crawled under my skin. Tji-Tji meowed and jumped on the bed. Laura yelled in delight and picked her up. I stood and turned on the light, and when I did, the strange awareness filled the room again. I looked outside, where I'd seen the energy earlier.

"Do you feel that, or am I crazy?"

I peered into the darkness, stupidly trying to see something. For the first time in my life, I longed to shift, wondering if I would see it then. I snorted and closed the curtains. *See through that.*

"I've been feeling it for about two or three weeks." The feeling eased when the curtains were closed, but it still loomed. Like throwing a thin cloth over a lamp only slightly dims the light. Laura was worried that I had told no one else about it. She insisted I be more careful since we didn't know what sociopaths could be out there. I remembered her calling Adrian a sociopath earlier and the dark tinge in her song when he came to mind. I caught myself before blurting out how different his energy was from hers. A chill ran through me. Why did it look so different? I struggled to swallow and pushed the question away.

She found the movie, and we settled in on the bed; Tji-Tji happily snuggled between us. It was just after nine when my trapdoor creaked, and we almost screamed. My senses fell, and I saw Laura's heart hammering in the air. We stared as the door edged open. I thought I imagined a shadow emerging from the opening. The next moment, dark red hair appeared, and I inhaled sharply.

Adrian opened the trapdoor and stepped onto the landing, regarding us with an amused smile. I wasn't sure whether I was freaked out or happy to see him.

"Aren't you two comfy?"

Tji-Tji woke with a start, and when she saw him, she jumped up and ran from the room. He stared after her with a strange expression.

"Well, this isn't creepy," Laura remarked, shrugging. "You know, Adrian, cats can sense things humans are too caught up to see." An edge hid beneath her playfulness. His glowering expression drifted from the hollow to her and, within milliseconds, his features softened, and he smiled at her.

"You are right. Perhaps she could sense that I would like to be alone with Josilyn." He smiled sweetly. They were at it again.

"And maybe, *some* people also sense things but choose to ignore them." I did love her sass, I must admit. And audacity.

"We all feigned blindness when it suits us."

"All right, I think we can all see perfectly well—didn't expect you tonight."

"I did say I'd come by. I missed you too much to wait until tomorrow."

My heart swelled at his admission. Laura made a gagging sound and slipped from the bed. She picked up her vanity case and approached the stairs, scowling at him. I imagined her attacking him with it and suppressed a smile.

"Excuse me," her voice sprouted thorns.

"Enjoy." He smiled, blissfully, at her as she disappeared under the hatch. I was acutely aware that it was just the two of us now. He looked magnetic in his black button-up shirt, sleeves rolled up over tanned arms, and dark jeans. I wondered if he'd been out somewhere. His scent suffused the room, and I inhaled it deeply.

"Hi." His mouth pulled into that wickedly crooked smile and my heart skipped a beat. I smiled at him; my tongue frozen. His gaze drifted to the mirror, and he walked towards it. I cleared my dry throat and slowly approached him as he investigated the frame.

"Where is the compartment?" His voice was remote.

"There," I repeated the earlier routine, but he wouldn't need the chair. He reached up, and my eyes drifted over his admirable frame. He touched the top without difficulty. Sometimes I didn't realise just *how* tall he was. This position highlighted the contours of his shapely back and caused his shirt to pull up at the bottom, revealing his toned lower back muscles. I felt my face grow hot. He said something, but my thoughts were too occupied to register them. His posture relaxed. I hoped he hadn't noticed. He chuckled.

"Josilyn?" His voice was low and bemused, his eyes shone.

"Hmm?" My heart raced, and the breath burned inside my throat. He gave a low, throaty chuckle again.

"I asked where the diary is."

"We don't have it anymore."

He frowned.

"What do you mean?"

"They took it away for authentication."

"Who?" His expression slipped from mirth into solemnity. A peculiar shift.

"I don't know, I was in town. Some guy from the mayor's office." His eyes glinted as he looked at me.

"What did the diary say?" Something about his tone put me on edge and I felt my brain fog up.

"Like I said this morning, I didn't read it. Just the dates and her name." A lie. His eyes narrowed, and my heart skipped a beat. He remained quiet as he looked at me, and the *Pulse* thickened inside my bones, my senses poised to be undone. I gave a step back right as he gave a step forward. My pulse climbed with the apparent change in the atmosphere. I kept backing away, and he didn't halter his approach. I swore the light in the room darkened a fraction, and the *Pulse* rolled beneath my feet. My back hit the windowsill. An inexplicable form of panic ran through my limbs. I lifted my head to look up at him.

The heat licked at me, and I could swear I felt his heartbeat in the air, even though my senses remained intact. When I met his gaze, my legs numb, his expression startled me, and I thought I was mistaken. His mouth was set in a line, and his jaw flexed as his eyes bore into me in a way they never had before. He was close but distanced compared to previous times. I was confused. Something about it brought back the angry man from the faculty. He took a step closer, the heat intensifying, and lowered his head, holding my gaze.

"You're still trying to run from me." Menace inside the folds of his whisper. Fear draped over me, and I looked away. The air was heavy.

"I'm not," I whispered, but it came out like gravel. He pinched my chin and lifted my face to look at him. My heart burned. A deep frown was carved on his forehead. His eyes held distress, maybe even woe.

"Why are you afraid of me?" His whisper was raw and thick, but it contained a trace of irritation too. The mere fact he said it aloud sent adrenaline through me. The *Pulse* burned up my legs and I tried to look away, but his hand held me firm, his penetrating gaze deeply unsettling.

"I'm not." Both a lie and the truth. I felt a paradox of emotions, both fearing him and believing he'd never hurt me. He scrutinised my face as if he could read my thoughts if he looked hard enough.

"I could never harm you, Josilyn." Even saying it seemed to disturb him, and I hid my shock at hearing him speak my mind.

"I know."

His expression shifted into bepuzzlement, and he turned his head towards the window, releasing me. He held his breath, walked to the far window and moved the curtain away, peeking outside. Where I'd seen the glow earlier.

"Did you get neighbours?"

Just like that, the atmosphere lifted, and I walked to him.

"No, but I feel it too." He seemed pleased that I'd come closer.

"Peculiar."

He looked at me again and my lungs were warm, my heart melting, even though I couldn't decipher any of the thoughts swirling behind those eyes. He lifted his hand to my face and gently, touched my neck and jaw, his expression soft now.

"She's almost done. Do you want me to come again?" I wondered how he knew she was finished.

"Yes," I breathed, feeling stupid for the way I'd reacted earlier. Of course, he would be upset that I was afraid of him. That would be a completely natural response. The smile reached his eyes this time. He bent down and brushed my cheek with his lips.

"Good." He paused. "I would have been unable to keep any promises otherwise." He stepped away and opened the trapdoor, disappearing from sight before I could react. I touched my cheek where his kiss still burned. Seconds later, Laura appeared wearing her pyjamas. She hesitated halfway and scoped the room.

"Is the big bad wolf gone?"

I laughed and rolled my eyes.

"He is." Their dislike was mutual, I suspected. But I liked them both, so they would just have to put up with each other. She climbed into the room and frowned at me.

"What?"

She came closer and touched my face, where it blazed.

"Is this your way of blushing? It only happens when you've been with Match-head. It's weird."

The veins. Chills pricked at my skin. I had forgotten about them. It seemed that every time he touched me; they became visible. Why?

"Um, he gave me a kiss." My voice timid and hollow.

"Well, see? He's a walking warning. Even his kiss is poisonous." She was half-joking, but I mused the statement. Could it be an allergic reaction to his potent cologne that always permeated the air around him?

We camped out on the floor with the mattress and cushions we collected from the second-floor sofas. I only hoped nothing weird happened during the night with Laura there. We finished the movie and settled for the night.

"I want to say something," Laura started. "It's not my place, but I think you should hear it in any case. It's about Adrian. You may have noticed, I'm not a big fan. He's good-looking, sure. And maybe not *terrible*—I get you like him, but there's just something about him. I don't know how to explain it. He has a weird vibe, as if he's guarding you so no one can steal you away from him. Like, possessive. I guess that could seem charming, but I don't know. I trust your judgement, just make sure you're seeing clearly."

I felt delighted that she cared enough to speak so freely, but my heart hammered, and I found myself listening as if he might come into the room again. I had the anomalous impression that he could hear us even when he wasn't near.

"I appreciate your honesty. And I see where you're coming from—I can't fault you for it." That seemed enough for her, and we talked about other things until we fell asleep. Tji-Tji never returned, but nothing strange happened during the night, and I woke up feeling rested and calm. We prepared a big breakfast, and then I showed Laura the pier, having flashbacks of the day Adrian took me there. Late in the afternoon, Laura remarked on Andrew's habit of disappearing into the forest on his own. We considered following him to at least check that he was safe, but instead, she began searching for Tji-Tji, whom no one had seen. She ended up staying Saturday night as well, and we watched another movie. I'd be lying if I said I wasn't expecting Adrian to arrive in some dramatic fashion again, but he didn't.

By Sunday, Tji-Tji still hadn't shown up, and we launched into a proper search. Having looked in every corner of the house and even my car, we decided to search the forest around the house. We split up, keeping our phones close. Finding a cat in a forest seemed like a near-impossible task, but we had to try. I ended up near the place where I had met Adrian for the first time. Hesitant, I walked down the narrow passage, remembering how it had looked in the glow of the full moon and the lanterns. Like revisiting a place with memories from a different lifetime. It seemed much more sober now.

The clearing with the smooth rocks was still beautiful but didn't hold the same mystery as that night. Tji-Tji wasn't there. I searched the treeline, and something caught my attention. It looked like a breech into the forest, and when I walked closer, saw a path leading deeper into the forest. The hairs on my body rose, and the *Pulse* curled around my bones. I couldn't remember there being a path. Why would there be one? It wasn't a hiking trail. My heart thrummed as I followed the path until the trees and brushes became too thick to continue. I looked around at the knots of infinite green with a sinking feeling. I would never find her in this green ocean. Giving up, I turned around before I lost my way. Something caught my eye, incongruous with the foliage and shadows, and my gaze flickered back. It was a little way off the path I was on. A branch blocked it and I ducked to get a better view.

And then I froze.

My brain deciphered the image and, senses shaking, seared horror into my throat like a branding iron.

Chapter 13

A cacophony of emotions barged through me. I tasted iron and stumbled back to distance myself from the horrific sight. My senses tangled as the *Pulse* shot through me. The world around me glowed, but she didn't. The small white body, high above. Pierced through by a broken branch, a trail of browned blood down the green bark. My stomach churned. Dread wrapped around my heart like murderous hands, yet I couldn't look away. My lungs itched to scream, but only hysterical wheezing escaped. Tears streamed as I staggered back, feeling my legs give way. I fell back, but something slammed into me, preventing me from hitting the ground. The nightmarish sight was blocked by a massive chest and warm arms enveloped me. My first reaction was to push away, but the arms tightened, and I sagged into the embrace. Tears soaked the shirt against my cheek. Adrian's warmth poured over me. I knew it was him, by his scent and the way my heart melted into him. My hand clutched at his shirt restlessly. He stroked my hair as he swayed me. I thought I heard rustling further off.

Against my hair, he whispered words that my traumatised brain couldn't make sense of. As if I weighed about as much as a feather, he lifted me and started to walk. Cradled against his chest, I felt his rapid pulse in the air, and it drew me in, lulled me into a semblance of calm.

What felt like a mere second later, we exited the forest. I must have phased out. My parents' voices approached across the clearing. Their words didn't register. I heard my mom's sharp intake of breath as he told them how I'd found Tji-Tji. Carrying me into the house, he told them she might have stumbled into a wildlife trap. When he laid me down on the Chesterfield, the absence of his heat made me shiver and roll into a tight ball. So cold. My vision was hazy, and I tried to blink it clear. I could only just make out my dad and Adrian's blurred shapes looming over me. Hurried footsteps neared, and then my mom was there, pressing a glass into my hand. The sweetness caught me off guard, but I gulped it down.

"You said it was a trap, Adrian? Why would there be a trap?" Chills ran down my arms.

"Laura." My voice was raw. I fished my phone from my pocket. Adrian took the glass as I called her. It cut off. "It's dead." Panic rose in me. If there were random traps hidden inside the forest, she was unsafe. I just about jumped up, but Adrian stopped me.

"I'll find her." Before I could ask how, he was already out of the room. My parents blinked after him, too. Dad's lashes fluttered as he blinked and frowned, then shook his head and turned to me.

"I'm sorry you saw that, Honey," my dad said after a while. "No one expected something like that." Mom launched into a rant that there could be such dangerous contraptions near our house, saying she'd call the mayor, or whoever, to find out what was going on.

"We don't know for sure that it was a trap," I interrupted.

I heard distant voices outside and turned to see Adrian and Laura coming from the forest. So small next to him. She jogged towards the house, but he diverged and headed back in the direction where I'd made the horrible discovery. Why was he going back there?

Laura ran into the room, a worried frown on her forehead. She stopped and looked at me, a pained grimace distorting her features.

"He filled me in… I'm so sorry." She shook her head and plopped down, hugging me. Still shaking her head, she said, "I don't know how you found her."

"Why is he going back?"

Her eyes widened, and filled with emotion, like she didn't know what to say.

"Um. He said he wanted to take a closer look and, uh, bring her back." She frowned. "How did he even find you?"

I shrugged. A good question, but I couldn't explain it.

"Shouldn't he rather leave the scene intact, so we can have someone look at it?" My mom asked.

"It might be nothing, Evelyn. I'm sure Adrian will be able to tell. I'll see if I can help." My dad turned and left the room. I expressed doubts about how they'd be able to get so high without a ladder, just as Dad disappeared into the forest carrying a tool bag and a cardboard box. I pondered where the proper place to bury her would be. My mom herded us into the kitchen and brewed a pot of tea. The scene was seared into the back of my eyelids, and the more I tried to push it away, the more it wiggled into my thoughts—a grim intrusion.

When Adrian and my dad came down the hall later, a thick silence entered with them. He came to stand beside me, his heat spilling over me like comfort. I almost reached out to him but caught myself. Mom asked Dad about the trap, and Adrian slid closer, distracting me as he touched my shoulder and whispered.

"Don't linger on what you saw." We moved back into the parlour after a while, but Laura's mom called and she left soon after. Adrian sat beside me, and it seemed that whenever my thoughts wandered to the forest scene, he would touch me in some way or clear his throat. I thought about the eyes I'd felt watching me the past few weeks. And the glow I'd seen Friday evening. It was in the same area. I wondered if it was an animal. But what kind of animal would stalk me for weeks? When my parents left the room, I asked Adrian if another animal could've done it. He seemed taken aback by the question, but after considering it, said it was possible, though unlikely. A storm of thoughts lashed at me from behind a thin membrane.

I thought back on how Tji-Tji had looked on Friday when I shifted. Different from the glow I saw outside, but then I didn't know how the energy register of animals looked. Perhaps cats were different. He implored me not to wander off into the forest alone, and left soon after, reluctantly. I had no appetite, but Mom insisted I eat something, the tasteless lumps dry in my throat. When I retired early, I realised she'd never jump on my bed again. I'd never again feel her warm fluffy body against me, and sorrow weighed on my heart like a stone. As I lay awake, my thoughts crystallised, and I recalled the sight again—every detail seared into my brain. I decided it could not have been an animal. They stayed behind the volcano. Even the Mjesecai were confident of that. And though I struggled to wrap my mind around it, Tji-Tji must have been thrown, or thrown at. No animal could do that unless they were apelike. But why leave her there?

I woke up on Monday to pouring rain, and the drive into town was slow going. A thick swirl of clouds concealed the mountain. Adrian met me by my car, drenched dark auburn tendrils on his forehead. My heart raced at the sight of him. The long-sleeved, dark green t-shirt clung to him in a way that made me tear my eyes away, cheeks burning. Cold air rushed in when he opened the car door, and I climbed out. His crooked smile and fiery eyes were almost too much to bear.

"I'd hug you, but I need a few minutes." Were he anyone else, I would have asked if he wasn't cold. He wove his fingers through mine and my pulse spiked. The rain reduced to a drizzle as we approached the building. He asked me how I was feeling, and I replied I was okay, but withheld what I'd concluded the night before. Unsure why I kept it from him. By the time we reached the building he was dry. It boggled my mind, but then again—much about him did. He attended Dagworth's lecture, but while we changed classes, I realised he was gone. I looked around, confused; Laura hadn't noticed his sudden exit either. Somehow, I managed to concentrate on the rest of the lectures, perhaps grateful for the distraction. After Giovaniello's class, she called me as I walked past her to leave. I was a little annoyed and wondered what she wanted from me this time. The *Pulse* bristled beneath my feet; the air purple. My senses were slippery, and I inhaled a deep, sobering breath. A small crease formed between her brows, but she smiled as I approached.

"You are well?" Her tone came across as puzzled.

"Yes?" I answered, equally confused. Her smile flickered, and she looked down, shaking her head as if at some private thought. She seemed so young, compared to the first time I saw her. Even her hair seemed less grey. It dawned on me for the first time how tall she was. She cleared her throat and looked away for a moment.

"I've wanted to speak with you since your practical, but you have seemed uneasy lately," She paused, but I was uncertain what she was waiting for, and continued when I remained silent. "In my… many years of experience, I've never seen anything quite like you. I wonder if you would indulge me and tell me how your extraordinary gift functions?"

The blunt enquiry took me aback, but it was understandable that she'd want to know. The *Pulse* responded, as if self-aware that it was being discussed, and wound around my ankles. I could swear she looked directly at the spot where I felt it for a second, but her eyes flitted back to mine. My brain fogged up, and my pulse flared. I tried speaking, but my throat was frozen. I cleared it and pushed against the fog.

"Uh, I don't know how it works exactly." Not a complete lie. My senses slipped, and, as usual, I looked away. The purple hue was thick, and for a fractional second, I saw black mist entwined with it, and it felt like something was pushing into my mind. My senses resettled, but I felt claustrophobic. When I looked at her, her frown had deepened to the point where she almost looked angry.

"Describe it to me. I'm sure I can keep up." Her smile felt forced. My heart hammered against my chest.

"I can feel the music." The words came out unbidden.

"Feel it?" She cocked her head.

"Yes. No one really knows how it works. Maybe I'm a savant." I smiled, hoping to end the conversation.

"Not quite," though she smiled, a glint shimmered in her eyes. I yearned to escape the stifling room. "Were you born with it?" She asked after a pause.

"As far as we can tell, yes."

"Does anyone in your family have anything similar?"
The question surprised me; I'd never thought about it.

"Not to my knowledge. No one has mentioned anything like that." She smiled and nodded.

"A singular endowment, then." Whatever that meant.

"I guess so." My pulse raced and I felt a headache coming on.

"You are a singular individual, Josilyn," her voice sounded odd for a second, and I thought I was dreaming.

"Uh, is there any other type?" Feeling awkward, I giggled. She searched my face, smiling.

"I would like to know more when you're ready. Your mind is elsewhere today." She drew in a deep breath and stepped back. I nearly sagged as if something had been holding me up and had just disappeared. My lungs expanded. I greeted her and left, pondering the somewhat bizarre interaction.

Only on the drive home did I realise Adrian never returned. Strange that he'd left without a word. Disturbing thoughts scratched at my mind, but I refused them entry.

My dad was in his study, absorbed by his laptop.

"Hi, Dad," He jumped in his seat and gasped.

"Jeepers, Kid, you scared the life out of me." He rolled the chair back, clasping his chest.

I hadn't meant to sneak up on him.

"Sorry."

"I didn't even see you drive up." He took off his glasses and rubbed his eyes.

"Are you writing?"

"Yes. And reading."

I looked at the screen and saw an enlarged image of a diary page. Now I understood how he had been reading it a third time.

"I took them when Hector said he's sending someone to collect it." He confessed.

I nodded—lungs heavy in my chest. He studied me for a while. "Do you want to sit?" I nodded again, and we moved to the adjoining parlour. He asked how I was, with all that had happened, but after talking trivialities for a spell, I could bear it no more.

"Do you think the Dwellers are real?" The question took him aback, and he frowned.

"Do I believe there are mysterious creatures living inside the mountain? I'm not sure. Is there something peculiar and inexplicable about this town? Yes."

"Is it still inexplicable if the Dwellers exist?" He raised his eyebrows.

"I guess not. But that would open a whole other door, wouldn't it?"

"We both read the diary. The door is already open." Thoughts raced behind his eyes as he looked at me.

"Summarise the inexplicable things about the town," I asked. He took a deep breath and seemed to collect his thoughts.

"The Mjesecai believe that panther-like, invisible creatures live inside the mountain, stalking dreams and snatching people on occasion. The townspeople believe this too, though more as folklore than fact. They've incorporated silver into their thresholds, to protect them from being snatched. A trail of unexplainable disappearances litters the town's history, though the last one occurred around twenty-five years ago. No bodies were ever found, but victims often reported dreaming about being trapped in fog and being watched in the weeks leading up to their disappearance. They were called D-cases, though there's a dispute about what the 'D' stands for. Ostia has drawn paranormal investigators for a while. They registered irregular electromagnetic waves coming from inside the mountain. But since they were amateurs, no further investigation took place.

My stomach dropped like a guillotine at the mention of the dreams and fog. The *Pulse* simmered underfoot.

"Sounds pretty explicable to me." My voice was strained. He shrugged, and I continued. "And what does the diary say?"

A shadow passed over his face.

"You read it too, didn't you?" A wry smile on his mouth.

"I did, but I'd like to hear what you took from it."

"Well, a great deal. But on our specific topic, Aurelia dreamed of being visited by her lover, amongst other peculiar things, including fog. Helda protected the house with magic, and the dreams stopped."

I wondered if he'd brushed over the critical parts on purpose. The taste of blood tainted the back of my throat, my senses lilted, and the room tinged with purple.

"So, you agree with Aurelia that her experiences were mere dreams?" He frowned.

"Yes, I believe her sanity did slip."

Interesting.

"So why does her experience match all the other cases?" He blinked.

"She didn't disappear."

"That we know of."

"I guess it's irrelevant." He shrugged.

"What about the man Helda saw at the lake?"

"She didn't see a man. Even if she did, it's just a man; it doesn't mean anything."

What? I searched his face. It was like he could not see what was right in front of him. Had we read the same diary?

"What if the man is a Dweller?" The hairs on my neck rose as I voiced what I'd contemplated for days.

"Enough about monsters and immortals." He clipped the conversation short and stood. "Let's get coffee." I stared at him. I hadn't said anything about immortals.

"Dad?"

"Hmm?"

The *Pulse* flowed over my skin, and I saw the slight purple tinge around him again.

"Are you okay?"
He snorted and waved it off.

"Yes, I just haven't had coffee in four hours. No wonder I have a headache."

I was at a loss for words. Something was off, but I couldn't place it. Still dubious, I followed him to the kitchen. I tried to broach the topic a few more times, but he was having none of it. I wondered if he was that serious about the non-disclosure agreement or if Hector had told him more than he was letting on. After a time, I gave up.

Adrian didn't stop by.

I dreamt Tji-Tji jumped on the bed, and my heart was heavy when I woke up and I realised it was impossible. The day passed in a blur. Adrian formed a habit of greeting me just to disappear again. When I asked what was going on, he just smiled and said not to worry about it. He didn't come by the house anymore.

The Wednesday was different. He stayed close, though I found myself anxiously glimpsing at him, expecting he'd vanish once more. His fixed attention made it a struggle to concentrate on the lectures. He was acting peculiar, more so than usual. He kept looking at me as if memorising every inch, a sheen of urgency in his eyes.

"I have found something I'd like to show you." He said as lunch ended, his voice low and tinged with an unidentifiable note. He'd been so quiet the whole morning that it took me by surprise.

"What?"

"Have you been to Shell Beach?"

"I've never heard of it, so I doubt it. Where is it?"

"On the opposite side of the lake from your house, where the foot of the mountain meets the water."

I'd seen it from my window and wondered what it looked like.

"Oh. No, I haven't been there."

"Could you meet me there after class?" Persuasion seeped into his voice, more potent than I'd ever heard from his lips. It was unnecessary; his normal voice would've sufficed for the request. As if I could refuse him.

"Uh, sure. Do I need different clothes or shoes, though?"

His languid gaze flowed over me, accompanied by a wicked, mischievous smile that made me blush.

"Oh no, this will do. I'll meet you there. Follow the main road on the other side and take the first gravel road to the left. Continue until you reach the end of the road. I'll be there." He pulled me closer and kissed my hair.

"You're leaving?"

He smiled, walking backwards.

"I'll meet you there."

Paying attention the rest of the day proved a struggled, as I kept wondering what he wanted to show me. I drove through the other side of town, which I'd never been to, and remained on the main road. When the houses fell from sight, the road curved right, but a grey gravel road branched off to the left, bordering the lake and flanked by trees. It looked like our stone path, but the forest was less dense between the road and the lake, and I could see the blue water through the trees. The road was straight for the most part, dipping and climbing occasionally. The further I drove, the thicker the forest became on both sides until the green corridor swallowed the lake from view. My heart rate rose, and the *Pulse* prickled along my spine as I drove in shadows. Seeing the cul-de-sac where the road ends ahead, I slowed down. The trees were so high they obscured the sky above, shrouding the area in shadow. I saw no hiking trail or any other opening.

I looked around—the car idling. An abrupt movement at my window startled me, and my senses dipped. Adrian was hunched down next to me, smiling through the window. He'd come from nowhere, eyes shining like flames, an exuberant smile on his lips. I smiled back, my heart palpitating. He opened the door, and I climbed out. His other hand was on the roof, caging me between the door and his body—my pulse flared. The air was cold, but his heat spilt over me, his fragrance sticking to my tongue like honey. Perhaps he possessed an internal faucet with which he could unleash both, and it was turned all the way open. Inebriated, head spinning, it was like standing near a sun dipped in intoxicating cologne. I swayed a little, and the *Pulse* sloshed inside my legs. A deep, low laugh vibrated in his chest, and the hue of it twisted my stomach.

"I'm glad you came." His voice smouldered like a suffocated flame and my heart clenched. Something was different about him, a subtle current. I wasn't sure how to interpret it.

"Of course." My lungs expanded and felt warm inside me. I felt perplexed about what was underway. He smiled and retreated. I tried to look at my hands, but while still mid-air, he grabbed one and rounded the car. Heat burned up my arm. He felt somehow warmer than usual. We neared the forest, and I swallowed, the *Pulse* rolling, my heart galloping. My senses overwhelmed, I could not distinguish if it was him or the forest as he led me towards the trees. At the brim, he stopped and turned around, cupping my face between his enormous hands. His eyes shone with a strange light. The *Pulse* ran through my skin and, knees buckling, I fell into him. His scent thickened, and he kissed me so abruptly it seemed as if he feared it was his last opportunity. I was taken aback and expected him to pull away like he did all the other times, but he didn't. His mouth was warm and urgent on mine and left me intoxicated. Blindsided, I pushed against his chest, but he pulled me to him with such force it knocked the breath from me. His heat smothered me like a thick mist. It felt like he was trying to absorb me or press me into himself. The *Pulse* exploded, my senses flashed around, and I tasted red oil. He pulled me up to my toes, one arm around my waist. My brain was overloaded and about to explode. The last time he'd kissed me like this had been our first kiss. It felt like the earth moved beneath my feet, and I wrapped my arms around him, tears burning from the intensity and the heat. His fingers raked over my back and sent chills through me. I was entranced, drawn in by his raw need, his nearly tangible ardour. So overpowering and dominant was he then, it sent a sliver of fear through me. Pain stung my lip, and my head shot back, my eyes flashing open. His was open, too, burning like abyssal magma. He was breathing fast, his expression wild with exhilaration. He allowed me to pull free from his arms. A frown pulled at my brows as I touched my lip. Blood stain on my finger. An eerie feeling twisted my gut.

"You just bit me," I heard myself say, my voice hollow. His eyes shifted like blazing coals.

"Sorry, I got carried away," he apologised, his voice thick. The apology evaded his features. The *Pulse* built up, threatening an explosion again, and my senses edged. Chills breathed down my neck. I blinked. A network of thin veins covered his nostrils. I stepped closer, squinting. His eyes swarmed at the action, and my throat tightened. I'd seen the veins before but couldn't remember when. The taste of blood flavoured my mouth.

"Why does your nose do that?"
He frowned; his eyes cooled a shade.

"Do what?"
I stretched out to touch it.

"There's a network of veins—" so fast it blurred—he snatched my hand mid-air as I was about to touch him, then stalked off into the forest, dragging me after him. My heart hammered, and the *Pulse* itched inside my bones. I stumbled trying to keep up, but his powerful grip prevented me from falling. Something had inhabited him. He kept his face fixed forward, and all I saw was thick burgundy hair and the occasional view of a flexed jaw. My pulse throbbed in my throat, my hand sweaty and numb in his. With each step, fear thickened in my limbs. I wasn't sure I wanted to go wherever he was leading me.

"You're crushing my hand," I managed after mustering the courage. The pressure lessened, but he did not slow down.

"Sorry." His voice detached, cold. I swallowed. Something was off, and adrenaline coursed through me; the *Pulse* rolled down my spine. The trees thinned ahead.

"Why are you in such a hurry?" My voice tense as a string. He slowed and turned around, a smile on his face. The veins were gone. Was I losing it?

"Sorry." His voice had lost the edge from earlier. But his eyes were different. He turned back and started walking again—slower this time. My breathing was erratic, and not just from the fast walking. Subtly, I tried pulling my hand from his, but he wouldn't let me. We descended a gentle slope, and the trees ended, opening onto a light grey beach. As we stepped onto it, I noticed the myriad of small shells cracking and breaking under our footfall as we walked towards the lake. Hence the name, but the shells puzzled me because the ocean was miles away. I looked up and searched for the object of his hurried interest but saw nothing but the blue water. The sun hovered above the mountain, about to disappear behind it. I couldn't suppress the panic rising like the tide within. Why did he bring me there? He kept walking towards the water with a disturbing determination. The *Pulse* vibrated within me like it never had before. I tried stopping but couldn't, and when I tried freeing my hand, he tightened his grip.

"Adrian?" Panic rose in my voice, and I tried stopping again, but my feet ploughed through the sand. The *Pulse* shook me, my senses scurried, and I closed my eyes. The air felt red, and my head like something was pushing into it.

"Adrian, what are you doing?!" The scream was jagged and raw. He stopped and froze, stiffening. I just about ran into him. Frightened, I stared at his back. I felt his rapid heartbeat in the air, like micro shockwaves on my skin. He stood like a statue, with only his spine seeming to stiffen. I was about to speak again when his head jerked to the right, and he peered into the forest, or the mountain, as though he'd heard something. My pulse climbed, and I stopped breathing, listening, but heard nothing. I extricated my hand from his, surprised when he let me, and backed away. He remained unaltered, seemingly not realising my abandonment. The hairs on his neck were raised. I looked at where he was staring, but saw nothing.

"What's going on?" My whisper was a broken breath. The *Pulse* induced goosebumps over my whole body, and I shivered.

"Josilyn, you'll have to run. Very. Fast." A whispered command—strained and clipped. Shock filled my bones and raged inside me like an electric storm. My feet backed away of their own volition. My senses quivered in their sockets.

"Why?" It was a mere breath. Movement rustled in the forest where his gaze was fixed. A man emerged a moment later and I gasped—confusion and shock twined together. The angry man from campus. He had a perplexed expression and didn't notice us at first.

For a second.

Then he looked up and saw Adrian, and stopped—eyes wide and mouth agape. His face demonstrated the astonishment I was feeling. Time seemed suspended until Adrian turned to face me.

"*Run!*" he spat, and I froze, my senses falling like a stone. His face was distorted into something ferocious and blood-curdling—his forehead thickened with deep creases. Midway through the scream, while I stared into those wild eyes, he morphed into concentrated, black mist. I stumbled back, my senses dipping in and out of order, as Adrian and the large man shifted between their human form, into black mist in an ultraviolet world; the lake behind them now a summoning black hole. They crouched like animals, teeth bared, before their natural form disappeared and I heard a thunderous collision. I shifted and saw an entangled black mass fly across the beach at inhuman speed.

Snarls and growls echoed throughout the forest. A storm of icy needles pricked me, and I ran. Slow as a snail compared to them. Blood blazed in my throat as my legs struggled over the sand towards the tree line. In the distance, I could hear trees crack, here, then there. Reaching the forest, I ran faster than I ever had—green blurring past as I jumped over roots and brush. The echoing snarls grew fainter as I ran. They were at each other like animals. I broke into the clearing, and relief washed over me at the sight of my car. My legs ached as I ran for the door—clumsy fingers fishing in my pocket for the key. Did I drop it? Fear feasted inside me like crows as hot tears of relief spilt in torrents when I finally grasped it. Flinging the door open, I felt a change in the atmosphere. An eerie silence hovered. I had no idea what that implied, but fear possessed me, drove me to shove the key into the ignition and ram the engine to life. I swung the car around, tyres spinning, grey dust clouding the air. My pulse thumped wildly in my neck, the taste of copper thick on my tongue. The pedal was floored, but the car still moved much slower than I liked. I glanced at my hands on the steering wheel, wondering if I was having a nightmare again.

I could not believe what I'd just witnessed. Their feline features. Panthers. Dwellers. They could only be Dwellers. I was right. They were not invisible. Helda was right about the tall man who visited Aurelia. The trees blurred, and I pushed the car to her limits, a thick dust cloud trailing me. I had been ignorant. I thought of how Laura had glowed white, pure, and solid and how the energy of these… things, was black mist. As if they weren't *here*. Not fully. I shook my head, tears blurring my vision. Realising neither of them would have any trouble catching up with me, I took a frantic peek in the rearview mirror, but all I saw was dust.

The car sagged and drifted, and the sound of a door cracking open, then slamming shut, slashed through the air. My senses fell, and a black mist filled the car. I swerved the car, screaming. A second later, the black mist settled into the stranger who had stepped out of the forest. His back hunched, neck bent against the ceiling—squeezed into the passenger seat. *He was in my car.* He cussed under his breath. Tremors rolled through my arms, and a banshee scream ripped from my mouth, hurting my own ears. The car swerved dangerously. He cringed at the sound, covering his ears. I strayed beyond madness as the scream exhausted itself, leaving my throat raw and pained—I felt empty. I was an observer of horror, but not its participant. He was going to tear me to pieces, and I could do nothing about it.

His face was no longer distorted as he stared at me, dark eyes roving over my face. His expression was unreadable, and I looked ahead, tears streaming down my face. I found myself suspended in a dark, quiet hollow within—reality too much to bear. Trapped inside a moving car with a creature whose abilities I could only guess at. I knew he was strong. And fast. Both terror-inducing on their own, but I knew he was more than that. I floored the pedal—if I could just reach the town, where people are… He kept quiet and perfectly still, which made the whole situation even more horrifying. Probably contemplating the best way to kill me. That gave me an idea: to drive full speed into a tree.

He cleared his throat, and my nerves froze.

"Calm down." His calm, deep voice startled me. It was almost soothing. *Unexpected.* My mind tripped over itself. It had not been a suggestion but an order, an order which my body obeyed. My tears dried, and my heart rate slowed. Panic and fear left me. I could think how bizarre this development was, but I didn't feel any of it. My senses shuffled, and the air was tinged with purple and smelled like incense. I felt dumbstruck as my muscles relaxed and all the tension seeped from me, as if someone had pressed a button. His eyes weighed on me, but I refused to meet his gaze.

"Stop the car. Please." The words radiated authority and the certainty that I would comply. And I did. My foot eased off the pedal, and the car slowed down, but although my heart itched to beat faster, it couldn't. My head swam. I didn't understand why my body reacting the way it did. The magnitude of his abilities expanded. The car stopped, and though my mind raged with questions, my body was unaffected. Silence hovered like a guillotine, and though I should've descended into madness, I didn't. Morbidly, I wondered how he would end me—if he had killed Adrian. The thought tightened my throat, but only for a second. I felt numb from my body's indifference to my thoughts.

Reactions stemmed from emotion, which came from thought. Now, thoughts were all I had.

"If you're going to kill me, get it over with," I heard myself say, surprised at how strong it sounded. I could not believe I'd said it out loud. He sighed.

"I'm not going to kill you. Get out of the car; my neck is breaking." I blinked, and he was already outside, by my door, the car rocking from the sudden movement and weight change. No running then. I obeyed his instruction and climbed out, my legs aching. He was massive. Taller than Adrian even. I thought of how he'd glared at me on campus and kept my eyes down. I could feel his body heat radiating over the distance between us.

"You don't have to be afraid of me, Josilyn. I intend no harm."
A shock ran through me. How did he know my name? The *Pulse* simmered beneath my feet, even as my legs trembled from exhaustion—the air purple. I still avoided looking at him.

"Perhaps you should sit."

Of course, I did as suggested and plopped onto my car seat, my legs outside.

"May I have my body back, please?" My voice was flat and hollow now.

"It's yours. You don't have to sit if you prefer not to, but your legs are shaking, and you're not in the right state to make decisions."

A bold statement, assuming autonomy over my choices. If I didn't know running would be fruitless, I would be at it like a fox.

"Why do I do everything you say?"

He stayed silent. I waited. It wasn't like I was going anywhere. I almost looked at him.

"What are you?" Confusion laced his voice. For a second, I thought he'd spoken my thoughts out loud. I looked at him, dumbfounded. And received a double shock when I met his gentle gaze. So different from our previous encounter. *Unexpected.*

"What are *you*?" I shot back, but it was like he didn't hear me.

"You have a peculiar scent registry, one I've never encountered, which is unusual." Although I didn't even know what that meant, it sounded like he was speaking more to himself than addressing me.

"Don't know what that means, but I'm just a normal person. Well, relatively normal."

"No, you're not human. Not fully, anyway."
The words fell on me like a landslide.

"Then what am I?" I frowned at him, and he at me. How the tables turned.

"That is the question." He was zoned in now.

"Why does my body obey your words?" I repeated now that I had gained his attention. He stared at me, searching my face, and sighing, sat on the ground. I noticed his low hairline and heavy brow ridge above hooded, deep-set eyes.

"How much have you been told?" I wondered if he assumed Adrian had told me things. It stung to know Adrian had withheld all this from me. But I had known. That he was different. How easily I had rationalised events into normalcy.

"Nothing."
He snorted.

"You don't know nothing."
My pulse flared, and I met his steady gaze. I had no idea how to respond, so I didn't.

"We are the ones who live inside the mountain." My heart hammered against my throat, and I could only stare at him in shock while registering that my body was at least reacting normally again. The *Pulse* crackled on my skin, my senses dipping. His black cloud sat before me, a dormant storm. A knot in my throat, I looked away.

"I don't know what that is, but I can feel and smell it."
I looked at him—a frown carved into his forehead. He kept talking about smells and scents, but I was still processing the fact that a Dweller was sitting before me. Not that I knew what that even meant. Myth?

Hallucination? Reality? Not a panther, not invisible. Not four-legged—as far as I knew. A shiver ran through me.

"No, we don't turn into animals." Shock rippled through me. Um?

"What?" I whispered, incredulous. His gaze was steady.

"We don't turn into panthers. And no, we're not invisible. Not literally."

I blinked at him, my brain struggling to process what had just happened.

"D… did you just read my mind?" My voice was low and tense, and I felt lightheaded.

"Did you see me at the university?" He cocked his head, curiosity plastered over his face. My heart burned with the memory.

"Yes."

"You weren't supposed to."

I swallowed; my tongue dry as sandpaper. I remembered Laura saying she didn't see him. It wasn't lost on me that he ignored my questions.

"Did you read my mind?"

"That is an oversimplification, but in essence, yes."

My face burned, and a chill ran down my spine.

"Can you hear all my thoughts?"

"It's not that straightforward. Each person's mind works differently. Some think in pictures, others in voices. It's a different type of language. If I played you an audiobook in an unknown language, you wouldn't comprehend anything. Just like humans, some are better at languages than others. I'm pretty good." He frowned. "Though I'll admit, you're quite… enigmatic. As I said, you have a register I've never come across."

"Earlier, you said scent register."

"Yes."

"So, I smell weird?" I felt self-conscious, and I slouched a little. He snorted, smiling.

"No, not like that. Just in a way which tells me you're not a normal human. It's difficult to put into words, but we can smell, or taste, your thoughts from the scent you exude. But I have years of practice because it's my job. Thoughts emit a smell, or it affects your scent. So, reading them is like standing before a wall with a million small doors. Your scent leads me towards the right thought."

Ice prickled down my back. Not only because he could read my thoughts, but because I understood what he meant. It was not dissimilar to my own gift when I composed a heart song. I became restrained with my thoughts, to not let them stray. Curious that there was a similarity between us. I wanted to keep him away from that thought.

"So, super speed and strength. Controlling and reading minds. What else can you do?"

"It's not mind control. More like… biological programming."

"Same outcome."

He shrugged.

"In a way, I guess."

I wondered what he meant by it being his job. A sober thought came. Why was he so willing to tell me all this? What did it all mean?

"I'm telling you because you can't tell anyone anyway. But I must warn you, and for you to be warned, you must be aware.

He wasn't threatening me.

"Aware of what?"

He searched my face.

"There was a train of thought you suppressed earlier. What was it?"

"I suppressed it for a reason." I felt a little smug that he couldn't pick up everything. But I soon suspected it had been a trick because it was a struggle to keep it from peeping into my consciousness. I jiggled my head as if it was an Etch A Sketch I could clear.

"I'm asking for a reason." He frowned at my avoidance tactic. "That won't work…"

"You don't have to know everything. And you keep ignoring my questions."

"I am sorry. You are a curiosity to me. It's like listening to one conversation, but another interesting one is taking place a few feet away."

"Except, I am both conversations."

His crooked smile reminded me of Adrian. My heart ached and faltered.

"No, that's impossible. Though I suspect you might have a dormant gene." He frowned. "But they always remain dormant in—" He stopped himself. At first, this comment confused me, but I realised he must've accessed the thought I'd tried to suppress. I had been wondering if I was somehow like them. I blushed. Underdeveloped thought. Where would such a dormant gene even come from?

"What did you ask?"

Keeping track of the actual conversation was taxing—I had to think back about what I'd asked.

"What did you mean it's your job? And why did you look at me like you wanted to kill me that day on campus?" I slipped that one in there. His dark eyes swarmed as he looked at me.

"I didn't want to kill you. That's not what I do. I am a surveyor of sorts. A keeper. Let's just say I realised at that moment I'd been tricked—duped—into leaving town. You wouldn't understand, but that is quite a feat, and quite worrisome. The butterfly tried to give you a message, which you were unaware of, but it drew my attention. I felt the peculiarity inside you, caught your scent. And the lingering remnant of my kind on your mind. We can conceal ourselves from others of our kind to a certain extent, and I was baffled by who it could be. Your memories were locked up. Until I saw you on the beach."

The *Pulse* swirled inside my bones. I wondered what the butterfly had tried to say. Unbidden, my thoughts turned to Aurelia and the messages they'd given her. But I shut that down fast. I thought of him and Adrian colliding on the beach, and my stomach churned. Adrian's distorted face—had he been the one who tricked him? Why? Where was he taking me? And for what purpose?

"What did you do to him?" It forced itself out, and I battled to keep my voice even.

Not answering, he stared at me for so long, my cheeks flushed.

"Forget about him."

A strange response. But as his words sunk in, all the memories of Adrian flashed through my mind in reverse, up until the night I'd first met him in the forest clearing. He stepped back into the darkness of the trees and faded away. I sat there, wondering what had just happened— why I felt empty. Confused, I touched my cheek where a warm tear ran down.

"What just happened?"

"I'm sorry about that. It's necessary." Before I could ask what he meant, he continued. "As for the warning… It's essential you never, ever, under any circumstances, enter the mountain again."

Shocked, I stared at him. How did he know that? I wasn't even thinking about it. But it confirmed the worst: it had not been a dream. I speculated if he was the thing that followed me when I was there.

"No, it wasn't a dream. And no, it wasn't me in the woods. But you are lucky to be alive. I'm surprised you got away."

"But you are a Dweller?" What else would it have been?

He frowned, contemplating. His eyes were unlike any I'd seen before. As dark as they were, they swarmed with life and wisdom.

"That's a word they use for us, yes. Amongst others."

"What word do you use?" I had the fleeting thought my dad would love to know and a chill ran through me, his face expressionless for a second.

"You won't be able to do that, I'm afraid." It wasn't a threat or a warning. Just a simple statement of fact. I wondered if he'd command me into silence.

"Tell me, how many people have you told about your *'dreams'*?" His peculiar emphasis on the word made it clear what he meant. I considered it—except for minor details—I didn't remember my dreams when I was around people. And what I *did* remember, I was reluctant to tell anyone. Except… someone… but my brain could not lay hold of the rest of that thought—stung as it tried.

"Not a human, so doesn't count. But you get the point. That's also why I can tell you what I'm telling you—you won't be able to share it with anyone."

I remembered how weird my dad had acted when I tried talking about Dwellers.

"Did you do something to my dad?"

He frowned and looked so deep into me, that I felt naked.

"You saw it in effect, then. No."

"What do you mean?"

"Your father came to the same conclusion you did but couldn't speak about it."

How did he know that? The thoughts gushed. I was about to speak about it with my dad. Why could I?

"Are you stalking our house?"

"What? No." He was blindsided.

"Did you kill my cat?"

He frowned and shook his head, lifting his hands as if in surrender.

"Why would I kill your cat?"

"That is what I would like to know."

"Can't help you there, I'm afraid." He shrugged.

"I would still like to know what you call yourself."

"Myself or our kind?"

Um.

"Both." I watched him closely as his facial expressions shifted and changed—fixed on him for a while. As impossible as it seemed, I felt comfortable and... safe with him. He must have jinxed my mind.

"I haven't charmed you."

My cheeks flushed. It seemed he was becoming better at reading me. A perturbing thought.

"Names?"

"No." His jaw flexed, his lips tightening.

"Why not?"

His eyes bore into me, heavy as planets. I caught my breath but held his gaze.

"No human has heard it spoken and remained."

The *Pulse* coursed over my skin.

"Remained?" Was he going to take me away? I thought of the reports about people disappearing after dreaming the same things as I had.

"You've got it all wrong. But no, I won't take you into the mountain. That would be counterproductive."

"Counterproductive to what?"

He stared at me. I got the impression he sometimes spoke his thoughts aloud without filtering them.

"As I said, *you* should not be going into the mountain at all."

"Because I smell weird?"

He laughed but cut it off by pursing his lips.

"Yes, because that means I don't know what you are."

"So, if I was normal, I'd be inside the mountain?"

"Well, yes, probably. But again, not in the way you think. You've got it all wrong."

"Then why do people disappear?"

"I'm only telling you things you need to know. That isn't one of them."

"But I won't be able to tell anyone."

"Doesn't matter."

Our conversation was ending, I could feel it. And I realised I didn't want it to. I still had so many questions.

"The names?"

His eyes narrowed a smidge before he rose to his feet, dusting himself off. My heart dipped at the size of him.

"You can call me Caleb, even though we hopefully won't speak again. As for our kind… We are guardians. V'le Cremah." It rolled from his tongue in a way that evoked a thrill inside my bones, and the *Pulse* simmered. Enthralled, I gazed up at him.

"V'le Cremah," I repeated under my breath. It sounded like an incantation, even though I was probably saying it wrong. A memory gnawed at my brain but was incapable of coming into the light.

"Don't waste your time. It's getting dark; you should go."

My legs moved into the car, and I closed the door, turning the window down. I did not appreciate him telling me what to do. Unnecessary, this time. Still, I couldn't deny the disappointment at him saying he'd hopefully not see me again.

"Don't worry. If there were a next time, you wouldn't even know I was ordering you around. Drive safe." He retreated. There was a crackling pop sound, and he was gone.

"Bye," I spoke into the void. My senses dipped into the ultraviolet world and there were no dark mists to be seen. Undecided, I switched on the car and drove. Slowly. No matter how I tried, I was incapable of speeding up.

Chapter 14

I reached home long after sunset and parked beside Mom's car. I sat there a while, collecting myself—considering the day's events. How I would face my parents—my dad—after what happened. Something was amiss, but when I tried thinking about it, my brain fogged up. Why did I visit the beach alone?

"Josilyn." A whisper. I turned.

I stood inside the foyer, my dad in the parlour doorway. Gasping, I took a step back, my senses falling out of place. His solid, white, glowing form, was surrounded by an ultraviolet world. Purple mist hung over his head. He put his hands up as if in surrender.

"Sorry, kid, are you okay? Are you awake?" The sound waves from his words vibrated through the air, coming out orange. Freaked out, I looked away, my breath racing as I waited for my senses to recalibrate. He took a step towards me.

"Give me a sec." His footfall sent liquid mist vibrating over the floor, and chills rolled through me. He stopped, and I watched the waves ripple out and die. I controlled my breathing, and after a few long seconds, normal sight returned. I looked at his familiar form with relief. Concern scrunched his forehead.

"You good?"

I felt uncomfortable and confused. Something I could not identify gnawed at my insides. The afternoon's events slunk back and faded into the shadows.

"I… yeah."

Mom came from the hallway.

"Oh, hi Honey! You're back late. Were you with…" she paused, frowning, "uh, Laura?"

I wondered if I was but was stumped.

"No…"

We three stood frowning at one another. Comical, in a way.

—I was sitting at the kitchen counter, eating. The fork dropped from my hand, startling everyone. Dazed, I looked around me. I was losing time fragments—far worse than ever before. I apologised and we continued with dinner. Dad kept eyeing me, and I tried to remain calm, but I just wanted to escape. Hide. An ache inside my chest expanded like a gaping wound and tears burned my eyes. I blacked out twice more while in the kitchen and I couldn't take it anymore, so I excused myself. When I entered the foyer, the air felt thick, and my heart hammered.

The *Pulse* smouldered beneath my feet as I approached the stairs slowly. On the first step, my foot submerged into a layer of fog flowing down the steps like dry ice.

A knock came from the front door. One. Two. Three. Slow and deliberate. My pulse raced as I turned and stared at the door, waiting. A tangible silence permeated the house. No one came down the hall, so I neared the door. Whoever it was didn't knock again. My heart racing so much that I felt warm, I opened the door. No one was there. I stepped outside and looked around.

"Hello?" I was certain I had not imagined the knocking, but there was nothing. And no car.

"Josilyn." A near inaudible whisper touched me, indiscernible where it came from.

"Who's there?" I asked into the dark with a jagged voice. A muffled response came, as if it were underwater, making the words indistinguishable. Panting, I looked around before rushing back into the foyer and closing the door.

—I stood before the stairs inside my hollow. The *Pulse* vibrated inside me, and I steadied myself against the wall. My heart pounded as I climbed, recalling the things Caleb had told me. Unfathomable, how I had forgotten it all while with my parents. The trapdoor was closed, and my pulse raced as I pushed it open into darkness.

I switched on the light quickly, feeling like someone else was in the room. But when the light flooded the space, and I scanned around, there was no one. I closed the curtains and I faced the mirror, thinking about Caleb's warning not to enter the mountain again. Because of what I was. The *Pulse* rolled beneath my feet as I walked closer, my senses fraying. I looked at my reflection, still normal, as the *Pulse* wound around my legs and my arms, and my senses fell. Resisting the instinct of flinching away, I looked at myself as the room changed into its ultraviolet spectrum, filled with neon colour and mist. To my surprise, the mirror transformed when I shifted—into the dark, fog-filled doorway and I stepped back, fearing the darkness before me. I couldn't explain it, but I felt nothing could exit from it. My senses clicked back into place, and I saw my regular reflection again. A conundrum, trying to see what I looked like when I shifted if the mirror changed too. But I had seen energies without a complete shift. I approached the mirror and pressed my palm against the cold surface, where the outline of my hand formed in fog after a second. I removed my hand, startled when the mirror wobbled like jelly. It stagnated when I stepped back. The outline of my hand disappeared before my eyes. It was as if the mountain wanted me to enter. I took a deep breath and focussed on my feet, where I usually felt the *Pulse* first, as if it came from the earth. All my life, I'd never tried summoning it this way, and I felt pretty silly. I'd always seen it as something beyond my control, something that happened to me, because of stimuli. The *Pulse* surfaced, like I'd called it forth by imagining it already there. But it buzzed inside my bones, and the next moment, the room's light changed. Not into the ultraviolet.

I caught my breath.

Still looking at the ground, I noticed something in front of me, where the mirror was. My heart hammered against my chest, and I saw the vibrations of my heartbeat warp the air around me like heat waves. Slow, I lifted my gaze to the mirror and looked at myself. Goosebumps rolled over my body, the *Pulse* oscillating through me from feet to head and back again. My eyes stung and I swallowed hard as I looked at the white glowing form reflected back at me. I was a cluster of white sparkling mist—not a solid humanoid shape like Laura and my dad. Shocked by this sight, I stumbled back, shaking my head in an attempt to push the *Pulse* away. I looked more like Caleb and—

—I was in bed, in my pyjamas. I drew in a sharp breath, staring at the voile fabric above my bed. My hands clenched into fists beside me. If these time lapses persisted, I would have to tell my parents. What did Caleb do to me? All I could remember was him telling me not to enter the mountain again, and from what I saw that afternoon, disobeying the order would be inconceivable. Troubled by these thoughts, I fell asleep at last. A gentle, sweet scent hung in the air, and I drew it into my lungs. The light seemed too bright behind my closed eyelids. I was walking and stopped as I opened my eyes. Disoriented, I wondered if I had blacked out again. The sun burned low through the trees behind me as I stood in the forest on the path leading to the pier. A splash of blue between the trees caught my eye. Beautiful, bright galaxy orchids. I wondered if it was their scent permeating the air. Then I was walking towards them, picking my way over roots, squashing the thick underbrush beneath my shoes. Though I expected birds at this hour, there were none—only a peculiar, thick silence. I reached the orchids—so beautiful, so irresistible, their scent heady. I bent to pick a stem. As I did, a reddish spray expelled from the ground, but vanished so quickly I wasn't sure it had happened.

I straightened and whiffed the flower with my eyes closed. When the light changed, I opened them again. I was on a shell-covered beach. The water sparkled in the light as the sun dipped lower, nearing the volcano on my right. The flower was still in my hand, and I was sitting on a blanket. I felt warm, even though the sun was so close to setting. Someone sat beside me, but I was incapable of looking at them. No matter how I tried, they remained a blur in my peripheral vision—there, but not. They spoke, but the words were muffled.

"What?" I asked in a hushed tone. Trying to look at them was like trying to make two same-poled magnets touch. They spoke again but the words remained unintelligible—frustrating.

"I can't hear you."

A butterfly settled on my knee. A *Morpho*. Its body was turned towards me, and I remembered Aurelia saying they were messengers. I didn't know how to listen, but tried to focus. I heard nothing audible, but there was an impression in my thoughts.

"You can't trust him."

A shadow fell over me, blocking the sun. I looked up to see a massive man looming over me, dark eyes fuming with hate and malice. Gasping, I scurried back, my hands digging into the sand and sharp shells. He followed and, grabbing my ankle with a burning iron grip, pulled me towards him. I tried screaming, but the air caught in my throat. I kicked and I turned on my stomach, clutching at the ground for anything to resist him and crawl away, but it was useless. As if I weighed nothing, he dragged me towards the lake as I scraped my fingers on the sharp shell fragments. My chest and throat burned from the intense fear. I kept kicking, but as I looked over my shoulder, saw we were near the water. The next moment, someone crashed into him, and I knew somehow it was the stranger who'd been on the blanket with me. The impact freed my leg, and, feeling the earth fall away beside me, I turned onto my back.

—I was on my bed, Mom lying beside me—I sat up with a start. She had a fright too and jolted upright.

"Sorry, Honey! Didn't mean to startle you. You were so fast asleep."

Heart pounding, breath racing, I scanned the room, unsure what I was looking for.

"Are you all right?" She touched my arm. I took a deep breath.

"Yeah, I was just… deep in a scary dream." It didn't feel like a dream. Concern touched her brows, but she managed a smile.

"Perhaps it's better you woke up then."
It felt unusual for her to be in my room like this.

"Is everything okay?"

"Oh yes. I just haven't seen much of you. So, I wanted to check in. How are you? How's Laura? Ever since Tji—"

—I was standing in front of the mirror, dressed. My mom was gone. I looked at the clock on my bedside table. I needed to leave. An unexpected sight stood beside the clock—a galaxy orchid, and a floating lotus in a little glass bowl. I didn't remember it being there the previous night. I stepped closer, drawn towards them. Their display on the bedside table triggered a memory—someone gave me flowers like these. And I saw them in the forest, walking to the pier with…

"So, now I'm supposed to walk home, which is, you know—great and all. But not the whole week. So, thanks, I'd really appreciate you dropping me off."

I stopped in my tracks and gazed around me, dumbfounded. Laura. We were near the main building on campus. The *Pulse* shot through me, sending my senses into a tumble. It hit me so hard that I doubled over, hands on my knees, feeling nauseous. Laura placed a hand on my shoulder.

"Hey, are you okay?" concern shone from her voice. My pulse drummed wildly, a knot in my throat. I could only shake my head.

"Is that… thing happening to you?" Hesitant, she asked. I nodded. After a while, my senses fell back into order, the Pulse shrunk back, and I straightened.

"How did I get here?" I looked at her, on the verge of completely freaking out. She blinked at me. My fingertips throbbed.

"What?"

"I don't know what's going on, but I'm losing chunks of time. The last thing I remember is standing in my room right before I had to leave. How did I get here?"

Her eyes were saucers.

"I… don't know. I walked here from my mom's office and saw you standing by the fountain." She glanced behind me. "But your car is here. I'm assuming you drove."

I turned and saw my car in the usual spot, felt the key in my hand.

"Does this… happen often?"

"Not to this level, no."

"So, you don't remember anything before right now when you stopped walking?"

I wracked my brain, but there was nothing.

"No. Nothing. I was in my room one minute, and the next I was here walking with you."

Walking to class, she told me I had offered to drop her off later. I asked if there'd been anything strange about my behaviour but, apparently, I'd been acting normal. That freaked me out even more. When she started asking questions to figure out what triggered it, I stopped her because my heart was aching, and it felt like something was about to happen. I blacked out for most of Dagworth's lecture, and a few more times throughout the day. According to Laura, there wasn't any notable difference in my behaviour.

When I parked by the kitchen door, my parents' cars were not there. I had not blacked out on the drive home but noticed that, right before it happened, my heart would ache as if a sudden sadness had crept up on me. So, when that sensation arose, I redirected my thoughts to happy memories, like drinking coffee on the porch with Dad. It loomed now again. I got out of the car and hurried to the front door.

"Josilyn." That whisper again, reaching out like a hand, and I turned, shaken. No one was in the clearing, though I searched around me, my pulse erratic.

"Who's there?" I yelled in a shaky voice, my throat tight. No answer came. The opening in the trees that led to the pier path pulled me closer and, feeling the ache again, I tried redirecting my thoughts, backing away. But I found myself standing at the mouth of the opening into the forest. I looked around, the *Pulse* bristling beneath my feet like needles, and saw no one. I looked at my hands—trembling, but I was awake. Birds chirped in surround sound. I dropped my bag and walked onto the path. The musty forest fragrance filled my nostrils as I descended over root and stone, my heart hammering like crazy. I was unsure what I was doing. Halfway down, a flash of blue off the path drew my gaze. Galaxy orchids. As I stared at them, the ache bloomed inside my chest. It felt like déjà vu, walking into the forest and picking one and...

—I stood on the pier, right at the edge. Startled, I tried to pull back, but lost my balance and instead fell forward. I braced for the cold and shallow water, throwing my hands out, but the impact never came. I opened my eyes to the first-floor parlour. Stupefied, I turned around as if I could find an answer somewhere in the room. My heart raced, lungs burned. Indistinct whispers swirled around me and I spun around like a madman searching for ghosts.

"What are you?!" the hysterical question burst out. The chaos quieted, but the silence that followed was pregnant. A more solid whisper reached me, though the words were indistinct. A warm breeze drifted over my arm and back, and then something touched my face. I flinched, my breath quickening.

"Don't touch me!" I scrutinised the room, certain I wasn't alone. I resolved to use the *Pulse* to see and tried to summon it. Nothing came. Peculiarly, my senses weren't shifting either. I looked at my hands.

My heart dropped.

I had too many fingers on each hand, blurring as I tried to count them. They moved lethargically slow as I rolled them around. I was dreaming. Shocked, I stared at them until it freaked me out too much. The presence lingered, watching me. What was I supposed to do now? I didn't know how to wake up. I ran from the room. Maybe I was crazy, but I thought I could pinpoint the silent observer's location. Through the foyer, towards the ballroom, all the while feeling it follow me, quiet and controlled. As I burst into the ballroom, music played, and the room was filled with people dancing. The Masquerade. I stopped in my tracks and looked down at the sparkling red tulle on my body. I wove through the crowds, looking for something, or someone.

"Josilyn," I heard my name whispered and turned, looking straight at Laura. She waved at me, but something about it felt off, and I turned back around. And then saw myself, wearing the golden dress. When the other me turned to face the dancing people, I saw the snaking scar on my back. She felt like a stranger. I was dreaming about a memory. This was the night I met… someone. My heart started aching again, and I backed away, running through the crowd and out the door—right into something solid. I staggered back but saw nothing before me. Tentative, I reached into thin air and touched a fabric with warmth behind it. I recoiled, and as if it had been cloaked for a second, the presence was right before me, and I'd just touched it. It felt like a person blocking the front door. I stumbled back, my eyes roving over empty space between me and the door.

"Who are you? Why are you chasing me?" I screamed; my voice raw. An answer came, but the words remained mumbled still. Tears burned my eyes.

"I can't hear you!"
Heat radiated over me suddenly, and I snapped back, but a massive, blazing hand cupped my face, searing my neck and jaw. To my utter confusion, the touch was tender. My heart ached the way it did before a blackout, and my skin prickled under the heat. A low, deep voice spoke, but I still could not make out the words. Shaking my head, I stepped back, but I slipped on something wet, and then I was falling.

"… I'm not sure what to do with you, Honey. Your dad won't be back for a while. Why are you wet?"

My mom stood beside me, a hesitant hand on my shoulder. Startled, I jerked away.

"Sorry! I tried leading you back home. Are you all right?" Her eyes were huge.

Disoriented, heart hammering and aching, I looked around—outside, near the path to the pier. I looked at my hands—I was awake.

"I didn't know you were sleepwalking again. Why are you wet, Hon?" She was right; I was soaked. I swallowed.

"What's that?" My skin burned where she touched my face. "Your veins are visible here… Did you touch something poisonous?" Concern radiated from her eyes.

"N—no." My heart ached.

—I came to, sitting on the porch wrapped in a towel. My only reaction was a sudden inhale as the shock of teleporting through time wore off. In my hands, I held a cup of coffee. Mom and Dad were sitting with me, chatting as if nothing had happened. I don't think they noticed. I touched my face where it had burned. My heart ached, and I thought about birds soaring through the blue skies, pushing away whatever thought was clawing at the surface. At bedtime, I chose to rather sleep in the guest room adjoining Andrew's. Dad thought it was a good idea, probably so he wouldn't worry about me falling down the stairs. I drank warm milk with honey before bed, somewhat fearful about what would happen. If I dreamt, I couldn't remember it, but I woke up Friday morning with a burning sensation around my throat. No marks were visible in the mirror and the next second, I was on campus. I half-shifted in Giovaniello's class, and though the room was hued in purple, I thought I saw subtle red around her. She paid little attention to me, which seemed strange after our last encounter. I remained attentive to the ache inside me and regulated most blackouts by doing so, but not all of them.

I remained in the guestroom that evening.

At some point during the night, I woke up with a racing pulse. The heat was stifling, and I kicked my duvet, feeling something weird around my ankle. I sat up to get a look but could see nothing. I wiggled my foot—something was wound around my ankle. The moment my fingers brushed against it, I flinched in surprise. Warm and thick, it felt like what I can only describe as dense air. Wary, I reached down again, exploring it with my fingers. It felt like a cuff attached to a rope. I rose with the invisible string in hand and followed it to the door. Wild heart, I pulled on it. It gave only a little before pulling taut. I straightened and turned the doorknob. The door opened into an empty hallway. I pulled on the rope again. This time, it was slack, and I followed it past Andrew's room, through the second-floor parlour, and into the hallway where my secret door was. My pulse spiked when I realised it led to my room. I hesitated. What was I doing? The rope tightened until I stepped forward and continued walking, following it to my hidden entrance. I climbed the stairs, my hands sweaty, heart racing. I questioned myself, wondering why I was following an invisible rope locked around my ankle. The hatch was closed, but the light was on, and I wondered if I had forgotten to turn it off earlier. My heart ached, and I paused on the steps, expecting another time jump. But it didn't come. I pushed the trapdoor open and stepped onto the landing. The line was taut towards the back of the room, and I turned around and froze.

An enormous man stood by my desk, his back towards me. His hair was the darkest, richest red I'd ever seen. Dark chocolate and wine. I dropped the invisible rope, though it made no sound. My chest heaved, my heart clenching. He turned around, and I was breathless. Our eyes met, and for a second, he seemed taken aback, emerald eyes framed by dark lashes swarming. He was the most beautiful thing I'd ever seen. Tan skin, strong jaw, aquiline nose. He was perfection. He spoke, and I realised it was him; the one I couldn't hear. I still couldn't. My heart ached and tears burned my eyes.

"I—I can't hear you," I whispered, and he frowned. He started towards me, and his sheer size invoked the desire to back away, but I was immobile, entranced by the way he looked at me. A storm raged inside me, both confused and terrified by this stranger who looked at me as though we knew each other intimately. He reached me and, bending down, cupped my face in his colossal hands. My heart dipped with the heat of his touch. The fear burned away, but not the confusion.

"Who are you?" I whispered again, my throat burning. Pain flashed across his face, intensifying the ache in my heart. He spoke and the warm breath spilling over my face was somehow intoxicating, but the words were indiscernible. His eyes felt familiar.

I shook my head.

"I can't hear you."

He stroked the back of my ear with his thumb, his eyes calculating but wild. Then he pressed his flaming lips against mine, and my heart exploded. His lips were gentle against mine at first, and I felt him draw a deep breath. His fingernails over my skin sent a thrill through me before he bunched my hair in his fingers and pulled me against him. My lungs swelled inside me. He exhaled a quick breath against my mouth, pressing his feverish forehead to mine, and his kisses became urgent and desperate. Crushing. Possessive. His heat permeated my bones, his scent a heady potion. I was transfixed, absorbed. *Our first kiss had been like this.* He'd taken me to the lake, out on a boat. He'd given me a lotus flower by the water. Memories swarmed through my head and tears flowed down my cheeks. *Adrian.* I wrapped my arms around him, making an unintelligible sound, and he caught his breath, enveloping me with burning arms. Even as he held me so close, I felt his muscle relax. He moved his lips away from mine and kissed my cheek.

"Can you hear me now?" A hoarse whisper against my ear—hot breath sending a thrill through me.

"Yes." My voice matched his. He blew out a breath and pressed his fiery forehead against mine. All the veins within me reached out to him. More memories fluttered into my head.

"I thought I'd lost you forever."

"Why couldn't I remember you?"

His lips pulled into a severe line.

"He tried to take you from me." His eyes held an icy glint, a dark malice. Ice ran down my neck.

"Who?"

He pulled back, frowning.

"What do you remember?"

I thought hard, seeking clarity through the haze.

"Um, I was on the beach. And this man came out of nowhere, dragging me to the water."

"And then?"

I remembered running as fast as I could and reaching my car. Grey dust billowing behind me. My heart ached again, and I pulled back, lifting my hands to look at them, but he grabbed them, his eyes locked on mine.

"It doesn't matter."

My wrists burned beneath his fingers. A strange moment. How did he know I looked at my hands to tell if I was dreaming? Why didn't it matter?

"What happened next?"

I concentrated with all my strength. His name was Caleb.

"He found you."

"Yes," I breathed. Some memories came, but they were vague.

"You're a Dweller." I tried pulling away, realising he wasn't human like me. But he held me close.

"But you're not."

I frowned. Why would he say that? Of course I wasn't a Dweller.

"No, Josilyn. You're not fully human either."

Shock burst through me for two reasons: first, he told me I wasn't human, and second, he had read my mind. I pulled away and he let me. His eyes shone. More memories came. Caleb had told me this, too. We were in the forest clearing now, where we'd first met, and not my room anymore.

"V'le Cremah."

"Yes."

My pulse raced as I looked at him, my thoughts running wild. I remembered looking in the mirror and seeing myself, white and misty—his opposite.

"And what am I?"

He shook his head and closed the distance between us.

"I don't know. But if you were human, there would be no way you could have remembered."

"Did he do something, so I'd forget you?"

"Yes, he deceived you. He made you trust him and twisted your memories. But I don't think he realised it won't work with you."

"But why would he do that?"

He shook his head.

"I'm trying to figure that out. It has something to do with the diary." He gave me a pointed look. I remembered that I'd kept the content of those pages from him because I suspected he was a Dweller.

"You live inside the mountain."

"Yes."

"You stay there your whole life?" I wondered if it was a prison.

"Technically, yes, I must stay inside the mountain. It's complicated."

"Can… can he come through my mirror?"

"No, the silver is charmed. We cannot pass through."

His frankness took me aback.

"But, Josilyn, you must avoid Caleb at all costs while I figure out what's going on—what he wants with you. Block your thoughts; you've done it before. Especially thoughts about me. If he realises you remember me, it will cause more trouble."

I recalled Caleb telling me my thoughts were difficult to follow. I nodded.

"I'm not sure how, but I'll try."

He smiled and pulled me against him.

"Just follow your instincts." He took a deep breath and squeezed me. "I must leave."

My heart ached at the thought, and I clung to him. He pulled back and gave me the softest kiss he ever had–my breath catching. His lips still burned on mine, but, when I opened my eyes, he was gone.

I woke up in the guest room to a knock on the door. During breakfast with my family, I noticed the blackouts were fewer, though not gone. I wondered why he must stay inside the mountain. Comforted by the fact they couldn't enter through the mirror, I moved back to my room. But I declined an invitation into town with Dad, afraid Caleb would materialise from nowhere. The thought that he could show up at any time produced an uneasiness that simmered beneath the surface throughout the day. Of course, I couldn't stay home for the rest of my life. On Monday, I returned to class, though I was anxious and kept looking around. To my deep relief, not much happened, apart from the random low-grade blackouts. Until Wednesday.

Sitting in class waiting for the lecturer, my senses shuffled without warning and with no apparent stimuli. The *Pulse* burst through me, but something felt wrong. Everything around me contorted and swirled and I became nauseous, chills running over me.

"I need fresh air." Sounding drunk as I grabbed my bag and stumbled from the room, feeling as if my consciousness was slipping. I shoved past people while fleeing, but all I could hear was the blood thumping in my ears. Outside, the cool air pushed into my lungs, and my brain felt like being crushed under enormous pressure. A yelp squeezed itself out, and I grabbed my head. Murmured whispers drifted into my mind—I thought—but I didn't understand the words. I stumbled down an alley, unsure where I was going but feeling compelled to keep moving. Through the blur of senses, I heard a crack and saw black. I moved, the air rushing over me as if I were falling from a skyscraper. And then I stopped. I hunched over, hands on my knees, breath racing. My senses were manic, spluttering around. I didn't know what just happened or where I was, but I felt dizzy.

"Settle down." The last voice I wanted to hear. My senses dragged back into place and the nausea subsided. But the panic rose as I frantically tried to avoid the one thing I must not think about. Swallowing, I straightened and drew a deep breath. We were standing in the forest.

"I didn't think you'd react this way." He sounded almost apologetic. What was he talking about? Telling myself to focus and play it cool, I looked into his brown eyes. They seemed calm enough. All deception.

"The blackouts?"

A frown creased his already heavy brow.

"Blackouts? No, I mean, I didn't know you'd react this violently when I summoned you."

"You… summoned me?" I was both confused and incredulous.

"What did you mean by blackouts?"

"What do you mean by summon?"

He blinked at me, annoyed that I'd disregarded his question.

"I made you exit the building." He waved his hand like that was inconsequential. "Blackouts?"

My heart raced. It was a tricky subject to navigate, especially in thought.

"You did something to me the other day. When I got home, I began blacking out. Like, I don't know what happens, but I lose hours where I don't know what I was doing. No one noticed, which is terrifying."

Shock shone from his eyes as they studied me, calculating something. He shook his head.

"No, that shouldn't happen."

"Well, I mean… It does."

"But it shouldn't, Josilyn." He gave me a pointed look. "You don't understand, this has never happened before."

"You often warp people's memories?"

A shadow passed over his eyes.

"How did I warp yours?" He spoke slowly, intentionally. Realising I'd made an error, I swallowed and tried backtracking.

"I mean, what else could it be? You can read my thoughts, and you can coerce me into doing things I don't want to do, like *summon* me outside. That would mess with anyone's head." My heart raged; it took everything I had to avoid the thing I shouldn't think about.

"Why did you call me out? I thought we wouldn't speak again."

His eyes were alive and bright.

"What do you know about memory warping?"

I shrugged.

"It was an assumption. What did you do?"

His eyes were sharp.

"You shouldn't even realise I did anything, Josilyn."

"I mean, it's logical, though? The blackouts began after our interaction." My heart hammered so much that I was lightheaded, and my senses drifted. I saw his black form, infused with a red tinge for a second before it normalised.

"Your heart is beating faster than normal."

I folded my arms over my chest.

"Of course it is. This is a weird conversation."

His gaze was steady, but it felt like he was unwrapping my mind.

"What are you hiding?"

Tricky, how the mind works. *Don't think about what you mustn't think about. Don't think of a purple elephant riding a monocycle. Don't think about…*

"Nothing, I'm hiding nothing." I doubted I could be more obvious. He took a slow step closer, and I backed away. And I thought about what I shouldn't have. He stopped and the light darkened around us. The *Pulse* swirled inside my feet, and my heart ached again. I inhaled sharply, feeling my eyes widen, and I put my hands on my chest and tried thinking about something else.

"No, no, no, no, no." Blacking out now would be the worst possible scenario. Radiating heat came closer and settled on my head. The heat seeped into my heart and the ache dulled, though I still anticipated a blackout. He stepped back, releasing me.

"That's impossible." The look of sheer horror and panic on his face startled me.

"What?" My pulse flared, even as I wondered what could possibly horrify him.

"How do you remember him?" He looked and sounded utterly shocked.

I swallowed hard—my mouth suddenly dry. "What do you mean?" My heart hammered against my throat, and I took a deep breath.

Whatever he was thinking about took him to a different place and he looked at me like I wasn't even there.

"Something's not right." He frowned, and I saw a thought drop into his mind. "Unless… No. No, it can't be. That's impossible." He shook his head, repulsed by whatever thought it was.

"What's going on?"

"But he's re-bound… He can't reach…" He seemed to be thinking aloud.

"Caleb, what are you talking about?" At last, he looked at me.

"What I did was for your own safety. You shouldn't remember him at all."

"Maybe you did it wrong."
He shook his head, snorting.

"No, I wish. That would be an easy fix."
That angered me.

"Oh, yeah. I guess messing with people's memories is an easy fix, isn't it?" A mirthless laugh rang out. "I mean, who cares if they lose hours of their waking life, right? As long as they don't remember, everything is fine."

He stared at me, looking perplexed.

"You had no right to take from me."

"This isn't a game, Josilyn. I can't risk anything. Not with what you are."

"Oh!" I emitted the same laugh. "Oh, it's *not* a game, is it? I'm sorry. I got confused since you seem to think my mind is a toy you can toss around as you please. And I thought you don't know what I am."
He blinked, but then sighed and shook his head.

"I don't know. You wouldn't understand."

"You have no idea what I would and wouldn't understand."
His eyes narrowed.

"You do realise I'm not your enemy, right?"
Surprised by the comment, I repressed the peculiar anger I felt.

"Forcing me into forgetting someone seems like enemy behaviour."

He nodded.

"I can see why you'd think that."

He was so calm, so reasonable. But he knew how to glean what he wanted, even though it felt like he wanted to help. He cleared his throat.

"Did you remember on your own, or did he craft your recollection?" I swallowed—unsure myself.

"I'm not sure. But why am I blacking out?" He shook his head.

"I have an inkling, but I'll withhold that until I can confirm it. You realise you can't trust him, right?"

"I'm not sure what or who to trust at the moment." It wasn't a lie. He nodded and looked off to the side.

"Trust your instincts." I snorted, catching even myself off guard.

"Yet, we're here having this conversation. I can't trust my instincts."

"If you'd trusted your instincts, you wouldn't have come to Ostia."

A chill ran down my spine. He was right. Something about the town had put me on edge from the start.

"Do you mean to say I must leave town?" He looked at me with an unreadable expression. His cleft chin scrunched.

"Might not be a bad idea." My heart ached at the thought.

"I have nowhere to go." The ache became worse as I thought of fleeing and my breathing grew rapid. He frowned at me. Panic rose within, and I feared I'd black out again.

"What are you doing?" He asked and, in a flash, he stood before me, dissecting me with his heavy gaze. A gust of wind spilled over me from the rapid spurt, and the scent it carried reminded me of Adrian. The ache sharpened, emotions welling up like a torrent. A frown was carved between his brows. He reached out his hands, but I stepped back, not wanting him to touch me. The *Pulse* swirled inside my feet and my senses edged. He stepped closer again.

"I'm trying to help you." He seemed determined.

Tears burned my eyes, and I stepped back.

"You don't know what you're doing either. You could make it worse." My voice was tight, and, evading him, I bent over, hands on my knees, and focussed on controlling my breathing. The earth moved beneath me, the ache as strong as a black hole inside me. I expelled a loud grunt— an almost-scream—the *Pulse* sloshing through me like chaos. "What are you doing?!" The raw exclamation burst out. I crouched lower, feeling unstable.

"Nothing, I'm doing nothing." His voice sounded close, and I opened my eyes to slits. Sitting on his haunches nearby, he continued to stare at me. My sight drifted from seeing his black form to his natural form, imbued with red. I wondered what it meant, but it felt like my head would split open and I closed my eyes. A hesitant heat touched my head and it felt like it extricated the pain right from it. I breathed deep relief as the *Pulse* subsided and my senses settled. The heat lifted off my head, though I could still feel him radiating near me.

"Thanks," I breathed and opened my eyes, but was unstable in my crouched position and stumbled forward. He caught my wrist and held me up, his hand searing. As warm as Adrian. Perhaps it was a Dweller thing. When I was stable, he released me, and I looked at my arm. The veins were visible beneath my skin although not quite at the level I had seen it before. I glanced up and saw him looking at it too, a slight crease between his brows. He moved his arm closer and pressed it against mine. An unexpected action. The veins reacted and became more pronounced. I looked up, wondering what he was thinking, and he looked intrigued.

"I've never noticed this before."

The heat spread through my blood, and my heartbeat sped up. It felt weird. I thought only Adrian would have this effect on me. I cleared my throat.

"Why does it happen?"

He pondered for a moment.

"We live on scent energy or elemental aroma, and life is in the blood. Right now, yours is more concentrated. It makes sense."

"You… you live on what?"

"Basically, the energy fragrance emanating from your soul."
I'd never heard anything like that. My tongue stuck to the roof of my mouth.

"Like a… mystical vampire or something?"
He gave me a sharp look. I blinked, and he suddenly stood a few feet away, arms crossed.

"No."

"Is that why people disappear? You take them into the mountain?"
His expression was unreadable.

"No."

"Does it… hurt us?"
He shook his head.

"No." He sighed and shifted his weight. "I must go. But if you're undecided about who to trust, you know he shouldn't have been outside in the first place. Which should tell you he's up to something."

"Why are *you* out, then? Shouldn't all of you stay inside?"
He blinked.

"No," he said, shaking his head. "We have different dynasties. Ours reigns outside. On this plane. But you don't need to know any of this."

"Different dynasties?"
He threw his hands in the air.

"Not for you," He stepped closer and pulled me to my feet. "I'll try something else."

"What?" The shift came so fast that I was caught off guard.

"This is for your own good. Perhaps even the greater good."
His hands were on my head, and I was about to protest when everything went dark and silent.

I came to, standing in the forest, with no idea how I'd ended up there. Or where exactly I was. I looked around. How was I going to get out? My pulse climbed. I didn't even know where the heck I was; home, campus? I had the thought that someone had led me here, and I would kick them when I saw them again. Luckily, I realised my bag was with me, and I checked my phone for the location—surprised to see I was just across the street from the faculty. Eleven thirty-five. No wonder my legs ached. Dazed, I followed the map towards the road. The sun hit my eyes like razor-sharp darts when I exited the forest and I closed them and covered them with my hands. They were extra sensitive to light. As if someone had woken me in the middle of the night and shone a spotlight right into my eyeball. I dropped my hands and opened my eyes.

—Walking towards our house. I stopped, heart banging in my chest. Mom opened the kitchen door and stopped, frowning when she saw me.

"Hon? What's the matter? Why are you home so early?"
I forced a smile.

"Oh, don't worry. I'm just feeling a little dopey. Didn't feel like struggling through class like this." Or being in public when I was technically unconscious. She offered to stay home with me, but that was the last position I wanted to be in. I distrusted my mental absence.

"No, it's fine. I'm just going to sleep it off."

She seemed reluctant but left after making me promise to call if I needed her.

I watched her drive through the stone arch and into the forest. As she did, something like a switch flipped, and in a trance, I walked towards the trees, the side where—

—I stood at the brim, facing the trees. My senses shuffled long enough for me to see a faint glow deeper into the forest. Human-sized. I shifted again, and it was closer than a moment before. My pulse climbed when I realised it was a person. Senses still shifted, I noticed the air looked strange and thick. I lifted my hand, feeling a peculiar elasticity beneath my touch and I pushed my fingers forward into whatever it was. It gave way but didn't break. It felt like I was inside a strange bubble. I squinted, wondering if I could see it. My senses dug deeper than ever and the neon colours around me intensified tenfold, my ears ringing loudly. At my fingertips was something resembling a soap bubble, but with more intense colours swirling in waves from my finger outwards. Astonished, I backed away and followed the colour lines, tripping as I did—all around the clearing and the house. What was it? Freaked out, I ran to the house, senses jerked, the *Pulse* bristling as the world kept changing from this to that. Anxious that the person in the forest would follow, I looked back, but they were frozen in place. I ran up the porch steps, yanked the door open and slammed it behind me.

I turned around—inside my room. Staggering back, I plonked down on the windowsill. My reflection in the mirror was spooked and whiter than usual as I stared at myself, at a loss for what to do. Traces of memories flitted through my thoughts, but they fled my grasp, and I was incapable of looking at them clearly. The only plan I could think of was to write down the vague images slinking through my consciousness. Lightheaded, I approached the desk and opened the drawer. Inside, right at the top, was an ivory envelope with a red wax seal. I frowned at it, unable to recall seeing it before. I picked it up and removed the page inside.

Josilyn

My apologies for the abrupt departure...

I skimmed the rest.

... Adrian

"Adrian?" Inexplicably, my heart ached as I recited the name, whispering it out loud. A chill rolled down my spine and I swallowed. My mind became even foggier, and I felt a pressure in my head. Flinching, I put the letter on the desk. Panic rose inside me like a whirlwind and my breathing became rapid. The indentations and marks on the letter indicated I had read it multiple times yet had no memory of its contents. I would've remembered meeting an '*Adrian*' at the lake. My pulse was erratic as I wracked my brain, trying my darndest to remember this Adrian, and if I'd met him at the lake. A blinding headache pummelled me, my vision swam and I shrieked, grabbing my head. Nausea pushed up my throat, so I stopped trying and took a deep, panicked breath.

"What the hell?" I asked the room. It was like having a word at the tip of your tongue but being unable to grasp it. Except, your brain kept stabbing you if you tried to remember. After returning the letter to its envelope, I hid it beneath the other documents. I retrieved a notepad and wrote down what I was experiencing, including discovering a weird letter from a person I couldn't remember.

I blinked, and the sheet before me was empty, even though I had written a whole page. Dumbfounded, I stared at the blank page, then at the ground, my bin, and the drawer. Nowhere. Dread pulled my stomach into the earth and I stared ahead into nothing. I folded my hands together and pressed them to my mouth. Hopeless tears burned my eyes. Something came over me and I threw the notepad across the room. Expecting to hear it hit something, I turned in the chair when I didn't. My heart dropped at the sight of a massive man with dark red hair standing at the foot of my bed. Though it hurt my head, I thought he must be Adrian. Hand hovering in the air, he was holding the notepad like he'd caught it mid-air. I absorbed all of him, every detail, confused by how I could have forgotten him. He stared back at me with a frown carved between his brows. My heart bashed against my chest.

"I… know you, don't I?"

The frown deepened, and he closed his eyes with a sigh. When he opened them again, his lips pulled into a thin line.

"You do."

He came closer, and my blood warmed at every languid, graceful step. He kept his eyes on mine as he put the notepad on the desk in front of me. His heat spilled over me like a bonfire. Unnerved by his height and proximity, I swallowed. It felt so intrusive, yet also familiar somehow. The greenest emerald eyes gazed down at me—a melting pot of emotions boiled in them. I could not name a dominant one. Sadness? Tenderness? Malice… What a cocktail.

"I told you to stay away from him." His whisper held no accusation, just deep emotion. Stay away from who? Was there something between us? The way he looked at me and spoke made me think there was. My cheeks flushed.

"Yes, there is. You are mine." Darkness tinged the words as they came out like heavy clouds. My heart simultaneously expanded and ached. He knew what I thought. A word slipped into my stream of consciousness. *V'le Cremah.*

"I am." He lifted his hand and delicately touched my cheek with the back of his fingers, and they burned on my skin. Feeling self-conscious, I pulled back, and he dropped his hand.

I cleared my throat.

"There's something outside, around our house."

He frowned and blinked.

"I'm aware." He breathed, seeming dubious, "How do you know?"

"I saw it. How do you know?"

Now he looked stunned.

"Saw?"

"Yes?" I felt as confused as he looked.

"I don't think it should be visible."

"I see many things." Why did he know about it? What is it?

He nodded and sighed, looking away.

"I know because I put it there. It's a protection charm since I can't be here."

My mouth went dry, thoughts jumbled.

"I'm not sure what any of that means." He was right in front of me?

"It doesn't matter." Shaking his head, he bent down, clasping my wrists with his hand, and pulled me up against him. My heart ached and I blushed, taken aback. I pushed against his chest to create space between us, but his arms around me were iron. A peculiar fear slithered around my spine. I recalled being dragged through the forest. Ice prickled down my back, and I felt him stiffen a slight.

Again, I tried wriggling loose to no avail. His hold tightened. A strange silence thickened the air.

"Let me go, please," I managed in a bare whisper.

"Why do you fear me?" His voice was low and held an unidentifiable tone.

"I don't know. My mind is fractured and tired. I don't even know what's going on anymore. Let me go, please."

He didn't.

"You'd rather choose to forget me?" A cold edge to his voice now.

"Let me go, please." It was a near inaudible whisper.

"What has he done to you?" His words fell like stars, and my pulse hammered against my neck.

"I don't know who you're talking about." I tried pulling away again, but he tightened his embrace, and I felt his gaze weighing on me, though I looked away. We were frozen, and I listened to his rapid heartbeat. I remembered how it had slowed as I'd listened to it on the couch. My heart dipped.

"Stop that."
He held his breath.

"I didn't do anything. You're supposed to remember me. I know you feel it."

With an unexpected move, which surprised us both, I dipped to the ground, slipping from his arms. I twirled back, facing him. He looked taken aback, standing awkwardly with empty arms before dropping them.

"Look. I'm not stupid. Yes, I can feel I know you. But every time a memory prods me, it feels like my brain tears itself apart, which, I hate to tell you, does not feel great. I'm questioning my sanity, and I have no clue what's actually going on here. You keep talking about *someone* who's done something. I don't know who you're talking about, but my mind needs recalibration. And if remembering you hurts me, then maybe I shouldn't."

He was close again, though I hadn't noticed his approach, his burning eyes roving over me while I spoke. I stepped back, and he followed, and we did this dance across the room.

"You'd choose to forget?" The whisper was dark and with an undertone. I caught my breath as my heart ached at the impact of it.

"Only until it stops hurting."

"I'd rather endure torment for eternity than forget you." My eyes burned.

"Because you remember." I shook my head. "It's not a fair or balanced scale."

"A fair scale doesn't exist. What if remembering takes the pain away?"

I considered it but shook my head.

"No."

"Just let me kiss you." The urgency simmering beneath the surface took me aback.

"No. Remember, despite our obvious familiarity, in many ways—most ways—you're a stranger to me."

"Let me show you that's not true."

The next moment, I was running down the steps—down the foyer stairs. I looked back, and he was descending the steps at a stroll, following.

"You can't run from me." Neither a threat nor malicious, just a statement. I opened the front door and ran outside, unsure of what my plan was. I felt for my car key in my pocket and found it. As I crossed the lawn towards my car, I looked over my shoulder. Adrian was still walking, his gait determined. But just before disappearing behind the gazebo as I rounded it, his body sprang into a running pose. There was a whip crack, and then he was suddenly right behind me. I caught my breath and tripped over my feet at the shock. He closed the distance between us in half a heartbeat and, grabbing me around the waist, scooped me up from the ground and into his arms. I squealed, my stomach twisting as the adrenaline pumped through me. I burst out laughing and covered my face with my hands. A heavy but exuberant laugh droned through him as he swayed his body, rocking me side to side. His thick scent seeped into my head like a drug.

"See, I'm not the bad guy." His voice yielded as he pressed his nose against my hair, his lips burning against the fingers still covering my face. My heart hiccupped. I removed my hands and looked at him. A soft smile curved his lips and his eyes shone. My heart felt heavy and ached. A different ache. I touched his face and clouds passed in his eyes. Just thinking about what I wanted to do made my lips tingle, and I blushed. I slid my hand to the back of his head and pulled him closer, his chest heaving. Our lips met, and I heard him catch his breath. The ache inside my chest was loud, and the veins swelled under my skin. I opened my eyes and we were by the pier. His eyes were closed. I remembered him carrying me there once. His eyes flashed open, and he pulled back, looking at me with eyes on fire. I drew closer and kissed him again, feeling the fire erupt. He bent to put me down, though I was on tiptoes. He pressed me to him, leaving me breathless. Memories flitted through my mind, but they were unfocused and vague. I caught my breath when his burning hand touched the skin of my back. My hands travelled over his chest and around his waist, feeling his back muscles move beneath my fingers.

We were lying on the grassy bank, his hand cupping my face as he kissed my cheek down to my neck. A shiver ran through me.

"Don't bite me again."

He stopped and pulled back, staring at me.

"What?" A breathless whisper. I froze. Where did that come from?

"What?" I echoed, more at myself. We frowned at each other. He'd bitten me once, and there was blood. I reached out and touched his nose, remembering the veins that had formed there. Frantic, he studied my face.

"Why did you do that?" The question came out raw, like an open nerve.

His blazing eyes didn't cool, but the next instant he was standing. I shivered with the absence of his heat and sat up. He had a peculiar expression on his face. I couldn't tell if it was confusion or shame.

"I… must leave."

"Adria—" I didn't get to finish his name before he vanished right before my eyes. Flabbergasted, I looked around, playing back what had happened. It dawned on me that I didn't black out while he was with me. But as I thought about it, my heart ached and my brain seared.

Chapter 15

The full moon glowed gold and bright in the night sky on Saturday evening. All the days prior had been drunken blur, the nights restless and filled with dreams that I forgot upon awakening. My heart ached still—raw and suffocating. But one adapts to pain when adapting is the only option. I felt a numbness, a detachment, from everything and everyone around me, and I spoke little. Even though I couldn't remember my dreams, I sensed they were recurring, with someone specific consistently showing up, but no matter how I tried, I could not bring them to mind. I hid in my room as often as possible, but Saturday evening Dad coaxed me out to the porch to have hot chocolate and look at the full moon as it rose over the forest hills. He'd brought out blankets to ward off the biting air and wanted to know how I was doing, but it was difficult to answer without my heart aching and my head pounding. I perceived the eyes lingering on us from the usual place, but for some reason, I felt certain they would be unable to come closer. The moon was larger than I'd ever seen it and so bright that it cast an eerie, day-like glow on the trees, dark indigo coated with gold.

Peculiar, how the night could turn even the most familiar setting into something sinister. But the mystery of darkness held a potent allure, I must admit. Something about it seemed familiar, but my heart ached, and I sighed, thinking about something else. Mom and Andrew joined us, and as the moon rose, a double halo formed around it. My dad called it a moonbow. They were delighted with the enchantment of the night sky, but something about it stirred deep emotions within me, and my eyes stung. Unsettled, I excused myself right after finishing dinner—pizza— and hugged everyone good night, seeking the comfort of touch.

The *ache* intensified as I ascended the foyer stairs, uncertain if it was the now regular pain or something new. The moonlight shining through the skylight thickened the night's already ominous air. A headache materialised when I reached the second-floor landing, and I stopped, wincing. My pulse climbed and I felt hot. Whispers swirled around me., and I buckled against the balustrade post, the *Pulse* shooting through me—senses falling out. The world shifted into the ultraviolet. Red tinged the air, and I wondered if my eyes were bloodshot. I took deep, steadying breaths as my head throbbed. Nausea stuffed my throat, and I stumbled towards the bathroom as fast as I could, gulping down a pill with water. The whispers grew louder, sending goosebumps rolling over my skin, the hairs standing on end like antennae. My heart drummed like an angry bee. My insides heated up so much that I clambered into the shower, fully clothed, and turned on the cold water. I trembled—not from the cold—as my breathing accelerated. Pressure wrapped around my brain and with a loud groan, I gripped my skull in both hands. Right before squeezing my eyes shut, I noticed the dark network of veins on my hands.

"Stop!" I snarled at nothing, my heart still aching. Still burning up, I quit the shower and patted myself dry, clothes and all. A memory itched, small and erratic, about me, fully clothed and wet. But my head hurt even more as I tried to recall. The mirror told me the veins were all over my neck and face. As I stared, they retreated, along with the pain and the heat. My energy sapped, and I sagged against the counter, taking deep breaths.

"Josilyn?" someone called from what sounded like the second-floor hallway.

"Coming." My voice was raw, and I cleared my throat. I ensured I was not dripping, but it would still be difficult to explain why my clothes were wet. Off-balance, I trudged down the hall, into the parlour, and then into the hallway. No one was there, but I picked up the pace.

"Coming!" I repeated, louder, in case they hadn't heard me the first time. The moon cast a peculiar aura ahead, and by a trick of the light, it looked like mist or dust swirled around the stairs. A sweet fragrance suffused the air, fresh and alive. I slowed, wondering if someone had opened all the windows and let the forest seep into the house. As I neared the landing, I saw it sitting on the post. I stopped. The *Morpho* shifted its body as if to face me; then lifted off, circling around the staircase opening. The mist had thickened and filled the stairs like a cloud. My pulse climbed.

"Josilyn?" The impression seeped into my mind, and I thought it was the *Morpho*.

"Yes?" I whispered, feeling foolish. It kept circling, the mist forming a soft vortex beneath it.

"It's time."

A shiver ran through me. In the back of my mind, I was aware of dribbling liquid.

"For what?"

No answer came, but it dipped lower, and the mist retreated. To my own surprise, I stepped forward. The fresh scent thickened like an intoxicating potion as I reached the first step and descended. The mist retracted, the butterfly a few steps lower than me. My lungs thickened and warmed inside me. I followed it down and down until I realised our stairs didn't wind down this far. I thought to stop but was incapable. Ahead, the butterfly dipped into the mist and disappeared. The fog melted away, and below, the steps submerged into a rippling silver pool.

I stopped, swallowing hard. Beneath the surface of the silver water, the butterfly fluttered, waiting. The sight evoked a memory, like I'd seen something like it before, but it just slipped my grasp. I stepped closer and stooped to investigate. It settled on the water as if it were glass, its underside facing me from the other side. Curious, I reached down and poked my finger at the surface, which had a thick and cold consistency. The *Morpho* flew up—or under—and away, disappearing. I retracted my finger. The silver water stilled into a mirror surface before me, and in its reflection, I noticed a shadow, someone on the steps behind me. Startled, I jumped up to face whoever it was but lost my footing and fell back into the pool, submerging into the dense liquid. I flailed around and inhaled a deep lungful of… air. I was backing away from a wall, stumbling, and fell on my butt.

Confused, I stared at the wall before me, breath burning my throat. And then the scent registered, thick and sweet and earthy. Life buzzed around me, and I turned. I was sitting in the middle of a white stone pathway amidst an ancient forest. My heart skipped a beat. I… thought I had been there before. As I rose, the noise became clearer, though distant. I held my breath and listened. It sounded like drums and chanting. I backed away until I hit the wall, rough and jagged beneath my hands. The path stretched straight before me until it disappeared into the darkness. My head hurt as I looked at the beautiful forest around me, my heart aching. I turned around to face the wall. It felt wrong to expose my back to the vast, sinister unknown. I stared at it unseeing for a while, before I calmed myself and focussed. Dark crystals covered it, beautiful but somehow terrifying. I touched them, but they were sharper than expected, and I pulled away quickly. Some were chipped away only where I stood, as if by strong claws. Cold sweat beaded on my forehead and neck thinking about what could cause such marks. And why. I suspected I was inside the volcano, as implausible as the idea was. My gaze followed the wall up and up. It seemed boundless as it blended into the dim-starred sky. Except, it wasn't the sky, was it? The crystals glimmered above: dark blue, green, and purple. Black. The canopy curved up and, for the first time, I noticed a thick ray of light breaching through a large hole at the top. The crystals shimmered inside the cavity, illuminating the forest. I caught my breath at the sight too spectacular for words. My heart swelled when fireflies swarmed from the trees, moving in waves like sparks of fire. A shift occurred; I felt it. But what?

From deeper inside the forest, a low horn resounded through the trees, and I jerked back, feeling the wall's sharp edges bite my skin. It quieted again, and I swallowed. My heart jolted and thrashed like a wild horse as I wondered if I was the reason. I faced the wall again, poking it first, and then pushed my palms to the surface. Nothing happened. Anxious, I glanced around. I shouldn't be there. I closed my eyes and rested my head against the wall, trying to focus and call forth the *Pulse*. Even wiggling my toes, but nothing came. Tears were burning in my eyes and nose, and I tried to slow my breathing. As my predicament sunk in, I was at a loss for what to do. But after a spell, I found myself turning back to the stone path and trudging forward, step by illogical step. I kept walking until the dreary road narrowed; the trees closing in, swallowing us both. They were tall and ghostly, shrouded with a sinister bluish gloom. Startled by movement above, I looked up to see a large butterfly circling overhead, then slowly spiralling downwards when noticed.

When it was close, I reached out to touch it, but it moved away. A thought seeped into my mind, and my muscles solidified. I had been there once or dreamt that I had been. A four-legged creature had stalked me. It could be lurking anywhere in the surrounding darkness. My head swayed, and I held my breath to listen better, but my pounding heart was all I heard apart from the gentle forest sounds. I expected my senses to fall, but they remained nominal. I crept ahead until the white stone path turned into a footpath where the undergrowth crunched beneath my feet. My heart ached and I stopped, expecting a blackout. The worst possible event in this circumstance. But it didn't come; nothing did. I opened my eyes and glanced over my shoulder back down the path. Through the darkness, the wall seemed unchanged, still closed. I took a deep breath and continued forward. The path narrowed so much that the trees touched above me, blocking the sky. My unease intensified with each step deeper into the mountain. A mouse expecting a cat to jump out of nowhere any second. But something drove me further. My footsteps were rhythmic, and I expected a shift, but my senses remained stagnant. The light changed ahead, and I stopped. About twenty metres away, the path opened into a clearing. My heart thumped inside my chest, fear raw in my throat. A cool gust of wind pressed against my back, and I whirled around, tripping over my feet and falling. Pure adrenaline coursing through my veins, I scanned the area but there was nothing in sight.

For a moment. Fresh fear gripped me when a thick mist formed between the trees and flowed over the path, obscuring it. I scurried back, stopping only when I became aware of the distant chanting. Trying to be quiet, I rose to my feet. It came from deeper within the mountain and sounded like a choir. Trembling, I approached the opening, slower as I neared the brim. I peeked out, left and right. It was a gallery of some sort, lain with smooth white marble, too well kept for a road. Perhaps a promenade. Pulse erratic, I took a few hesitant steps onto the slab and scanned its length. The mist filled the space as far as I could see, preventing me from seeing much else. I noticed, however, that the mist retreated when I stepped forward—more than just air flow. It withdrew until it revealed a shiny black marble line about two feet wide. I followed the line left and right. It ran parallel with the white promenade, like a centre line on a road. Though it was black as night, it contained some luminosity, making me think it might be liquid rather than stone. I could hear nothing now. Curious, I stepped closer and knelt beside it, the hairs on my arms standing on end. It was flush with the white stones alongside it. I reached out my hand but yanked it back when the blackness spiked up towards it, and I almost toppled backwards. Shocked, I sat back on my heels and stared at it. It settled back into stillness so fast that I wondered if I'd imagined the movement. Cautious, I stretched my hand out again and let it hover above it. It radiated warmth and spiked up again, and I orchestrated it around, moving my hand up and down, left and right.

A nervous smile spread over my lips. It was mesmerising. I had no idea what it could be. As my hand drifted closer to touch it, my finger just about to graze the surface, something slammed into me, yanking my hand back and gripping my arms as I became airborne. The breath left my lungs from the impact and terror. This was it. This was how I died.

The mist blurred past, and the next moment, I stood between trees. The pressure confining me released, but I stood frozen stiff, trembling. I was just lucid enough to recognise the heat withdrawing from me. My chest heaved as I listened for a sound, but none came. Milliseconds dragged by—my mind exploding with unfathomable terror. I half-expected my body to shut down from the intensity of it. I heard something too indistinct to name, and as I turned my head, heat wrapped around my arm, and then I was propelled through the air again at an unnatural speed. My stomach churned and twisted, nausea thickening in my throat. If there was any pain, it eluded my awareness. I stood beside the black mass again. *What was going on?* I tried to whirl around to look for the assailant, but my body remained motionless as if I had no control over it. Maybe this was an actual shutdown. A burning tear at my wrist and a warm trickle down my hand. That pain did register. A whimper escaped as I watched the rivulet of blood run from the glowing wound to the tip of my finger and drip. It hissed as it mingled with the black liquid. A scream clawed at my throat but couldn't escape. A warm pressure on my arm. Heat at my back. Whatever was behind me was massive. My heart ached as a thought tried to dislodge. A chill ran through me despite the warm air flowing over me from the back.

"Zardi'Val mec nah." The voice was deep and urgent but not threatening. I gulped, wondering what strange language I'd just heard. The pain and heat vanished from my wrist, and I was whirled around with such speed I felt like I had whiplash, warm hands grasping my shoulders. I looked into frantic brown eyes. His lips moved fast, but the words sounded muffled and I frowned, wondering if I'd gone deaf. I tried pulling free from his grasp, but strong fingers dug into my shoulder.

He stopped speaking, pulled back and frowned, noting my ineptitude, and then he shook me.

"What are you doing?" I inexplicably found myself unafraid of this huge stranger. His lips moved, but the words still sounded like he was speaking underwater. I shook my head.

"I can't hear you." The ache in my heart surged. With eyes framed by shock, he released me and took a step back. Strange—why could I hear him when he spoke earlier but not now? Stepping closer again, he put his hand on my head. Instinctively, I tried to pull away, but his other hand grabbed my shoulder. The heat filtered into my mind, a headache pulsing through my brain, and I squirmed.

"You're hurting me!" A burning hand covered my mouth as he pulled my back against his chest, his other hand still on my head. The pain seared like a fiery dagger into my skull right down to my spine. I cried out, going limp. He held me up, and, after what felt like an eternity of hellish torment, the pain faded. I took a deep breath, my throat raw. He released me, but I was shocked into petrification.

"I'm sorry I had to do that." Raw emotion laced his voice. Numb, I stood staring into the trees, trying to process what I'd just gone through. He came around and stood in front of me.

"I told you never to come here again. How did you override the command?"

I blinked at him, wracking my brain.

"You… you did?"

He looked taken aback.

"You can't remember?"

I took a step back.

"I don't know who you are."

Horrified, he stared at me, eyes scanning my face as if reading it, his chest heaving.

"You're right, you don't." A whisper. "Something is very wrong. I don't understand." The taste of iron tainted my tongue. He shook his head as if forcing himself to focus. "You can't be here. Ad—he... is here. If he senses your presence, he'll possess you."

His words were nonsensical, yet still, my heart ached again.

"As in, own me?" What a weird thing to say. I wondered who he was talking about. And why would someone want to own me? He frowned.

"No." He looked as confused as I was and shook himself again. "We have to get you out before he notices—if he hasn't already."

My heart raced.

"Who?" It came out hysterical, and he put his finger to his lips, brushing the air dismissively.

"It doesn't matter, but you have to be quiet." He whispered again.

"What is this?" I pointed at the black mass he had bled me into. He blinked, disoriented by the subject change.

"Surveillance."

"Why is it warm?"

His eyes sharpened.

"Did you touch it?" His alarm was evident, and I quickly shook my head.

"No."

"They're living organisms. Their movement causes friction. But we don't have time for expositions. We need to get you out."

Disgust flooded me at the realisation.

"Ew! Why'd you feed them my blood?"

"The intruder's blood must be spilt, or an alarm will be triggered. The kind you wouldn't survive. Enough. We need to—" The arm that was reaching out to me dropped to his side, eyes going dim. He turned away with an exasperated sigh.

"I've been summoned. You must stay here. I'll return as soon as I can."

"Summoned? What? No! You can't leave me here!" A desperate whisper, but he was already backing away.

"A summoning cannot be denied. I'll shroud you as best as I can, but don't move."

He held his open palm towards me, and I felt pressure on my brain. His influence tainted me, and my heart rate decreased. I backed up until I hit a tree trunk. In the blink of an eye, he whip-cracked from sight, swaying leaves the only evidence he'd been there. How did he know that someone had summoned him? What did that even mean? Perplexed, I stood against the ancient tree, wondering why I was suddenly so calm. Who had he been speaking about? My heart ached, and I redirected my thoughts. As time ticked on, the effect of whatever he'd done to me wore off, and I felt fear creeping up on me like a ghost. My mouth was dry, pulse climbing.

What did he mean by "shroud" me? The thought crossed my mind to return down the path and see if I could escape on my own. But I was unsure of where I was, and the mist was thickening through the forest again. Heavens knew what else lurked inside this ancient cavity. Fear congealed as the forest sounds dwindled into silence. I held my breath, heart pounding, my palms clammy against the mossy bark. I pushed my back against it harder, as if I could render myself invisible by doing so. The hairs on my body rose as goosebumps rolled over me in waves.

"Josilyn…" A whisper on the wind. I drew a sharp breath—heart aching. Clamping a hand over my trembling lips, I scanned around but saw nothing through the thick mist. I looked up, wondering if I should climb the tree. A *Morpho* sat on a branch above, fixed on me. I had the sense that other eyes were on me too, and my stomach twisted. Unfocused, I looked ahead, wondering where the man… where *Caleb*… was. Strange how the name dropped into my consciousness. Maybe I knew him after all. My pulse climbed again, and my body warmed as if I was standing beside a fire—or, rather, as if there were a fire inside me. Pressure wrapped around my brain, and I cringed, shaking my head. Though painless, it felt uncomfortable, like wearing a too-tight helmet. As I lifted my hands to my head, I stopped. They were covered with a network of veins. I shook them as if it would help. It didn't. I pushed back my sleeve—they went all the way up my arm, just like earlier. I felt the same way I did in the bathroom, too. What was happening?

"Josilyn." The voice was crystal clear and right inside my head. Startled, I jumped around to look and fell. My heart ached at the sound of that voice, though unrecognisable, and I pressed my hand against my chest.

"Who's there?" I whispered so low it barely registered as I scampered back to the tree. I wondered if it somehow played a part in the shroud Caleb said he'd cast—whatever that meant. No reply came as I scanned around, searching for the source of the voice. It had sounded like it was right against my ear, or inside it. Then, for only a second, the mist flowed over the shape of a man. Then I stood up. The heat inside me was searing, and my heart pounded. I moved to the left, undecided to do so. Panic rose as I walked away from the tree, which had felt like a safety zone. But my body was not my own. Any attempt at stopping was futile. The only control I retained seemed to be over my thoughts and my eyes. I walked through the mist, unable to see anything. It was like my body was on autopilot, and I was a spectator. Before long I reached the white promenade and, walking right up to the black mass, jumped over it. It remained as still as stone. A scream scratched at my throat, but I could not open my mouth. How did one war against the relentless will of one's own flesh? I was dumbfounded by what was happening, and I wondered about that voice. At first, I'd thought it could have been the butterfly, but I doubted that now.

An awareness seeped into my consciousness, a sensation I could only describe as being watched, but from inside my mind. It felt like I shared it with someone, or something else was lurking within my body. A deeply disconcerting thought, and I suppressed it. I reached the edge of the forest and broke into a run. But it was not *my* run. I ran at an unnatural speed; one my body was not supposed to achieve. Soundless as a ghost, I sprinted through the forest. The chanting seeped back into my hearing, growing louder as I ran. Somehow, I knew it was exactly a hundred and ninety-three metres away. With my sharpened sight and hearing, every leap brought the forest to life, each scuttering bug drawing my gaze as if I could zoom in with my eyeballs. It freaked me out. When I slowed and stopped, I wasn't even out of breath. I stood at the forest's edge under the trees, bordering an oval-shaped basin or valley, and had the illogical impression that the mountain was larger than it appeared from outside. The moon's light pierced through the opening above, casting a spotlight on the crystals, refracting magnificent purples and blues everywhere. It almost looked like the world when my senses shifted. The chanting was coming from the basin. As I focussed there, a giant, jagged, dark structure took shape before my eyes. It was… odd. As if not retaining its own architecture. One moment it looked like a gothic palace, the next like an iridescent knife with all its sharp edges, levels and sides. Something about its aspect called to mind refined coral, with all its protrusions and fingers reaching towards the sky. It evoked an outlandish gnawing at my core. At the base—sunken into the earth— was a huge, greyish stone structure that looked like an amphitheatre surrounding a pond—movement around it. As I watched, I felt those eyes on me, inside me. The valley was dark, with a few lanterns scattered around the sharp structure. Vibrant green grass covered the steps of the amphitheatre. A scattered beam hit the gothic structure and lit it up like a blazing iridescent fire, shapeshifting like a flame. It probably would've taken my breath away, if I still had my autonomy. It was crystal, but unlike any crystal I had ever seen. To my dismay, my body set off into a run again, this time around the perimetre of the forest. Drums hammered like a fearful heart; an energy of anticipation permeating the air. The chants were thunderous, in a language which churned my blood—hauntingly beautiful, yet dark and horrific. For a second, I thought I understood what they were singing, but it escaped my grasp in the next instant. *Who are you?* Directed at the presence hijacking me. I looked back at the scene and noticed for the first time the hundreds of people dancing. The brilliant robes they wore shone in the same way as the structure. Men and women danced with perfect, synchronised, and inhumanly fast movements. A hypnotic sight, and the energy pulled me like a magnet. I could feel my body yearning to move closer, but something resisted it. The amphitheatre spiralled down and submerged into an electric blue pool. Right in the centre, there was something on the water. Padded on what looked like a thick green leaf was something resembling a pearl in colour and form, except it was massive, perhaps as high as my waist. As a ray of moonlight hit it directly, it folded open, and the chanting grew louder and more intense. But at that moment, I ran back into the forest, the scene lost from sight. From what I'd seen, it looked like a huge lotus-like flower. It was all kinds of freaky. This whole episode took maybe thirty seconds.

Speeding through the forest, Caleb's earlier words came to mind: someone would possess me if they knew I was here. This must be what was happening, but to what end? I crossed the stone promenade with the black canal again. It must run in a circle around whatever was happening at the centre. For only a second, I felt overcome by excitement and longing rushing through my flesh, but it wasn't mine. It disturbed and confused me, though it caused heartache as I felt my body being pushed even faster. The roar of rushing water grew louder just before I breached the forest into a clearing beside what I thought was the volcano wall. My body slowed down into a walk. A waterfall gushed from the wall into a dam-like structure, similar to the one from earlier. It looked ancient, like something from Mayan architecture. Large boulders and trees bordered the area to my right. A shadow slid down one of the boulders beside the dam, disappearing behind it, and I stopped. *I stopped.* Relief washed over me as I realised I had my body back, but then a wave of panic soon followed. What to do now? Something, or someone, had slipped from that boulder.

Someone was waiting behind it. Although every fibre in my body wanted to run, I knew it would be futile. Heat bled through me again, and my body walked forward. I wanted to cry from sheer helplessness, walking towards who knew what. Whatever it was hadn't taken me fully, because my heart raced and the fear distilled as I approached the opening between two-storey-high boulders. I rounded the boulder onto a narrow path, and there he stood waiting, dressed in black like a deathly omen, hands behind his back. He released me again, and I stopped in my tracks, swallowing hard as I took him in—so beautiful, so terrifying. Though his expression was inscrutable, his eyes teemed with power, a touch of darkness shining amidst the green. His dark red hair evoked emotions deep within me, and my heart ached so intensely that my eyes burned.

"Josilyn." His deep voice caused a fluttering in my stomach. My name was a prayer on his tongue, a seductive spell which compelled and confused me.

"Do… I know you?" It came out as a raw whisper. An emotion flashed across his face, too fast to name.

"No, it seems not." Disappointment was evident in the statement as his eyes devoured me. "I guess I should thank Caleb." His name was spoken with corrosion. "I wouldn't have been able to do this if he hadn't taken it upon himself to… 'help' you."

"What do you mean?"

His lips pulled into a thin line, and he straightened, shaking his head resolutely.

"It doesn't matter. It will be over soon."

This sent a shiver through me, and I wondered if it meant he was planning on killing me. Before I could voice the question, he turned his back and walked down the path ahead. I followed. The trail was rough moss-covered stone and sloped down towards the waterfall. The spray became heavier as we neared. Was he planning on drowning me? *I'm not going to kill you.* The thought rang clear inside my mind, startling me so that I lost my footing on the slippery moss. The next thing I knew, his burning arm was encircling my waist, and his warm hand was flat on my ribs. As inexplicable as it was, his touch was delicate, making my heart flutter in an unexpected way. I was on the boulder side now, away from the water. He continued forward, and when we reached the waterfall, we were both drenched. He swiped his free hand through the air, and the water parted like a curtain. Shocked by the obvious magic I'd just witnessed, I wriggled to escape him, but he tightened his hold. The warmth of his body seeped into me, and I could see the moisture evaporate because of it. Behind the water lay a black hollow, a beckoning darkness. Unseeing, I stared into it, my pulse flying. What lurked inside there? When we entered the blackness, I could see nothing; my eyes never adjusted. Completely blind and disconcerted, he led me forward, deeper and deeper into the belly of the cave until the roar of the waterfall was far and distant, almost inaudible. I caught myself when I was about to cling to him in desperation at the loss of my sight, and now even sound. He stopped and released me. As his heat seeped away, I felt cold, wet, and alone. The silence was a thick oil.

"Barloech dam lah." His deep voice echoed within the hollow, and a faint blue glow lit up the space. A rectangular room, about four metres wide, the ceiling even higher, maybe six. The strange blue light came from a substance which looked like small jelly pods stuck to the wall as if it grew there. I stood before a grooved wall. As my eyes adjusted, I realised the grooves formed motifs of a foreign kind. He was leaning against the wall, gazing at me with a peculiar, dark intensity. Self-conscious, I shifted my weight and cleared my throat. A particular detail in the pattern caught my eye—a crack slithering down the length that looked somehow familiar. His gaze was heavy on me still, I focussed on it and after a moment, a chill ran down my spine and I gave a step back. It was the same elongated 'S' I had on my shoulder.

"Curious, isn't it?" He moved away from the wall, circling me before coming to stand behind me. His heat spilled over me. My breath chased as his fingertip touched my shoulder, tracing the scar—my skin tingled beneath his touch. I nearly leant into him before I caught myself. Shocked by this, I stepped forward, and his hand dropped. Who was this man? With a heavy sigh, he came back around and placed his palm against the crack.

"I've waited for this moment, and you, a long time." He shook his head, "I'm not even sure how long." His voice a whispered sigh, and he stepped back. "Time unravels into chaos when you pull at its strings." Something about his voice sounded ancient—almost grave—and my heart ached. Though the meaning was sinister at best, hearing him say he'd waited for me made my stomach churn.

"I don't understand." A layered statement.

"You wouldn't, no." He pulled in a deep breath. "It's time." I saw the flash of a blade and my heart stopped. In a removed sort of way, I wondered if he'd stabbed me, and I looked down, but I was fine. Puzzled, I looked up to see him trace his bloodied finger along the slithering crack. It startled me when it sang, just like when you run a wet finger along the rim of a glass filled with liquid. I inhaled a sharp breath. His blood trickled into the crack, glowing a dim blue, as the sound rang and echoed around the room, sending goosebumps over my body.

"I need you to sing."

… What? I stared at him, gobsmacked by this weird development. But somewhere in the back of my mind, something clicked.

"No." I heard myself say. His back was still towards me as he looked at the crack.

"I can make you." The words fell like heavy stones, low and controlled as they were. I knew it was true.

"I can't feel the *Pulse* here." I assumed he knew about that, and it was the only thing I could think of.

He nodded.

"That makes sense." A low, strained whisper. The crack still sang. His body turned askew and without taking his eyes off the wall, he reached his right arm towards me as if beckoning me closer. My heart longed to close the distance, but I wouldn't.

Except, I did. His fingers moved behind my neck, weaving through my hair, his hot blood searing my skin. My mouth was dry. He put his left hand on the crack and a current flowed through us. My heart dropped and chills rolled over me. The *Pulse* simmered beneath my feet, and my senses fell out. The wall before me changed, just like my mirror had, into a dark doorway. He was a black mist… *Adrian*… his name came to me. I was trembling and looked down, noticing I appeared like a glowing white mist. His thumb stroked the back of my ear, and a memory tried to dislodge itself. He'd done it before. Heat flooded me, and the *Pulse* shot through me as my body hummed the note which rang inside the hollow.

Try as I might, I could do nothing to stop. My eyes closed as the notes vibrated through me, through the air. My mouth opened and I sang, a dark eerie melody which rattled my bones. Moments dragged by amidst the darkness as I sang.

Something cracked.

I stopped and his heat disappeared. My heart beat violently as I opened my eyes.

Alone.

Petrifying fear washed over me as I stared at the slithering crack into utter darkness.

Chapter 16

Tremors assaulted my body as cold air rushed over me from the void. I stumbled back, hitting the ground so hard that the wind knocked out of me. I had no idea what lay in the darkness–if something would emerge from it. So I kept my eyes locked there as I clawed backwards, my fingers digging into the soft, damp earth. The only audible sound was the faint waterfall. The crack had become an open passageway. With burning lungs and shaky legs, I hoisted myself up, utterly depleted as the physical exertion from earlier took its toll. My biology was not made for such speed. I came to a stop, feeling like any movement would throw the world into chaos, and I waited, bracing for something to happen. The deafening stillness rang in my ears, my throat dry. I wondered where the redhead, Adrian, had gone. Something about his sudden abandonment wore heavy on my heart. Vibrations rolled through my feet and took hostage any other thought. I didn't exactly *hear* it, but it sounded, or felt, like a growl. Multiple growls. My heart stopped. It came from the passage before me. I took a step back, realising that the blue pods on the wall were glowing brighter and brighter. I thought something became visible and squinted, heart pounding. The air moved, bending around a shape… a shape that looked like a wolf.

I turned and ran.

My legs were jelly, and I knew I could not outrun whatever that was, but I wouldn't just stand there. I tried to map out the path forward in my head, wondering how I'd navigate the pitch-dark cave on my own, but my surroundings shifted and the dense humidity lifted. Crickets sounded around me—my senses scrambled.

Caught off guard by the *shift*, I tripped and fell. Why now?

I was in the forest again, surrounded by trees, thick roots, and bushes. A strange light cast down on the trees. My heart exploded at the thought that perhaps I was no longer inside the mountain. But where was I then? The faint rustling of stealthy movements slinked through the bushes around me. I stumbled back to my feet and ran—uncertain how far I would manage. Tears burned down my cheek, but I tried not to whimper. I jumped over roots and rocks, feeling like every jump would be my last. With my cheeks wet and cold in the wind, I thought about my dad, my mom, Andrew, and Laura. If they'd ever find me, what they'd suffer through and the questions they would have. I hoped it would be over soon.

The rustling closed in around me. I tried to avoid thinking about the imminent pain. Something cold and wet wrapped around my ankle and I slammed into the ground. I lay there, wondering if I snagged it on a root or something. It felt like an icy ribbon clinging to my skin— the touch sent a shiver through me. The next moment, a force pulled me backwards, and I clawed around, trying to grab hold of something, anything. The ribbon tightened and dragged me back with jolting force.

"No!!" The scream tore from my throat, piercing even my own ears. I dug at the ground—earth and mush squeezing under my nails—and kicked, but it was futile. I managed to flip onto my back as I was dragged across the ground. Horrified, I followed the thick, black whip contorted around my leg.

My fight expired.

At the other end was the warped-air, wolf-like creature's mouth. The sleek whip was its tongue. My body went limp with shock. I saw the vague, distorted outline jump around as it pulled me closer. Panic wrapped around my chest like a python. With one last tug, I slid right in front of the air mass, its tongue unwinding from my leg. The tongue had been the only distinct part of it, and I struggled to see where the creature was now that it was no longer visible. Moments dragged by as I lay there, petrified, awaiting death—my heart a wild, thrashing animal in my chest. I could hear and see nothing. I moved, assessing.

Nothing happened.

I held my breath and listened, not wanting to miss any sounds. Slow, I scooted back on my butt. A growl vibrated close by, and I froze. Warm, foul breath spilt over me, and I stopped inhaling. The paw prints in the soil were larger than my outspread hand. Was it keeping me hostage? Why didn't it attack? It shifted around, paws padding circles around me, panting like a dog. A quiver ran over me. The suspense of waiting was death.

More determined, more terrified, I scampered further back.
A mistake.

The tongue whipped around my neck, squeezing. Choking for breath, I clawed at it, trying to loosen its hold. My heart throbbed in my neck and the blood surged in my head with nowhere to go. I gasped for air, but my windpipe was shut. Panic spread through me like biting insects. The trapped air burned my lungs.

With terrible force, it yanked me through the air, so close to its mouth, the breath was wet on my face. Its hold tightened. Filled with dread and panic, I slipped from consciousness. Tears ran down my cheeks as my senses dulled and the autonomy flowed from me—went limp.

Darkness.

The compression around my neck slackened as something slammed into the creature with such force, that its yelp faded far into the distance. I gagged, the painful first breath scraping down my throat like broken glass. My vision swam as I drifted back, and I tried to steady myself with numb hands on the ground, every swallow an agony. I had no idea what was happening, but I still heard snarls and whelping in the distance. Trees creaked and broke under a heavy beating. It sounded like wolves fighting. The hair on my body stood on end. I thought I heard hissing as well. Cold sweat pricked over my whole body.

Woozy, I scooted back until my back hit what I hoped was a tree's stable support. The world was spinning, and unable to stay upright any longer, I slumped sideways. The *Pulse* simmered beneath me; I could hear it, and the fight. Could almost imagine *feeling* it. Could never outrun. I fought to keep my heavy eyelids from closing—my short and shallow breaths unsatisfying. Hot tears ran down my face as I listened and realised I had no strength to escape before the pack returned. I couldn't even sit.

It went silent.

I held my breath. Sluggish, I pushed myself up again. The world swayed, though less than earlier. I could see or hear nothing as I scanned the enveloping forest. An eerie quiet had settled. I felt electricity where my hands rested on the earth.

A sound cracked in the distance, and my heart jumped. A gust flowed over my skin. Heavy hands grabbed my shoulders and pulled me up onto wobbling legs. My shoulders burned at the touch. I could hear someone speaking, but their words were stifled. The adrenaline rush had worn out, and my vision blurred—eyes slits. My head bobbed back, my body wanting to follow, but whoever was holding me up didn't let go. I heard my name, and my ears rang. My legs had no strength to stand. I managed to open my eyes wide enough to recognise Caleb's panicked face before they closed again. Why was he shaking me? I scowled at him.

"Stop that." My voice was a raw, awkward squeal that sent a sharp pain down my spine. I opened my eyes long enough to notice a dark silhouette on a branch high above. Hallucinating? Caleb seemed unaware, as he kept shaking me and speaking in hysterics. I squinted. The figure adjusted; perhaps aware it had been spotted. Couldn't tell whether it was a person or an animal. My lips tingled as I opened them to speak. It lurched towards us.

Caleb remained oblivious right up to the moment the figure slammed into his back. Shock flashed across his eyes before I dropped to the ground like a rag doll when he released me as he stepped back. Pitch-black limbs wrapped around him, and his hand flew to where a dagger shimmered against his throat.

He was too fast.

He grabbed the arm wielding the dagger and threw the whole being over his head. It somersaulted and landed in a crouch. My throat stung and ached when I gasped.

Xorvelca. My heart dropped. What was she doing here? Her icy eyes—almost glowing in the dark—locked on him. The sudden adrenaline rush woke me up enough to absorb as much as I could.

He had the dagger now, which, by his posture, he seemed ready to use. Without hesitation, she jumped upwards and, grabbing hold of a branch, pulled herself up, and launched at him with a blood-curdling scream. She moved like a panther. Sounded like one, too. I remained frozen in place, flabbergasted by the whole situation. Was she insane? Didn't she know what he was? He jumped too, disappearing into the trees above.

She landed near me, not so gracefully, shock evident on her face. Perhaps she realised just now what she had got herself into. We were both dead quiet, staring up at the trees, listening. My heart drummed in my throat. Her eyes were giant saucers as they searched the canopy above, breath racing. Airwaves rippled around her as her heart raced. The *Pulse* pushed against my skin like a bulging dough in a plastic wrap.

"Bre teri?" She looked at me with a horrified expression, still crouched like a biped forced on all fours.

"I don't know," I heard myself say in a whisper, but I wasn't sure what I meant. I tried to swallow, flinching at the pain. My heart rate was dropping for some reason.

Leaves rustled above; a shock wave ran through the ground, and Xorvelca yelped. Caleb held her in a vice grip, her back against his chest and her own dagger pressed to her throat. The sight shocked me.

"No!" I screeched and coughed, shocked by the pain. After a moment of paralysis, she clawed at him, swinging her legs around, trying to trip or throw him off balance. Valiant, but ultimately useless—he was too quick. They blurred for a second, and when they reappeared, he had her pinned to the ground, sitting on her legs, her arms stretched above her head. She tried to wriggle but was trapped. The dagger was no longer in his hand.

Seconds dragged by and the suspense sent my pulse into a tizzy. *What a night.*

"Brjelte clo. Sharlon tjast mjiaco." Caleb spoke. It sounded like Nomraj. As if spell-cast suddenly, she stopped moving, looking as shocked as I at hearing him speak their tribal language. She looked almost fragile, and perhaps even scared. Which was fair. I wondered again what she was doing here. Were we near the village? Maybe she heard the noises and came to investigate.

"Brjelto clo?" Her voice was soft yet still held the mysterious depth. The fierce warrior had met her match. I suspected being overpowered was a novel experience for her. He nodded once, and I saw the tension leave her body. I was dying to know what he'd said. With slow movements, he released her and rose. She lay there an extra moment before getting up. He blew out a long breath and slipped his hand behind his back, retrieving the dagger, and offered it to her, handle first. I was surprised by how fast the atmosphere had changed, but remembered he could induce people into doing whatever he wanted them to.

He was wearing his dark jeans and khaki t-shirt, which hung loosely over his broad shoulders. I thought about the ones dancing at the amphitheatre in their iridescent clothes. In the blink of an eye, he was standing before me again, holding out his hand. When I took it, he pulled me up, gentler than before. More careful. His dark eyes were unreadable as I looked at him, seeking answers. Seeking a light tower in all the murky haze I was caught in. His eyes flitted away.

"I have to get you back." The words were still settling when he scooped me into his arms. Caught off guard, I jerked back, and he had to re-establish his hold.

"Where?" I swallowed, wincing from the pain. My heart muscle squeezed with every pulse as if struggling.

"The mountain. But don't use your voice, I'll take care of that later." The mountain? Why would he take me back there? He looked at me and what I saw in his eyes scared me. My heart clenched, in a more visceral way than I had ever experienced. I frowned at him, but he avoided my gaze. Energy crackled in the air as he turned, and goosebumps rolled over me. I caught sight of Xorvelca's distressed face and what followed was so unexpected, it made me blush. She ran towards us and grabbed his arm with a pleading expression.

"Krjeki, tvos bleka! Bleka!" Gone was the mighty warrior. He shook off her hand.

"Xras." He seemed cold and distracted.

"Bleka!" She fell to her knees, begging. Shocked, I stared at her, wishing I knew what would reduce her to this. To see her like that distressed me. I willed the question towards Caleb, uncertain if it would work. He seemed discomfited by her begging too, and he hovered. This was the last position I ever thought I'd see her in, and it twisted the emotions inside me. I willed the question again, and he looked at me. The conflict was written all over his face. I mouthed 'what' to him, without using my voice. He gave a deep, long sigh, squeezing his eyes shut.

"She wants to come with us." He whispered. Befuddled by the idea, I thought, *why?* He shook his head.

"No time." He looked at her. "Zsar." That was the answer she wanted. Her teary face radiated relief and delight. He turned around and walked off without another word. She stayed mum, rose and followed us. I looked at her over Caleb's shoulder, and our eyes met and I held her gaze. The rules had changed, and we both knew it. A searing pain shot through my ankle, and I winced. My heart contracted as my eyes fell shut, a heavy slumber overcoming me.

"Oh no," was the last thing that blurred through my consciousness as I slipped from it.

I had feverish, restless dreams about running through the forest, chased by wolves as their long, black tongues licked at me, and the redhead, Adrian, watching me from a distance. Then, all went dark.

After a lifetime of darkness, my awareness clawed back into the light. Deep warmth wrapped around my entire leg, which had stung like liquid fire before I'd blacked out. That pain was gone now, and I was lying on my back, on a hard surface covered with fur. A potent aroma of herbs permeated the air and cooled my lungs as I inhaled deeply. I pricked my ears but heard nothing. I did, however, realise the heat on my leg came from someone's touch. The hands burned, so I knew it was a… V'le Cremah. I couldn't tell if it was Caleb or someone else. Curious, how fragments of memory seeped into my mind. A soft murmur confirmed—not Caleb. The voice was older, gentler. This would be the third of their kind I would meet. With much effort, I lifted my heavy lids and met a penetrating yet soft blue gaze. The smile tugging at the corners of his mouth touched his eyes. He looked much different from Adrian and Caleb, with pale skin and silver hair. *Was* he V'le Cremah? He seemed simultaneously young and old.

"Welcome back, Josilyn." The words were clear but toned with a heavy accent. His hands still lingered on my leg.

"H—hi," I croaked, glad to find that it no longer hurt to speak. Gingerly, I propped myself up on my elbows.

"My name is Tricus. Tonight, I am your Healer."

"Th—thank you." My head spun with the strange new world which opened before me. I wasn't even sure what a *Healer* was. A kind of doctor, I'd guess. He looked at his hands and the warmth spread through my leg. I looked down and noticed my pants were torn halfway up my thigh. I was glad I had shaved. My skin glowed red, and a white scar coiled around my ankle where the tongue had wrapped itself around it. The veins were visible beneath my skin.

"You had a mild encounter with the Brecah. The tongue cut your skin and some poisonous saliva entered your system. Caleb noticed in time to stop the spread, so you should be fine within a few hours. The scar will fade with time."

I could only nod. Taking a deep breath, I absorbed my surroundings. Tricus wore a rich, dark blue tunic embroidered with spiralling silver patterns. He radiated comfort, calming my psyche. The room was white and round, the ceiling fan-vaulted as if built between four trees that melted into the structure. White jelly pods like those inside the cave glowed along the branches of the fan-vault veins. Incense burned in a stone firepit at the centre. The faint trickling of water came from somewhere. It all felt too surreal, as if I'd woken up on a movie set. I looked back at Tricus.

He seemed as tall as Caleb and Adrian. His features were regal yet subdued, and his face had a delicateness about it. I wondered why he looked so different. A smile tugged at his lips again.

"I look different from the others, yes."

A shiver ran down my spine and blood rushed to my cheeks as I realised he, of course, could also hear my thoughts.

"I'm sorry."

He shook his head.

"No need. We are the same but different and take pride in it."

"Where's Caleb and Xorvelca?"

He straightened up slightly, his eyebrows lifting, and sighed.

"They are at the Dwelling, discussing matters."

"What matters?"

"Let's rather wait for Caleb to fill you in, shall we?" He removed his hand from my leg and stepped back, signalling he was done. I sat up more.

"Am I in danger?" My pulse climbed. I had trespassed here, sure, but it wasn't my fault. Not completely.

Avoiding my eyes, he thought for a few seconds.

"It seems you have been for a while. But right now, the danger has passed. You are not at risk of harm."

I believed him and calmed a little. I looked outside, wondering what time it was. My parents would freak out if they went into my room and I was missing. It must've been near dawn. I longed for it all to be over soon so I could return home and sleep.

"Are we near a river?"

"Yes." He smiled, "Nerlak prefer the calm of water. It is peaceful."

"Nerlak?" It was the first time hearing that word… I thought.

"Yes. I look different from the others because I am Nerlak."
A thought shook itself loose, something Caleb said once.

"Dynasties?"

He smiled and nodded.

"I saw you knew, though it might be hidden from you for now. We are three. I am Nerlak, Caleb is of Crema, and Adrian," he hesitated the name, "is of Brumagcht."

My pulse climbed as he spoke so casually of something so foreign and strange, so new to my mind. The names sent a shiver through me, particularly the last one. The way he'd said it. He said I knew already.

"Why are they hidden from me?"

"Mistakes were made, in innocence and pure intentions. But do not fear, all that is lost shall return, as you've noticed already."

"What mistakes?" Mine, or someone else's? He shook his head.

"Caleb is your Keeper and shall tell you all that needs telling. It is not my information to share."

"I don't understand the secrecy. Why can't I remember? How did I end up here? What happened in the cave? I must understand what's going on because it's all a blur, and I don't know what's real and what isn't." I was thinking about it all, anyway. He studied my face with a knowing smile.

"What is the prerequisite for something to be *real*?"
I blinked at him, taken aback by the question. I thought about it. Hard.

"Um… I guess something which can be experienced by many people at the same time, in the same way. Like… standing in the rain and hearing thunder. Something physical."

He nodded, still smiling.

"So, an event is only real if multiple people experience and corroborate it?"

"In a way yes. That's why we always want witnesses for a story."

"And yet, people don't remember the same events the same way. Memory is untrustworthy because everyone looks at the world through their own lens."

"Different perspectives."

"Exactly. So, I must ask then, if there is no one to witness it, does it still rain or thunder?"

"Of course." I frowned. "There is physical evidence. The ground will be wet, or there will be mud."

He squinted, half nodding, half shaking his head.

"And when it dries up, how will you prove it rained?"

"Well, the water would change the surroundings. Perhaps plants will grow."

"How will you prove the thunder occurred? If memories are forgotten, did it still happen?"

I came up short and shook my head.

"You got me there."

"Reality is subjective to your own experiences. As we get older and look back on events earlier in our lives, the perspective seldom stays the same. So even your own realities shift and change as time goes on and as you change. One might argue then, whatever you perceive as reality, *is* reality. Reality is not stagnant or solid."

I shook my head, tapping out of this peculiar conversation.

"I'm just trying to understand what's going on, not question reality."

"Well, you said you were questioning reality as it were. And I'm trying to tell you they are woven together. The clarity you seek lies within the haze you want to avoid."

"That's a lot to process. And I still don't quite know how it applies to me."

He smiled. "As I said—it will become clearer as you walk into it." He turned to a desk near the wall, filled with papers and potions, and picked up a steaming fine silver chalice. "Now you're awake, drink this."

I dangled my legs off the slab and took the chalice from him. It had a warm, sweet, citrusy aroma and I inhaled a deep nose-full before taking a sip. It flowed down my throat like raw peace, and I drank the sweet substance with glee.

"When will Caleb come?" I was eager to know more, and it seemed clear Tricus would not be the one to enlighten me on the matter.

"As soon as he can."

"Is the Dwelling close?" I didn't even know where we were.

"In a way, yes." A small smile tugged at his mouth.

"What do you mean?"

His smile broadened.

"If you disliked the conversation about reality, you'll like this even less."

"Is distance also just a state of perception?"

He laughed, eyebrows lifting.

"Well, of course! My perception of running a hundred kilometres and yours would differ greatly."

A shiver ran down my spine.

"Right. It may be the same distance, but what would take me days would take you seconds."

"Yes."

"So, the Dwelling is far for me, but not for you?"

He cocked his head and thought for a second.

"How big do you think this mountain is?"

It felt like a trick question, but I remembered how, earlier—when Adrian had possessed me—the mountain seemed more extensive than it appeared from the outside. After a second, Tricus smiled.

"Our gut is right most of the time. Humans have just learned to ignore it. The mountain is like a house with many rooms. You need only enter the right door. All you've seen is the foyer and the hall."

I blinked at him, trying to remember different sections or entrances within the mountain, but I'd only seen the white promenade and the iridescent structure at the centre. And the waterfall, which appeared to be on the opposite side of where my room was.

"He is almost here."

My stomach dropped. I heard a whirlwind approaching through the trees. The sound of him running was scary. I'd barely heard the whip crack outside when he appeared at the arched doorway. Our eyes met, and something like worry flashed across his face before he rearranged his expression to neutral. He looked at Tricus, and they exchanged unspoken words. Caleb nodded.

"Can you stand on your leg?" He put down the bag he had with him. I put the chalice down and tried to slide from the slab. It was constructed for someone of V'le Cremah height, not mine, and when I blinked, Tricus was helping me down. I tested my leg.

"It feels a little weird but not sore." I was self-conscious about their eyes on my naked leg and torn pants.

"That's good. We stopped the poison in time," Caleb said with a peculiar, declaratory tone, and I looked at him. He cleared his throat and looked away. The atmosphere was thick and awkward, but I had no idea why.

"Excuse me," Tricus said after a beat and left. Caleb gave him a pursed smile and avoided looking at me.

"What's going on?" I asked after Tricus was gone and presumably out of earshot. He sighed and approached a fur-covered stool by the firepit and sat, resting his elbows on his knees, and rubbed his eyes. He looked up and laughed, a maniacal sound that built up and bounced around the room. I adjusted my weight to the other leg, unsure how to respond to the peculiar reaction.

"You're being weirder than usual." As if I knew what *usual* was. He folded his hands together and pressed them against his nose, locking eyes with me. His dark eyes flitted over my face, as if calculating, but the emotions were unidentifiable. After a long pause, and me clearing my throat and looking away, he spoke—voice heavy and coarse.

"I made a mistake." The weight of those words hit me like a bus. Though I didn't know what mistake, I felt the magnitude. I swallowed, feeling a little dizzy, and took the stool across from him.

"What mistake?" I whispered as if we were exchanging scandalous secrets. He covered his face with his hands, sighed, rounded his shoulders, and stretched awkwardly. Composing himself, he straightened, placed his palms on his knees, and looked straight at me. I froze in place.

"I made a mistake with you, and the consequences are far-reaching." It felt like a blunt dagger pushed into my heart. Tricus had said mistakes were made in innocence and with pure intentions. My palms were clammy.

"What did you do?" I breathed, unsure why I was incapable of speaking above a whisper. He closed his eyes, shook his head, and raised his eyebrows. When he opened them, he looked at the ceiling.

"When I saw you at the lake with Adrian, I didn't think too much of it. Sure, he was trespassing, and what I thought he was doing is forbidden, but it was a minor offence, as it were." My brain hurt as I tried to remember being at the lake with Adrian. He continued. "I knew you had a peculiarity but thought little of it. It's been years since we last had a situation like this. Back then, we'd just let the victim forget the perpetrator and reseal them within the mountain. That would be the end of it." He said all this as if it were the most normal conversation in the world, but I was lost.

"Caleb, you're saying all these things as if I should understand and be following along, but I'm not. Pretend I know absolutely nothing—because I don't."

He took a deep breath and nodded.

"You're right. I've never had to explain the basics before. And I avoided giving you much information because I hoped it would not be necessary. Another mistake." He paused. "There is no easy way to explain this, and it will be a lot to process, so try and keep up."

I nodded, inhaling deeply as if I could force clarity into my mind.

"I'll start from what you know, whether or not you remember. We are V'le Cremah, which means Guardians, or perhaps a better translation would be Gate Keepers. Tricus has expanded your knowledge that we are three, Nerlak, Crema and Brumagcht. Translated, these would be Healers, Keepers, and Dreamers." He paused and looked at me as I absorbed all this. Tricus was a Healer, Caleb a Keeper. And Adrian was a Dreamer. A shiver ran over my skin, wondering what that could even mean. He was watching me and continued when I nodded.

"Perhaps you ask what's the point, what we are a Gate Keeper to?" Though rhetorical, I nodded, but he did not continue for an extended moment. His jaw moved as if he was grinding his teeth.

"Two realms exist on this planet. Well, two and a half. They are not visible to one another, though one knows about the other's existence. And one has no idea." He paused and looked at me, "Yours." He let that settle before continuing, "The one in the know is an eerie world filled with ghostlier creatures, amongst other things. Dangerous. Malevolent. The rules are different on the other side."

My mouth was dry. Goosebumps all over my body.

"The realms were once merged, but humans are the most fragile intelligent beings and the Ancient split the realms into two, erasing the memory of those haunted, terror-filled days for humankind. Gave them a fresh start. But some entities can still influence your world, even though entering fully is difficult. Sometimes, when they are strong enough, they can occupy a human, but never completely. A membrane, for lack of a better word, splits the realms. It is strong, but like with all things, there are weak spots. When the creatures notice them, they use it."

He stopped and allowed me to take in what was just relayed; such foreign knowledge to hear so casually. My head spun and felt aerated, throbbing, and I put my hand on my mouth, over my nose, as if I could hide from the truth. Speechless, I stared at him with wide eyes.

"So, where does the V'le Cremah fit into all this? Well, we are the Gate Keepers between the two realms. This mountain is the half-realm I mentioned. I say it's half a realm because it's not as constricted and solid as the other two. More fluid. Incomplete. Gauzy. In a way, a neutral realm. As Tricus told you, it's larger here than it appears. In fact, there are entire worlds layered here, different realms. But they work differently from yours. As a Keeper, I have more access to your realm than the other V'le Cremah. For reasons I won't go into now, it is specifically locked to Brumagcht. As I told you, our dynasties rule over different realms. Crema keeps your realm, Nerlak the other, and Brumagcht… Well. They're a little different. But my job as a Keeper is maintaining the structural health of the membrane which divides the realms. We search the world for weak spots or tears and seal them before they can be exploited."

I shook my head, horrified. "Stop."
My stomach churned. I rose and paced.

"Give me a second."

"All right."
I walked around the room, digesting and filing everything he'd said. My whole understanding of life and the world was just upturned. I had many questions, but one pricked my tongue.

"How do I fit into all this?"
He pursed his lips into a thin line and sighed.

"Sometimes, weak spots go unnoticed and tears, like a tattered cloth. This is called a Gape Hole. They emit an energy signature when they open, which is how we know. As soon as this happens, we close them; in part the reason we can move so fast. Sometimes, they self-correct fast enough, requiring no intervention from us. But when they are open, it's a clear access point for the other creatures to enter your realm. Some have, which is why you have mythical creature lore. We removed them, though. Hence there's no physical evidence. They are incalculable and can open at any place, at any time. That's where you come in. By ridiculous chance, you were born at the exact moment, at the exact spot where a Gape Hole tore open. Which means you were born into both worlds simultaneously. This has happened only twice before, that we know of. The phenomenon is called Seers because you see what others can't."

I steadied myself against the slab as chills rolled over me. The idea of being born into two worlds boggled my mind. Everything I had seen, the music, the ultraviolet world, were aspects humans weren't supposed to see. It didn't seem so malevolent, though.

"No, it's not all bad, of course. It would be unbalanced if it was. Good and bad exist on both sides." His eyes shifted, and he adjusted his weight. "There's more, though. A complication."

"What?"

"I think you may have already figured it out, but you were born with dormant V'le Cremah DNA. This happened in the past, when V'le Cremah, uh… bedded humans. But it stayed dormant since the gene is unreadable by the human body, and it has never been a problem. But—" he looked at me, "because you were born touched by a Gape Hole, the dormant gene was activated. So, you might not have all our traits, but some will come out. One which makes you a Treader. You can, in theory, switch between any realm at will. You just haven't because you're oblivious about what you possess. There's never been anything like you."

My head spun with a tornado of questions begging to be answered.

"How is all this linked, and what did Adrian want from me?"
He raised his eyebrows and looked away.

"Well, I think that question has multiple layers, which I'm not going into with you. But this mountain is the rim of a double-edged sword, the cornerstone. What he attempted, and achieved, was to cause the membrane to dissolve from this point forward, until the realms are one again. Within, approximately, four of your months."

I trembled, feeling dizzy. I didn't quite understand the implications of what he'd said, but it could be nothing good. So much to unpack—I could spend a week asking questions, just for the answers to lead to more questions.

"How did he do that?" Even as I asked, it gnawed at my mind. He gave me a pointed look.

"You, Josilyn. He used your gift. You are the only being from both realms, *and* you have V'le Cremah DNA. Your blood speaks, sings, to both. You are at an equilibrium between them. You alone could initiate the decay." He pulled back and shook his head. "If Adrian's actions weren't so diabolical, I'd call him a genius. I'm not sure how, but he knew you tied into this somehow. And here I thought he was after frivolous pleasures, but it turned out his intentions were apocalyptical."

I sagged to the ground against the solid marble slab, goosebumps rolling over me like waves.

"Is there no way to undo this?" I shook my head as if it was something I could reject. "I tried to stop him, but I couldn't."

He held his hands up, as if in surrender.

"No, you couldn't have stopped this. I should have. I was mistaken in assuming his intentions. But, yes, there is a way to prevent or reverse the thinning."

I knew. I knew as he spoke, though I refused to believe it.

"You are the only one who could cause the decay and the only one who can stop it. This was not the plan, of course. But sometimes, things just diverge unscripted. You are the skeleton key which opens and closes."

I stared at him, mouth agape.

"But then, just take me to the cave, and we'll close it. Why is it such a big deal?"

His eyes swarmed, and he shook his head, looking down.

"No, Josilyn. It's a failsafe. It's not supposed to be so easy to undo. Another stone talisman exists to reverse this one's effect. But it's in the other realm. We must go there."

The idea freaked me out, but I reckoned at the speed Caleb could travel, we could cross the world a couple times in the next hour.

"Okay, so we go there at your super speed, reverse the effect, and come back. We can be done within the next few hours, right? You said we have four months. That's more than enough time."

Mirthless laughter escaped him.

"What part of failsafe don't you understand?"

I frowned. What did he mean?

"Things work differently there, as I said. And the talisman's exact location is unknown because it keeps changing. So, yes, I might be able to travel fast, but it'll be a dangerous scavenger hunt and a race against time. Adrian won't leave you be."

My heart clenched. I felt like I was floating outside of my body.

"How can you not know where it is?" My voice was shrill. He shrugged and gave another incredulous laugh.

"This was never supposed to happen. It's been aeons. No one ever dreamt something like this would ever happen, unless the Ancient induced it and, well then, there'd be no need to know where the twin talisman was."

"This *Ancient* you keep mentioning… I assume he—it—is still alive. Can't he just fix this? That seems like the more logical step."

He blinked.

"No one's seen him in centuries. We have no idea if the more detailed myths about the realms' origin are real or just sprung up with time."

"Well, that's just reckless," I heard myself say. He was taken aback. "How long will it take us then?"

He shook his head.

"I don't know. I don't know. We'll have to be as fast as possible, but we have a mere four equivalent months. So, in the other realm, *should* have about six. Maybe three."

"I'm sorry, what?"

"Remember I said the other realm works differently? Time does too. There isn't a linear correlation between the two. What feels like days there might equate to weeks in yours. Or the inverse."

Cold ran over my body, chilling my bones to the core. My pulse sped up.

"What?" it came out in a whisper. I couldn't just disappear for weeks or months. "So, I can tell my parents, right? I must tell them; they'll freak out if I'm just gone for months. What about my life?"

"Life as you knew it has ended. Best to accept your new normal, as strange as it is."

Hysteria rose inside me as I thought about everyone at home. Poor Laura. My *dad*.

"Look, I understand this is a lot, but it will be taken care of. It's difficult for you to see, but that's the least of our problems."

"Right. Because the bigger problem is not just that we have to find a *mythical* talisman inside another dimension within months when you have no idea where it is. But one of your own will also hunt me. One who you couldn't even figure out was up to no good, right under your nose." My throat burned with the fury in my blood, and I rose.

"Adrian deceived me too."

I gaped at him, incredulous.

"Deceived you?" My voice was shrill and loud. "*How* did he deceive *you*? Couldn't you read his mind? Did none of you pick this up? How is that even possible?"

He stood.

"That is the true horror here, Josilyn. Tampering with another V'le Cremah's mind is forbidden, and yet he did it, despite the difficulty. He warped my memories too. And another—a violation of the highest order. In retaliation."

"In retaliation for what?" I almost yelled.

"For making you forget him!" His anger flared, the ground vibrated, his voice bounced around the hut before and all went silent. I stepped back, trembling. The atmosphere dissolved back to normal quickly, and I had a moment of objective realisation—how funny it was for me to think my rage could match his. He could snap me like a twig—or worse, make me snap myself. What he'd said sunk in. Caleb was the reason my memories were gone, why I couldn't remember Adrian clearly. I swallowed the burning knot in my throat. It didn't explain why I couldn't remember Caleb earlier.

"He warped your memories too. Gave you a false reality by twisting what actually happened. Adrian is what you'd call an Architect or a Scholar. We knew he was powerful, but we had no idea at what level he could operate. You were immune against his devices to a large extent due to what you are. Until I compelled you into forgetting. It fractured your resolve, for reasons I'd rather not disclose, but it created the opportunity to pull you into this realm tonight. Something he's been trying to achieve since he met you. I pieced it together too late. So, I played right into his game without even realising it."

My mouth fell open. *Adrian was pulling me towards the lake.* Ice trickled down my back. My heart clenched, and I put my hand on my chest.

"Yes. Your true memories will return, bit by bit."

"Why?"

Shadows flickered across his eyes.

"Multiple reasons."

A shift came over him, and he straightened, his eyes distant. I frowned at him.

"Caleb?"

His shoulders sagged, and he looked at me, focusing. Wordless he studied my face.

"The Council has summoned us."

Before I could ask anything, he handed me the bag he'd brought with him.

"I brought you some of your clothes. When you're ready, come outside."

He left before I could say anything. My heart dipped, thinking he'd snuck into my house—my room—while my parents slept on, blissfully unaware of all the chaos. His practical and thoughtful selection of items impressed me. I wondered if he had a sister. Were there even any female V'le Cremah? I'd only seen men. When I was done, I stepped outside into an open, forested area beside a wide river, feeling numb and distanced from it all. I caught my breath. Thousands of fireflies and butterflies, in every imaginable colour, swirled overhead, painting the sky with a slow-moving kaleidoscope. It was the most beautiful sight I'd ever seen.

"Wow!" I whispered.

Caleb was staring at the sight, troubled—a concerned frown carved between his brows. I looked up again. The slow, swirling mass seemed to vibrate. I could hear a low thrum, but couldn't tell if it was their wings or something else. As I stared, the display had the hairs on my body standing on end.

Caleb?

My heart pushed into my throat.

"What are they saying?" My strained whisper came out.

His chest heaved with rapid breaths. In the next heartbeat, he scooped me up, and we were running.

Afterword

As I close the chapter on *Charmed Vigilance*, I find myself reflecting on the incredible journey that brought this story to life. Who I was when I started in 2010 versus who I am now in 2024 are worlds apart. Writing this book was not just an act of creation and perseverance but a voyage of self-discovery, revealing much about the world I sought to build and about myself.

Since completing the manuscript, I've gained new perspectives on the themes and characters that shaped this narrative. I had a strong sense of who Adrian was, and the atmosphere I wanted to create for Ostia, but I didn't yet have the life experience to fully capture it. The enigmatic town of Ostia and Josilyn's journey has continued to resonate with me, reminding me of the power of storytelling to explore the unknown.

I would like to extend my heartfelt thanks to everyone who supported me throughout this process. Your encouragement and feedback were invaluable, and I am deeply grateful for your belief in this project. As I move forward, I am excited about the possibilities that lie ahead. The story of Josilyn and her gift may continue in new ways, and I hope you will stay tuned for future developments. Thank you for joining me on this adventure, and I hope you carry the magic of *Charmed Vigilance* with you.

I promise to not take another 14 years to publish the sequel.

About the Author

In the spirit of mystery and intrigue, Skylar believes some tales are best left untold, including her own.

Acknowledgements

Over the course of 14 years, Charmed Vigilance has had many fingerprints that touched it. Like pottery, each of those fingers helped to shape this story into what it is today. I would like to name fingers and point names in chronological order:

My mom – thank you for being there from literally day one, and for the hours of listening to me read the chapters I've written over the phone.

Colette Bradford (nee de Beer) – The MVP, for being honest with me about the book not being up to standard, after I basically published a first draft. I know—yikes.

Early inputs/readers – Telisha du Plessis, Nanine Steenkamp, Ilse Ferreira, Simon Jacobs, Alicia Strydom, Danice Blatt (nee Bezuidenhout) Dimone de Waal (nee Wilke.

Johan Erasmus – For your enthusiasm and getting me back on the horse to start rewriting.

Micha'ell Petrus Kruger – What can I say… Thank you for your proper read-through, feedback, support, and friendship. It was invaluable, and to have someone who doesn't read this genre actually enjoy the book—a true compliment.

Laurita le Roux – For your enthusiasm and encouragement.

Estelle Grunewald – An angel amongst people. Thank you for your more than a year-long dedication and work to edit this Novel and your fantastic input, without which it would not have been what it is today. I am eternally grateful to you.

www.ingramcontent.com/pod-product-compliance
Lightning Source LLC
Chambersburg PA
CBHW032037050726

47590CB00001B/32